LIGHTNING STRIKE

ALSO BY WILLIAM KENT KRUEGER

This Tender Land

Desolation Mountain

Sulfur Springs

Manitou Canyon

Windigo Island

Tamarack County

Ordinary Grace

Trickster's Point

Northwest Angle

Vermilion Drift

Heaven's Keep

Red Knife

Thunder Bay

Copper River

Mercy Falls

Blood Hollow

The Devil's Bed

Purgatory Ridge

Boundary Waters

Iron Lake

LIGHTNING STRIKE

A Novel

William Kent Krueger

ATRIA BOOKS

New York   London   Toronto   Sydney   New Delhi

ATRIA
BOOKS

An Imprint of Simon & Schuster, Inc.
1230 Avenue of the Americas
New York, NY 10020

First Atria Books hardcover edition August 2021

ATRIA BOOKS and colophon are trademarks of Simon & Schuster, Inc.

For information about special discounts for bulk purchases, please contact Simon & Schuster Special Sales at 1-866-506-1949 or business@simonandschuster.com.

The Simon & Schuster Speakers Bureau can bring authors to your live event. For more information or to book an event, contact the Simon & Schuster Speakers Bureau at 1-866-248-3049 or visit our website at www.simonspeakers.com.

Interior design by Yvonne Taylor

Manufactured in the United States of America

1 3 5 7 9 10 8 6 4 2

Library of Congress Cataloging-in-Publication Data is available.

ISBN 978-1-9821-2868-5
ISBN 978-1-9821-2870-8 (ebook)

For Danielle Egan-Miller.

For more than twenty years, you have offered me hope,

and that has made all the difference.

LIGHTNING STRIKE

AUTHOR'S NOTE

A significant element of this story involves the Indian Relocation Act of 1956, the brainchild of a group of men appointed by President Harry S. Truman to solve what lawmakers in Washington, D.C., called "the Indian problem."

For a century or more, the United States government had attempted to eradicate Native cultures in this country through various means: outright war, forced relocation onto reservations, and finally the cruel Native American boarding school system, whose effect was meant to shatter families and whole tribal groups. Still, the indigenous people of North America struggled forward, holding together, maintaining their cultures within reservation communities. The cost of supporting these communities, of keeping the promises the government had made, was seen in Washington, D.C., as exorbitant. The Indian Relocation Act of 1956 was one of the solutions to this "problem."

Under the Relocation Act, many reservations were terminated. On other reservations, governmental services were reduced or canceled altogether. In return, the government promised to provide transportation for families willing to relocate to urban settings,

and promised as well help in finding housing, jobs, and job training. As so often has been the story, the promises turned out to be
worthless. Many Native families who relocated found themselves
in the worst neighborhoods, with inadequate housing and either
low-paying jobs or no jobs at all. Because the Relocation Act
provided no money for return travel to their reservations, these
families found themselves stuck in cities far from home, separated
from other tribal members, floundering in a world alien to them.

Despite the government's positive spin on this program, it was
at heart simply another effort to crack apart Native communities
and families and force assimilation. Reservations disappeared.
Many Native communities were practically abandoned. And the
flood of Native people to cities created a legacy of hopelessness for
many urban Native Americans which, even today, more than half
a century later, they continue to struggle against.

PROLOGUE

On his first day as the newly sworn-in sheriff of Tamarack County, Minnesota, Cork O'Connor seated himself behind the desk that came with the badge. The desk, clear at the moment of all but a morning paper, a ceramic mug that held pens rather than coffee, and a framed family photograph, was a mosaic of scars and cigarette burns, the legacy of his father and the other men who'd sat behind that desk before Cork. He wore the khaki uniform he'd ironed himself for the swearing-in ceremony, which had been held that morning in the county courthouse a block away. His wife, Jo, had been there, along with his three young children and his sister-in-law, Rose. Sam Winter Moon had come, and Cork had been especially pleased to see Henry Meloux at the back of the courtroom. The old Mide had sat erect and expressionless, but his presence—and Sam's—in that place where the Anishinaabeg had sought but seldom received justice spoke to the hope they now held.

Cork felt the solemnity of the moment. It came to him with a sense of satisfaction but also with a profound sense of burden. Wearing the badge his father had worn, he felt the heavy responsibility of measuring up to a man who'd given his life in the line of duty and, in doing so, had left his son with a hard road map to follow into his own manhood.

Deputy Ed Larson appeared in the doorway. He was tall, laconic, and nearly a decade Cork's senior. They'd worked alongside one another for years.

"Care to take a victory lap around town?" the deputy said, then added with a grin, "Sheriff."

It was January, and there was a bracing chill in the air outside the Tamarack County Sheriff's Department. The sun was a melt of yellow in an aster blue sky. On the streets of Aurora, which were banked with plowed snow, folks greeted him in a neighborly way. Despite the badge and the nature of all that came with it, he was still one of them and had been his entire life. They ate alongside him and his family at the Friday night fish fry in Johnny's Pinewood Broiler. On fall evenings, they cheered with him among the local fans at the high school football games and sat next to him in the bleachers of the school gymnasium during basketball season. They took communion with him on Sundays at St. Agnes. Yes, he was one of them. And yet, not quite. Because there was something different about Corcoran Liam O'Connor that didn't show in his face but ran in his blood. And he was reminded of it on that first day he wore the new badge.

As he and Deputy Ed Larson made the rounds of the small business district, an old man stepped from the Crooked Pine, and with him came the musty odor of stale beer. He jammed a cigarette in the corner of his mouth, cupped his hands around a match flame, and blew smoke toward the sky. Then he caught sight of the two officers and gave a drunken grunt.

"Never thought I'd see the day when a Redskin was sheriff here," he said.

"I take it you didn't vote for me, Lyle," Cork said.

"Hell, didn't vote period."

"Not much cause to complain then," Larson said. "And I've got a question for you, Lyle. How do you intend to get home? Because it's clear you're too drunk to drive."

The old man swung his eyes to a mud-spattered pickup parked at the curb. "Guess I'll have a cup of coffee at the Broiler first."

"Better make it three or four," Larson said. "And I'll be watching."

The two officers walked on, a rough circle that brought them to the courthouse, where they stood looking at the structure, which had been built of red sandstone in the days when the wealth from the mines had fed the county's economy and ornate public buildings were de rigueur on Minnesota's Iron Range.

"You promised lots of changes in your campaign speeches. Going to change that?" Larson said, nodding toward the courthouse.

As was often the case with county courthouses, at least in Cork's experience, a cupola crowned the structure and a large clock face was set within it. The hands had not moved in twenty-five years. The clock had been hit during the exchange of gunfire in which Cork's father was killed. Periodically, the county commissioners would entertain a motion to have the clock repaired, but so far that motion had never passed. In its way, that frozen clock face was considered a memorial to Sheriff Liam O'Connor.

"Not up to me," Cork said.

"I didn't know him," Larson said. "But he sure left a mark on this town."

"Tell you what, Ed. Why don't you go on back to the office? I'd like to spend a few minutes here alone."

"Sure thing, Sheriff." Larson gave him a little salute and crossed the street.

As Cork stared up at the frozen clock face, a cool breeze passed over him, which felt to him like the visitation of his father's spirit. His father would have scowled and said something like "That's your heart talking. If you're going to be a good lawman, you need to listen to your head."

It was a piece of advice in keeping with the kind of man his father had been. Or at least as Cork remembered him. In Cork's memories, Liam O'Connor had been a lion, powerfully built, with hands like huge paws and a thick mane of red-gold hair. Although not typically given to displays of emotion, when the situation demanded, he was a ferocious, towering figure. Yet these days, whenever he studied the family photographs of his father, Cork saw a man much smaller than he remembered and with a much gentler face, different from the father Cork remembered, a stranger in so many ways.

There was a bench on the sidewalk, and he sat and allowed himself the indulgence of reverie. Beneath a blue sky and a butter yellow sun, with a cool breeze on his face, the weight of a new badge on his chest, and the responsibilities that came with it resting on his shoulders, he considered a summer long ago when he'd first begun to try to unravel the mystery that had been his father.

PART ONE

SUICIDE

SUMMER 1963

CHAPTER 1

Before they discovered the body, Jorge had been singing.

"Sixty-six bottles of beer on the wall, sixty-six bottles of beer. Take one down and pass it around, sixty-five bottles of beer on the wall."

That droning ditty had gone on longer than Cork O'Connor could stand, and he finally said, "Will you just shut up."

"Sixty-five bottles of beer on the wall, sixty-five bottles of beer . . ."

It was late July, hot and humid. In the North Country of Minnesota, everything under the blaze of the sun sweltered. The afternoon was a miserable biting of blackflies, and to keep from being eaten alive, the two boys had done their best to maintain a brisk pace. They were hiking an abandoned logging road through the Superior National Forest, at the edge of what was then officially known as the Quetico-Superior Wilderness, though most folks simply called it the Boundary Waters. This was one of the ten milers required for their hiking merit badge, their destination a place known as Lightning Strike. They both carried packs topped with rolled sleeping bags, intending to spend the night, then hike back into the town of Aurora in the morning, completing the second of the required ten milers. They'd set out at noon, and it was now nearing three o'clock.

". . . take one down and pass it around. Sixty-four bottles of beer on the wall."

"Geez, just can it for a while."

"Okay. What do you want to sing?"

"I don't want to sing."

"Guess what I watched on television the other night."

"You already told me. *The Thing*."

"That creature was so cool. Know who was inside the monster suit?"

"No idea."

"James Arness. You know, Marshal Matt Dillon on *Gunsmoke*."

"You're kidding me."

"I swear."

"Why would he do something stupid like that when he's already Marshal Dillon?"

"This was before *Gunsmoke*. Everybody's got to start somewhere. Check this out."

Jorge shrugged off his pack, reached under the flap, and pulled out a rolled sheet of drawing paper. He unfurled it and showed it to Cork. It was a pencil sketch of the creature from the movie they were discussing. Even at twelve years of age, Jorge was a terrific artist, and his interest for a long time now had been in things that go bump in the night, especially those things pumped out by the Hollywood B-movie horror factories.

"That's really good," Cork said.

"I've already sent away for the model kit. When I put it together, I know exactly where it will go. Right beside the Wolfman and the Creature from the Black Lagoon." Jorge stopped talking for a moment, sniffed the air, wrinkled his nose, and said, "What died?" Cork smelled it, too, the foul odor of rotting flesh, brought to them on a weak breeze. "Probably a deer or something," he said. "Somewhere in the woods."

A hundred yards down the grown-over logging road, the two boys could see the meadow where the ruins of Lightning Strike lay. "Let's go," Cork said. "We're almost there."

Jorge put away his drawing, reshouldered his pack, and they walked on.

Lightning Strike sat in a clearing in the middle of a great stand of old-growth white pines and mixed hardwoods on the shoreline of Iron Lake. Cork had been there many times, usually in the company of Billy Downwind, a friend from the rez, and Billy's uncle, Big John Manydeeds. Because of his deep knowledge of the great Northwoods and the skills it took to survive there, Big John was a man Cork respected and admired. But the first time Cork visited Lightning Strike, he'd been only six years old and in the company of his grandmother Dilsey. From the reservation, it was a three-mile hike, and though Cork's legs were small, they'd carried him to Lightning Strike and back easily. The whole way, Grandma Dilsey had pointed out plants and trees and the signs of animals, telling him the Ojibwe names for these things. She was true-blood Iron Lake Anishinaabe, and one of only a handful of elders left who spoke the language of her people fluently. She was always trying to convince Cork to learn to speak as his ancestors had, but he complained that it was too hard.

"Only to a lazy mind, Corkie," was her usual reply. She'd been a teacher most of her life, and although she chose not to push him in his learning, she would generally add something along the lines of "When I die, and the other elders, too, the language dies with us. And there will go everything we've ever been as a people." Which always made Cork feel guilty, but not enough that he'd knuckled down yet to learn a language his father had complained was the second most difficult on earth behind Mandarin Chinese.

In the center of the clearing stood the burned remains of a large log construction. The walls had long ago collapsed and only a stone hearth and chimney remained intact. The clearing was filled with rattlesnake ferns and club moss and fireweed that bloomed in spiked clusters of brilliant purple blossoms. The boys crossed the meadow and went directly to the burned-down structure.

Jorge stood looking at the charred scene, then at the sky. "Hope there's not a storm tonight. I don't want to end up like this place."

"This is a sacred place for the Ojibwe, a place of power," Cork told him. "Grandma Dilsey says no one should have ever logged here. That's why the spirits caused it to be hit by lightning. You and me, I think we're okay." Cork gave a skeptical look. "Well, I'm okay anyway."

Jorge punched Cork's shoulder, then contorted his face in a look of revulsion. "That dead stink is following us. Maybe we should camp somewhere else. I don't want to smell that all night."

Cork wasn't listening now. He was looking toward the south end of the meadow. Through the trees there, the surface of Iron Lake shimmered as if it were made of mercury. But it wasn't the lake that had caught Cork's attention. He was focused on a huge maple tree that stood alone inside the clearing. "Jorge," he whispered and nodded toward the tree.

Jorge followed his gaze, then whispered back, "Jesus. That's no dead deer."

The boys dropped their backpacks and walked slowly toward the solitary maple, unable to take their eyes away from what they saw there. They stopped a dozen feet from the hanging body.

The man at the end of the rope was huge, a goliath. His long black hair lay draped over his shoulders like a mourning shawl. His face was swollen, his tongue distended and black. Foamy, blood-colored liquid leaked from his mouth and nostrils. His eye sockets were empty holes from which maggots crawled down his cheeks like milky tears.

The breeze shifted strong in their direction, and they recoiled at the smell that overwhelmed them.

"God!" Jorge turned and stumbled away.

Despite the stench and the grotesque, rotting figure, Cork couldn't move, couldn't take his eyes away, because he knew this man. And although what hung before him was in no way his fault or his doing, Cork began to cry and said, "I'm sorry, Big John. I'm so sorry."

CHAPTER 2

Four men stood in the clearing, three of them in the uniform of the Tamarack County Sheriff's Department. With the toe of his boot, Deputy Joe Meese tapped one of the two empty whiskey bottles lying in the meadow grass near the hanging man. "Had to build up his courage first, looks like."

Sheriff Liam O'Connor gave a sad shake of his head. "I thought he'd kicked the booze for good."

Sigurd Nelson, who owned the only funeral home in Aurora and was the county coroner, stepped back from the cursory examination he'd been doing of the body, which still hung from the tree. "Dead awhile, Liam. Long enough the crows and maggots and decomposition have been at work. Four or five days would be my guess. Around the time of the long Fourth of July weekend."

Cy Borkman, another Tamarack County deputy, was circling the body with a Polaroid camera, shooting the scene from every angle. He finished, placed the camera and the photos he'd taken into a carrying bag, and joined the other men. "When are we gonna cut him down, Liam?"

The breeze was blowing west to east. Liam O'Connor and the others stood on the upwind side of the body. When the breeze let up, the stench came back to them.

"You finished here, Sigurd?" Liam said.

"I've seen what I need to. I can do an autopsy, if you want, but cause of death is pretty clear. You could save the county a chunk of money."

Liam studied what was left of the body of Big John Manydeeds. As the coroner had pointed out, the crows and maggots had done their work. Add to that the bloat of decomposition, the rupture and oozing of the flesh, and the god-awful stink, and what remained was the repulsive final horror that had been a man he'd known and had respected.

"Skip the full autopsy, Sigurd. I need to get his body to his people as quickly as possible. Ceremonial reasons. But I'd like to send blood samples to the BCA for a toxicology report, just to be on the safe side."

"Will do. I'll be waiting at the mortuary with a gurney." The coroner turned and walked back to his car, which he'd parked on the old logging road next to a Sheriff's Department cruiser and Liam O'Connor's pickup.

"Cut him down now, Liam?" Borkman said.

"Let me get a tarp from my truck."

Liam walked slowly across the meadow as the coroner's car swung around and headed back to Aurora. He dropped the liftgate on his truck, climbed into the bed, and opened a large cargo bin attached to the back of the cab. He pulled out a canvas tarp and returned to his deputies and to what was left of Big John.

"Help me get this under him, Joe."

The dead man's booted feet hung only six inches above the ground. Liam and Meese slid the tarp beneath the body, arranged it, and Liam said, "Cut the rope, Cy. Where it's tied around the branch."

"I'm not sure I can reach that high. Can't I just cut it somewhere above the noose?"

"That'll leave rope on the branch. I don't want anything left behind here that will attract ghouls."

Borkman shrugged. "You're the sheriff."

A four-foot section of rotting trunk from a fallen pine lay near where the body had hung. The lawmen had already speculated that Big John had dragged it there and used it to reach the branch where the rope was tied, then had taken his fatal step. Borkman mounted the trunk section, reached up on tiptoe, and sawed at the rope with his pocketknife. The body dropped suddenly. It hit the tarp with an odd squishing sound, and fluid oozed onto the canvas around it.

"Jesus," Meese said. "Sometimes I hate this job."

Liam carefully worked the noose off the man's neck and laid the rope aside. The two deputies each took a corner of the tarp. Liam pulled the other two corners together and gave the order to lift. They carted the heavy body to the pickup truck and maneuvered it onto the bed. Liam folded the tarp over and secured the ends, so that what remained of the dead man would be completely covered on the ride to the funeral home.

He closed and latched the liftgate, then stood looking at the sky. The sun was already nearing the western horizon, its rays peach colored and sharply slanted. The meadow lay in the long shadow of the old pines that edged the clearing.

"I'll drive the body in," Liam said. "When you come, bring the rope and the bottles. And before it gets too dark to see, look around for anything else."

"Like what?" Borkman said.

"Anything Big John might have left behind."

"You mean like a note?" Meese said. "Seems to me those whiskey bottles say it all. You've seen this before, Liam. We all have. Too many times."

"Just do it."

The two deputies exchanged a glance and Meese said, "Whatever you say, Sheriff."

Liam had snapped at them, and now he softened his tone. "His truck's not here. Check the lakeshore, see if he came by canoe."

None of the men moved right away. They stood together, their own shadows long across the wild grass that grew in the meadow around the burnt ruins of the old logging camp.

"I thought he'd put the booze behind him," Meese finally said. "I thought he'd dealt with his demons."

Liam O'Connor didn't reply. But he was thinking, and what he thought was this: *Do our demons ever go away for good?* And he was thinking, *No one should have to look at something like this. Especially a kid.* And he was thinking, *Especially not my kid.*

Liam stood on the sidewalk outside his house on Gooseberry Lane. It was dark now. The interior lights shone through the windows, and although they were inviting, he was reluctant to enter. Upstairs, only one room was lit, and that was his son's bedroom. As he stood looking up, the light died. There was still much to do that day, but first he had to talk to Cork. He wasn't sure what to say to a boy who'd looked on the kind of horror he'd seen at Lightning Strike.

Liam O'Connor had fought his way across Europe with the 82nd Airborne Division. He'd seen death and its aftermath in a hundred hideous forms. Although he'd been a grown man then, or thought of himself as such, those disturbing visions still sometimes visited him in the night, and he woke shivering in a sweat. What would it be like for a twelve-year-old boy?

He mounted the front steps, and at the sound of his boots on the wooden stairs, his wife appeared at the door. She opened the screen and studied him.

"You look awful," Colleen said and put her arms around him. "How's Cork?"

"Quiet." She stepped back and let her husband into the house. "He's been upstairs since you left."

Dilsey, Liam O'Connor's mother-in-law, came from the kitchen. She was slender, short in stature, but, as Liam liked to say, "tough as ironwood." Although she was well into her sixties, her hair was still panther black, and she usually wore it in one long braid that hung down the center of her back. "Did you talk to Big John's family? His brother?"

"I went out to the rez and knocked on Oscar's door, but he didn't answer. Nobody I spoke with seemed to know where I could find him or any of Big John's cousins for that matter."

"You went out like that, in uniform?" Dilsey said.

"Official duty."

"Did you tell them why you were looking for Oscar?"

He shook his head. "I didn't want word spreading until I had a chance to notify someone in the family."

Dilsey gave a little eye roll. "No wonder they wouldn't tell you anything. They probably thought you were going to give Oscar a hard time or arrest him again."

"I did get the number for his sister in California, and I'll call her as soon as I've talked to Cork."

"When you go back to the rez, I'll go with you," Dilsey said. "I'll knock on doors. They'll talk to me."

The house smelled of meat loaf and Liam realized that despite the unappetizing work of that evening, he was hungry.

"I'm going up to Cork's room, then I need something to eat. Still a lot of work ahead tonight."

Colleen leaned to him suddenly and kissed him, a response that seemed to come out of nowhere and surprised him.

"What was that for?"

"For being a good man in a hard job. I'll have a plate of meat loaf waiting for you."

Upstairs, the door to his son's bedroom was closed, and Liam gave a gentle knock.

"Who is it?"

"It's Dad. Can I come in?"

"Yeah."

Cork lay on his bed in the dark. The light from the hallway cut a blade across him. Lying peacefully next to the boy was Jackson, the family dog, who raised his head and blinked at the light.

Liam sat on the bed. "How're you doing?"

Cork shrugged. "I keep seeing him."

"I know. You will for a while, I'd guess. A hard thing to unsee."

Cork looked away, out the window into the dark. "Why?"

"Because it's a horrible thing and horrible things stay with us."

"I mean why did he do it?"

"That I don't know, Cork. Alcohol was involved, so . . . I don't know."

"He stopped drinking. Henry Meloux cured him."

"When you're an alcoholic, you're never cured. You're always in recovery."

"You don't kill yourself just because you're drunk."

"No."

"Then why?"

"I don't know."

"Are you going to find out?"

"I'm not sure there's any point in that."

"People will want answers. His family."

"They may be the ones best suited to understanding the why of it. I think it might be best to let them work it out."

"Does Billy know?"

"I have the number for his family in California. I'm going to call them."

Jackson jumped off the bed, stretched, shook himself, and trotted out of the room.

"Have you eaten?" Liam asked.

"Wasn't hungry."

Liam put a hand on his son's shoulder. He was a slender boy and Liam felt the bone beneath his palm. "What you saw today, I wish you hadn't seen. But I can't help you unsee it. If you want to talk about it, I'll listen."

"Jorge saw it, too."

"I'll talk to him and his mother."

His son gave a nod, then turned his face again to the window.

"I'm going down to have a bite to eat. Want to come?"

Cork shook his head and lay there, staring out the window.

Liam O'Connor went to the doorway and stood with the light in the hallway at his back, his shadow falling long and dark across the bed. He wished there were a way to make the grotesque image that his son was seeing disappear from his head. He knew there was no magic to wipe clean the slate of memory. You just learned how to move on.

CHAPTER 3

It was Billy Downwind who, four days later, asked Cork to return to Lightning Strike. Cork didn't want to go, but Billy pretty much insisted. He said he had to see the place where his uncle had died, see exactly where Cork had found him.

The two boys followed the shoreline of Iron Lake north out of the reservation town of Allouette. It was a three-mile hike through dense woods to the ruins of the burned-down logging camp, which had been abandoned for nearly half a century. Although a tragedy had brought Billy back to the Iron Lake Reservation, Cork was looking forward to this time with him, a chance to catch up with a friend he hadn't seen in almost two years.

Billy had been giving him a rundown on Los Angeles, what a different world it was from the rez. So many cars and they all went so fast. Bright lights everywhere that stayed on all night long so you couldn't see the stars. Showers with hot water. Taco stands on every street corner.

"Tacos?" Cork said. "What are tacos?"

"Mexican food," Billy said. "Spicy meat and cheese in a crunchy shell. You can get burritos and enchiladas, too."

"What about movie stars? Did you see any movie stars?"

Billy stopped and knelt to retie the laces of his Keds. "I think I saw Johnny Weissmuller once on Venice Beach, but he was kinda far away, so I wouldn't swear."

As always, the biting blackflies were a nuisance. "Hurry it up," Cork said.

Billy stood and they resumed their journey.

In the two years his family had been absent from the Iron Lake Reservation, Billy had grown. When he left, he'd been a little shorter than Cork and thinner. He was two inches taller now and his upper body was showing enviable muscle. Cork was still waiting to get his own growth spurt. When he'd turned twelve, his father had promised him this would probably be happening soon, but Cork was still anxiously waiting. His father's good friend Sam Winter Moon had advised patience; manhood came in its own time, he'd said, and then he'd cautioned that it wasn't always what it was cracked up to be. And old Henry Meloux, who was a Mide, or healer, and who was known to be wise, had offered, "A bird is not ready to fly until it has all its feathers. I have seen you naked in the sweat lodge, Corcoran O'Connor, and it is clear that all your feathers have not sprouted." Which had made his father and Sam Winter Moon laugh, but Cork hadn't found it funny.

"Does it ever snow?" Cork asked.

"Up in the mountains, not in the city."

"Do you ever go to the mountains?"

"Naw, Pop's always too busy."

"Do you miss the snow?"

"About as much as I miss the mosquitoes and blackflies."

"I don't think I could live anyplace that didn't have snow. What about Disneyland? Been there?"

"Not yet. Costs an arm and a leg to get in."

"But you go to the ocean?"

"Sometimes. The ocean's free."

"Got any friends?"

Billy said, "Stop with the questions already."

At Spider Creek, a clear run of water through tall reeds, they took off their sneakers and socks and rolled up their pant legs and crossed the stream. A quarter of a mile beyond that, they came to Lightning Strike. Billy walked ahead slowly, as if reverently. When they reached the hearth and chimney, Billy stopped and shoved his hands into the pockets of his old Levi's. His troubled eyes took in the ruins, then he turned to Cork.

"Where?" he said.

Cork knew exactly what he meant, and he pointed toward the lone maple tree near the edge of the clearing. He was relieved when Billy held back from going there.

Billy closed his eyes, took in a deep breath, and said, "He's here."

"He's dead, Billy. Walking the Path of Souls."

"That's not what Broomstraw says." Billy used the nickname given to Elsie Broom by kids on the rez. She was an old woman, exceedingly thin and of a brittle nature, hence the uncomplimentary epithet. "She says he's been dead more than four days without a ceremony, so his soul doesn't know how to walk the Path of Souls. She says even if he had a proper ceremony, he still couldn't walk the path because he took Mass from Father Cam out at the mission."

"Lots of Indians take Mass," Cork said. "You take Mass."

"She says none of us will walk the Path of Souls. She told me Uncle John will just hang around the places he hung around when he was alive. Like a ghost."

"Broomstraw's old and crabby. She doesn't know what she's talking about."

Billy said, "He used to bring me here all the time."

"I know. I was with you sometimes."

"Remember? He would tell us stories about Grandpa Willis working the camp before the lightning burned it down. We'd lay out sleeping bags, look up at the stars. We saw the Northern Lights a lot."

"I remember," Cork said.

"Do you remember what he told us they were? The dead, dancing in *Gaagige Minawaanigoziwining,* the land of everlasting happiness. He should be headed there on the Path of Souls. Instead, he's stuck in, I don't know, limbo or someplace." He turned a full circle, his eyes sweeping slowly over everything and finally settling again on the solitary maple. "Why here?"

Cork knew what he was asking. Why Big John had chosen this particular spot to end his life, a question Cork couldn't even begin to answer.

Billy finally sat down among the rattlesnake ferns, plucked one from the ground, and began idly to pull off the leaves. Cork sat beside him.

Billy had told him how they'd got the news in California from Cork's father late at night. His mother had cried until the sun came up. Billy admitted that he'd cried, too.

The afternoon was still, no birds singing in the trees that walled the clearing on every side. Even the blackflies seemed to be avoiding the area.

"My uncle told me this place has power. They weren't supposed to be logging here and that's why the lightning struck." Billy took a deep breath. "He was right. I can feel it. And I can feel him. He's here."

Cork felt something, too, but for him it was tied to the image of the hanging body, a horror that still haunted him. At least Billy had been spared that.

"But he's not in limbo," Billy said. "He wants something."

Cork scanned the trees, almost expecting to see someone or something step from the shadows. "Wants what?"

"I don't know."

Cork wasn't certain if it was the suggestion put into his head by Billy or if it was the residual sense of tragedy that seemed now to permeate the place, but he thought he sensed something, too, something menacing. He was suddenly eager to get out of there. He stood and said, "We should talk to Henry Meloux."

Billy didn't move.

"Come on," Cork said. "The Mide will help us. He'll know what Big John wants."

Billy finally stood and followed. When they reached the edge of the trees, Cork paused and turned back for a last look at the burned ruins of a building that, if the Ojibwe were right about this place, should never have been constructed there. A cloud passed over the sun and a darkness swept across the boys. At the very edge of his vision, among the shadows of the tall pines on the far side of the clearing, a much greater darkness suddenly arose, and Cork's gut balled into a fist of fear. He spun to grab his friend's arm. "Geez, Billy! Look!"

But when the boys turned back together, the sun had reappeared, and the great darkness was gone.

"What?" Billy said.

Cork took a moment to gather himself. "Nothing," he said. He put his back to Lightning Strike and started walking. "It was nothing."

CHAPTER 4

Law enforcement for the reservation of the Iron Lake Band of
Ojibwe was the responsibility of the Tamarack County sheriff. This
was due to the passage of Public Law 280 by the U.S. Congress in
1953, which gave sovereign Native people the right to choose the
agency that would have jurisdiction in criminal matters. Many reservations had opted to remain with federal law enforcement, which
meant the FBI, or with state agencies. The Iron Lake Ojibwe had
chosen the Tamarack County Sheriff's Department. Why, Liam
O'Connor couldn't say. He so often felt helpless and frustrated in
the face of their resistance when he tried to do his job.

He stood in the small cabin that belonged to Big John Manydeeds, not surprised at all by the neatness of the place. Manydeeds,
once he'd become sober, had lived in a way he believed was in
keeping with the spirit of his real home, which was the vast wilderness that stretched north into Canada. He possessed nothing that
wasn't necessary to his survival and what little he owned he maintained with a respect for its value in his life. The cot was made, the
blanket tucked neatly under the thin mattress, which was stuffed
with the floss from milkweed. The cooking surface of the cast-

iron stove in the center of the cabin was clean. Big John appeared to have swept the floor before heading to Lightning Strike for his final visit. The place smelled a bit musty, but that was because the windows had been closed for some time, and Liam figured his friend had taken a moment to see to that detail as well. It was clear that Big John hadn't gone to his end thoughtlessly.

Liam stepped outside and closed the door behind him. There was no lock. Almost no one on the rez locked their doors. Big John's old Ford pickup was still parked on the narrow lane to the cabin. He turned and looked toward Iron Lake, only a couple of dozen yards from the cabin. Big John had built a small dock where he landed his canoe when he came off the lake. Next to it was a canoe rack, which he'd constructed of birch. At the moment, the canoe wasn't tied up at the dock, nor was it resting on its gunnels on the rack.

Liam half-circled the cabin and, in a Dole pineapple cardboard box below the back window, found what he was looking for. The box was half filled with empty whiskey bottles, Four Roses, just like the two empties at Lightning Strike. How long had Big John been off the wagon?

He returned to his cruiser, which he'd parked behind Big John's truck, and started back to Aurora.

When he entered the Sheriff's Department, which was located in the basement of the county courthouse, Deputy Joe Meese looked up from the contact desk. "Got something for you from the BCA. Big John's blood alcohol level. You asked for that first. The full toxicology report'll take a bit longer."

He handed Liam the manila envelope. The sheriff opened it and slid out the paper inside. "Did you look at this?"

"Yeah. Just like we figured. Through the roof."

"I was just out at Manydeeds's cabin. His truck's there but not his canoe. And you didn't find his canoe when you searched Lightning Strike, right?"

"Nada," Joe said. "Probably loaned his canoe to somebody. You know the Ojibwe. Generous people. So he probably had to walk."

"A long last walk for a man carrying a couple of bottles of whiskey and a rope just the right length to hang himself. He had to have passed through Allouette. Someone would have seen him with the bottles and the rope. Why hasn't anyone said anything? What are they hiding?"

"Got me. Going to the wake tonight?"

Liam nodded.

"Won't be easy, I expect," Joe said.

Liam said, "In this job, not much is."

He went to his office, closed the door, and sat at his desk. He placed the manila envelope on the desktop and stared at it as if it were a scorpion.

Folks on the rez had to have known, didn't they? But no one had said a word to Liam, not even his wife. And why would they? He understood perfectly. Big John Manydeeds was Anishinaabe, which meant "The First People," though Dilsey often shortened it to simply "The People." Big John was one of them. But Liam O'Connor? Although he'd married a woman who was half Anishinaabe, that didn't make him one. And there was nothing he could ever do that would change it.

CHAPTER 5

Allouette, the larger of the two communities on the Iron Lake Reservation, was grieving the loss of Big John Manydeeds, but the grieving went back long before that. In truth, it had begun with the white man's earliest encounters with the Anishinaabe people, who were also called Ojibwe or sometimes Chippewa. The killings, deceptions, and theft of all that was dear and sacred came soon after that. The ancestors of the Ojibwe of the Iron Lake Reservation were Algonquin and had lived along the Atlantic coast. Long ago, they'd been driven west by their enemies, the Iroquois. According to the old stories, they'd followed the sacred Megis shell until it brought them to the great lake they called Kitchigami, which white men knew as Superior. They'd finally come to rest and for a long time had been happy.

But the white men followed, came in such numbers they were like swarms of blackflies. They took what they wanted, by force or deceit or through twisted laws. In the end, what was left to the Ojibwe people was only a small parcel of what they'd once called home.

This wasn't the history taught in schools, but it was a history Cork knew because he'd been told it by Grandma Dilsey.

Cork and Billy Downwind found her in the Allouette community center, a plain wood construction painted white and with "Ain Dah Yung," which meant "Our Home," burned into a large plaque of polished maple and hung above the door. At one time, it had been the school where she'd taught the children of the reservation. Those, at least, who hadn't been dragged off to one of the government boarding schools. Along with several other women from the rez, she was helping prepare the center for Big John's wake that evening.

"There you are," she said when she saw the two boys enter. "We thought you'd been eaten by wolves."

"Billy wanted to go out to Lightning Strike," Cork said.

Grandma Dilsey had been putting a cloth across one of the tables where food would be set for the communal meal which would accompany Big John's wake. She scowled at the boys.

"Why in heaven's name would you want to go there?"

"It used to be one of my favorite places to go with my uncle," Billy told her. "I just wanted to see it again, and see where . . ." But Billy couldn't finish.

Grandma Dilsey's face softened. "Your mother's been looking for you."

"We want to talk to Henry Meloux first," Cork said.

"He's gone back to Crow Point to prepare himself for tonight. You can talk to him then. In the meantime, your mother needs you, Billy. And, Cork, don't you have papers to deliver?"

Outside the center, Billy said, "Thanks for going with me."

"Sure. See you tonight at the wake."

In parting, the two boys solemnly shook hands, as if they were grown men.

Cork didn't leave right away. He waited until Billy had gone, then went back inside the community center and shadowed his grandmother for a moment until she realized he was still there.

"Those newspapers won't deliver themselves," she said. "Here, take the end of this tablecloth and help me spread it." After Cork had done as she'd asked, she looked at him closely. "Something on your mind?"

"Broomstraw says—"

"She's an elder, Corkie. Show her respect."

"Mrs. Broom says that Big John's spirit can't walk the Path of Souls."

"And why not?"

"It's been more than four days since he died."

"I'm sure the Creator understands the circumstances."

"Besides that, he took Mass."

"And I'm sure the Creator has more important things on his mind than how we pray."

"What do you think, Grandma?"

"About what?"

"What happens. You know, after we die."

"Sit down," Grandma Dilsey said.

They sat in folding chairs at the table and Cork's grandmother took his hands. Because she'd been a teacher much of her life, she had a lot of experience with the questions of children, though Cork was no longer a child.

"I don't know if there's anyone who can answer that question truthfully, Cork. I don't know if there's anyone who's actually come back from the dead to tell us."

"I saw a story in the *National Enquirer* in the drugstore."

"Forget that claptrap."

"What about the Path of Souls? What about heaven?"

"In the absence of evidence, we have faith, Corkie."

"Do you believe in the Path of Souls? Do you believe in heaven?"

"What I believe isn't important. It's what you believe, what you feel in your heart."

But he didn't feel anything in his heart at that moment except a great emptiness, and he didn't know how to give that emptiness words of explanation.

"Talk to Henry tonight," Grandma Dilsey said. "Now, I have work to do, and so do you."

Cork had left his bike leaning against the side of the community center. He mounted it and began the long ride back to Aurora. The bike was a ten-speed Schwinn Varsity, which Cork had purchased himself after nearly a year of saving all his earnings from delivering newspapers and cutting lawns and from gift money at Christmas and his last birthday. On his Schwinn, he felt like he was riding the wind, and the ten miles between the Iron Lake Reservation and his house in Aurora were nothing. Or almost.

Allouette was a crisscross of a few streets, none of them paved. The homes were a hodgepodge of drafty old cabins, flimsy houses built by the Bureau of Indian Affairs, trailers set on cinder blocks, and a number of sturdy little houses with flowers and medicine gardens, his grandma Dilsey's among them. With LBJ's "war on poverty," electricity and phone service had finally come to the rez, but no running water yet, and outhouses were the norm. There wasn't much enterprise—Frank's gas station, the Wild Rice Café, LeDuc's General Store, the small tribal building, and the community center. It had never been what might have been called a bustling town, but these days, with so many families like Billy's having been lured away to distant cities by the promise of jobs, it sometimes felt deserted.

Cork was quickly outside town and cycling his way along the gravel road that paralleled Iron Lake itself. The vast blue sparkle of water came in bursts between the birch and aspen lining the shore. To Cork's left rose rugged hills covered in a mix of evergreen and hardwood, stretching east more than sixty miles to Lake Superior. This was the great Northwoods, the country he'd known since birth, and he felt the pulse of its life in the same way he felt the beat of his own heart.

He'd gone three miles when he came to a spur that cut left and led to the old mission, where Father Cameron Ferguson from St. Agnes still held Mass every Sunday afternoon for those in Allouette who'd been confirmed. It was also the place where many of the Ojibwe of Allouette buried their dead.

Without thinking, Cork took the spur and biked the quarter mile to the mission. It was small, built seventy years earlier of white pine logs, and still stood sturdy in a little clearing circled by wooded hills. Behind it was the cemetery, enclosed by an old picket fence. Cork got off his bike and leaned it against one of the fence posts. Among the markers and headstones stood a number of traditional spirit houses, which were small planked structures that rose two feet above the grave. Each house had a hole at one end, allowing the spirit to escape, and a little shelf where offerings could be placed to help the departed in their journey to *Gaagige Minawaanigoziwining*.

Cork walked to a mound of dirt that marked the place where Big John's casket would be lowered the next day. The open grave had been covered with a canvas tarp held in place by four heavy stones at the corners. Cork removed the stones and pulled the tarp away. This was more than idle curiosity or a morbid interest. It had to do with the swirl of questions in his head about death, and not just Big John's. He questioned the Ojibwe belief in the soul walking a path to a better place, and he questioned the Christian view of heaven. Staring into that square of vacant earth, which felt to him like a cold, unwelcoming box, Cork considered that maybe everything he'd been told about death and what came after was no better than a fairy tale. That waiting hole, where even now he could see earthworms wiggling along the edges, told the real story. There was life, all of it aboveground, in the freedom of the air and sun and moon and stars, and then there was death, which was nothing but a hole in the ground waiting to be filled. A dark, senseless forever.

He was about to put the tarp back into place when he saw a small pink square in a corner at the bottom of the grave. It stood out in dramatic contrast to all the raw, dark earth around it. Cork peered more closely and could see that it was a piece of folded paper. The hole was six feet deep. Cork eased himself over the side, dropped to the floor of the grave, and picked up the paper. He carefully unfolded it and saw that it was a piece of stationery with flowers along the edges. One word had been written on it: *Goodbye.*

There were little gray stains on the paper, and Cork realized they were from tears. Then he caught the scent of something exotic, something lovely and floral, and he lifted the paper to his nose. The perfume, whatever it was, was strong. Cork had never smelled anything quite like it.

He knew this was an intrusion, a trespass on someone's private grief, and he refolded the paper and put it back where he'd found it.

Getting out of the grave was a bit of a struggle, but he finally scaled the side and put the tarp back in place. He mounted his bike and started again for town, feeling an enormous sense of sadness. But surrounding that emotion was a lingering disquiet because of the great darkness he'd glimpsed—or thought he'd glimpsed—rising above the shadows at Lightning Strike.

CHAPTER 6

When Cork returned from Allouette, his mother wasn't home. Jackson was gone, too, and he thought maybe she'd taken him to the vet. There were reports of distemper in Tamarack County, and his parents had discussed the importance of making sure the dog was well protected.

Cork wrote a note saying he'd gone to deliver his papers and attached it with a magnet to the refrigerator door. He walked to the newspaper drop box on Dahlia Street, where he found Jorge Patterson sitting cross-legged on the ground, reading a magazine. The publication was called *Famous Monsters of Filmland* and featured photographs of creatures from movies, old and new. The boys loved monster movies, but while Cork saved his money for things like a Schwinn Varsity, Jorge bought monster magazines and monster model kits. His bedroom was decorated with his drawings of frightful creatures, not only re-creations of those dreamed up by Hollywood but also many that came directly from Jorge's vivid imagination.

"Check this out," Jorge said.

The picture in the magazine was of a woman with snakes sprouting from her head.

"The Gorgon," Jorge said.

"Yeah, I know," Cork said. "Greek myth."

"But this one terrorizes an English village. Stars Christopher Lee and Peter Cushing. It's gonna be great, man. I can't wait to see it."

Cork pointed out that the film wasn't going to be released for a long time yet, then added, "It'll take forever to get to the Rialto, if it ever does." Aurora's small movie theater showed mostly family-oriented films, usually long after they'd hit the screens in the Twin Cities. "Come on, let's get these papers delivered."

Between them, they shared three afternoon routes, delivering the *Duluth Herald*. Cork also had a morning paper route for the *Duluth News-Tribune*, but that job he did alone. They divided the streets, Cork taking one side and Jorge the other, and in this way, the whole process was finished in a little over an hour.

Cork liked the job in part because it took him through a small town he knew as well as he knew his own face in the mirror. But Aurora was changing. It had once been a booming iron-mining community, as were so many towns along Minnesota's Iron Range. But the iron mines had begun to close—cheaper foreign steel, everyone complained—and Cork had watched families leave, kids he'd grown up with gone forever. It sometimes felt to him as if the ground under his feet was shifting, and it scared him. If he had the power, he would have frozen everything in place forever.

When the boys finished their routes, they headed, as usual, to Sam's Place. This was a Quonset hut constructed during World War Two, but it had been purchased after the war by Sam Winter Moon and converted into a thriving burger joint on the shore of Iron Lake. Sam was Ojibwe and a family friend. He was a frequent dinner guest at the O'Connor house, and Cork's father and Sam often hunted and fished together. But maybe the tie that bound them most was that they'd both been in the war. They'd fought their way across Europe into Germany in many of the same battles. They seldom talked about their war experiences, at least in Cork's presence, but they seemed to understand each other in a deep and, to Cork, mysterious way.

When the boys arrived, Sam was standing in the dirt parking area looking at his Quonset hut. He turned when he heard them coming. "Think I should paint it red?" he asked.

The hut was dull gray, the color of the corrugated metal from which it was constructed, the color it had always been. Cork had never given it a thought one way or the other. It was just Sam's Place and served up the best burgers in the North Country.

"Daisy says it would be more appealing if I painted it red." Sam shook his head.

Sam Winter Moon stood just under six feet tall. His hair was black and he kept it in a crewcut. His eyes were two dark almonds in a face the color of deer hide. When he smiled, which was often, you could see that his teeth were porcelain white.

He ran a hand along his jawline. "Daisy's got an eye for things like that. What do you boys think?"

Before Cork could answer, Daisy Winter Moon, Sam's niece, who'd just graduated from high school, leaned out the serving window of the Quonset hut and called, "Or blue. Would match the lake, don't you think?"

Sam shook his head. "Come on, boys, let's get you something to eat."

Most folks who visited Sam's Place took their orders and left, or they ate at one of the two picnic tables placed near the lakeshore. Cork and Jorge usually ate inside, in Sam's personal, private area. In his remodeling, Sam had divided the Quonset hut into two sections—the front for food preparation and serving, the back as his living area from spring until late fall, when he closed up for the winter.

Sam threw a couple of hamburger patties on the griddle and

Daisy made two chocolate shakes. When the food was ready, the boys sat down at the table in back where Sam ate his meals. Sam called out to Daisy, "Give me a holler when the rush comes," and he sat down with the boys. "So, Jorge, how are things out at Glengarrow?"

Jorge's father had died in the Korean War, one of the many Marines killed at Heartbreak Ridge. Jorge's mother had moved from San Diego to Aurora with the idea of raising her infant boy among his father's Minnesota relatives, an idea that soured as soon as she arrived.

"A bunch of religious crazies," Jorge had told Cork more than once. "Because Mom's from Mexico, they think she's dirty. And because I look Mexican, I'm dirty, too. When we bump into them somewhere, they pretend they don't see us. The hell with them."

To support herself and her son, Jorge's mother had taken a position at the big estate called Glengarrow, which belonged to Duncan MacDermid, who owned the North Star iron mine.

"Everything's fine, Mr. Winter Moon," Jorge said. "But old Mrs. MacDermid's health isn't so good."

"Never has been, truth be told. But you help out?"

"I do what I can."

"All anybody can ask." Sam turned his attention to Cork. "You look like someone with a question on his mind."

"Big John," Cork said.

"Ah." Sam nodded. "Anything specific?"

"I stopped by the mission today. I saw where they'll bury him."

Sam waited and Jorge went on eating.

"He was baptized and confirmed Catholic," Cork said. "He went to Mass pretty often. But he committed suicide, which is a mortal sin. So, I didn't think he could be buried in the cemetery."

"Probably couldn't in the Catholic section of the cemetery here in Aurora. But the mission's on rez land. On the rez, we can do what feels right to us." Sam's dark eyes held on him for a long while, then Sam said, "But I'm guessing there's something else."

"Yeah," Cork said. But before he was able to tell Sam about what he'd glimpsed at Lightning Strike, Daisy hollered from the serving area, "Rush coming."

Sam stood and put a hand on Cork's shoulder. "We'll talk more at the wake tonight."

When they were alone, Jorge reached into his back pocket and brought out a folded sheet of drawing paper. He opened the sheet and swung it around on the tabletop so Cork could see it clearly. "My newest monster creation."

Cork was chewing the last bite of his hamburger, but nearly choked when he saw the drawing. He coughed and coughed and finally rasped, "When did you draw that?"

"After we went out to Lightning Strike and found . . . well, you know. It's kind of vague at the moment. I don't know what it'll become. But I love those scary eyes."

Cork stared down at Jorge's drawing. It was just a vague scratching of charcoal, a kind of dark cloud, but in the middle of all that darkness two burning eyes stared out.

"You okay?" Jorge asked, seeing the look on Cork's face.

Cork wasn't okay, not at all. Because what Jorge had drawn looked very much like the thing Cork had seen, or thought he'd seen, towering among the shadows in the pines at Lightning Strike.

CHAPTER 7

Home, Liam had often heard, is where the heart is. If that was true, his heart was in a white, two-story frame house on Gooseberry Lane. There was an elm out front, still young as elms go because Liam had planted it to celebrate his son's birth. A roofed porch ran the length of the home's front and a swing hung there, suspended on two galvanized chains. Lilac hedges served as property boundaries on either side.

The house had been built by Colleen's father, an O'Connor who was a distant relative to Liam's father. He'd come to Aurora as a teacher and had become the superintendent of schools. He'd worked with Dilsey, Colleen's mother, to improve education on the rez, and they'd fallen in love and married. He'd built the house on Gooseberry Lane and had raised his family there. When her husband died, Dilsey had moved back to the small house on the reservation where she'd spent her childhood, leaving the big house in Aurora to Colleen and Liam. She often visited, however, and sometimes stayed the night in the guest room.

Colleen was at work in the kitchen. The house smelled of hamburger stew, one of Liam's favorites, a concoction of ground beef, corn, green beans, stewed tomatoes, onions, lots of savory spices, and because his wife was half Ojibwe, wild rice, of course. It was more typically a winter meal, but Colleen often prepared it for large gatherings because it was quick, easy, and popular. The stew was for Big John's wake that evening.

He found her at the sink, washing up the bowls and utensils she'd used in the stew's preparation. He liked that she was full-bodied, with lots of soft, rounded areas. Her hair was auburn, a genetic mix of her father's Irish red and the darker tone that came from her mother's Native heritage. When she heard him enter the kitchen, she turned, and her earth-colored eyes settled on him warmly. Liam took a spoon from a drawer and dipped out a bit of the stew to taste.

"If you're hungry, I'll make you a sandwich," she told him. "It will be a good long spell before you eat."

He knew what she meant. A wake could go on for quite a while before the ceremonial sharing of the meal.

"Got the report today on Big John's blood alcohol level," he said.

"And?"

"He was definitely intoxicated when he died."

Her back was to him, but he saw her go stiff. Like everyone else on the rez, she refused to believe what the evidence indicated.

"I was out at his cabin. He left his truck there. His canoe was gone as well. It wasn't at Lightning Strike either, so I think he must have walked. Which means he had to have passed through Allouette carrying two bottles of Four Roses and enough rope to hang himself, but nobody on the rez admits to having seen him."

Colleen stirred the stew. "Maybe he didn't want to be seen. It strikes me that suicide is a very private act."

"Which he seems to have thought out well."

That wasn't unusual, Liam knew. As a cop in Chicago, he'd worked enough suicides to understand that some attempts had been meant as calls for help and were poorly carried out. But people who truly wanted to die often spent a good deal of effort in ensuring their end.

Colleen turned from the stove. "Dilsey called while you were out. She told me Cork was at Lightning Strike today. Billy Downwind asked him to go."

Liam closed his eyes. "Oh, God. That'll just feed his nightmares."

"But you can understand Billy wanting to go."

"I suppose. Only why did he have to take Cork?"

Before his wife could answer, Cork came in through the mud porch door. Jackson, who'd been lying sleepily in a kitchen corner, bounded to him, tail wagging a mile a minute.

"Hey, boy." Cork gave the dog a good patting, then went to the refrigerator, pulled out a bottle of milk, and poured himself a glass. Then he said "Hi" to his parents.

"Have a seat." Liam nodded toward an empty chair at the table.

Cork must have heard something in his voice because he looked concerned. "Am I in trouble?"

"Like I said, have a seat." Liam waited until Cork had taken a chair, then he sat down at the table, too. "I understand you went out to Lightning Strike today."

"Billy wanted me to go with him. To show him—you know."

Liam gave a nod. "He wanted to see where it happened."

"He's trying to figure out why his uncle did it." Cork looked into his father's face, then turned and looked at his mother, who was watching from the stove, the wooden stirring spoon in her hand. "Why do you think he did it, Mom?"

Colleen laid the spoon on the stovetop, came to the table, and sat down beside their son. "You know that Big John had struggled with a drinking problem."

"I thought he licked it."

"It's hard to know what someone's going through, the demons they wrestle with. I know some of what drove Big John to drink in the first place. When a lot of men came back from the war, alcohol was a way they tried to forget what they'd seen and what they'd done."

"Not Dad. Not Sam Winter Moon."

"Every man is different," Liam said.

"Okay, so maybe that's why he started drinking, but he stopped. What made him start again?" When his mother didn't reply, Cork looked to Liam, who shook his head.

"I never saw him drunk, not once," Cork insisted.

"That doesn't mean he wasn't drinking," Liam said.

"I'm never going to drink."

"I hope you hold to that." Colleen leaned and kissed his forehead. "Finish that milk, then get yourself cleaned up for the wake."

CHAPTER 8

A fire burned in a ring of stones outside the community center in Allouette. The fire had burned for four days, ever since Big John's body had been discovered at Lightning Strike. It would burn until the next day, when Big John was laid in his grave.

Cork and his parents walked past the fire and entered the community center. The coffin sat atop a low table surrounded with flowers. It was positioned with the head to the west, the direction a spirit would follow on the Path of Souls. Though an open casket was more typical, the lid was closed. Cork had seen what remained of Big John and understood why.

In one corner, a prominent display of photographs of the dead man had been created by his family, all of them showing a great bear of a human being, generally with a broad smile across his face.

Rows of folding chairs had been set up, two separate sections, one for family of the deceased and one for friends and others. When the O'Connors arrived, there were already a dozen people in each section, talking quietly among themselves. Though death was no stranger to any of them, they all seemed to eye the coffin in disbelief. Because Big John was special. Big John had battled his whole life, and in a way, his huge spirit embodied the struggle of his people. Or that was Grandma Dilsey's assessment, and one she'd shared with Cork on numerous occasions, along with the larger-than-life history of the man.

In the days when so many Native children were wrested from their families and forced into government-run boarding schools, Big John had resisted. He'd run away many times from the Pipestone Indian Training School, and always they'd come to the rez and hauled him back. Until the last time he escaped. He was twelve years old then—the same age Cork was now—and to ensure his freedom, Henry Meloux had helped him flee into the Northwoods and had taught him how to make his way there, hunting and fishing and foraging. At the age of sixteen, he began to earn a living guiding others, mostly white men, into the Quetico-Superior Wilderness, an area he'd come to know intimately. At nineteen, he was tapped by the federal government and drafted. Though he could probably have disappeared again deep in his beloved Northwoods, he went to war instead, as did many young men from Tamarack County, white and Native alike. When he returned, he was a man who drank mightily.

From his own father, Cork had been given a general understanding of what might have driven Big John Manydeeds to hit the bottle. As an officer of the law, Liam O'Connor had seen some pretty bad things, but he'd told Cork that war was far worse than anything he'd ever encountered in civilian life. Whenever his curious son had pressed him for more information, he refused to share the horrific details of his experiences. Big John was different. When he drank, he grew angry and bitter and loud and violent, as if he were still fighting in the war. Which landed him in jail on many occasions, some of those arrests made by Liam O'Connor.

Grandma Dilsey had told Cork that it was Henry Meloux

who'd guided Big John out of his darkness. He did it with ceremo-
nies and with medicines and with compassion and with persistence.
By the time Cork was old enough to have memory, Big John, it
seemed, had put the drinking behind him.

But from comments he'd heard in Aurora, Cork understood
that in the opinion of a lot of white people, Big John would forever
remain just another drunken Indian.

So, there were not many white faces in the community center
at Allouette. Mrs. Pflugleman, the pretty wife of the pharmacist
in Aurora, was there, because like Cork's mother, she was half
Anishinaabe. Mrs. Andersen and Mrs. Krabill, two widowed sisters
who owned Borealis Outfitters—they were known as the Borealis
sisters—were there because they'd employed Big John as a guide
for years. Although he was to have no part in the wake ceremony,
Father Cameron Ferguson was there because he'd given the Holy
Eucharist to Big John at the mission for the last several years; Cork
understood that the two men were friends.

Cork's mother spent a few minutes with Billy Downwind's
family. Billy and Cork said "Hey" to each other, but that was it.
His parents greeted many of those already present, then sat in the
area designated for friends of the family and spoke little as they
waited. For an hour, in the quiet of the big room, folks drifted in,
paid their respects, and found chairs. There were more than a few
who gave Cork's father a cold eye, men he'd arrested or the families
of men he'd arrested. Cork knew his father had a few friends on
the reservation and among the Ojibwe who lived off-rez, but he'd
also heard Grandma Dilsey caution that many saw only one thing
when they looked at him—the oppressive authority of white law.

The chairs were mostly filled when Henry Meloux entered.
Cork felt something enter with him, the sense of a great presence,
and there seemed to be a change in the room, like the ripples that
went out from a stone dropped in water.

Meloux was not a big man. In height, he was well under six feet, and slender, like a young birch tree, and like a birch, he stood straight and strong. Although he was fifty years Cork's senior, his hair was still as black as a moonless night, and he wore it long and flowing down his back. He was a member of the Grand Medicine Society, a Mide, a healer, and Cork had always felt something calming in his presence, soothing in his voice, magnetic in his deep brown eyes.

The Mide walked to the family of Big John and spoke to them quietly, then went and stood next to the coffin. Abby Manydeeds, one of Big John's young cousins, moved about the big room with a clay dish in which sage smoldered. As she passed, each person drew the smoke to their bodies, cleansing themselves. Billy Downwind and one of his cousins, Skipper Manydeeds, rose from their chairs and took two bowls from a small table next to the casket. The bowls were filled with loose tobacco, and the young men moved among the rows of chairs, dropping pinches of the tobacco into the opened palms of those who'd gathered.

Meloux spoke in Ojibwemowin. Cork had been to many wakes, and although he couldn't translate most of the words, he understood that the Mide was explaining the importance of the tobacco. Then Meloux said in English: "Take your tobacco to the fire outside and give it to the flames, along with your offering of prayers so that the smoke may carry them to the Creator."

Cork and his family joined the long line that snaked out of the community center, circled left around the fire, delivered their tobacco to the flames, and returned to their seats.

Meloux spoke again in Ojibwemowin, and Cork understood that he was talking about the path to *Gaagige Minawaanigoziwin-ing*, which lay far to the west, and how it had been created. Then Meloux explained in English that the spirit of Big John needed to eat on his long journey, and food had been prepared for him and also to share with those who'd gathered. If those present didn't eat, the spirit of Big John would not eat. He encouraged everyone to join in the feast.

They took their time with the meal, and when they were finished, they sat again. The Mide spoke once more in the language of his people and after a pause, interpreted what he'd said for those who couldn't understand. He explained that he was helping to guide the spirit of Big John Manydeeds to *Gaagige Minawaani-goziwining,* telling the spirit what he would see in order to be sure that he was on the right path. Cork knew it was a long journey and wouldn't be completed that night but would end with Meloux's final guidance at the funeral the next day.

Meloux concluded with a prayer spoken in Ojibwemowin which he didn't translate into English. At last he said, "That is all I have to say for tonight."

People rose and talked quietly to one another and began to move toward the door. Mrs. Pflugleman walked past Cork's family and spoke for a moment with Cork's mother. In that moment, Cork caught a powerful scent that, when he recognized it, gave him a jolt. It was the same fragrance he'd smelled on the folded piece of stationery in Big John's grave. The woman strode out the door before he could pull himself together enough to speak, but even if he'd had his senses about him, he had no idea what he might have said.

"Liam, why don't you and Cork wait for me at the car," Cork's mother said. "I'm going to give a hand cleaning up from the meal."

Cork followed his father outside. There was still light in the sky, a soft, evanescing blue reflected on the placid surface of Iron Lake, which was visible through the trees along the shoreline. Billy Downwind was waiting, and he gestured to Cork to join him. In the dying light, Billy looked pale.

"You okay?" Cork asked.

"Yeah. Mom's pretty upset. And Uncle Oscar isn't helping any. He's been drinking again, and he keeps getting her riled up. All she does is cry." Billy looked away. "He called your dad a damn *chimook*. Says he's just sitting on his ass."

"*Chimook*." Cork gave a shrug. "Well, he is white. But heck, he's been called worse by other *chimooks*. He isn't just sitting on his ass though."

The boys caught sight of Henry Meloux as he exited the community center. After he'd spoken a moment quietly with Father Cam Ferguson, they approached him.

"Mr. Meloux, could we talk to you?" Cork said.

"What is it, Corcoran O'Connor?"

People were still coming from the community center. "Maybe over by the fire?" Cork said.

Meloux followed them, and when they were away from the others, Cork said, "Billy and me, well, we went out to Lightning Strike today."

He waited for Meloux to comment on a move that everyone else seemed to think was a big mistake, but the elder said nothing.

"Go on, Billy," Cork said. "Tell him."

Billy Downwind stumbled a little as he said, "My . . . my uncle was there."

Although the old man's face showed nothing and he didn't speak, Cork thought he saw a change in Meloux's eyes.

"His spirit's not on the Path of Souls, like you said tonight," Billy insisted. "He's out there at Lightning Strike."

"You saw him?" Meloux asked.

"Not exactly," Billy replied.

"You felt him?"

"Yeah, more like that."

"And you, Corcoran O'Connor?"

Cork thought about the huge, dark shape he'd seen, but decided to refrain from saying anything about it. Instead he said, "I felt something, too."

"Do you know about that place?" Meloux asked.

"My uncle said it's a special place, a spiritual place, and they should never have been logging there," Billy jumped in. "He said that's why the lightning hit."

"Maybe it was just that you sensed the spirit of that place itself," Meloux said.

"It was more than that. It was Big John. And he wants something. I could feel it." Billy was almost in tears. He looked earnestly at Meloux, then said, "Ah, hell, I should've known no one would believe me."

"I did not say that. Sit." Meloux indicated the ground near the fire.

The two boys sat and Meloux joined them. He stared a long time into the flames. It was a warm night with no breeze, and the smoke from the fire rose straight up toward the arc of the heavens, which was sugared with stars.

"I have read in the Bible how people have been brought back from the dead," Meloux finally said. "But I have never known a man or woman who has made the journey over and then returned to tell us what is true and what is not. What we believe about the spirit of a human being or the spirit of anything shaped by the Creator's hand is only what we believe. So, I will not say that what you felt at Lightning Strike was not a true thing."

Meloux lapsed into another long silence, and Cork and Billy waited, and the fire crackled as it burned, and the smoke followed its own path upward, and beyond the firelight the night was becoming as dark as a blind man's sight.

"To this world, we listen with our ears," Meloux said at last. "To the world beyond, we listen with our hearts. What your heart has heard and told you, Billy Downwind, is true for you, and so I believe you must do your best to understand what has been spoken. I do not know what that is. But I will say this: Your own spirit will not rest until you have your answer."

"How do I get there?" Billy asked.

"Do you know the story of Hansel and Gretel?"

"Sure."

"Follow the crumbs and see where they lead," the old man said.

"What?"

But Meloux didn't explain. To Cork, he said, "What did your heart tell you at Lightning Strike?"

Cork wasn't sure that his heart had told him anything at Lightning Strike, but his eyes had picked up something. "I saw . . ." He hesitated, trying to find the right words so that he wouldn't sound childish or crazy. "A shadow thing. A big shadow thing."

"Big John?" Billy asked eagerly.

"Bigger. Gigantic."

"Where?"

"In the trees on the far side of the clearing. It was there for a second, then gone." He looked to Meloux for confirmation and, he hoped, for explanation.

Meloux said, "The eyes are different from the heart."

"Different how?" Cork asked.

"They can be tricksters."

"My eyes fooled me?"

"You saw what you saw. But maybe you should ask yourself why did you see it."

"Isn't that the same question you put to Billy? Why did his heart speak to him?"

"Follow the crumbs. The trail will take each of you to the answer you are looking for."

"What crumbs?" Cork asked.

Meloux stood, looked down at the boys, and gave them what seemed to Cork a careless shrug. "Your trail. You figure it out."

Meloux turned and walked away, blending into the night.

"What the hell?" Billy said. "That didn't help at all."

Cork had to agree. They'd got no real answers from Meloux. But at least he hadn't called them crazy.

"What do you think we should do?" Billy asked.

"Let's meet tomorrow morning and figure things out," Cork suggested.

"Where?"

"Can you get into Aurora?"

"I'll borrow my cousin's bike,"

"Sam's Place. Ten o'clock."

They were still at the fire when Cork heard the raised voices.

"Like hell! What do you care? You're just another damn *chimook*."

"Oh, geez," Billy said. "That's Uncle Oscar."

CHAPTER 9

On the job, Liam O'Connor usually drove a cruiser from the Tamarack County Sheriff's Department. Because he wanted to do his best to keep his personal relationship with folks on the Iron Lake Reservation separate from his duty as an officer of the law, whenever he visited the rez in a nonofficial capacity, he used the family automobile, a red Ford Falcon station wagon. Most of those who'd attended the wake had scattered, but Liam had been stopped as he walked toward the car, and he stood now in the soft blue light of evening, facing an irate Shinnob.

"What do you want me to do that I haven't done, Oscar?" Liam tried to keep his voice even.

Oscar Manydeeds leaned threateningly across the few feet that separated them. Manydeeds could very well have carried the same epithet as his brother because he was every bit as huge as Big John had been. The difference was in their natures. Big John wasn't just enormous in body; the name had applied to his spirit as well.

"Ask questions, goddamn it."

"I've asked, Oscar, believe me. No one out here admits to knowing anything."

"Maybe you're asking the wrong questions."

"What should I ask, Oscar? You tell me."

Manydeeds simply glared a moment, his face a mask of anger, then he shouted, "My brother didn't go to Lightning Strike to kill himself!"

"And why is that?"

"Because it wouldn't be right and he knew it."

"Is there a right place for a man to kill himself, Oscar? If so, I'd love to hear it."

"Lightning Strike is a spiritual place. Every Shinnob knows that."

"A man who's thinking of killing himself probably isn't thinking straight. Especially a man who's been drinking."

"Big John didn't drink. Not no more."

"I think he did."

"Then the hell with you. You don't know nuthin." Manydeeds took a menacing step, closing even more the narrow gap between them. Liam braced as if for a blow. But it never came.

Sam Winter Moon stepped between them.

"A wake is meant to offer comfort and the hope of a peaceful journey along the Path of Souls," he said. "It's not a place for anger. You should go home and cool off, Oscar. And, Liam, you should leave."

Colleen and Dilsey had come from the community center. Cork joined them, and they walked to the station wagon through what remained of the gathering.

Before he left, Liam faced Billy Downwind's mother, who'd stood by wordlessly watching the exchange between the two men. "I'm truly sorry for your loss, Jeanette."

He thought she might thank him for his condolences, but she just stared at him until he turned away and walked to the car.

Colleen had made coffee, and now Liam and his wife and his mother-in-law sat at the kitchen table. Cork was upstairs in bed, but there was a heat grate in the kitchen ceiling that opened onto their son's bedroom, so they kept their voices low.

"Oscar Manydeeds was upset, Liam," Colleen said.

"Oscar Manydeeds had been drinking," Liam said. "He reeked of whiskey. Even so, he wasn't alone in his thinking. I could see it in a lot of the faces there tonight. They believe I haven't done enough."

"Only some," Dilsey said. Then she said, "Do you think you've done all you can? And do you really think he killed himself?"

"I go by facts, Dilsey. Here are the facts. He was called Big John for good reason. If he didn't want that noose around his neck, it would have taken a small army to put it there. But I found no signs of a struggle, no sign that anyone had been there with him. He had a history of alcoholism, and two empty whiskey bottles were lying at his feet. I know that Lightning Strike was a special place for him. When I was a cop in Chicago, I responded to a lot of suicide calls, and it wasn't uncommon for someone to end their life in a place that had some special meaning for them."

"You talked with his family and his friends?" Dilsey asked.

"You know I did."

"And they told you they didn't believe he killed himself?"

"It's a hard thing for anyone to accept."

"We've seen a lot of our people take their own lives, Liam,

and we can accept that it's a reality in our community. But when someone like Big John kills himself, that's different."

Liam was worn out, but not just from that day and the long ceremony that evening and his confrontation with Manydeeds. He was tired of asking questions on the rez and getting nowhere, tired of people saying the same things but not giving him any useful information.

"Different how, Dilsey?" he said, unable to keep his voice from betraying his frustration.

"Big John had been sober for years. He was respected on the rez and respected even among *zhaagnaashag*," she said, using the Ojibwe word for white people, which she almost never did unless she was angry. "We'd have known if he was drinking again or thinking of suicide."

"People can be pretty good at blinding themselves when they'd rather not see something."

"You knew Big John. You liked him. What do you think?"

"I think I let the facts, not my feelings, guide me."

Although her voice was calm, Dilsey's tone was all frost now. "You're the sheriff. I guess that has to be good enough."

"All right, Dilsey, here it is." Liam heard the iron in his voice, but he had no intention of softening what he was about to say. "After we brought his body in, I went to Big John's cabin. Out back, I found a box full of empty whiskey bottles. It was clear he had a fondness for Four Roses."

"I can't believe that."

"When he died, his blood alcohol level was through the roof. I have the report from the BCA."

"I never saw one indication of his drinking."

"My guess is that he did it in solitude, at his cabin. Maybe because of the trouble it got him into in the past, he'd learned to stay home when he was drunk. I wish everyone who drank did that." It was quiet in the kitchen for an uncomfortably long time. Then Liam said more gently, "Even good people, if they're alcoholics, can fall off the wagon. And Big John had demons. We all knew that."

"It's been a long, difficult day," Colleen said. "I think it's time we all got some rest."

CHAPTER 10

"Four-thirty, Cork. Time to rise and shine."

He'd set his alarm clock and it had gone off, but he knew, as he lay there drifting back into dreamland, that his father would make certain he didn't oversleep. His father always rose before first light, a lifetime habit. When Cork had taken on the additional responsibility of delivering a morning paper route, his father had assured him that he'd get used to the early hours, and even more than that, come to appreciate the quiet world that he would have to himself before the rest of Aurora awoke.

Jackson jumped on the bed and licked Cork's face.

"I'm up," Cork said. "I'm up."

His father had recommended that before Cork went to bed every night, he lay out his clothing for the next morning. It would make getting dressed that much easier. While Jackson sat watching patiently, Cork slipped into his jeans and T-shirt and socks and sneakers.

"Okay, boy, let's go."

His father was dressed in his khaki uniform and already had coffee percolating on the stove.

"I'm going to have a cup of joe, then, if you'd like, I'll drive you to your drop box," his father said.

"Okay." Cork sat at the kitchen table, idly petting Jackson's head. "Something I want to ask you, Dad."

His father had opened a cupboard and was reaching for a coffee mug. "Ask away."

"You know I went with Billy Downwind out to Lightning Strike yesterday."

His father leaned against the kitchen counter, cradling the coffee mug in his hands. "Yes. And?"

"Billy swore he could feel the spirit of Big John out there. He believes Big John isn't on the Path of Souls. His spirit's hanging around because he wants something."

"Does Billy have a sense of what that is?"

"I don't think so. But Henry Meloux said we should follow a trail of crumbs to the answer."

"You talked to Henry?"

"Last night."

"All right." His father moved to the stove and filled his mug. "What is it you want to ask me?"

"You do a lot of investigating."

"Goes with the job."

"How do you do it?"

"I begin by gathering all the facts I can. Physical evidence. What witnesses, if there are any, have to say. I try to look at the context of a situation so that it's not isolated from other events that might have some bearing. I try not to make assumptions but let the facts lead me." He sipped his coffee. "What does Billy think about his uncle's death?"

"That Big John didn't kill himself."

"What about you?"

Cork shrugged. "Mr. Meloux said Billy and I should follow the trail of crumbs, like Hansel and Gretel. He said it could lead us to the answers we're looking for."

"Do you have any crumbs for that trail?"

"Maybe."

His father seemed to look at him with deep interest now. "Care to share them?"

"They're nothing really. Not yet."

His father let some time pass before he spoke next. "When someone dies like Big John died, the result is usually a lot of hurt for those left behind. You have to be careful not to make that hurt greater for them than it already is."

"I know."

"And you have to be careful not to get in the way of the anger that also comes from being left behind and being left in the dark." Cork wasn't sure what this meant, but his father continued to explain. "When someone you love leaves you suddenly, the hurt can run deep, so deep that it makes you act out in destructive ways. I've seen it happen."

"You mean like Oscar Manydeeds?"

"Him in particular. But there's a lot of grief on the reservation right now. So, if you follow your trail of crumbs, and I suspect nothing I can say will keep you from it, I want you to be careful. I want you to check in with me every day. Okay?"

This did two things. It made Cork feel as if his father had allowed him into the investigation, and that gave him a profound sense of pride. But it also made him feel a tremendous sense of responsibility for finding the truth, and from the moment the weight of that duty settled on his shoulders, he was never quite the same again.

When Cork began his route, it still felt like night. The new day was just a vague suggestion of a lesser dark along the eastern horizon.

He'd folded all the papers and stuffed them, front and back, into the canvas bag that Mr. McCreary, the distribution manager, had given him. His paper route was essentially a square of more than a dozen blocks that included the downtown of Aurora. He always delivered to the residences first, so that the papers would be waiting on the porches of the early risers, then strolled through downtown, where the businesses would open much later.

Cork had taken on the morning route months before, when he was still trying to earn money for his Schwinn. He was already doing three afternoon routes with Jorge, and he'd invited his friend to join him. Jorge had reacted as if he thought Cork was crazy. "Only thieves, geeks, and freaks are up at that hour," he'd said. So when Cork walked his morning route—it was way too dark to ride his Schwinn—he usually walked alone, except for Jackson, who sometimes trotted along.

He was thinking about what his father had said, how the quiet of the morning was something he had almost entirely to himself, something he would come to appreciate. It was true. On the streets of Aurora in that early hour, he was almost always alone. Sometimes lights were on in a room, usually a kitchen, or on rare occasions, a car might drift past, but he and Jackson owned the sidewalks and the morning was his.

He was consumed with thoughts about Big John's death. Maybe it was exactly what it seemed, what his father believed it to be, the suicide of a drunken, troubled man. In the dark of that morning, Cork imagined what it must have been like for Big John to be alone at Lightning Strike. He imagined Big John slipping the noose over his head, snugging it around his neck. Did he hesitate before he stepped off the log he'd hauled there to stand on? Was there a moment when his muscles wouldn't move, wouldn't yield to his intent? Or was that what the empty whiskey bottles were all about, to help in breaking down every barrier between this world and the next?

Cork was deep in thoughts so terrible that he didn't notice at first the sound in the trees. Or rather, the lack of sound. Usually in the mornings, at the first hint of light, the birds began their chatter. Only a few at first, but by the time Cork was halfway through his route, it usually seemed as if the whole of avian existence had been aroused. As he walked now, he suddenly became aware that the soft click of Jackson's paw nails on the pavement and his rhythmic panting were the only sounds. He stopped and listened more carefully. Not a single bird.

He was on Beech Street, still two blocks from the businesses of Aurora. There were streetlights at intersections, but no lights between. Cork stood in near darkness, the town of Aurora—houses and trees and the distant courthouse tower—nothing but black silhouettes against the promise of dawn, the thinnest hope of a new day.

Then he saw it. For the second time. Among all those predawn silhouettes. The towering shadowy shape from Lightning Strike. Bending as if preparing to leap at Cork.

Jackson must have seen it, too, or sensed it, because he let out a low, threatening growl, then commenced to barking up a storm. Part English setter and part bulldog, Jackson was a canine with a fighter's heart. Cork knelt and threw his arms around his dog, seeking both to be protected and to protect.

Nothing came at him, and when he looked up, the shape was gone. Just as it had been gone in an instant at Lightning Strike. In its place was the silhouette of a tall spruce swaying in the wind that had risen. From far to the west came the low rumble of thunder, a summer storm moving in.

Jackson ceased his barking but, like Cork, continued to stare at the swaying evergreen.

"Come on, boy. We still have papers to deliver."

Cork went on, his eyes darting toward every shadow. He

peered long into darkened alleyways, and he glanced over his shoulder constantly.

The business district of Aurora was three blocks of shops, all small enterprises—Johnny's Pinewood Broiler, Glint's hardware, Marv's Men's Clothing, the First National Bank. At the corner of Oak and Fourth, he passed the red-brick structure that was the North Star Veterinary Clinic, and he thought about distemper and reminded himself to ask his mom about getting a booster shot for Jackson. In the next block, he passed Pflugleman's Rexall Drugs, and he thought about the scent he'd caught when Mrs. Pflugleman passed him at the wake, the same fragrance that had been on the folded note in Big John's grave. He paused a moment, trying to put those two things together in a way that made sense, but a big drop of rain hit his forehead, and he moved on quickly, wanting to get the route finished before the storm came. As he tossed the last of his folded papers into the doorway of The Novel Idea, the town's only bookstore, a Tamarack County Sheriff's Department cruiser pulled up to the curb.

"All hell's going to break loose in a few minutes," his father called to him. "Want a ride home?"

"No birds this morning," Cork told his father as they drove. "I didn't hear a one."

"Probably sensed the storm coming. Hunkered down like most intelligent creatures."

The storm had indeed broken, with a fury of wind and lightning and thunder. The wipers on his father's cruiser worked furiously to keep the windshield clear in the deluge. Liam O'Connor drove slowly, the headlights illuminating a curtain of rain.

"You know Mrs. Pflugleman, Dad?"

"Babette? Sure. Why?"

"She smelled good last night."

"Really?" His father glanced at him and smiled. "She's pretty, isn't she?"

"I guess."

"Not as pretty as your mom."

"I was just wondering about that smell."

"Probably some cologne or perfume."

"Which one?"

"Even if I'd caught the scent, I'm sure I wouldn't know."

Cork wanted to tell his father about the huge thing he'd seen twice now. But they'd been only glimpses and then they were gone. He wasn't sure if his father, a man who demanded hard evidence, would believe him. He wasn't sure he believed it himself.

His father dropped him off at home. Cork and Jackson ran through the downpour to the garage, where Cork kept the canvas bags for both his morning and afternoon routes. He hung the bag on the peg where he always hung it and was about to leave when he spotted the Louisville Slugger, which his father had given him on his tenth birthday, leaning against the wall next to the door. He picked it up and swung it and liked the solid feel of it in his hands. He set it beneath the canvas bag he'd just hung, thinking he'd take the sturdy baseball bat along with him on his route the next morning. Although he wasn't sure of what he'd seen that day, it had scared him plenty. And if it turned out to be more than just his imagination, he wanted to be ready.

CHAPTER 11

By the time Liam O'Connor knocked at the door of Sam's Place, the storm had passed. The sun was well above the horizon and the sky was showing a promising blue. Sam Winter Moon had a cabin on the Iron Lake Reservation, but midspring through late fall, he usually slept at the Quonset hut, the better to get the place ready every day for business.

Liam and Sam Winter Moon had become friends, joined by a bond that two reasonable men could form out of their reasonableness, but solidified further by their shared experience in World War Two. They almost never talked about the war, but there was a tacit understanding that they'd been scorched by the same fire, and it made them, in a way, brothers.

Sam opened his door immediately and, despite the early hour, seemed pleased to see his friend. "Good timing, Liam. The coffee's just finished perking."

There was something enormously comforting about Sam's Place. Some of it was the good aroma of hot fry oil that permeated the place and always made Liam think of French fries. Some of it was the simplicity of what Sam needed for his own comfort, the few well-chosen furnishings. And some of it was, of course, the man himself, one of those welcoming souls who seemed able to put even the most contentious spirit at ease.

Sam poured them both coffee and they sat at the small table, which Sam had made himself of birch.

"What's on your mind?" Sam said.

"I want to run something by you."

"I figured you were after more than just my coffee, good as it is."

Liam said, "Cork and Billy Downwind hiked out to Lightning Strike yesterday afternoon. Cork told me Billy Downwind felt something there. He believed it was the spirit of Big John."

Sam gave a single nod. "So?"

"You don't seem surprised."

"It could be just a kid missing a man he loved and imagining that he hasn't gone away completely. That seems understandable. But it's also possible that what he felt was exactly what he thought it was."

"The spirit of Big John lingering there?"

"Why not? Look, in the war, I often heard the voices of men I knew had been killed. There's a reason that we Ojibwe believe it takes a while for a human being's spirit to find its way to a final place of peace."

"No one on the rez believes Big John had fallen off the wagon, but it's clear that he was drinking again."

"Those whiskey bottles at Lightning Strike?"

"I also found a box of empties behind his cabin. When Sigurd Nelson was preparing Big John's body for burial, I had him take some samples so that I could send them to the BCA for a blood alcohol level at the time of death. I got the report, Sam. His blood alcohol level was extremely high."

"Hard to believe he could keep folks from knowing something like that. There are no secrets on the rez."

"Stay with me on this a bit, Sam. Suppose Big John had gone back to drinking, any idea what might have caused it?"

"In my experience, for a lot of unfortunate folks, Indian and white, it's simply that alcohol has set its hook and won't ever let go of them completely. If not that, then maybe a great disappointment of some kind."

"Has anyone that Big John cared about died recently?"

"Not that I know of."

"What about a broken heart?"

"Lots of women on the rez wouldn't've minded taking up with Big John, but I haven't heard of anyone lately. And believe me, I'd know. Like I said, no secrets on the rez. By the way, how's Cork doing? Going back to Lightning Strike after what he saw there, that couldn't've been easy for him."

"He's got it in his head that Big John's spirit is sticking around because there's something he wants. And he thinks he and Billy Downwind are supposed to find out what that is."

"Does he have a clue?"

"Crumbs, he says, but that's it."

"Crumbs?" Sam Winter Moon smiled.

"Something Henry Meloux told the boys. Follow the crumbs."

"When Henry suggests you do something, there's always a reason, Liam. Just let go of your rational thinking for a moment. Just be willing to accept that maybe the boys are right. What is it, do you think, that the spirit of Big John might want?"

"Sam, I'm not even going to entertain that thought. If I let myself be guided by spirits, I might as well stop calling myself a cop. Something I can hold in my hand, examine with a magnifying glass, run a ballistics test on, those are the kinds of crumbs I deal in."

"What are you going to do about Cork? He seems set on finding his own answers."

Liam shook his head. "One thing I know. If something scares

you, the best thing to do is take action. Give yourself a sense that you have a measure of control. I'm thinking that's what Cork is doing here. So I'll let him play his game."

"That's what you think it is? A game?"

"If it becomes more serious than that, I'll step in. Thanks for the coffee, Sam."

Liam stood up and headed toward the door. At his back, Sam said, "Sheriff O'Connor."

Liam turned.

"Know what I think it is that Big John wants?"

"What's that, Sam?"

"What we all want. Just the truth."

CHAPTER 12

By ten a.m., the time he and Billy Downwind had agreed to meet at Sam's Place, Cork was bicycling over the Burlington Northern tracks that lay between the business district of Aurora and the Quonset hut on the shore of Iron Lake. The rain had cleaned the July dust from the air, and the morning felt fresh and new. Under the bright morning sun, Iron Lake was a great shimmer of welcoming blue. There were boats cutting the surface, a few moving slowly, trolling, a couple of small sailboats catching the light breeze that had continued after the passing of the storm. No fast powerboats yet, but there would be later.

Billy Downwind was already there, and he stood with Sam in the gravel parking area, both of them eyeing the Quonset hut.

"Billy here thinks yellow," Sam said without prelude when Cork dismounted from his bike. "Thinks it'll make the place pop."

"You know, catch the eye," Billy said. "The Mexicans in California paint everything bright colors."

"It looks fine the way it is," Cork said. "People don't come for the color. They come for the hamburgers."

"My thinking exactly," Sam said. "But it never hurts to try new things."

Cork wasn't so sure. Usually, he liked things just the way they were.

"So, what are you two up to today?" Sam asked.

Billy glanced at Cork, who shrugged and said, "Just goofing around. You know."

Sam gave him a half smile, which Cork couldn't quite interpret. "I haven't just goofed around in years. Sounds inviting."

Cork was afraid the man was going to suggest that he join them, but Sam said, "Have fun. Me, I've got work to do." He headed back toward the Quonset hut, but before he reached the door, he called out, "I'll see you at the funeral this afternoon."

After Sam had gone inside, Billy said, "So, what do we do now?"

"Exactly what Mr. Meloux told us to do."

"What's that?"

"You'll see. Come on."

They mounted their bikes and Cork led the way. At the corner of Elm and Second, where the post office stood, a voice hailed them from behind. "Cork! Billy!"

Jorge biked toward them, pumping his pedals to beat the band. They waited, and after he came abreast of them, they waited a bit more while he caught his breath.

"Hey, Billy," he finally said between gasps.

"Hey, Jorge."

"Heard you were back. Sorry . . ." Jorge paused and took a deep breath. "Sorry about your uncle."

"Thanks. I heard you were with Cork when . . . you know."

"Yeah," Jorge said.

They shared an uncomfortable quiet until Jorge said, "What's going on?"

"Yeah," Billy said. "Where are we going, Cork?"

"Some of this is going to sound a little crazy."

He filled Jorge in about Lightning Strike and what he and Billy had sensed there. Then he told them both about the scent of the note in Big John's grave, which had also wafted off Mrs. Pflugleman at the wake. What Cork didn't share was the towering thing he'd seen in the shadows that very morning. He couldn't say why exactly

"So, what are we going to do?" Billy said.

"Talk to Mrs. Pflugleman."

"And ask her what?"

"I don't know. We'll figure that out when we get there."

"Okay if I come?" Jorge asked.

Billy gave a nod. "Sure."

And so they became three.

Cork's mother and Grandma Dilsey occasionally talked about Mrs. Pflugleman, who, like Colleen O'Connor, was half Ojibwe. The other half of her genetic makeup was Italian. As a young man, her father had worked quarries in Italy, and after he came to America, had found work in the North Star Mine. Mrs. Pflugleman always looked to Cork like a movie star. Her hair was black and long and silky, her cheeks prominent, her eyes dark and sparkly. The pharmacy was the only store in town that handled anything near high-end cosmetics, and Mrs. Pflugleman's face always looked flawless.

When Cork and the others walked in, she was arranging face creams on a shelf. She turned and bestowed on them a smile outlined in luscious red.

"Good morning, boys."

They all said good morning back, and she waited, holding that perfect smile on her lips.

"A good ceremony last night," Cork finally said.

"Yes." A cloud of sadness crossed her face. She looked at Billy. "I'm so sorry. Your uncle was a good man."

"Thanks."

"I haven't had a chance to talk to your mother," she said. "How's everything going in California?"

"It's nothing like here," Billy said, his tone bitter. It was the first time Cork had heard him speak so sourly of his new home.

"You're not the only ones who've left the rez. Every time I visit Allouette, the town seems so empty. They say the Relocation Act was a good thing, but I wonder."

Like many other Ojibwe families, the Downwinds had abandoned the reservation because of the Relocation Act of 1956. Grandma Dilsey had explained the legislation to Cork, an act of Congress that funded relocation of Native families from reservations to certain designated cities. The government paid for the move, promised to help each family find housing, and offered to foot the bill for vocational training, if necessary. On the surface, it seemed like a pretty sweet deal.

But Grandma Dilsey had said that it was simply another attempt to eradicate the Native cultures.

"They tried blankets tainted with smallpox. They tried guns. They tried boarding schools. Now they're trying this. It's all meant to separate us from one another, to wring out of us what makes us who we are. Anishinaabe, Navaho, Dakota, Blackfeet. We are the legacy of our ancestors. We are the vessels of all their learning, all that they held sacred. No one tries to drive Ireland out of the Irish who've come here. There are so many damn polka bands oompahing around that you'd think everyone in America is Czech. And I swear, Franco-American spaghetti has become our national food. But God help you if you're one of The People."

Mrs. Pflugleman had been holding a jar of face cream. She set it on the display shelf and said wistfully, "When I was a girl, I dreamed of going to California and becoming a movie star. My senior year in high school, I was Aurora's Blueberry Princess." She half-turned and struck the pose of a starlet, one hand on her hip, her face lifted, her red lips in a coquettish smile. Cork thought she was every bit as pretty as Elizabeth Taylor.

"You could still be a movie star," he said. "You wear perfume like one."

"It's called White Shoulders. You like it?"

"Yes, ma'am," Cork said. "But I liked the one you wore last night better."

"That was Shalimar." She leaned to him in a conspiratorial way. "My husband owns the joint, so I get to wear whatever I want. Shalimar is my favorite. I always wear it for special occasions."

"So you wore it special for Big John?"

"I guess." Again, that cloud of sadness cast its shadow over her face.

"Did you know Big John pretty well?"

"I thought I did." Her eyes took on a faraway look. "He was so handsome when he was young. Most of us girls had crushes on him. Even girls who weren't Indian. I would never have suspected . . ." She glanced at Billy and didn't finish.

"Did you maybe visit Big John's grave yesterday, Mrs. Pflugleman?" Cork asked.

"His grave? No. Why?"

He'd seen detectives on television ply people with question after question until they cracked. But Cork had hit a dead end in his own questioning, and he stared at her dumbly.

He was saved when her husband hollered from behind the pharmacy counter, "Babette! Customer in hair care!"

"Duty calls. I'll see you two at the funeral," she said to Cork and Billy, then she walked away, leaving the ghost of White Shoulders behind her.

"Well," Billy said. "Where did that get us?"

"It wasn't much," Jorge agreed.

"But it was a crumb," Cork said. "Let's go."

CHAPTER 13

It was nearing lunchtime, and Jorge suggested they head to his house to grab a bite.

"Mom fixed fried chicken for dinner last night," he said. "I know she'll let us have the leftovers."

Jorge and his mother lived at Glengarrow, the big estate outside of town. It was the grandest home and grounds Cork had ever seen. The house was gray stone, three stories, a great central square with wings stretching off either side and so many windows that on clear days the reflections of the sun made it seem as if there was a fire in every room. The old carriage house had long ago been converted into a garage large enough to hold four vehicles, with a living area above it. When Jorge wasn't much more than a toddler, his mother had been hired as a companion and caregiver to Aurelia MacDermid, the doddering old matriarch of the family, who was sliding into dementia, and they'd moved into the apartment on the second floor of the carriage house.

The boys leaned their bikes against the wall of the carriage house and clambered up the outside stairs. Music flowing through the screen door greeted their arrival. Cork recognized the song from all its play on the radio: "It's My Party." Jorge's mother was singing along at the top of her voice about how it was her party and she'd cry if she wanted.

Cork knew her story. Across their long friendship, he and Jorge had shared everything about their families. She'd been born in Chihuahua, Mexico. Her parents, who were dead now, had migrated north and worked the agricultural fields of Southern California. She'd met Jorge's father and married him while he was training at Camp Pendleton. He'd been deployed to Korea during that war and had come back in a coffin draped with an American flag. Although Jorge had never known him, he kept a framed photograph of his father dressed in his Marine uniform on the desk in his bedroom, where he did all his drawing. In a snap case in the top drawer of his dresser was the Bronze Star his father had been awarded posthumously.

"Jorge!" his mother said with a smile when saw him. She was at the kitchen counter, washing strawberries in a colander. "Hello, Cork!" Her eyes widened in surprise when she saw their companion. "Oh, Lord, is that you, Billy?"

"Yes, ma'am."

"I heard you and your mother were back." She wiped her wet hands on a dish towel, walked to Billy Downwind, put her hands gently on his shoulders, and said, "I'm sorry about your uncle."

Billy looked down at the linoleum floor and said, "Thank you."

"My, how you've grown. Are you here long?"

"Not long, no. We'll probably go back after . . ." He didn't finish.

"We're hungry, Mom," Jorge said. "I told the guys we could have the leftover fried chicken."

"Of course. Sit," she said, indicating the chairs at the kitchen table. "It's hot out. Are you thirsty?"

"Yes, ma'am," Cork said.

"I'll fix a pitcher of Kool-Aid, then put out the chicken."

She talked to them gaily while she worked. Cork liked her immensely. She was, he thought, a woman of great energy and goodness, and he believed it a tragedy that she'd lost her husband so young and that Jorge had never really had a father.

"So, Billy," she said as she prepared the Kool-Aid. "How do you like California?"

"It's all right," he said with a shrug.

"Sunshine all the time, yes?"

"Mostly."

"And do you eat the good Mexican food there?"

"Some."

"Frijoles? Tacos? Burritos?"

"Sometimes."

"How about menudo?"

"Not that, no." Billy's face scrunched up in disgust.

"What's menudo?" Cork asked.

"A delicious dish," Jorge's mother said. "So aromatic, so tasty."

Jorge whispered, "It's tripe soup."

"Tripe?" Cork said.

"Cow's guts," Jorge said.

His mother put ice cubes in glasses and poured them grape Kool-Aid. She was just turning to the refrigerator when there was a knock at the screen door.

"Carla?" a man called out.

"Come in, Nicholas," Jorge's mother called back. She said "Nee-ko-las" in a way that made it sound a little like happy music.

A moment later a man in a charcoal suit stepped into the kitchen. His hair was glossy, slicked down with cream oil, and his cheeks were shiny as if he'd just shaved. He wore black-framed glasses and his eyes behind the lenses were steel blue. He wasn't tall but was powerfully built, reminding Cork of a football line-backer. He smiled when he saw the boys sitting at the table.

"Hey, guys," he said. "Qué pasa?"

"Hi, Mr. Skinner," Jorge said.

"How many times do I have to tell you, Jorge. Just call me Nick."

"It's the boys' lunchtime," Jorge's mother said. From the refrigerator, she pulled a plate of fried chicken covered in waxed paper and set it in the middle of the table.

"For them, maybe," the man said. "You're wanted in the big house. Aurelia is in a bit of a temper, and you're the only one who seems to be able to calm her down these days."

"Plates are in the cupboard," she said to her son. "Napkins in the drawer. And you're welcome to the strawberries I just washed, boys. Or there are apples in the fridge."

"Adios, muchachos," the man said as he escorted Jorge's mother out.

"Muchachos?" Cork said after they'd gone.

Jorge shrugged. "He thinks it's cute."

"Who is he?" Billy asked.

"Mr. MacDermid's lawyer," Jorge said.

"He's sweet on Jorge's mom," Cork said.

Billy raised an eyebrow. "What do you think of him?"

"I don't know," Jorge said. "He really seems to like my mom, and she seems to like him. She gets lonely sometimes. So . . ." He let it go with a shrug.

"Is he rich?" Billy asked. "Cuz that suit didn't look cheap."

"I guess," Jorge said. "Mr. MacDermid is rich, so his lawyer probably is, too. Come on, let's eat."

When they'd finished the chicken and each of them had eaten a handful of strawberries and had drunk all the Kool-Aid they cared to, Billy said, "I gotta get back to the rez."

"My mom's driving out to help set up the community center for the funeral," Cork said. "She'd probably give you a ride. Thanks for covering my paper route this afternoon while I'm at the funeral, Jorge."

"What friends do."

The boys took their plates to the sink, and Jorge rinsed them off and stacked them neatly for washing. Then he put the pitcher of Kool-Aid in the refrigerator. Jorge was always good about helping out his mom. Cork was always thinking he'd try to be better in the same way with his own mother, but invariably he seemed to falter in the follow-through.

The boys bounded down the steps outside and had just grabbed their bikes when a deep, commanding voice hailed them.

"You hold it right there, George!"

Along with the others, Cork turned and watched Duncan MacDermid cross the yard and approach them.

Mostly, Cork saw Duncan MacDermid on Sundays at St. Agnes. The MacDermid family had a pew of its own at the very front of the sanctuary, so the man was usually a figure at a distance, larger than life to Cork because of how everyone spoke of him. He was tall, with an angular face that seemed chiseled from the kind of rock found deep in his family's vast iron mine. His hair was thick and grayed, his eyes sharp and dark, his mouth like a thin scratch across the stone of his face. He was the only person who insisted on calling Jorge by the English version of his name.

"What is it, sir?" Jorge said in a quiet voice.

"I've been looking for your mother. My mother needs her." The man stood above the boys, smelling of whiskey, which Cork figured might account for the way he leaned, as if pushed by a strong wind. His eyes shifted to Cork. "I know you."

"My father's Sheriff O'Connor."

"Of course." The man nodded. Then he glanced at Billy Down-wind. "You I don't know."

"William Downwind," Cork's friend said.

"Downwind," MacDermid said coldly. "Indian."

Billy didn't reply. Everyone on the rez knew how Duncan MacDermid felt about Indians. He'd never hired any to work in his mine, not one. Cork had occasionally heard people in Allouette call him a *maji-manidoo*, which meant devil.

"Friend of yours, George?" the man asked Jorge.

"Yes, sir. He lives in California now. He's back for his uncle's funeral."

"Funeral?" He studied Billy again. "Your uncle, was he John Manydeeds?"

"Yes, sir."

"I don't want you coming around here again. Ever."

Billy took a moment, then said, "I wouldn't even if you paid me."

The man swung his attention back to Jorge. "Your mother?"

"Mr. Skinner came to fetch her a little while ago."

MacDermid gave a nod, then a last glare at Billy Downwind, turned, and walked back toward the big house.

"Asshole," Billy said under his breath. "*Chimook* asshole."

CHAPTER 14

The funeral that afternoon, like the wake the night before, was held in the community center in Allouette. When Liam O'Connor stepped inside with his family, he saw that the chairs were arranged as they'd been the evening before, and the casket was in the same position.

By the time Henry Meloux began the ceremony, all the chairs were filled. Most of those in attendance were Native, but Father Cameron Ferguson was there again, as were the Borealis sisters and Mrs. Pflugleman. After the smudging with sage, after the tobacco and prayers had been offered, after everyone had shared in the meal, Meloux spoke to the spirit of Big John in Ojibwemowin. Then, for those who'd never learned to speak their language, the Mide explained in English that he'd told Big John's spirit what to expect as he completed his journey in the next world. He ended with a long prayer, spoken in that beautiful language and in a cadence that made it seem like a song.

"That is all I have to say," Meloux concluded. "The spirit of Big John Manydeeds has completed his journey. It is time for his body to return to Mother Earth."

Six men rose, all of them relatives of the deceased and, like Big John, veterans of military service, evidenced by the khaki VFW caps they wore. Each took his place beside the casket and lifted. Liam, who'd been to many Ojibwe funerals, knew that in accordance with custom, the coffin had been carried into the community center through the eastern door, and as he watched, the six men carried it out through the west-facing door.

The gathering remained quiet as they followed, but once outside in the waning light of the late afternoon sun, Elsie Broom, whom Liam had heard his son and so many others on the rez refer to as Broomstraw, muttered, "It's a lie. He was never on the Path of Souls."

"Hush, Elsie," Dilsey said.

"Mark my words, we'll be seeing his ghost," Broomstraw said, paying her no mind. She wagged a bony finger at Liam's son. "You make sure you don't talk to him, boy. He'll grab hold of you and snatch you right out of this world and into his."

Dilsey looked ready to spit, but before she could say anything further, her attention, and everyone else's, was grabbed by Oscar Manydeeds, who spoke loudly at Liam's back.

"Know what I did today, Sheriff?"

Liam turned and faced the big, angry man. Manydeeds's sister, Jeanette Downwind, and her son, Billy, stood next to him.

"You mean besides drinking too much, Oscar?" Liam replied.

Manydeeds ignored the comment. "I went out there to Lightning Strike. Know what I found?" He held out his hand. In the opened palm lay a cigarette lighter, silver, expensive looking.

"You found that at Lightning Strike?" Cork's father said.

"Right near where he was killed."

"My men went over that area. They didn't find anything."

"Well, they sure as hell missed this. Big John didn't smoke, unless it was for ceremony. This lighter's got writing on it, nothing like what my brother woulda put there."

"I'd like you to give that to me, Oscar."

Manydeeds drew his hand back quickly. "Finders keepers."

"That's not how the law works. That lighter may be evidence."

"Of what? You finally willing to admit it was no suicide?"

"Give me the lighter, Oscar."

"Not till you tell me what else you 'didn't find.'"

"Let's go somewhere and talk this over quietly."

"Why not here? What you tell me I'll tell all of them anyway." He swung his hand toward the gathered crowd.

"Okay, here it is," Liam said. "I sent a sample of Big John's blood to the Bureau of Criminal Apprehension lab in Saint Paul. When the report came back, it indicated that Big John's blood alcohol level was nearly two hundred when he died. Do you know what that means?"

"Why don't you tell us?"

"He was drunk, Oscar. Really drunk."

"He gave up drinking."

"Have you looked behind his cabin?"

Manydeeds didn't respond.

"You'll find a small mountain of discarded whiskey bottles. Big John fell off the wagon quite a while ago. I talked to Ben Svenson at the Crooked Pine. Apparently, Big John had become a regular customer lately."

"I don't believe it."

"The evidence is clear."

Manydeeds turned in a circle, addressing the crowd. "I haven't seen him drunk in years. Have any of you?"

"I'd like that lighter, Oscar."

Manydeeds spun back. "You'll have to take it."

The two men stared at one another. Although he was a white man in the center of a great circle of mostly Anishinaabe faces, Liam didn't back down.

Henry Meloux stepped between them. "This is the time for us to say goodbye to the spirit of our brother, our uncle, our grandson, our cousin. Saying goodbye to Big John Manydeeds should not be done with anger in our hearts."

"That's all there is in my heart right now, Henry." Manydeeds turned, and as he stormed away, the crowd made way for him.

During the confrontation, Sam Winter Moon had stood near enough to Liam that he could easily have interceded, if necessary. Now he leaned close to his friend and said, "You should leave."

"Go on," Colleen, who'd also been standing near, said. "I'll find a way home after the burial." She glanced beyond Liam at her son. "You go with him, Cork."

With Cork at his side, Liam made his way through the gathering, his spine rigid. The looks of those he passed covered a broad range of responses to the presence of a white lawman in their midst, even one they all knew well. On some faces, Liam saw deep concern, in others outright hostility. He and his son got into the station wagon without a word and drove away from the community center and out of Allouette.

They didn't go far. After five minutes, Liam turned off on a spur that cut away from the main road and led down a dirt track to Big John's cabin on the shore of Iron Lake. He killed the engine and sat staring at the simple structure.

"What are we doing here?" Cork asked

Liam didn't answer but finally opened his car door and stepped out. His son did the same. Liam walked to the cabin, opened the door, and went inside.

"What are you looking for?" Cork asked.

"I don't know. Sometimes something jumps out at you. Something you didn't see before."

"Do you really think he killed himself, Dad?"

"That's what the evidence shows. At the moment. But

maybe . . ." Liam stood still and turned in a slow circle. "Maybe I missed something."

He finally shook his head and moved past Cork, walking out into the sunlight. He went to the back side of the cabin with his son a few steps behind.

"Geez," Cork said when he saw the box full of empty whiskey bottles. "Big John? I wouldn't have guessed."

"You can't trust appearances, Cork. People can be awfully good at hiding what they don't want others to see."

"How do you ever know what's true?"

"Wait here," Liam said and headed back to his car.

Cork stood looking down at the evidence of weakness in a man who'd seemed to be all about strength. He hadn't been called Big John for nothing. In physical stature and in the esteem of his people, he'd stood tall. He was known to be the best guide in all of the North Country, much in demand by anyone wanting to journey into the Quetico-Superior Wilderness. In his dealings with Big John, Cork had always found him to be a generous spirit, but quiet, in the way of a man who was comfortable in the solitude of the great Northwoods.

The cabin stood alone in a grove of aspen on a small cove off Iron Lake. Beyond the opening of the cove, the broad blue of the lake stretched away under the afternoon sky, the surface as smooth as glass. The little cove had a calm feel to it, a place of intimacy or, depending upon how you looked at it, isolation. It fit Big John, Cork thought. Then he looked again at the box of empty bottles, and that thought twisted into a suspicion of the true reason for the man's solitude.

Cork's father came back wearing the pair of work gloves he kept in the station wagon. He lifted one of the bottles from the box, held it up to the late sun, and studied it. He put it back in the box and lifted another and turned it in the sunlight.

"What are you doing?" Cork asked.

"What I should probably have done in the first place," his father answered. "He was right, you know."

"Who?"

"Oscar Manydeeds. He may have been drunk tonight, but he was right. I made assumptions. A rookie mistake." He looked at Cork and said, "You asked me how you ever know what's true. The only way I know to the truth is to consider all the evidence, not just some of it. I haven't done my job in that regard, Cork." His father put the bottle back with the other empties, lifted the box, and carried it toward the station wagon. "It's time I got started. Let's go. I'll drop you at home."

CHAPTER 15

In the dark of the next morning, after he'd taken his canvas newspaper bag from the peg where it hung in the garage, Cork grabbed the Louisville Slugger he'd put beneath it the day before, and he and Jackson headed off to deliver his route. The sky was clear and star dusted, the air still, the first birds already anticipating dawn with timorous calls. The baseball bat was unwieldy and, as it turned out, unnecessary. Cork saw nothing like the towering shadow thing he'd seen the previous morning.

When he finished his route, a thin, pale light lay along the eastern horizon. Returning home, he found his father, out of uniform, alone in the kitchen sipping freshly brewed coffee. Cork slipped his canvas newspaper bag off his shoulder and leaned the baseball bat against the wall.

"Practicing your swing while you deliver papers?" his father asked.

Cork didn't want to tell him the truth, that he'd taken it because he was afraid of a shadow. "There's a dog on the route that sometimes gives me trouble."

"Wouldn't talking to the owner be a better idea than anything you might do with that Louisville Slugger?" His father waited. When he didn't get an answer, he said, "Two things on your agenda today. First, we promised to help with the Cub Scout training at St. Agnes."

"Do I have to?"

"You agreed. We both did. And second, don't forget your mother's birthday is tomorrow."

Cork filled Jackson's bowls, one with fresh water and one with Purina dog chow, then dropped a couple of slices of Wonder bread into the toaster. He poured himself a glass of milk and joined his father at the table.

"Have you bought anything yet?" his father asked.

Cork shook his head. "But I kinda know what I'm going to get her. What did you get her?"

"What I always do, and what she expects. Wind Song cologne and bath powder."

"Why do women think they have to smell nice?"

"Don't you like that they smell nice?"

"I guess. But I'm glad I'm not a girl. I don't have to worry so much about how I smell."

"Maybe you should," his father said and waved a hand in front of his nose. Then he smiled. "You'll be worrying about it soon enough."

The toast popped up and Cork spread the pieces with peanut butter and gooseberry jam. "What are you going to do with those bottles you found at Big John's?"

His father took a few moments to respond, and Cork thought maybe he was considering whether he'd answer at all. Finally, he said, "I'm having them dusted for fingerprints."

"Why?"

"Everybody on the rez tells me that Big John didn't drink.

His blood alcohol level says they're wrong. If he was drinking, I want to know if he was drinking alone. If not, who was with him."

"What if his are the only fingerprints?"

"Then I'll have to accept that maybe folks on the rez didn't know about his drinking and weren't just covering for him."

There was a knock at the back door. Cork's father looked surprised and when he got up to answer, found Sam Winter Moon standing there.

"Saw the kitchen light on, Liam," Sam said.

"Come on in." Cork's father stepped aside to let his friend enter.

"*Boozhoo*, Cork," Sam said, using the Ojibwe greeting.

Jackson trotted to him, and he gave the dog a good petting. When they were all seated, Sam reached into his pocket and brought out a silver cigarette lighter. He slid it across the tabletop to Liam O'Connor.

"Got that from Oscar after he sobered up and cooled down some," he said.

Cork's father picked up the lighter and turned it over and over, studying it.

"Fingerprints," Cork said, because his father was always talking about care in handling evidence.

"It's been through too many hands now, Cork."

"See the inscription?" Sam said. "And the initials?"

" 'Alba gu bràth, D.M.' " his father read.

"What?" Cork said.

"It's Gaelic, Cork. In Irish, we'd say 'Erin go Bragh.' Means 'Ireland Forever.' I'm pretty sure this is Scottish and probably means basically the same thing about that country."

Cork thought a moment. "D.M. What's that?"

"Initials, maybe," his father said.

One name came quickly into Cork's mind. "Mr. MacDermid? He's Scottish, right?"

"Bright boy," Sam said.

"Did Oscar pick up on that?" Cork's father asked.

"He didn't say anything, and I suspect if he understood he would have said plenty."

"A crumb?" Cork said, nodding toward the lighter.

"Crumb?" Then his father got it. "I don't know, Cork." He stood the lighter on the table, and it reminded Cork of a headstone in a cemetery. "Maybe."

"I'm heading out to talk to Henry," Sam said. "Something I want to run by him. Care to come along, Liam?"

"I've got a few questions I wouldn't mind putting to him."

"Can I come?" Cork asked.

His father and Sam exchanged a look, and his father said, "Don't see why not. But let's leave your mom a note so she doesn't worry."

Henry Meloux lived alone in a cabin he'd built as a young man on Crow Point, far north on Iron Lake at the edge of the reservation. Sam Winter Moon parked his pickup truck on the side of a narrow, graveled county road, and he and Cork's father and Cork set out along a path that wove two miles through thick forest. They crossed Wine Creek, and not far beyond that broke from the trees and entered a broad meadow full of wildflowers and timothy and thistle. Meloux's cabin stood on the far side. As the visitors approached, a dog set to barking. This was Makwa, Meloux's only companion.

Meloux met them at his cabin door, Makwa at his side. In the language of the Ojibwe, Makwa meant "bear." The dog was huge and shaggy, a mix of breeds, none of which Cork had ever been able to identify. Despite the great beast's fearsome appearance, Makwa's bushy tail wagged eagerly, and he came forward to nuzzle Cork's outstretched hand.

"Hey there, boy. How you doing?"

"He has spent his morning worrying rabbits," Meloux said. "It keeps him from other mischief." The Mide looked at Liam O'Connor and Sam Winter Moon. "The day has barely broken. This must be important."

"It is, Henry." Sam and Cork's father both gave Meloux tobacco, which they'd brought to thank the Mide for his time and his wisdom.

Meloux said, "Let us smoke and talk. Wait here."

He went into his cabin and a minute later, returned with a beaded pouch and a long-stemmed pipe. He led the way along a path that cut across the meadow and between two outcroppings of high rock. On the other side of the rocks lay a circle of stones with a great bedding of char and ash at the center. Beyond a line of aspen, the water of Iron Lake burned with the gold light of early day.

Cork and the others sat cross-legged on the sparse grass outside the fire ring. Makwa trotted past them and sniffed his way down the shoreline. Meloux offered tobacco to the spirits of the four directions, then filled his pipe from the beaded pouch and, once it was lit, passed it to the others. The pipe came to Cork last, and he looked to Meloux for permission to smoke with the men. Meloux shook his head. When Cork handed him the pipe, Meloux gave him a pinch of tobacco to offer the spirits instead.

After they'd sat in silence for a while, with the sun on the rise and the morning air warming and the smell of countless sacred fires all around them, the Mide said, "Ask."

Sam said, "On the rez, people are talking. They've seen something that scares them. They're saying Big John's spirit didn't make the journey on the Path of Souls."

"I saw it," Cork said. "First out at Lightning Strike, then in town yesterday morning, when I was doing my paper route."

His father said, "I'm guessing that Louisville Slugger you hauled around this morning wasn't because of a worrisome dog."

"No, sir."

Sam said, "On the rez, they're saying you might have an idea why he hasn't walked the Path of Souls, Henry. Word is Big John was troubled about something and did a sweat with you just before he died."

"Do you know a human being who is not troubled?" Meloux replied. "If you do, I would like to meet that person."

"People are wondering if his death had anything to do with the reason for his sweat, and maybe the reason his spirit isn't at rest. They're wondering what he might have prayed for in that last sweat."

"If you came to me for a sweat, Sam Winter Moon, and I heard your prayers spoken to the Great Mystery, would you want me to tell others what was in your heart?"

Cork's father said, "If it helped get to the bottom of a death that might not be what it seems, I would certainly want that."

Meloux's dark eyes leveled on him. "You think you know what the heart of a dead man would want?"

"What I think is that you're not going to tell us anything, Henry," Cork's father said. "I wish to God you would just say that plainly."

"You talk about what the heart wants, Liam O'Connor, what the heart knows. Do you listen to your own heart?"

"I try."

"That is what you tell yourself, but I think you do not do this often enough."

"I'm a cop, Henry. I'm trained to look at evidence, and evidence is what I'm looking for here."

"Which you will interpret with your brain."

"Logic. Reasoning. It's what a good cop uses. He collects facts, collects evidence, and tries to put things together so that they make sense. It's the only way I know how to get to the truth."

"The heart has its own logic, its own reasoning, its own way to the truth."

"Just tell me, Henry. Do you think Big John killed himself?"

"You ask for a shortcut in your own understanding of the truth. The only truth worth defending, Liam O'Connor, is the one you find on your own."

Cork's father reached into his pocket and pulled out the lighter Sam Winter Moon had given him. "Oscar Manydeeds claims he found this at Lightning Strike. I'm pretty sure it belongs to Duncan MacDermid. Do you know why it might have been found where Big John died?"

"I do not."

"You know of nothing that might tie Duncan MacDermid to Big John's death?"

His father's tone was harsh, tight with frustration, and Cork thought Meloux might respond with anger. Instead, the man said, "You are like a deerfly, Liam O'Connor. No matter how many times I shoo you away, you keep trying to bite me. I have said all I will say on this matter. Now go, or I will be forced to squash you like a deerfly."

"*Migwech*, Henry," Sam said, thanking the Mide. He stood, and the look he gave Cork's father said it was wise for him to follow.

"I may not know the truth in another man's heart, Henry," Liam O'Connor said, "but I know when a man is keeping secrets. I don't know who you're trying to protect or why, but I swear to you I'm going to find out." He stood brusquely. "Let's go, Cork."

They trooped in silence across the meadow, into the trees, and back along the path that would take them to the place where Sam had parked his truck. From the way his father held his fists clenched, Cork could tell he was angry.

"I would like to have seen that," Sam Winter Moon finally said, in a way that made Cork think he was about to laugh.

"Seen what?" Liam O'Connor said.

"Henry squash you like a deerfly."

Cork's father walked on several more steps, then relaxed and unclenched his fists. "He could do it, couldn't he?"

"And you'd never know what hit you."

Sam laughed. After a moment, Liam O'Connor joined him in that, and Cork thought his father should do as Meloux had advised and listen more often to his heart, because it was a good one.

CHAPTER 16

The first book Cork had ever bought with his own money was *Treasure Island*. He'd purchased it on the advice of Sandie Herron, owner of The Novel Idea. Since then, at her urging, he'd bought *Journey to the Center of the Earth, The Time Machine, The Call of the Wild*, and *The Hound of the Baskervilles*. He'd checked out other books by the same authors from the library, but these five he owned and kept on a shelf in his bedroom and he'd read each of them at least three times.

When he walked into the bookstore that Saturday morning, Sandie—she'd told him never to call her Mrs. Herron; that was too formal for two people who shared a love of books—was helping another customer, Astrid Lankinen, a nearly deaf old woman who was also a customer of Cork's on one of the afternoon paper routes he shared with Jorge. She always put off paying him when he came monthly to her door to collect for the delivered papers, and when she did finally cough up what she owed, there was never a tip included.

"You're sure I'll like this?" the old woman was saying. "Because I don't want to waste good money on trash."

"I know how much you appreciate Agatha Christie, Astrid."

"What?" The old woman leaned nearer and cupped her hand behind her ear. "Speak up. I can't hear you."

"Agatha Christie, Astrid," Sandie said patiently and with greater volume. "I know how much you like her work. P. D. James is a bit different, but she writes a marvelous mystery, and like Christie's, her stories are set in England. This is her second novel, and I believe it's even better than her first."

"And if I don't like it?"

"Well, Astrid, I guess you can always go somewhere else to buy your books."

"Hmmm." The old woman looked at the novel as if it might bite her. "I'll take it, but you'll hear from me if it's a disappointment."

"But you won't hear from me, will you?" Sandie said quietly. "Because you never wear your damn hearing aid."

"What?"

Sandie spotted Cork and put up a hand, signaling him to wait while she finished with Mrs. Lankinen. After the old lady had tottered past Cork and out the door, Sandie came to him smiling.

"How's my favorite young reader? Here for another recommendation?"

"A birthday present for my mother."

"It's Colleen's birthday?"

"Tomorrow."

"Do you know what you'd like to get her?"

"Not really. I just know she loves to read."

"I think I might have just the thing. Follow me." She went down an aisle and pulled a book from the shelf. "You know Charles Lindbergh, yes?"

"He flew across the Atlantic. Jimmy Stewart played him in the movie."

"That's right. This book is by his wife, Anne Morrow Lindbergh. It was published a few years ago, but it's timeless, and I believe it would speak meaningfully to your mother."

The book's title was *Gifts from the Sea*. Cork liked the cover.

"And I'll tell you what. Wait here." She left him for half a minute, and on returning, placed a paperback novel atop the Lindbergh book. The cover was dark, full of mist half-hiding an old castle and a woman who seemed terrified and looked to be running away. "I know Colleen has a weakness for Gothic romance, so I'll toss this in as a birthday gift from me. I'll even wrap them up for you."

Sandie had just handed him the beautifully wrapped books when the bell above the door jingled. A woman stepped up next to Cork at the counter, and Sandie said, "Good morning, Mary Margaret."

Mrs. MacDermid, wife of the mine owner, always moved in a way that reminded Cork of a doe in a forest meadow, graceful but ever alert for danger. On Sundays, when Cork saw her sitting beside her husband in their family pew at St. Agnes, she never looked happy. He'd sometimes wondered if her somber appearance was simply the effect of the Mass, that long, sacred ceremony, or if it was the result of having to sit so near a man whom most of the population of Tamarack County either feared or hated. He'd never spoken to her, nor she to him, and he thought she probably had no idea who he was.

But when she glanced down at him, she said brightly, "Good morning, Cork."

Despite his surprise, he managed to reply, "Good morning, Mrs. MacDermid."

"Gifts, I see."

"For my mother," he said. "Tomorrow's her birthday."

"Well, please wish her a happy birthday for me."

"I will, ma'am. Thank you."

She smiled politely and waited, and he realized she was dismissing him.

He stepped outside, paused in the shade of the awning, and

tried to make sense of something. Because wafting off Mrs. Mac-
Dermid in the bookstore had been the same scent Mrs. Pflugleman
had worn at Big John's wake, the one she'd told him was called
Shalimar, the fragrance he'd smelled on the folded note in Big
John's grave.

When she exited the store, she didn't seem to notice Cork. As she
passed others on the sidewalk, they gave respectful nods and moved
aside for her, which made him think of how nobles were treated by
underlings in the books he'd read by Robert Louis Stevenson.

Liam had grown up in Chicago, Illinois, the son and grandson of Irish
cops. He was a city kid, but when he'd married Colleen, who was
adamant that she couldn't live in a city, he'd uprooted himself and re-
settled in her hometown of Aurora, Minnesota. He'd quickly become
enamored of the beauty, the isolation, and maybe especially the pine
fragrance of the great Northwoods, which was a far cry from the
odor of hot tar on the Chicago streets, the smell of exhaust fumes,
and the odious drift from the stockyards and slaughterhouses.

Sam Winter Moon had, in a way, taken him under his wing,
and Liam was soon well acquainted with the Boundary Waters,
with canoeing and portaging and everything that went along with
setting up camp. When Cork came along, Liam introduced him
early to the joys of roughing it. Once Cork was old enough for the
scouting program, Liam served in a number of adult capacities,
often accompanying the boys on their outings into the woods that
surrounded them.

On that Saturday afternoon, he'd volunteered, along with
Cork, to help teach some skills to Cub Scouts who'd never camped
before. They'd assembled on the lawn in front of St. Agnes, which
was where the Scout troop met every Wednesday evening and
where the camping gear was stored. Mostly he stood back and ob-

served the older scouts at work, offering advice when needed. He was pleased with his son's patience in helping the younger boys as they stumbled about setting up the canvas tents.

Father Cameron Ferguson was also there. He'd been an Eagle Scout and as soon as he'd been appointed to serve at St. Agnes, had thrown himself into helping with the scouting program. After the tents were all set up and Conrad Dordt, who was the current scoutmaster, was preparing to deliver a lesson on honing knife and ax blades, Liam signaled to Father Cam that he wanted to talk to him.

They stepped into the narthex of the church, where they could still see the gathering of scouts through the open front door.

"What's up, Liam?" the priest asked. He was thirty-three years old, handsome, with an athlete's build and blond hair as thick as a lion's mane. Liam had heard his wife comment that a lot of gorgeous manhood had been sacrificed in the name of the Church.

"You knew Big John," Liam said.

"Of course. We all did."

"You gave him the Eucharist."

"Many times."

"And heard his confessions."

The priest, who'd been following with nods, suddenly grew still.

The sheriff said, "He's dead, Cam. So the privacy of what he might have told you in those confessions seems a moot issue now."

"What are you asking, Liam?"

"I'm wondering about his confessions. I'm wondering what he told you that might help me understand why he killed himself." Then he added, "If, in fact, he did."

"Dead or no, Liam, the Seal of Confession still applies."

"Then tell me this. Do you believe he'd fallen off the wagon, as the evidence seems to indicate?"

"People in confession seldom confess to everything, Liam."

"Do you know of anything that might have driven him back to the drink?"

The priest simply stared at him and held to silence.

Laughter from the lawn rumbled through the open door, and Liam glanced out to where all the scouts seemed to be enjoying the antics of a stray dog who was scampering among them, disrupting Scoutmaster Dordt's lesson on honing.

"Okay, Cam, how about this? In the confessional, has Duncan MacDermid confessed to something that might cause you personally some great conflict of conscience?"

"I'm not going to answer that."

"Then there was something?"

"I didn't say that."

"Would you say that Duncan has some terrible sin weighing on his soul?"

"What man doesn't, Liam, including you? I don't tell others what you've told me in confession. Why would you think I'd behave differently with Duncan MacDermid or Big John?"

"I'm asking, Cam, because I have reason to suspect that MacDermid may know something about Big John's death. So, all I would like to know from you is this: Is it possible I'll discover something significant if I press Duncan MacDermid?"

The priest turned from Liam and gazed down the center aisle toward a life-sized crucifix that hung on the wall behind the altar. After a long moment, he turned again to Liam and said, "Duncan isn't the only MacDermid who enters my confessional."

Liam thought about this, then nodded. "Thank you, Cam."

"Will I see you at Mass tomorrow?"

"I'm on duty."

"Pity. You look like a man who could use a little spiritual comfort."

CHAPTER 17

Saturday night was the one time in every week when Liam O'Connor took over the kitchen. With his son's help, he prepared the evening meal, which was almost always hamburgers, baked beans, and coleslaw. In summer, dessert was usually hand-cranked ice cream.

Liam loved this tradition in which the men of the O'Connor clan fed the women. He mixed the meat and Cork shaped the burgers. Cork chopped the cabbage and Liam threw together the slaw. Liam prepared the ice cream mixture and settled the canister into the rock salt and ice of the bucket, and he and Cork took turns with the cranking. They absolutely wouldn't allow Colleen or Dilsey to lift a hand in the preparations. While Liam and Cork worked, they talked. Which was maybe the best part of the whole arrangement.

That Saturday, Liam was deep in thought, and he didn't hear Cork talking to him.

"Dad!" Cork finally said, his voice demanding.

Liam stood at the kitchen counter, slicing tomatoes for the

burgers. He glanced over his shoulder at his son, who was turning the crank on the ice cream bucket. "What is it?"

"I've been talking to you."

"Sorry. What were you saying?"

"I bought Mom's birthday present this morning."

"Good man." Liam returned to his work. "What did you get her?"

"A book. Two actually, but one's a gift from Sandie Herron."

"She'll like that."

"Mrs. MacDermid came into the shop while I was there."

Liam turned fully now, knife in hand, his fingers red from the juice of the sliced tomatoes. "Did you happen to talk to her?"

"Just to say hello. But, Dad, she was wearing this special perfume. It's called Shalimar."

Liam waited for Cork to go on, trying to keep his face unreadable.

"It's like this. Before they buried Big John, I went to the grave they dug for him out at the mission. There was a note all folded up at the bottom of the grave. I was curious so I opened it. There was one word written on it—'goodbye.' The paper was scented with perfume. Then I smelled that same perfume on Mrs. Pflugleman at the wake, and when I asked her, she said it was called Shalimar. And this morning at the bookstore, Mrs. MacDermid was wearing it, too."

"Just the one word on the paper, 'goodbye'?"

"Yes."

"How was it written?"

"What do you mean?"

"In script or block letters?"

"Script."

"If you had to guess, was it written by a man or a woman?"

Cork thought about how the word had been written, and it reminded him of the way his mother wrote, clean and delicate. "A woman, maybe."

"And this paper, was it regular paper?"

"Pink stationery. With flowers across the top."

"Why didn't you tell me about the note before this?"

"It didn't seem important before. But now I think it's a crumb, and like Henry Meloux said, we should follow the crumbs."

"Where exactly?"

"To the truth about Big John's death."

Liam put the knife down and came and sat beside his son, who went on cranking. "The truth about Big John's death is my worry, Cork. I don't want you involved in this."

"You said I could follow my own trail of crumbs."

"Things are getting a little more complicated now."

"It means something, Dad. The note and the perfume."

"What does it mean?" Liam's voice had become taut, and he saw his son draw back.

"I don't know. But that's what an investigation is about, right? You don't know what the crumbs mean until you follow them to the end."

"You're twelve years old, Cork—"

"Almost thirteen."

"Almost thirteen," Liam granted, working to quiet himself. "There's a lot about this world and how people behave in it that you don't understand."

"What don't I understand?" Now his son's voice was rising, challenging.

"I'm not going to argue about this, Cork. I don't want you doing any more poking into what happened to Big John. That's that."

Colleen stepped into the kitchen and smiled when she saw them sitting together. "Boys sharing secrets?"

"Something like that." Liam stood and went back to slicing tomatoes at the counter.

"How's that ice cream coming?" Colleen asked.

Cork said with a dismal tone, "My arm feels like it's about to fall off."

"I'd be happy to crank for a while."

"Out," Liam said. "This is men's work."

After dinner, Dilsey, who always came into Aurora to share the Saturday night dinner, set up a card table in the living room, and Colleen brought out the Parcheesi game, another Saturday night ritual.

They were deep into the game when a knock came at the front door. Liam answered and found Sam Winter Moon standing on the porch with another man, a silver-haired Shinnob with a deeply lined face.

"Liam, this is Calvin LaRose," Sam said. "From Leech Lake. They've got a girl missing over there."

Liam reached out and shook the stranger's hand. "Pleased to meet you."

LaRose gave him a guarded look. "Sam said I should talk to you. Sheriff," he added with a note that rang sour.

Liam understood. He'd heard that same tone enough times from folks on the rez. Not all of them, but there were those who lumped him in with all other white people, and especially with all other cops.

"Tell me about the girl," he said.

"Her name's Louise. Louise LaRose. She run away. We been looking for her nearly a month. Heard she might be over this way."

"Do you have a photograph?"

The man reached into his shirt pocket and drew out a snapshot. He handed it to Liam, who studied it, then shook his head. "I haven't seen her."

"She hasn't been seen on the rez either," Sam said. "I thought maybe you could have your guys keep an eye out for her."

"How old is she?"

"Fifteen," LaRose said. "But looks older. Acts older."

"Can I keep this photo?"

LaRose nodded. "She's a handful."

"Is she your daughter?"

"Granddaughter."

"Does she have friends up here?"

"None I know of."

"How'd you hear she might be in Tamarack County?"

LaRose glanced at Sam Winter Moon, who said, "Word travels, Liam."

Rez telegraph, Liam thought. "How can I get in touch with you?"

"I'll get word to him," Sam said.

"In my experience, kids return home, Mr. LaRose. It may take them a while to come to their senses, but eventually they return home."

The man's face was stone. "Not all of 'em. Not if they're Indian." He turned around, pushed the screen door open, and left.

"I'll do what I can, Sam," Liam said.

"I figured you would. Good night."

Liam returned to the card table, and Dilsey said, "We heard. What do you think?"

"There's not a lot I can do except make sure my men are keeping their eyes peeled for her. If she's in Tamarack County but hasn't gone out to the rez, it's probably because she doesn't want anyone Ojibwe knowing she's here, afraid word would get back to her people."

"She's just a child," Colleen said. "How can she stay hidden? She needs food, shelter."

"Kids are resourceful, Colleen. Especially if they're scared."

Nobody asked what the girl might be afraid of. The possibilities for a kid, any kid, were many, and for an Indian kid especially, they were legion.

After the Parcheesi game, which Grandma Dilsey won, they watched some television, then Cork shined his shoes for church the next day. After that, he took his usual Saturday night bath and got ready for bed. His mother came in while he was reading *Journey to the Center of the Earth* for the fourth time. Cork made room for her to sit at the edge of his mattress.

"You okay?" she asked.

He put the book down. "Sure."

"You seemed a little quiet tonight. Your dad, too. Anything you want to talk about?"

"I'm okay." But he could see she wasn't convinced. "Dad told me I have to stay away from anything that has to do with Big John."

"Did he tell you why?"

Cork shook his head.

His mother reached out and smoothed his hair. "He has a lot on his shoulders right now. I think he doesn't want to have to worry about you as well."

"I won't give him anything to worry about."

"He's also trying to understand the truth, and there's a lot more to that than just answering questions." She gazed at him a long time, then smiled gently. "Your father loves you, you know that?"

"I guess."

"Try to get some sleep, all right?" She leaned to him and kissed his forehead. "Night."

After she left, Cork lay with the book open on his lap, but he wasn't reading. He was thinking about the missing girl, about the lurking spirit of Big John, and about his father. All evening Cork had fumed over the way his father had treated him, as if he were just a kid, forbidding him from following the trail of crumbs. His anger had cooled some, and he was considering now what his mother had said, that there was probably a whole lot more to the truth than simply finding answers. But finding answers was the beginning, wasn't it?

He put the book away, turned out his light, and closed his eyes, thinking that there were still answers to be found, and he would find them. But he would have to be careful to make sure his father didn't know he was looking.

In the dark near midnight, Liam stood in the doorway to his son's bedroom. Moonlight fell through the window and lit the room in ghostly silver. Jackson lay at Cork's feet, the big dog sprawled all the way across the mattress. He blinked at Liam but didn't even bother to raise his head. Liam watched the slow rise and fall of his son's chest, listened to his soft breathing, heard him mumble briefly in his sleep.

They'd been angry with one another, something that sat heavily on Liam's heart. He loved his son with a deep, fierce passion, but that was an impossible thing for him to speak aloud. Growing up in a world filled with cops, in a house overseen by one, he'd never once heard his own father say the words *I love you, Son*. He wasn't cruel to Liam, not even when he'd been drinking heavily, but those words that help to armor every child against the indifference of the world were never spoken. Liam didn't know how to say them either, not even now, when there was no one to hear but a drowsing dog.

At last he turned away and headed back to his own bed, feeling as if he was losing something, as if something essential was slipping through his fingers, but try as he might, he couldn't say what that was. He just knew it left him feeling afraid and empty and alone.

CHAPTER 18

They always sat on the right side of the center aisle and always in the first pew. They were first to contribute to the collection plate, first to the altar for the Holy Eucharist, and among the first to leave the church when the service ended. They almost never stayed for coffee and fellowship afterward, and they almost never seemed happy to have been there.

That Sunday morning, Cork studied Mr. and Mrs. MacDermid more carefully than he ever had before. His father was absent, on duty, and his mother was singing in the choir. Though she'd been baptized and confirmed in the Catholic Church, Grandma Dilsey no longer attended. She said she'd had more than enough of religion from the nuns in the boarding school to which the government had sent her when she was a child. So, Cork would have been sitting alone if it hadn't been for Jorge, who'd joined him in the pew near the back of the sanctuary. Jorge's mother sat several pews forward with Nicholas Skinner, the MacDermids' lawyer.

Cork watched the regal couple in the first pew carefully as they went through the motions of the service. Although everyone in the sanctuary knew when to rise, when to kneel, when to cross themselves, knew every responsive refrain, as he watched the MacDermids, Cork thought of them as robots, stiff in all their movements, like the Tin Man, who went about his business without a heart.

He was intent on his own concerns but at some point became aware that, like him, Jorge wasn't paying much attention to the service. His eyes were on his mother and Nicholas Skinner, and the look on his face wasn't particularly Christian.

"You okay?" Cork whispered as Father Cam walked to the pulpit to deliver the homily.

"She didn't come home until this morning," Jorge whispered back.

Cork thought about that for a moment. "Was she with . . . ?" He tilted his head toward Nick Skinner.

Jorge gave a confirming nod. "She said they were watching an old movie on TV and she fell asleep."

"At his place?"

Another nod.

"So?"

Jorge turned his smoldering eyes on Cork. "Fell asleep watching television? And didn't wake up until morning? Come on."

Cork was pretty sure he knew exactly what Jorge was intimating, but it was an area of consideration in which he didn't feel at all comfortable lingering.

"I thought you said you liked him."

"I never said that. I said Mom likes him." Jorge turned his glare again toward the back of Skinner's head. "We were doing fine without him."

Mass progressed, and after he'd taken communion, Cork returned to his seat and closed his eyes, trying to give the sacrament he'd just received due consideration. He felt a body settle next to him on the pew. He opened his eyes and to his profound surprise found his father there, in full uniform. Liam O'Connor looked straight ahead, following the movements of the priest as the ceremony wrapped up.

"You're supposed to be at work," Cork whispered.

"I am," his father whispered back without taking his eyes off Father Cam.

Jorge leaned forward and whispered across Cork, "Morning, Mr. O'Connor."

Cork's father gave him a solemn nod in return.

When the service was over and the congregation rose, Cork's father went quickly to the narthex door, where the priest always stood to speak with his parishioners as they left. Cork followed close behind him and listened in on their conversation.

"A word, Cam. You've told me more than once that you get down-and-out people stopping by the church looking for a handout. Have you seen this girl?"

Father Cam studied the photo Cork's father gave him. "Yes."

"Where? When?"

"A couple of weeks ago, maybe a little more. As you say, she was looking for a handout. I gave her food and urged her to go back home."

"You knew she was a runaway?"

"She was so young."

"Did she say anything to you? Where she might be staying or going?"

Father Cam shook his head. "She thanked me for the food and was gone. I haven't seen her since."

People were coming up behind Cork, awaiting their turn to greet the priest.

"Her name's Louise LaRose. If she comes back, will you call me?" his father said. "Her people are looking for her."

"That I will, Liam."

Cork and his father moved out onto the steps and headed toward the church parking lot, where the Tamarack County Sheriff's Department cruiser was parked. Jorge tagged along.

When they reached the car, his father stopped and looked back toward St. Agnes. "What's up with you two this afternoon?" He spoke in a distracted way, his attention really focused on the church door as people exited.

"You know, just messing around," Cork said.

"Home by four. Cemetery visit, then your mother's birthday party." His father spotted something and said, "Excuse me, boys."

Cork saw that Duncan MacDermid had left the church and was walking toward his car, a huge black Cadillac Eldorado next to which his father had parked the cruiser. Not at all a coincidence, Cork figured.

"A moment of your time, Duncan?" Cork's father said.

MacDermid halted but clearly seemed put out. "What is it?"

The sheriff reached into the pocket of his khaki pants and brought out something, which he held out in the palm of his hand, flashing silver in the morning sunlight. "Is this your lighter?"

MacDermid studied it a moment, then said, "Why, yes. Where'd you find it?"

"I didn't. It was turned in. I thought from the initials it was probably yours."

"A birthday gift from Mary Margaret. I didn't even realize it was missing. Who found it?"

"That would be Oscar Manydeeds."

"Manydeeds?" MacDermid's surprise was obvious on his face. "Where?"

"I'd like to talk to you this afternoon. Perhaps at your house?"

MacDermid's eyes dropped toward the flashing of silver in Liam O'Connor's palm. "Something to do with my lighter?"

"More or less."

MacDermid glanced around. Other parishioners were drifting toward the parking lot. "All right."

"Would two o'clock do?"

"That would be fine."

Mrs. MacDermid, who'd paused to speak with Father Cam, finally joined them. "Good morning, Liam. I understand it's Colleen's birthday today. Will you pass along my good wishes?"

"I will, Mary Margaret."

"May I have my lighter?" MacDermid said.

"I'd like to hold on to it for a bit, Duncan. I'll explain this afternoon."

"At two, then." MacDermid opened the passenger door for his wife.

Cork's father's eyes tracked the big car as if it were a buck in his rifle sight. He finally broke his gaze. "Four o'clock, Cork. Don't forget." He got into his cruiser and headed away.

"What's up with the lighter?" Jorge asked.

Cork shrugged, as if he had no idea, and said, "It's hot. What do you say we go for a swim in the lake today?"

CHAPTER 19

Liam O'Connor's Irish ancestors came to America during the great potato famine. When he was a child, stories of the callous hearts of English landlords had been fuel for the tirades of his male relatives, policemen all, whenever they gathered to drink, which was often. Liam didn't inherit hard drinking from those men, but their bitterness toward people with money and power was deeply embedded in his heart.

Duncan MacDermid had money, and Glengarrow, his grand estate on the shore of Iron Lake, was as near to a castle as you could find in the North Country of Minnesota. It had been built by Duncan MacDermid's grandfather, Andrew MacDermid, who'd opened the North Star Mine in 1886. The property took up a whole stretch of shoreline just north of Aurora, a long curve that gave a grand view of the town, which was still greatly influenced by the MacDermid family. In the halcyon days of iron mining, North Star owned the small abodes that housed its workers' families and ran the store where they spent their scrip. There had been other mining barons on the Iron Range, but the MacDermid name was among the most prominent. To the mining families who lived under the thumb of MacDermid rule, it was a name they hated.

Liam entered the estate grounds, a large, cleared area carpeted with grass and dotted with gardens, drove past the old carriage house, and parked in the circular drive in front of the great stone fortress. He stepped into the shade of the portico and was about to knock when the door opened and Mary Margaret MacDermid stepped out.

"Hello, Liam."

She was lovely but the kind of woman Liam thought of as fragile. She was at least a dozen years younger than her husband. Liam had heard that she was the only child of a once prominent Boston family who'd lost its fortune in the Great Depression. Duncan MacDermid, so the story went, had been in Boston for business and had spotted her playing the piano, hired as entertainment for a social gathering to which he'd been invited. Her beauty, her breeding, and her musical talent had won his heart. It was a pretty story, but as with all stories, Liam suspected there was more to it. Colleen had told him that once, when she and Mary Margaret had worked together on a fundraising bazaar for St. Agnes, she'd mentioned that story. Mary Margaret's response had been "I dreamed of being a concert pianist. Now I play only for Duncan."

"He's waiting for you in the guest cottage, above the boathouse." She lifted a hand carefully, as if following a stage direction, and pointed toward the lake.

"Thanks, Mary Margaret." Before leaving, he said, "A question for you. Did you know Big John Manydeeds?"

Her face didn't change, didn't show surprise or consternation, just held to a look as placid as a doll's face. "Not at all."

He crossed the well-manicured lawn, weaving among islands of flowers, and followed a path of crushed limestone to the guest cottage, which stood among a grove of birch trees at the edge of the lake. Although the MacDermids deemed it a guest cottage, it was nearly as large as Liam's home on Gooseberry Lane. The boathouse was at lake level, and above it was the cottage. Liam mounted the stairs to the door. He used the brass knocker, got no response, and used it again with the same result. He employed his fist the next time, hard and constant, and at last the door opened.

Duncan MacDermid had been drinking. His slightly unfocused eyes and the way he stood, like an old fence post slowly losing its grounding, would have been indication enough, but he also held a glass of amber liquid on the rocks.

"Sheriff," he said. "I was just relaxing on the deck. Shall we?"

Liam entered and was reminded again that "cottage" had a different meaning for the MacDermids. It was like stepping into the lobby of some grand hotel where the furniture was so luxurious that the idea of actually sitting on it seemed like criminal trespass. MacDermid made his way through the living room area and as he passed the bar, paused, turned back to Liam, and said, "Care for something to drink?"

"No, thanks, Duncan. On duty."

MacDermid shrugged and led the way through French doors onto a broad deck that overlooked the lake and dock, where his huge motor launch sat moored, along with a small sailboat, the kind Liam had heard called a Sunfish. MacDermid plopped down in a white wicker chair whose back fanned out around him like the spread of a peacock's tail. He set his drink on a wicker table next to his chair, where a smoking cigar sat in an ashtray with gold edging. He held his hand out toward another wicker chair, indicating Liam should sit there. It was a much smaller chair than MacDermid's, with a simpler design. The deck—the whole cottage, for that matter—had a stunning view of the lake, which was sapphire at the moment, the same color as the cloudless sky.

"Million-dollar view," Liam said.

MacDermid took up the cigar he'd been smoking, inhaled deeply, and shot a cloud toward Liam. "My father had this guest-house constructed, a place to get away and relax, you know?"

"To get away from business? Or other things?" Liam's eyes darted north, where the great house stood seventy yards distant.

MacDermid didn't reply, simply puffed on his cigar and said, "I remember sitting here with him before I left for the war. He was in this very chair, drinking his whiskey"—he held up his glass—"and smoking a fine Cuban. I remember he kept his gaze on the town over there, telling me how proud he was that I was in uniform, but that he was even prouder of the fact that the ore from our mine was going to help us beat those Axis bastards. And it was true, O'Connor. America couldn't have done it without us."

"You were in the service, Duncan?"

"Graduated from Annapolis. Served five years, four of them in the war."

"I was a paratrooper," Liam said. Normally, he didn't like to talk about the war, but he thought the connection might open MacDermid up a bit.

But the man said no more about it. Instead, he stared across the water, where Aurora lay neatly along the shoreline, a half mile distant. "My family built this town. That was another thing my father was proud of."

Built it on the back of other men's labor, Liam thought. The words were almost on his tongue, but he reined them in.

"So, Sheriff," MacDermid said, holding out his hand. "I'd appreciate the return of my lighter."

"When did you miss it?"

"As I told you this morning, I didn't know it was gone. A gift from my wife, a silly gift. I never use it. I only smoke cigars, and any connoisseur knows that you never light a cigar with anything but a wooden match. So, may I have it back?"

"I'm afraid I can't give it to you yet, Duncan."

"Why not?"

"There are still some questions surrounding the death of Big John Manydeeds. As you know, his body was found at Lightning Strike. The same place where your lighter was found."

"At Lightning Strike? And by this Oscar Manydeeds, you said? An Indian with the same last name as that dead man. A relative, I presume."

"Brother."

"My guess is that he stole it, or someone did, and it ended up in his hands."

"How would he have stolen it? Has he been here?"

"Probably not him then, but maybe one of my employees. My groundskeeper or housekeeper or cook or the woman who takes care of my mother."

"Are any of them Ojibwe?"

"I don't hire Indians."

"You have something against the Ojibwe?"

MacDermid set his cigar in the ashtray, focused his eyes on Liam as well as he was able to at that point, and said, "I know you married an Indian woman, so you probably think you have to believe differently. But the truth, O'Connor, and every white person here knows it, is that you can't trust an Indian."

"Did you have something against Big John? Something more personal than just hating Indians in general?"

"I didn't even know the man."

"Have you ever been to Lightning Strike?"

"Sure. Anyone who's lived here has gone out to Lightning Strike at one time or another. But I haven't been there since I was a Boy Scout."

"You're fond of Four Roses."

MacDermid seemed caught off guard by the sudden switch in the direction of the conversation.

"I noticed the bottle sitting on your bar when we passed it. That's what you're drinking now?"

"It was a favorite of my father. I learned to drink it early. It may not be the best whiskey on the market, but I have a certain nostalgic connection with it." He took up his cigar again, puffed twice, then said, "When do I get my lighter back?"

"Just as soon as I've closed my investigation."

"Indians kill themselves all the time, O'Connor. There's nothing unusual about that."

"Duncan—" Liam began, sudden anger burning in his chest. But he caught himself and held his tongue. "Thank you for your time."

"I trust you can see yourself out, Sheriff. I'm going to go right on enjoying my whiskey, my cigar, and this million-dollar view, as you put it, of my town."

CHAPTER 20

As he'd promised, Cork was home by four. His mother's birthday celebration didn't begin immediately, however. There was another part to this annual ritual, one that his mother insisted on although it always made her cry.

The cemetery lay at the south end of Aurora. In the afternoon heat, Cork, his parents, and Grandma Dilsey gathered around two small markers set in the grass. On the first was etched simply *Baby O'Connor, April 3, 1952.* The inscription on the other read *Baby O'Connor, July 21, 1954.*

Cork had been the firstborn, but after him, there'd been two miscarriages. And after that, there'd been no other pregnancies. When he'd asked his mother about this, she'd been circumspect, but also upset, Cork could tell, so he hadn't pushed the question. It was Grandma Dilsey who'd supplied the answer.

"Do you know what a vasectomy is, Corkie?" she'd asked in response to his question.

He was nine years old and he didn't.

"It's a kind of operation a man can have that will keep him from making babies. Your father had a vasectomy."

"Why? Didn't he want more kids?"

"When you were born, we almost lost your mother."

Which was news to Cork. "What happened?"

"Sometimes a woman bleeds, bleeds a lot. Colleen almost died before the doctors were finally able to stop the bleeding. It scared us all horribly."

"So, Dad got that operation?"

"Not right away. Your mother wouldn't hear of it. Then she miscarried her next child. When she miscarried the child after that, it was on her birthday and quite late in her pregnancy, and there were extraordinary complications I won't go into. But that nearly killed her, too. So, over your mother's profound objections, your father had the surgery. It's a touchy subject between them, Corkie. I wouldn't bring it up again."

And he hadn't.

Each marker had a little vase, and into each vase, Cork's mother put a bright bouquet of flowers. She stood looking down at the two small rectangles of gray granite, and Cork saw, as he had in years before, tears gather in her eyes and spill down her cheeks.

His father, Cork noticed, stood a bit back, and as always on these visits, the look on his face was one Cork was not able to decipher.

By the time she opened her gifts that evening, his mother had brightened, and she claimed to love, love, love the book Cork had given her. Grandma Dilsey's gift was a beaded change purse— she'd done the beading herself—which pleased her daughter immensely. Liam O'Connor's gift to his wife was Wind Song dusting powder and perfume, and a cashmere sweater, which Grandma Dilsey declared perfectly matched her daughter's eyes.

It was seven o'clock when the festivities ended, and Cork said he was going out for a while. He promised to be home by ten, his usual summer curfew.

He biked to Jorge's place on the MacDermids' property. On Sunday nights, he and his friend had a standing date with a game of Risk. Jorge already had the board set up in his bedroom, and the two boys settled down immediately to some serious battling. They'd been at it awhile, Cork stockpiling armies in South America and preparing for an invasion of Jorge's stronghold in Africa, when the sound of sobs beyond the closed bedroom door made them pause in their playing.

"Your mom?" Cork whispered.

Jorge shook his head. The two boys left the game, crept to the door, and cracked it open. Through the narrow gap, Cork saw Jorge's mother sitting at the kitchen table with another woman, who was sobbing uncontrollably, her face in her hands. When she lifted her head, Cork saw that it was Mrs. MacDermid, and he saw, too, the large bruise that spread out from her left eye.

"I don't know what to do, Carla."

"You have family?" Jorge's mother asked.

"Not really. No one I could turn to."

"But you cannot stay with him. Not after this."

"If I leave him, I'll have nothing. He would divorce me."

"He would have to give you something."

"Adultery, Carla. Everyone, everything would be on his side. He would give me nothing. Any court would back him up."

"A woman can begin with nothing and still make something."

"A strong woman, maybe."

"You must tell someone about this. And you cannot go back into that house."

"It's okay. He's been sleeping in the cottage since we had the big blowup, drinking himself blind every night."

"His mother, maybe she can help you."

"When he's like this, even his mother has no control over him. Today's been the worst. He started as soon as we got home from church." Mrs. MacDermid looked away and stared out the kitchen window, where the last rays of the day streamed through and painted her face in pale orange light. "I lied, Carla. I denied him."

"I don't understand."

"The sheriff asked me about Big John. I said I didn't know him. How could I do that? I'm such a coward."

"You must think of yourself now," Carla said.

The screen door banged open, and Duncan MacDermid staggered in, his face glistening with sweat. His eyes were wild. In his right hand, he held a bottle of liquor, nearly empty.

"You," he said, pointing a finger at his wife. "Come with me."

"She is staying here tonight," Carla said. She stood up and put herself between MacDermid and his wife.

"I don't think so." He glared at Jorge's mother, then at Mrs. MacDermid. "What do you think, Mary Margaret?"

The woman raised her eyes to Jorge's mother and said, "I'm going with him. It will be all right."

"Leave the bottle, Mr. MacDermid," Jorge's mother said. "It won't help."

"Do as she asks, Duncan," Mrs. MacDermid pleaded. "You've had enough."

The man lifted the bottle to the light. It was still a quarter full. "All right," he said, then threw the bottle to the floor, shattering it into a hundred pieces. "It's left. Come," he said, reaching out his empty hand toward his wife.

Mrs. MacDermid rose slowly. "I'll be okay, Carla," she said.

They walked out into the late evening light together, hand in hand, Mary Margaret MacDermid holding her head high, as if nothing at all had occurred.

Jorge left his bedroom and Cork followed. Jorge's mother stood looking where Mrs. MacDermid had gone. *"Dios te proteja,"* she whispered. She turned when she realized the two boys were standing there.

"You heard?"

Jorge nodded.

"You must say nothing to anyone, do you understand?"

Without being asked, Jorge fetched a broom and dustpan from the kitchen closet.

"I will take care of that," his mother said.

"It's okay. I can do it."

Jorge swept up the glass, and Cork held the dustpan. By then, Jorge's mother had filled a bucket with water and soap, and she ran a mop over the floor to clean up what was left of the whiskey and any remaining glass.

"We'll finish the game later," Jorge said.

Cork bid them good night. He descended the outside stairway, got on his bike, and in the last light of that day, headed toward home.

CHAPTER 21

Even before he heard the voices coming from the front porch, Cork could smell the aroma of the Cherry Blend tobacco in his father's pipe. The other voice belonged to Sam Winter Moon. As Cork came from the garage, where he'd put away his bike, the two men stopped talking abruptly.

"Home early," his father said.

"Didn't finish the game. Hi, Sam."

The two men sat on folding chairs brought from inside the house. It was dark enough that the glow of the embers in the pipe bowl illuminated his father's face. Cork had the sense that he'd interrupted a conversation the men were reluctant to continue in his presence.

"There's something you should know, Dad, something that happened at Jorge's house tonight."

Although Jorge's mother had said the two boys should tell no one, Cork hadn't actually made her that promise. So, he told the men about what had occurred at Glengarrow. His father, as he listened, took the pipe from his mouth and leaned toward Cork, as if afraid he might miss something important.

"The court would be on his side? That's what Mary Margaret said?"

"Yes, sir."

"And she said adultery. She used that exact word?"

Cork nodded. "Like in the Ten Commandments."

"Big John? And MacDermid's wife?" Sam said, as if it were an impossible idea. "How would she . . . ?" He broke off his thought, scratched his cheek, eyed Cork's father, and finally said, "How would they even know each other?"

"There's something else, Dad. That bottle he threw on the floor? When I was helping Jorge clean up the mess, I saw the label. It's the same kind of whiskey we found out behind Big John's cabin."

"Four Roses," his father said, as if this were no surprise, then he was quiet for a long time while the embers in his pipe went dark. "He battered her. If I could, I'd put him behind bars for that alone. But if I press her about it, she'll deny everything, say she fell or ran into a door. I see this kind of thing way too often." His father stared west, where the sky held only the palest memory of daylight. "You still willing to do me that favor, Sam?"

"I think you're barking up the wrong tree, Liam, but I'll ask around the rez. See what I can come up with about that lighter Oscar claims he found."

"Thanks."

"What about you?" Sam said.

"I'm going after Duncan MacDermid."

Cork's mother and Grandma Dilsey sat at the kitchen table, each with a cup of coffee, and spread out between them on the tabletop was a jumble of photographs.

"Your grandfather," Grandma Dilsey said when Cork looked over her shoulder.

He was a man Cork had never known. Handsome and smiling, he stood with a much younger version of Cork's grandmother in front of a small white clapboard building, the one-room school-house on the rez where Grandma Dilsey had taught and which had been enlarged to become the community center. Patrick "Paddy" O'Connor had been superintendent in the Tamarack County School District then. He'd died shortly after Cork was born.

"Talk about Irish blarney," Grandma Dilsey said. "That man could sweet-talk a bee into giving up its honey. And this one," she said, holding up another photograph. "My mother, at our sugar bush camp, boiling down maple syrup." She looked long at the photograph of a woman in a plain country dress, stirring a big, steaming pot over an outdoor fire. "I used to love to help her. Before the government took me away," she added with a bitter note. "And here's your mother, Cork, in her First Communion dress, seven years old. Do you remember that dress, Colleen?"

Cork had seen most of the photographs before. This was a usual part of his mother's birthday celebration, a parade through time via the old photographs Grandma Dilsey had kept and treasured.

Cork went to the refrigerator and opened the door.

"Hungry?" his mother asked.

"When isn't he?" Grandma Dilsey said.

"There's cold meat loaf and potato salad from yesterday," his mother said.

Cork put together a plate of the leftovers and sat at the table with the women.

"Who won the game?" his mother asked.

"Didn't finish." Cork hesitated before digging into his food.

His mother seemed to sense that something weighed on him. "What is it?"

He'd made no promise to keep it secret, so Cork told them about what had taken place at Jorge's.

*   *   *

When Liam O'Connor walked into the kitchen, he was stopped in midstride by the look his wife and mother-in-law both gave him.

"Big John and Mary Margaret?" Colleen said.

"He was three times the man Duncan MacDermid will ever be," Dilsey declared.

"It's hearsay," Liam said. "Maybe Cork misunderstood."

"I didn't," Cork said.

"Who would blame her?" Colleen said. "Duncan was a bully as a kid, and he hasn't changed one bit. Can't you arrest him, Liam?"

"Maybe if Mary Margaret lodged a complaint, which she won't. Even then, it's unlikely he'd be charged. Bud Fassbinder, our county attorney, is pretty much in MacDermid's pocket."

"On the rez, we've been saying all along that Big John didn't kill himself," Dilsey said. "Seems to me, Liam, that you've got good reason to look real hard at Duncan MacDermid."

"Thank you for telling me my job, Dilsey. Now I've got a question for you. What do you think of Oscar Manydeeds?"

His mother-in-law seemed caught off guard. "What do you mean?"

"Before Big John stopped drinking, if in fact he really did, he and Oscar used to go at one another until they were both beat and bloody."

"Big John stopped drinking long ago," Dilsey insisted.

"If you say so. But not Oscar. And when he drinks, he gets mean. Everybody's seen that."

"What are you getting at?"

"They weren't brothers. They were half brothers. As we all know, not a lot of love lost there."

Liam had heard the story of Big John and Oscar Manydeeds from Colleen and Dilsey any number of times, especially when he'd had occasion to arrest one of the brothers. Same father, different mothers. Big John's mother had died while he was away at the government boarding school. He hadn't even been allowed to come home for the funeral. Not long afterward, Big John's father had remarried. His new wife gave him two children, Oscar and a girl named Jeanette, Billy Downwind's mother. The last time Big John ran away from the boarding school and, with the help of Henry Meloux, disappeared into the wilderness, Oscar was six or seven. Oscar was an adolescent when Big John went away to war, and his brother was already a bit of a legendary figure. Oscar often boasted of his big brother, and as he grew into the same gigantic stature, claimed he would be just like Big John. But Big John, when he returned many years later, was a changed man, a drinking man, and that's when Oscar started drinking hard, too.

That's also when the fights began, half brother against half brother, bitter accusations that ran back always to deep loves for two different mothers and on Big John's part, a profound feeling of betrayal by his father, who had done nothing to prevent him from being hauled off to boarding school again and again, and who'd re-married while Big John's mother was still warm in her grave. The brothers were equally matched in size, but there was something more brutal about Big John. The war, people said. The deep wound-ing of his spirit. And they said that if Henry hadn't stepped in, helped Big John to heal, one of the brothers was bound to end up dead.

"Why are we even talking about this?" Dilsey said.

"Because of the lighter," Cork blurted.

Dilsey gave him a look of bewilderment, then gave that same look to Liam. "The one he found at Lightning Strike?"

"Says he found," Liam put in, then scowled at his son in a way meant to keep him quiet.

"I don't understand," Colleen said.

"The lighter belongs to Duncan MacDermid," Liam told her.

"Whose wife was having an affair with Big John," Dilsey said, as if capping an argument. "Doesn't that prove that MacDermid was out there? Why don't you arrest him?"

"Awfully convenient, don't you think? Oscar just happening to find it at Lightning Strike?"

"What I think is that you're trying to shift attention from Duncan MacDermid."

"The rich, powerful white man."

"Exactly, Liam. Who cares about Oscar Manydeeds? He's just a drunken Indian. And isn't that convenient? So, what are you going to do?"

"I've asked Sam to talk to folks on the rez. There are questions about Oscar I need answered. In the meantime, I will, as you say, look real hard at Duncan MacDermid, if that's what you're concerned about."

"What I'm concerned about is justice, Liam," Dilsey said. "That's something I haven't seen much of across my lifetime, especially when it comes to standing up to people who think their money and power can protect them from everything. People who have county attorneys in their pockets. Maybe even county sheriffs."

"You think MacDermid could buy me off?" Liam's blood was rising, and his voice drew taut. "Do you even know who I am, Dilsey?"

"Mom, Liam," Colleen said, her own voice pitched near anger. "Let it go."

Dilsey set her dark eyes on her son-in-law with a steady gaze. "Deep in our hearts, I'm not sure any of us really know who we are. It's moments like this that force us to look at the truth of ourselves. Who are you, Liam? I think we're about to find out."

Grandma Dilsey, in her anger, had chosen to return to her home on the rez that night, and long after the others had gone to bed,

Cork rose, went to his window, unlatched the screen, and slipped out onto the roof of the porch, where he sat thinking, as he sometimes did at night when everyone else was asleep. The moon was high and bright, and the house cast a shadow across the front lawn, which looked to Cork like a big, empty grave. He hugged his knees and thought about the sharp tone Grandma Dilsey had used that evening in pressing his father about justice for Big John. He knew his grandmother hadn't been thrilled when her daughter married a lawman. Grandma Dilsey's husband had been a scholar, a schoolteacher like her, said to be firm but gentle, and although he was white, because of his tireless work in helping his wife educate Ojibwe children, he'd been embraced by the Anishinaabeg of the Iron Lake Reservation. But to Cork, his father's badge seemed like an iron fence, and although his father did his best to reach across it, he would never be invited to the other side.

Cork stared at the night sky. The glow of the moon ate much of the Milky Way, but in the west, the dusty trail of stars was clear. That was the direction Big John's spirit should have followed on the Path of Souls. But more and more, Cork agreed with the cracked, bitter warnings of old Broomstraw, that something of Big John remained in Tamarack County. If not his spirit, then the shadow of something he'd done, maybe some sin. Adultery? But that wasn't his sin. That was Mrs. MacDermid's. The sin Big John had committed was coveting another man's wife. Was that a cardinal sin? Whatever, it seemed to have brought with it a curse that threatened the peace in Tamarack County and in the O'Connors' house as well.

Cork knew that lawmen in the Old West had carried a Colt revolver nicknamed the Peacemaker. His father owned a .38 Smith & Wesson Police Special, but he seldom wore it. Yet on his shoulders seemed to rest the full responsibility for restoring peace, finding the truth, bringing justice. Sitting alone on the porch roof, Cork tried to imagine the awful burden of that great responsibility on a man who didn't believe in the Path of Souls or roaming spirits, a man who'd come from a long line of no-nonsense Irish cops in Chicago, a man who seemed to face with equanimity the hostility that often came at him from both the Ojibwe and the whites. It all felt overwhelming, crushing. In the end, Cork crawled back inside the house and into his bed and found sanctuary in sleep.

CHAPTER 22

Liam slept fitfully and was up long before it was time for Cork to wake and head off to deliver his newspapers. He brewed himself coffee, fed Jackson, and at four-thirty went back upstairs just as his son's alarm went off. He waited in the hallway until he was sure Cork was up and moving, then left the house. He could have delayed a few minutes, offered his son a ride to his newspaper drop box, but at the moment, he needed to be alone with his thoughts.

He'd always been sure of what he wanted. Early on, he knew he would be a cop, wanted that connection with the other men of his family. The moment he'd set eyes on Colleen, he'd wanted her for his wife. He'd wanted children, and he counted Cork a great blessing. He'd wanted the job of sheriff, and it was his.

But now he was unsure of so many things, unsure of what he really wanted going forward. He felt as if he was alienating all the people he cared about and who cared about him. Was the truth of Big John Manydeeds's death really worth the risk of what it might cost him?

He headed north out of Aurora, past the lane through the pines that led to Glengarrow, along a country road that went from asphalt to gravel, and seven miles later, turned off where the old logging road cut through the trees to Lightning Strike. The new day was just a faint suggestion of soft blue along the horizon, and Liam's headlights illuminated the high wild grass and the press of trees on either side. He hadn't been back since the day Cork and Jorge found Big John hanging from the maple tree. There'd been no reason to return, but something was different now.

He parked his pickup at the edge of the clearing. By then the low clouds in the east were flamingo colored from a sun that was still below the horizon. He got out and walked into the center of the meadow. The air was cool and a little damp against his face. Although it had been more than fifty years since the logging camp had burned nearly to the ground, he swore he could still smell the char.

His wife's people claimed this was a spiritual place and that was why the commercial enterprise had suffered the fate that had given the meadow its name. Big John had sometimes invited Cork to come along with Billy Downwind and spend a night in the clearing. Cork would come home with stories Big John had told about the wonders he'd seen in the great Northwoods. How many times had Cork returned gushing, "There are things out there, Dad, that you just can't explain. Seriously."

Cork was young and impressionable, and in truth, Liam was happy to have him learn about the part of his ancestry that was Ojibwe. Dilsey was always working on him, always pressing Cork to learn the language, to understand his rich and noble heritage. Hadn't Liam done the same thing on his side? Only last spring, they'd gone to Chicago for the St. Patrick's Day parade and had watched men from Liam's family march with their brothers in police uniforms, and had gathered afterward for drink and for stories, and he'd been proud of the heritage that had been shared with his son.

So Liam understood that it was fitting for Dilsey and Colleen and Sam Winter Moon and Henry Meloux to steep his son in an appreciation and acceptance of what it meant to be one of The People. Which was something Liam would never be able to share. He would always remain an outsider.

He knew that among whites in Tamarack County, his marriage was an issue. He'd first heard the term "squaw man" when he'd run for sheriff. Colleen had been educated at the Winona State Teachers' College. Had graduated cum laude. Had taught social studies in Aurora for nearly a decade. Yet to some people in Tamarack County she was still defined only by her ancestry. And only half of her ancestry. There were many people of mixed blood in the North Country, but a lot of them refused to acknowledge this publicly, because to be Indian at all was to be Indian completely.

Which was something Dilsey believed Liam didn't understand, this profound and enduring prejudice. They'd argued on occasion, and Liam had pointed out to her that his own people, when they'd first arrived from Ireland, had been spit on, too.

"But no longer," she'd pointed out. "Now you hold big parades to celebrate your heritage, and thousands of people turn out and cheer."

He understood her point. If you were white, it didn't matter where you came from, eventually you were accepted. Being Indian was quite different.

But dying was the same no matter where you came from. Liam walked slowly toward the lone maple. The sun had just begun to peek above the horizon, and as its red-orange rays hit the top of the tree, the leaves seemed to burst into flames.

"Why here, Big John?" Liam asked aloud.

He studied the section of fallen trunk Big John had put there as a perch for his fatal last step. There were no marks on the ground showing that it had been dragged to the place. It must have been carried. The section was large and heavy and would have been a chore to haul from wherever it had come. For anyone else, that would have been a two-man job. But Big John wasn't called by that name for nothing. If he was as set in his purpose as it appeared, he could have carried that log a mile.

And it did appear he'd been set on ending his life. It certainly looked like suicide. The evidence had been so telling. The whiskey bottles, the blood alcohol level, the history of alcoholism. And suicide was tragically common in Native communities. So, Liam had bought it.

Which may have been exactly what he was meant to do.

"Are you here?" He spoke aloud again. "What is it you want?"

What did he expect? That the spirit of Big John would appear to him as it seemed to have appeared to others, and that he would be given answers? If so, he was disappointed. Except for him, the clearing remained empty.

When Liam walked into the Sheriff's Department in the basement of the county courthouse, Ruth Rustad gave him a warm, "Morning, Sheriff."

Ruth was a civilian employee, taking care of clerical duties and responsible for arranging for the food to feed prisoners, when they had any, which they didn't at the moment. She also sometimes acted as dispatcher. She was in her early forties and of a motherly nature. She often brought homemade cookies to work and offered them to folks who showed up at the department with troubles.

"Has Cy checked in?" Liam asked.

"He's in the evidence room, finishing up with those bottles you asked him to dust for prints."

"Where's Joe?"

"Upstairs delivering some papers to the clerk of court."

"I want to see him as soon as he's back."

"Fresh coffee's in the pot, if you want some," Ruth said.

Liam grabbed a mug decorated with an image of a troll, a popular item in an area settled heavily by Scandinavians, filled it, and went to the evidence room, where Deputy Borkman was bent over the cardboard box containing empty bottles of Four Roses.

"How's it going?"

"Almost done."

"In my office in ten."

A few minutes later, Cy Borkman entered Liam's office in the company of Joe Meese. Liam gestured to them to sit.

"What did you get on those bottles, Cy?" he asked.

"Nothing."

"Nothing? You mean no identifiable prints?"

"No prints at all. Weird, huh."

Joe said, "How does a man drink whiskey without leaving any prints on the bottle?"

"Gloves?" Cy said.

"There were a dozen bottles," Liam said. "Why would he put on gloves every time he drank?"

"Somebody wiped 'em clean?" Joe said.

"His prints were on the bottles at Lightning Strike," Cy pointed out. "Why didn't they wipe those clean?"

"He was alone at Lightning Strike," Joe said.

Liam said, "You told me you found cigarette butts when you and Cy searched the area. Where are they, Joe?"

"In the evidence room."

"Get 'em," Liam said.

Joe came back with a small envelope on which he'd handwritten *Butts/Lightning Strike/July 20, 1963*. He gave the envelope to Liam, who opened it and emptied the contents onto his desk. There were four of them, all with lipstick stains on the filters.

"Where exactly did you find these?" Liam asked.

"Middle of the meadow, more or less."

"Anything else?"

"We picked up some old, scattered trash, been out there awhile. I bagged that, too, if you want to see it. But those butts looked new."

"Could've been anybody," Cy said. "Tourist, maybe."

"Maybe," Liam said. But he had a pretty good idea that it wasn't just anybody.

CHAPTER 23

Right after lunch, Cork, Jorge, and several of their friends threw together a sandlot baseball game at the diamond in Grant Park. Well into the third inning, Billy Downwind stormed across the field and came at Cork, who, because he was the only one with a proper glove, was playing first base. Billy shoved him hard to the ground.

Cork scrambled back to his feet. "What are you doing?"

"Your old man's calling my uncle a liar."

"What?"

"*Chimooks* lie, not Uncle Oscar."

"What are you talking about?"

The game had stopped, and the other boys stood watching.

"Sam Winter Moon's asking questions about my uncle, about that lighter he found. He's saying your dad thinks Uncle Oscar lied about where he found it. My uncle's not a liar."

"My dad never said that."

"Yeah? Then why's Winter Moon saying so?"

"You must have heard wrong."

"You calling me a liar now?"

"Did you know that your uncle and Big John didn't like each other? They fought all the time."

"Used to. Not anymore. Anyway, what's that got to do with anything?"

"It's something that's got to be checked out."

"Why?"

"It might be motive."

"For what?"

Cork didn't answer, but the implication dawned on Billy. "Your dad thinks Uncle Oscar might have killed Big John? That's bullshit."

"Like I said, it's got to be checked out."

"Screw you and your old man," Billy said and gave Cork another hard shove.

"Fight!" yelled Colby Kogut, a big athletic kid who was on the pitcher's mound.

But Cork had no intention of fighting, not over this. "Look, we can't talk here. Let's go somewhere else. I'll explain, okay?" He turned to the other boys on the field. "Gotta go, guys."

Jorge, who'd been up at the plate, dropped his bat, joined Cork and Billy, and the three boys walked away together.

"What about the game?" Colby shouted at their backs.

Cork lifted his hands in a gesture empty of any satisfactory reply, and they walked on.

They found a picnic table under a shady maple at the edge of Iron Lake. A hundred yards out on the water, a speedboat shot past pulling a young woman on skis. Farther out, a Sunfish sailboat sat idle in the breezeless afternoon, the limp white canvas of the sail mirrored perfectly in the water.

"So, explain," Billy Downwind demanded.

Cork tried to think of a way to say it that wouldn't be giving away too much, that wouldn't be such a breach of the confidences that had been shared with him.

"My dad's going after Duncan MacDermid, not your uncle, okay? But he's got to check out every lead. It's something I've heard him call 'due diligence'."

"MacDermid?" Billy squinted. "He thinks MacDermid killed Big John?"

Cork glanced at Jorge. "We heard something last night."

"At my place," Jorge said, and told Billy what had transpired there.

"Big John and the rich man's wife?" Billy said, as if he thought it was impossible. "But what about my uncle and the lighter?"

"It's a lead and my dad has to follow it up. But you gotta promise not to tell anyone any of this. Not until my dad's had a chance to check it out."

"Like hell. Uncle Oscar should know. And my mom."

"Come on, Billy. Keep quiet for just a little while. Remember what Henry Meloux told us? These are crumbs we're following. If we're not careful, maybe somebody'll kick those crumbs away."

"What's that mean?"

"If they know we're after them, they'll cover their tracks. You've gotta promise."

For a few long moments, Billy Downwind's eyes held on the lake, which had smoothed over after the passage of the speedboat and once again lay mirror smooth. He gave a single nod. "For a little while." Then he said, "What do we do now?"

The three boys looked at each other, clueless, then Jorge said, "You keep saying that Big John's spirit is hanging around."

"So?" Billy said.

"Maybe we should just ask him what happened."

"Yeah, right," Billy scoffed. "How do you talk to the dead?"

Jorge said, "I have an idea."

* * *

Liam parked in the gravel lot of Sam's Place long after the lunch rush was past. Sam's niece, Daisy Winter Moon, was at the serving window, and when she saw Liam approaching, she turned back inside and called to her uncle. She got a reply and called to Liam, "He'll be right out, Sheriff."

Sam came from the door of the Quonset hut and gestured for Liam to follow him. He walked to the picnic table on the grass near the dock, which folks who were boating used when they wanted to stop at Sam's Place for a bite to eat. The afternoon was hot and still. At the moment, there were no boats on Iron Lake and the surface looked as blue and soft as a baby's blanket.

"Did you find out anything on the rez?" Liam asked.

"Nothing," Sam said. "But I've got to be honest, it wasn't something I put my heart into. I don't believe for a moment that Oscar Manydeeds had anything to do with his brother's death."

"Half brother. And with a history of going at it like a couple of rabid wolves."

"Not since Big John got sober, Liam. I know Oscar can get crazy when he's been drinking, but going far enough to do what you're suggesting? I can't see it."

"Suppose, Sam, just suppose that something made Big John fall off the wagon, and he and Oscar were drinking together, like in the old days." Liam shrugged as if the conclusion was obvious.

"I don't buy it."

"Big John was like a mountain on two legs, Sam. If someone hung him from that maple tree at Lightning Strike, it had to be someone every bit as big as him. The only man I know who fits that description is Oscar Manydeeds."

Sam shook his head slowly. "Liam, you and I both did our share of killing in the war. You know how hard it was to kill a man at a distance. Think about what it takes to kill a man close up. And kin as well."

"Some of the worst violence I ever saw when I was a cop in Chicago was among family members. Husbands killing wives, wives killing husbands. Parents killing children. And brother against brother? Hell, that goes all the way back to the Bible. Just because they were kin doesn't mean Oscar Manydeeds couldn't have done it."

"And how about MacDermid?" Sam asked, hard bone in his voice now.

"I've got my sights on him, too."

Sam looked long at Liam and finally said, "Sheriff, you better believe every Shinnob on the rez is watching you right now. Every step you take."

It sounded as near to a threat as Liam had ever heard come from his friend.

It was late afternoon when Cork headed out with his collection book. This was the hardest part of delivering newspapers, trying to catch the subscribers and settle their bills. Mostly he tried to collect on weekends or evenings, when people might be home. If he was lucky, he got three-quarters of his customers without any problem. But there were those who seemed never to be home, or if they were, always had some excuse for putting him off, and he was forced to return again and again.

That afternoon his intent was to hit the businesses whose papers he delivered on his morning route, drop in during regular hours to catch the proprietors who hadn't yet paid him. He was successful at the hardware store and Marv's Men's Clothing. He was approaching the Crooked Pine when he saw a Sheriff's Department cruiser pull up and park in front of the establishment. Deputy Joe Meese got out.

"Hey, Cork, what're you up to?" Joe said.

"Collecting for my paper route."

"I know what that's like. I delivered papers when I was your age." Joe glanced at the Crooked Pine. "Ben Svenson still owe you something?"

"Three months' worth. He always claims the register's empty."

"Well, let's see what we can do about that." Joe headed toward the front door.

"I can't go in there," Cork said.

Joe looked puzzled. "How do you collect?"

"I go around in back and knock until somebody answers."

"Well, you're not going around back today."

As soon as Joe opened the door, the yeasty smell of beer poured out, a smell Cork wasn't fond of. The joint was dark and empty. From the jukebox, Roy Orbison was crying over lost days on Blue Bayou. Ben Svenson had his back to the door, taking stock of the bottles shelved behind the bar. He turned as Joe and Cork approached. The butt end of a lit cheroot was jammed into the corner of his mouth. The smell of it assaulted Cork's nose even above the stale odor of beer.

"A little early to be drinking, isn't it, Joe?"

"Not here to drink, Ben. I'm thinking of running you in. Bilking a kid out of his rightful due."

"Huh?"

"Cork says you owe him for three months' paper delivery."

"Three months?" Svenson removed the cigar butt from his mouth and scowled at Cork. "That can't be right."

"I've got it here, Mr. Svenson." Cork held up his collection book.

"Three months." Svenson shook his head as if in disbelief. "Well, if that's what your book says. How much?"

Cork told him the amount, and the man popped open the register drawer and pulled out the cash.

"How about a tip with that?" Joe said. When Svenson gave him a surly look, the deputy said, "Has he ever missed a day?"

Svenson set his cigar butt on the bar, reached back into the till, and gave Cork an extra dollar. When Joe didn't make a move to leave, Svenson said, "Are we done here?"

"Not yet." Joe pulled a photograph from the breast pocket of his uniform. "Have you seen this girl?"

Svenson took the photo and studied it. "Yeah. She was hanging around outside, begging booze from some of my customers. I ran her off."

"When was that?"

"Two, three weeks back, I guess."

"Has she been round since?"

"Haven't seen her."

"If she does come back, will you let me or the sheriff know?"

"Sure. What's she done?"

"Runaway. Her people are worried about her."

"She looks Indian."

"From Leech Lake."

"Guess they start 'em drinking early there. Doesn't surprise me."

Joe put the photograph back in the pocket it had come from and said, "One more question. You told the sheriff that Big John had become a regular. Drank Four Roses."

"Was hitting it pretty hard toward the end. You know Indians, once they get a taste."

"Anybody else drink Four Roses pretty hard?"

"Not as a rule. Except MacDermid."

"Duncan MacDermid?"

"He's got a standing order for a couple of cases every other month. His preferred bourbon. He also makes a special order on occasion. As I understand it, he hands those bottles out to his mine supervisors and foremen as a kind of bonus. Been doing it for years."

"When did he pick up his last cases?"

"Maybe three weeks ago."

"And Big John just happened to drink the same brand?"

"He told me whatever was good enough for MacDermid was good enough for him. Pissing contest, I figured."

The door opened and a couple of customers came in with the sunlight.

"Look, I got a business to run." Svenson stuck the cigar butt back into the corner of his mouth. "And that kid shouldn't be in here. We done?"

"So, he hands out booze to his supervisors and foremen, huh?" Joe gave his head a little shake. "Well, you know those miners, once they get a taste. Come on, Cork."

Outside, Joe said, "Dumb Devil Dog."

"Devil Dog?"

"It's what they call Marines."

"Mr. Svenson was a Marine?"

"Not was. He'd tell you once a Marine, always a Marine. Truth is, the only fighting that Devil Dog did in the war was with a typewriter. He was just a damn clerk. Spent his whole hitch shuffling papers in Yuma, Arizona. Headed home, Cork? Be glad to give you a lift."

Liam was on the porch, sitting in the swing, smoking his pipe when Joe pulled up to the curb with Cork in tow. They got out and walked up to the house.

"How'd the collecting go?" Liam asked.

His son shrugged. "Okay, I guess. Still some deadbeats."

"Ben Svenson isn't one of them anymore," Joe said with a laugh. "I made sure of that."

Cork started inside and Liam said, "How about we toss the football after dinner?"

"I'm spending the night at Jorge's," his son said. "I'm going over right after we eat. Mom told me it was all right."

"Sure," Liam said, feeling a little bite of disappointment.

Cork hesitated, seemed on the verge of saying something, and from the serious look on his face, something important, but in the end, he just swung the screen door wide and headed in.

Joe stood on the porch steps, silhouetted against a late afternoon sun. "Asked Svenson about the LaRose girl. He said she was hanging around outside the Crooked Pine two or three weeks back, trying to cadge drinks off the customers. He says he ran her off, hasn't seen her since."

"She might've wandered to Yellow Lake. Tomorrow, I want you to swing over there and ask around, okay?"

"Sure thing, Liam. You talk to Sam Winter Moon?"

"He didn't find out anything useful and he wasn't happy having to ask."

"I think you're barking up the wrong tree there. Me, I like MacDermid."

The tobacco in his pipe was smoked to ash. Liam stood up and knocked the bowl clear on the porch railing. "I've been thinking I'll make another visit to Glengarrow this evening."

"You really believe you'll get anything more out of Mac-Dermid?"

"Probably not him. But he's not the only one who lives there."

A slow smile spread across the deputy's face and he gave a little nod of approval.

Liam said, "See you tomorrow, Joe."

*　*　*

They stood at the kitchen sink, Colleen washing the dishes, Liam drying. Cork had already gone away on his bike to spend the night with Jorge. Dilsey hadn't returned since she'd left in a huff the evening before. The house was quiet and felt empty to Liam.

"What's wrong?" Colleen asked. "You haven't said two words since supper."

"He's growing up fast."

"Cork?"

"Used to be when I suggested we toss the football he was all over that. Now . . ."

"It's one night, Liam."

"My father never tossed a football with me."

"Tell you what. When we've finished with the dishes, we'll go into the backyard and I'll throw you the football."

He smiled, as he knew she intended, but shook his head. "Work to do."

"Cop work?"

"I'm going to talk to Mary Margaret."

"Alone?"

"That's what I'm shooting for."

"Will Duncan allow that?"

"If I'm lucky, he won't be there. When I talked to him in the guest cottage, it looked to me as if that might be where he's spending his nights now."

"If you ask me, after what he did to Mary Margaret, he should be spending his nights in jail."

"I'm doing my best to put him there."

"Does that mean you think Oscar Manydeeds is in the clear?"

"In the clear? You've been watching too many cop shows. But no, that's not what it means. Just following up on all the possibilities."

She paused in her work, her hands deep in the soapy water,

and looked at her husband steadily. "Liam, you're not from here. You're a wonderful cop and that's why you're our sheriff. But there are forces at work in this place that you can't possibly understand, emotions that run deep and go back to forever. You're walking a thin line. And . . ." She took a wet hand from the sink and put it to his cheek.

"And what?"

"There's a fire here that's raged for generations and you're walking right into the middle of it. I'm wondering what will be left of you when you come out on the other side."

Her wet hand was still held against his face, and drips of water crawled down his cheek with the same feel as tears.

CHAPTER 24

It was going on seven-thirty that evening when Oscar Many-deeds pulled into Grant Park in his 1945 Ford pickup. Like a lot of vehicles on the rez, it was a patchwork of salvaged parts—the body pale green, the cab doors brown, the hood cherry red. Manydeeds had pieced it together himself. In his wild youth, he'd spent a good deal of time in a juvenile detention center south of the Twin Cities and had learned the basics of auto mechanics there. Back on the rez, he'd continued to learn on his own, tinkering with vehicles suffering from all kinds of mechanical issues, until he'd acquired a reputation as a Shinnob with a knack for machines. Unlike so many other Frankenstein vehicle creations on the rez, his truck ran with a smooth hum.

Oscar said, "Find your own damn way home tomorrow. I got a job to do."

Billy hopped out, lifted a bike from the bed of the truck, and his uncle took off.

Cork and Jorge had been standing behind the framework of the park's picnic pavilion. When Billy was alone, they stepped into plain sight.

"Did you tell him who you were hanging out with tonight?" Cork asked.

"That would've got me nowhere," Billy said. "Just told him and my mom it was some friends."

"Let's get started," Cork said. "We should be there before dark."

Cork lifted his backpack, onto which he'd tied his sleeping bag and a canteen of water. Jorge had a sleeping bag, too, bound with twine to the carrier on the back of his bike. He also shouldered a knapsack. Billy Downwind had brought only a blanket, rolled and tied with a long leather cord that looped over his shoulder. They mounted up and headed north out of Aurora.

By the time they reached the meadow, a gentle blue twilight had settled over Lightning Strike. The air in the Northwoods had cooled after sunset, and the clearing was quiet and inviting. On the far side was a small bared circle filled with char and ash and outlined with stones in a ring, the place Billy and his uncle Big John and Cork, when he was with them, had built fires when they'd spent nights at Lightning Strike. The boys laid their bicycles down in the tall grass there.

"Let's gather wood," Cork said.

Ten minutes later, they were back at the fire ring, each with an armful of dead branches. Cork built a tepee of twigs and small limbs over a bed of dry pine needles, lit the needles with a kitchen match, and slowly added wood while the fire grew. By the time white stars began popping through the ink of the night sky, a good blaze was burning.

"Now?" Jorge said.

"Let's wait awhile," Cork said. "There's no hurry. How about something to eat?"

He'd brought Fritos and Oreo cookies. Jorge had brought peanut butter and jelly sandwiches and apples. They chowed down, then sat for a while, staring into the fire.

All his life, Cork would love the magnetism of a campfire, as did anyone who'd spent nights outside the glare of a city's lights. There was something elemental in fire, which warmed the heart as well as the body, mesmerized the eyes, cleared the brain of worry, let in a healing peace. He'd experienced this many times with his father and mother and Grandma Dilsey and Henry Meloux around the fire ring on Crow Point. Grandma Dilsey had told him that Nanaboozhoo, the trickster, had stolen fire and given it as a gift to human beings. Cork thought it was a generous gift.

"I'm not going back," Billy Downwind said out of nowhere.

"To the rez?" Cork said.

"Los Angeles." Billy stared at the fire and his eyes blazed. "I hate it there."

"You told me it was a great place."

"I just said that. It's noisy and it stinks and everyone hates us."

"But your dad has a good job, right?"

"Another promise they didn't keep. He doesn't work every day, and when he does, it's some shitty job. Pushing a broom or washing dishes or something. He could barely scrape together the money for two train tickets to get Mom and me here. There's no way he has the money to bring us back. I don't want to go back anyway. Out there, they think we're Mexican, call us Beaners."

"What's wrong with being Mexican?" Jorge said, sounding stung.

"Nothing. That's not what I'm saying. I'm saying they don't know who the hell we are. And out there, I wonder about that, too. Here, I know who I am."

"You can't just leave your dad there alone," Cork said.

"Mom says he can come back if he wants to. Me and her, we're staying."

Cork couldn't imagine what it would be like to live separate from his father. But Jorge said, "My mom and me, we do all right. You would, too, I bet."

"I could get a job," Billy said.

"Doing what?" Cork said.

"Anything."

"You gotta finish school first."

"Uncle Oscar could teach me to fix cars and stuff. I don't need school for that." Billy threw a stick on the fire. "At least I'd be here."

"People call you names here," Cork said. "Injun. Redskin. Worse. Being Ojibwe isn't exactly easy."

"Off the rez, it's hard. But on the rez, I'm with my people. We may not have much, but we've got each other. That's more than I can say for L.A."

They were quiet after that, listening to the crackle of the fire. Finally, Cork said, "It's pretty dark now. Let's give it a try."

Jorge reached into his knapsack and brought out a Ouija board, which he laid on the ground. The board glistened in the wavering firelight.

"You know how this works, right?" Jorge said.

"Not sure," Billy said.

"Okay, see this triangle thing here? It's called a planchette. I'm going to put it down on the board, then we're all going to put our fingertips on it, and you're going to call to the spirit of your uncle, ask him to talk to you. If he's here, the planchette moves to different letters and spells out what he wants to say. Got it?"

"Does it really work?" Billy said.

"Donna Markle used it to talk to her brother."

"The one got killed in a motorcycle crash?" Cork asked.

"Yeah, him. Okay. Put the tips of your fingers on it, like I said, but real light, so when it moves, it's Big John doing it, not one of us."

They all did as Jorge instructed.

"Now, Billy," Jorge said. "Talk to your uncle."

Billy looked beyond the small circle of light cast by the fire, looked into the dark where the ruins of the old logging camp lay. "Uncle, are you here?"

The planchette didn't move.

"Are you here, Big John?" Billy tried again. "Will you talk to me?"

Slowly, the planchette began to creep across the board and settled itself over the word YES. The boys exchanged wide-eyed glances of amazement.

"You didn't walk the Path of Souls?"

The planchette inched its way to the word NO.

"Why not?"

The planchette moved to the letter Y, then O, then X and paused.

"Yox," Jorge said.

"I don't understand," Billy said. "What does that mean?"

But the planchette didn't move.

"Ask who killed him," Cork said.

Billy gave a nod. "Who killed you, Uncle?"

The planchette held still a moment, then began to sweep in broad circles around the board, until it slipped right off into the grass.

"Put it back on," Jorge said. "Hurry."

But as Billy set the planchette back on the board, they all heard the sound of an automobile engine approaching on the old logging road.

Cork jumped up, grabbed his canteen, and emptied it on the fire, dousing the flames.

"What'd you do that for?" Jorge said.

"Why's somebody coming here this late at night?" Cork said.

"We're here," Jorge pointed out.

"Yeah, to talk to the dead," Cork said. "Let's see what they're here for."

The moon had climbed higher into the sky, the yellow of its early rising replaced by silver-white, the glow from it bathing the clearing in a milky iridescence.

Cork said, "Lie down."

They watched the headlights crawl between the pines. The car stopped at the edge of the clearing and the engine fell silent. The door opened, illuminating for a brief moment the driver inside, a woman. She closed the door and afterward became a small, pale wisp moving through the meadow grass toward the burnt ruins at the center of the clearing. She stepped in front of the stone chimney and knelt there, as if before some kind of altar. From where they lay, the boys could hear her voice but not her words.

"We need to get closer," Cork said.

On his hands and knees, he moved forward. When he was twenty yards away, he stopped and lay again on his belly. The other two boys had followed.

She was bent over, weeping so violently that it racked her whole body. Even without seeing her clearly, Cork knew who the woman was. He'd heard this same kind of crying from her only the night before. Her sobs were mixed with unintelligible words, but at last, she drew herself up and said clearly, "I miss you. I—I—" She lifted her face to the stars. "I'm sorry. I'm so sorry for everything."

A powerful wind rose, and the night, which had been so quiet, suddenly filled with a terrible moaning as the tree branches swayed and limbs rubbed against limbs. The wind made the tall grass bend as if pressed down by the passage of a powerful presence. The woman looked left, then right, then directly at the gibbous moon. In the stark light, Cork could see her face clearly, could see that her eyes had widened and her mouth stood open in surprise. Or maybe it was fear. She leaped to her feet and fled back across the meadow to her car. The wheels spun and the car swung around and sped away down the narrow corridor between the trees, taillights like little red eyes staring back at what had sent the woman fleeing. Cork turned toward the glow of the moon, just as Mary Margaret MacDermid had done, and he saw what she'd seen: a black shape towering above the treetops.

"Look!" he cried out and pointed.

Jorge and Billy saw it, too. As they watched, the wind died, and the black shape melted back into the broad shadow of the trees, and all was quiet once more.

"We called him up," Jorge said in a hoarse voice. "We really called him up."

"No," Cork said. "I think she did."

Billy Downwind continued to stare where the shape had been and finally said in a reverential whisper, "Son of a bitch."

They were still sitting in a state of amazement when the second set of headlights approached Lightning Strike. The boys lay down in the meadow grass as the truck parked and someone got out. Whoever it was left the headlights on. A dark figure was silhouetted against that glare and slowly it walked toward them.

Billy Downwind pressed his cheek to the ground and whispered, "Oh, crap."

The figure paused, and Cork held his breath, hoping the intruder would simply turn and leave. But in the next instant, he came on, and in ten more paces stood above them.

"Come on, boys," Liam O'Connor said coldly. "I'm taking you all home."

CHAPTER 25

His son sat on the far side of the cab seat, pressing himself against the passenger door of the pickup truck. Cork's two friends and the bicycles were in the truck bed. Liam's hands gripped the steering wheel as if he were trying to choke the life out of it.

"Dad—" Cork tried to say.

Liam cut him off. "We'll talk about this when we get home."

Earlier that evening, as he'd planned, Liam had driven to Glengarrow, hoping Duncan MacDermid was still isolating himself in the guest cottage and he could speak alone with Mary Margaret. When he rang the doorbell of the big house, Jorge's mother had answered and explained that Mary Margaret had stepped out and had asked if she would keep old Mrs. MacDermid company. Mary Margaret hadn't said when she'd be back.

Liam asked her one of the questions he'd intended to put to Mary Margaret: "Does she smoke cigarettes, Carla?"

"Yes."

"Do you know what kind?"

"Salems. Is that important?"

"I think so." Then he'd asked the simple question that had turned the night fateful. "How're the boys doing?"

Carla had given him a quizzical look. "Don't you know? Aren't they at your house?"

And it had become clear to them both. Cork had used Jorge as an excuse to be out, and Jorge had used Cork. And it didn't take a mind reader to know where they'd gone.

"Dad," Cork tried again.

"I don't want to talk about it right now."

"She was there, Dad."

"Who?" It was more like the snap of a whip, and Cork fell silent. After a moment, Liam said more reasonably, "Who was there?"

Cork had turned his face away, so that he was looking out the window at the darkness streaming past them. "Mrs. MacDermid," he mumbled.

"Mary Margaret?"

"You must have passed her on your way."

"I passed a car on the county road. I didn't know it was her. What was she doing there?"

"Crying mostly. And she was talking to Big John."

"What?" Liam eyed his son, then had to pull the steering wheel hard to the left because he almost missed a curve in the road.

"You know, all sad and stuff. Like how much she missed him and how sorry she was."

"Sorry for what?"

"She didn't say."

"Mary Margaret," Liam said, thinking he'd been right about at least one piece of the puzzle.

"And something else, Dad," Cork said.

"I'm listening."

"I saw Big John again."

This time Liam only glanced at his son. "His spirit?"

"Yeah. Big, Dad. I mean really big. Bigger than the trees even. Jorge and Billy saw him, too."

In his own family when Liam was growing up, they talked about the "little people." It was usually said in a joking way. Or if they wanted to give children a scare, they told stories of banshees. Nobody took these things seriously. The Ojibwe were different. Liam wasn't sure how he felt about that, this willingness of his wife's people to accept that they shared a world with spirits of all kinds.

But he said, "All right." Then again, more quietly, "All right."

He dropped Jorge off first, then continued to the rez and delivered Billy Downwind to his mother's place. At the door, she drilled Liam with a killing look, and after he'd given her a terse explanation, she gestured her son inside. She hadn't offered Liam a thank-you before she closed the door against him.

It was a long, silent ride back to the house on Gooseberry Lane. Colleen was waiting up and clearly surprised to see Cork enter ahead of her husband.

"Something wrong at Jorge's?" she asked, putting down the book she'd been reading and rising from the sofa.

Liam said, "The boys were out at Lightning Strike."

She looked at Liam with confusion, then at her son. "I don't understand."

"Do you want to explain to your mother?" Liam said.

Cork looked down at the floor and took a moment to gather his courage. "I didn't go to Jorge's."

"I gather," his mother said.

"We met at Grant Park—"

"You and Jorge?"

"And Billy Downwind."

"And?"

"We biked out to Lightning Strike."

"For heaven's sake why?"

Cork used his hands as if shaping something for her to see. "Jorge had this Ouija board and we conjured up Big John." He looked at her with hope, as if that not only explained everything but justified it as well.

"So you lied to me," Colleen said.

"Yeah, but we called up Big John's spirit, Mom. And Mrs. Mac-Dermid was there, too."

Colleen's surprise was clear. "Mary Margaret went with you?"

"No, she came later."

Colleen glanced at Liam, who said, "I'll explain it all in a bit. Right now, the important issue is that Cork lied to you. To us both."

His wife continued to look to him as if expecting some guidance in what lay ahead.

"Go on to bed, Cork," Liam said. "In the morning, we'll talk about an appropriate punishment."

Cork gave a nod, turned from them, and trudged upstairs. Jackson, who'd been with Colleen on the sofa and had sat patiently through the whole conversation, followed loyally behind him.

When they were alone, Liam explained what Cork had told him about the events at Lightning Strike that evening.

Colleen said, "What are you going to do?"

"About Cork or Mary Margaret?"

"Let's begin with our son."

"He needs to be punished of course."

"What did you have in mind?"

"My father would have taken a strap to me."

"You've never hit Cork."

"How about we begin by grounding him?" Liam said.

"All right. For how long?"

"I think a week will do. And how about we have him wash all the dishes after every meal?"

"For how long?"

"Until he goes off to college."

She smiled. "How about a week?"

"A week it is."

"And Mary Margaret?"

"She can do the dishes for as long as you want her to."

"Liam."

"I need to talk to her, alone. I'll try again tomorrow."

"It's so sad. Star-crossed lovers. When I was a girl, we all had a crush on Big John. He was handsome and sad and solitary. It was tragic to see what the war did to him, the drinking, the violence. Then he became Big John again. I understand what Mary Margaret saw in him. I just wish . . ."

"What?" Liam said.

"That it could be a different world than it is, I guess."

Liam put his arms around her and drew her to him. She embraced him and laid her cheek against his chest. "There's a lot of ugliness sure, Colleen, but I think about you and Cork, and I see so much beauty, too. We're lucky, you know."

Her body fit to his with such a wonderful familiarity that the anger and frustration he'd been feeling left him, and in its place, for one quiet moment, he felt peace descend.

"Cork has his paper routes," Colleen said, her cheek still against his chest. "And it'll just about kill him if he can't hang out with his friends, and he'd only be underfoot here. What if we hold his punishment to doing all the dishes?"

"Done," he replied and lifted her face gently to his and kissed her.

CHAPTER 26

Cork slept late the next day. Because he'd thought he would still be out at Lightning Strike, he'd arranged with a kid named Terrance Leonardi to cover his morning paper route. He'd done the same for Leonardi on occasion, and they had an understanding. But Leonardi didn't always see to his own route very well, and whenever he covered for Cork, there were problems.

When he came downstairs, the house was empty, but several notes had been laid out on the kitchen table, calls from customers whose newspapers hadn't been delivered. Cork ate a quick bowl of Cheerios, then took Jackson with him and spent an hour making sure everyone was satisfied. The last paper he dropped went to the Crooked Pine. Ben Svenson met him at the back door, chewing on a smelly cheroot and eyeing him like a criminal. "This is what I get for that big tip I gave you yesterday?" Svenson said. "Crappy service? If I treated my customers this way, I'd be out of business."

"The tip wasn't that big," Cork mumbled.

"What did you say?"

"Said I'm sorry, Mr. Svenson. It won't happen again."

"Better not," the man said.

Cork headed home, thinking a person must want a drink pretty bad to get it at the Crooked Pine.

His mother was home now, sitting at the kitchen table with a cup of coffee, reading the book Cork had given her as a birthday present, *Gifts from the Sea*. She was a schoolteacher and her summers were free. She spent a good deal of her time reading, "catching up" she called it, because when school was in session, she was busy every evening with lesson plans and such.

"I was in Allouette this morning visiting your grandmother," she explained. "Your father would like to see you. He said you should come to his office this morning."

"About last night?"

"Yes."

"Can't I wait until he comes home?"

"In my experience, Cork, it's best to get the bad out of the way quickly."

"It's going to be bad?"

"Not so much," his mother said. "Go on now. I'll call and let him know you're on your way."

Cork biked to the courthouse, dreading what was ahead. In the Tamarack County Sheriff's Department, he saw that the door to his father's office was open, but Ruth Rustad held up a warning hand.

"He told me to have you wait out here," she said.

Cork sat down in a chair at one of the desks the deputies shared. Through the open door of his father's office, he could hear voices, though he couldn't make out what they were saying. He glanced at Mrs. Rustad, who'd become involved in sorting through files in a cabinet, then he moved to a desk that was nearer his father's office.

"What was she doing out there?" he heard Cy Borkman say.

"According to Cork, crying mostly," Liam O'Connor replied.

"She went all the way out there to cry?"

"Cork said it sounded like she was talking to Big John. Or talking to his spirit anyway."

"Was she drunk?"

"I don't know."

"Could Cork hear what she was saying?" Joe Meese asked.

"Apparently telling Big John how much she missed him and that she was sorry. That kind of thing."

"So Lightning Strike was where they carried on?"

"Makes a certain kind of sense," Cork's father said. "If they met at Big John's cabin, someone on the rez might see them. Anywhere else in Tamarack County and they ran the same risk. It's isolated out there, and for Big John, a tryst under the stars doesn't seem out of character at all."

"Yeah, but what about Mrs. MacDermid? Not exactly a nature girl," Cy said.

"On the other hand, what's a few mosquito bites where true love is concerned?" It sounded as if Joe was warming to the idea.

"The rich man's wife and Big John," Cork's father said. "How could that pairing possibly have happened?"

There was a long silence, during which Cork stood up and walked to the doorway. Cy was staring at the ceiling, Joe at the floor, and his father at his hands, which were folded on his desk.

"What about her Sunfish?" Cork said in a small voice.

Liam O'Connor looked up from his folded hands and scowled. "How long have you been out there?"

"Couple of minutes."

Joe said, "What's that about her Sunfish, Cork?"

"Just a minute, Joe," his father said. "Cork and I have some business to take care of."

"What about the Sunfish?" Cy Borkman said at the sheriff's back.

Cork's father gave his son as stern a look as he could. "We'll finish our business at home. Right now, come into my office. Sit," he said and pointed toward an empty chair.

Cork sat down, awaiting instructions. His father retook his chair behind the desk, sat back, and said, "All right. What's this about a Sunfish?"

"You know the boathouse at Glengarrow, where Mr. Mac-Dermid keeps his big motorboat?"

"More like a yacht," Cy said. "And that boathouse? You could park a battleship in there."

"We know the place," Cork's father said. "Go on."

"She keeps a Sunfish tied up there."

"Sunfish?" Cy said.

"You know, a little one-person sailboat."

"Go on," his father said.

"Sometimes when I'm goofing around with Jorge, I see her take the Sunfish out on the lake. Jorge's mom says it's the only real freedom Mr. MacDermid allows her. And you know Big John, he was always out on the lake in his canoe."

His father frowned but seemed to be thinking this over. "They encounter one another on the lake, each of them alone. Maybe they strike up a conversation. Maybe she has trouble with her boat, and he helps her. Maybe over time things get more serious. In the end, Big John canoes to Lightning Strike, the woman meets him there in her little sailboat. And nobody's the wiser."

"I suppose it's a possibility," Joe said.

Cork's father drummed his fingers on his desktop for a few moments, putting elements together. "Okay, we have motive," he said to himself. "But we need method." He looked at his deputies.

"Suppose it was MacDermid. How is it Big John could let himself be hanged?"

"Remember his blood alcohol level," Cy said. "He was drunk as a skunk."

"He was twice the size of a normal man," Cork's father said. "He had a lot of alcohol in him, but he could still have fought hard."

"Drugged maybe," Joe said. "So he was helpless?"

"Drugged with what, Joe? Give me an idea."

Which, Cork knew, was well within the deputy's expertise. Before he'd been a lawman, Joe Meese had owned the Rexall Drug Store now owned by the Pfluglemans. He'd become a pharmacist only because his father was a pharmacist, but it wasn't what Joe really wanted out of life. Cork's father had often told how, from the moment he first set foot in Aurora, he'd listened to Joe complain that standing behind a counter with a mortar and pestle and doling out cough syrup all day was like a living death. What he wanted was action, to feel alive. What he wanted, had wanted since he was a kid, was to be a cop. When Liam O'Connor was elected sheriff, he finally challenged Joe to get off his ass and get the training. If he did that, a job would be waiting for him. Which was how Joe had come to trade in his white smock for the khaki uniform of the Tamarack County Sheriff's Department.

"My first thought would be one of the barbiturates," Joe said. "Phenobarbital, secobarbital, something like that. Easy to come by, and unless a full toxicology is run on the body, no one would suspect a thing. Even then it might not raise an eyebrow. Lots of folks use barbiturates these days. But a good dose would knock him right out. He'd be helpless if someone decided to string him up."

"Stringing him up out at Lightning Strike? That would be a

hell of a slap to the face of a wife who's been stepping out on you," Cy said with a shake of his head.

"Get him drunk, then drug him. Leave a couple of bottles of liquor at Lightning Strike, and a bunch at Big John's cabin, and it looks like just another rez suicide," Joe said.

"How would MacDermid get hold of a barbiturate?" Liam asked.

"He'd need a prescription," Joe said. "Or access to someone who has a prescription."

"Old Mrs. MacDermid takes pills to go to sleep at night," Cork said.

"How do you know that?" his father asked.

"Jorge told me. His mother gives them to her. He said they knock her right out."

His father sat back and scowled as he thought it through. "I'd like nothing better than to nail MacDermid, but there are some problems. Everyone on the rez believes Big John wasn't drinking anymore. If that's true, how did MacDermid get him drunk enough to be able to drug him? I can't even imagine the two of them sitting down together, let alone sharing a drink. And here's another fly in the ointment. MacDermid's got no real meat on his bones. Assuming he somehow drugged Big John, how the hell did he get him out to Lightning Strike and hang him? It would be like trying to haul a drugged buffalo."

Joe said, "He had help?"

"Who?"

None of them had an answer to that one. His father glanced at Cork in a way that told him he shouldn't be there, hearing all this. But it was too late now.

"Maybe we're looking at this all wrong," Joe said carefully.

"What do you mean?" Liam said.

"Okay, before you tell me I'm crazy, just hear me out. That

lighter Manydeeds found, maybe it wasn't MacDermid who
dropped it."

Cy scratched his jaw and said, "Then who the hell did?"

"Maybe his wife. Maybe she had more to do with all this than
just, you know . . ." Joe eyed Cork and seemed to think better of
how he was going to end that sentence.

"Mary Margaret MacDermid?" Cy said. "That little wisp of a
thing? I can't see it."

"Look, maybe Big John jilted her. And you know what they
say? Hell hath no fury like a woman scorned." Everyone in the
room stared at him and Joe said, "Shakespeare, I think."

"Jesus, if she was going to kill anybody it'd be that bastard of
a husband," Cy said.

"Cork, you told me that out at Lightning Strike she kept saying how sorry she was," his father said.

"That's right."

"But she never said what she was sorry about?"

Cork shook his head.

"If anything could knock a man off the wagon, it's a woman,"
Joe said. "She could have lured him out there, maybe for one last
hurrah, a few drinks together, one of them spiked, then when he's
out cold, she drags him over to that maple, puts the rope around
his neck, and hauls him up."

"A lot of ifs there," Cork's father said.

"Just saying it might be worth considering," Joe said.

Cork's father gave a slow nod. "I need to talk to Mrs. Mac-
Dermid alone, without her husband hovering. In the meantime,
Joe, check with the BCA and see if you can find out when we might
expect the full toxicology report on Big John. Make sure they check
for the presence of something like a barbiturate." He looked at his
son. "You've been a big help, Cork, but don't think it gets you off
the hook."

"No, sir."

"Go on home now. We've got work to do here."

Cork rose and left the room, but as he was walking away, he heard Joe say, "Go easy on him, Liam. He's a good kid."

"You don't need to tell me that," his father replied.

CHAPTER 27

Liam left immediately after supper and drove to Glengarrow. This time when he rang the bell, Mary Margaret answered. In her hand was a wineglass half filled with some vintage of a deep plum color.

"Liam?" She was clearly surprised to find him on her doorstep. "Are you looking for Duncan?"

"Actually, Mary Margaret, it's you I'd like to talk to. May I come in?"

She hesitated, and he could see her calculating. Which was a reaction he got mostly from people who had something to hide.

"Of course," she finally said, and stepped aside so that he could enter.

Liam had had occasion to be in the house only once before, a couple of years earlier, following a break-in; someone had jimmied the door to the veranda that overlooked the gardens behind the mansion. Several silver pieces had been stolen and Liam had never been able to nail the burglar. He'd pointed out to the MacDermids that they were lucky the thief—or thieves—had been content with taking what they could from the first floor and leaving unmolested those who slept upstairs. The silver had eventually been traced to a pawnshop in the Twin Cities and returned, but MacDermid continued to speak of the Tamarack County Sheriff's Department as a bunch of witless incompetents, though never within Liam's hearing.

The living room was high-ceilinged, with red-brown beams and wood paneling that Liam guessed might be mahogany. The floor was a dark polished wood, and at its center lay a large, ornate Persian rug. The furniture was all leather the color of creamed coffee. The fireplace was surrounded by tiles inlaid with soft brown designs, and above the mantel hung a portrait of Andrew MacDermid, the stern-looking Scotsman who'd built the family fortune. The room felt ancient and suffocating to Liam.

Mary Margaret asked if he'd like something to drink.

"I'm fine, thanks," he told her. "Could we sit down?"

She wore white capris and a blouse tied around her waist with a pattern that reminded Liam of a bandana. Her dark hair was bound with a white kerchief, red canvas espadrilles on her feet.

"You look dressed for boating," Liam noted.

"Oh," she said. "I just . . . it's just simpler."

"I'm going to tell you up front, Mary Margaret, that my son was with his friend Jorge at the carriage house the other evening when you came to Carla for comfort."

"I really don't know what you're talking about." She'd done her best with makeup to cover the bruise MacDermid had left on her face, but now she turned more in profile, in a clear attempt to make the bruise even less apparent.

"Adultery, Mary Margaret, that's what I'm talking about. Adultery with Big John Manydeeds."

All her body language told him she was going to deny it,

then everything changed. She seemed to wilt before his eyes. She turned her face to him fully.

"My version of the scarlet letter," she said, and lifted her hand to her cheek.

"Duncan?" Liam said.

She nodded.

"Could you go back to the beginning, Mary Margaret?"

"That would have been shortly after our wedding, when I realized the true nature of the man I married."

"I mean with Big John."

She put her wineglass down and closed her eyes. When she spoke, it was as if she were watching the scene play across the backs of her lids.

"I'd taken my sailboat out. There were storm clouds, and I should have known better, but I couldn't stand to be in this house with that man another moment. When the storm broke, I lost control of the boat. He came out of nowhere with his canoe and brought me safely to shore. We took shelter under some pines and huddled together under a tarp from my Sunfish." She opened her eyes and looked directly at Liam. "He was everything Duncan was not."

"How long ago?"

"Late May."

"The pines where you took shelter, was that at Lightning Strike?"

"Yes."

"And that's where you would meet?"

"It was isolated and beautiful. He told me it was a special place and there was a reason the storm had driven us there."

"You always boated to meet him?"

"Not always. Sometimes I drove. But he always came by canoe."

From his pocket, Liam took the silver lighter he'd brought and held it out to her in the palm of his hand. "Look familiar?"

She nodded. "A gift for Duncan, which he never used. Nothing I ever gave him was good enough. So I've been using it. Where did you get it?"

"It was found at Lightning Strike. Maybe you dropped it?"

"Probably. Sometimes when I left there, I was a little . . . well, focused on other things."

Liam put the lighter back into his pocket.

"When Big John died, was the affair still going on?"

She closed her eyes again, lowered her head, and spoke in nearly a whisper. "No."

"What happened?"

"I confessed."

"To Duncan?"

"To Father Cam first. He urged me to end it, to return to my marriage, which he reminded me was a holy sacrament."

She raised herself up, sat straight, and took a deep breath. "It couldn't have gone on anyway. We were from such different worlds. And the truth is, I didn't deserve him."

"So you broke it off? When?"

"A couple of days before the Fourth of July. I'd just put red, white, and blue streamers on the mast of the Sunfish."

"How did Big John take the breakup?"

"He was like a rock."

"Was this at Lightning Strike?"

She nodded. "I boated away and never saw him again. A week later, he was dead."

Little pearls of tears gathered along the rims of her eyes, then one by one began to crawl down her cheeks.

"And Duncan knows?"

"From the way I was behaving, he knew something was wrong.

He never took notice of me before, but suddenly he was at me all the time, and finally I broke down and told him. We had a huge blowup. He's been sleeping in the guest cottage since, getting himself stinking drunk every night."

"Did he know about the affair before Big John died?"

"Yes. And he went looking for him but couldn't find him. So he's been taking it out on me." She pointed toward the bruise as if it were her badge of honor.

"I can stop him, Mary Margaret."

"I'll do that on my own. I'm leaving him. He can divorce me. He has all the grounds he needs. I don't care. But I warned him that he's never to lay a hand on me again."

Like Big John, she was suddenly all rock, and although Liam understood her determination, the possibility of her confrontation with a man like Duncan Macdermid concerned him. "If he threatens you at all, Mary Margaret, call me."

She hesitated, then gave him a nod.

By the time Liam returned home, Colleen and Cork had gone to bed. Lights were still on in the bedrooms upstairs, and Colleen had left a light on in the kitchen. Liam flipped it off and mounted the stairs. He poked his head in his son's bedroom, where Cork had his nose in a book. Jackson lay across the foot of Cork's bed.

"Good story?" Liam asked.

"*War of the Worlds.* The Martians are everywhere."

"Sounds exciting. Don't stay up too late. Papers to deliver tomorrow morning. And did your mother tell you?"

"Tell me what?"

"You're responsible for the dinner dishes until we say otherwise."

Cork put the book down. "Why?"

"For lying to us."

"Oh. Yeah." As if he'd just remembered some long-ago trans-gression.

"Could have been worse, buddy. I wanted to ground you, too. Your mom pleaded for mercy. Like I said, don't stay up too late."

Colleen, too, was reading in bed. When Liam walked in, she set the book down and looked at him expectantly.

"How'd it go?"

"She admitted to the affair." As he took off his uniform, folded the pants and shirt, and laid them on the chair next to the bureau, he explained what he'd learned that evening.

"So Duncan knows?" Colleen asked.

Liam slipped into pajama bottoms but left his T-shirt on. "She confessed to him, too. Big mistake if you ask me. He's been using her for a punching bag since."

"That's a little glib, don't you think?"

"But accurate. You should see her face. I'm going to brush my teeth. Be right back."

When he returned, she was standing at the window. "I feel so awful for her, Liam. Isn't there something we can do?"

She held herself as if she were chilled by the night air, and Liam put his arms around her. "She said she's leaving him."

"Will she go through with it?"

"My guess is yes. Hell hath no fury," Liam said. Then he said, "Shakespeare."

"Congreve, actually," Colleen said. "Mom told me folks on the rez know about the affair. Billy Downwind has been talking."

"But did they know while it was going on?"

She shook her head. "Seems to have caught everyone by sur-prise." She stepped from his embrace and looked into his face. "Do you think Duncan MacDermid killed Big John?"

"I don't have enough evidence yet to prove that. But when

I find it, I swear I'll make certain that man never draws another breath outside a prison cell."

"I know you will." She smiled at him. "But you're off duty for this day. Come to bed now."

She took his hand and he was happy to be led there.

CHAPTER 28

When Cork came downstairs in the dark of the next morning for his paper deliveries, he heard voices in the kitchen. He stepped into the doorway and found his father and Sam Winter Moon standing at the counter, each of them holding a mug of coffee and so engrossed in their conversation that they didn't notice him.

"That's not what they want to hear on the rez, Liam. They want to hear that you've put MacDermid behind bars."

"I'll say it again, Sam. Until I have proof, my hands are tied. But listen, I've been thinking. Mary Margaret said that she and Big John broke up a few days before the Fourth of July, and she never saw him again. Do you know if anyone on the rez saw him after that?"

"I can't speak for everybody, but I don't recall seeing him for quite a while before the boys found his body."

"He'd been hanging from that tree at Lightning Strike four or five days before that. Between his breakup with Mary Margaret and when he died, at least four or five days must've passed? That's maybe nine or ten days total. If nobody saw him, where was he?"

Sam said, "He was the best guide in these parts. Maybe he had a job."

Jackson, who'd been lying on the floor in the corner near his water bowl, got to his feet and trotted to Cork. Cork knelt, ruffed the dog's fur and said, "Hey, boy."

His father turned from the counter. "Didn't see you, Son. We have company."

"Hey, Sam," Cork said.

With his coffee mug in hand, Cork's father moved to the table and sat down. Sam Winter Moon remained standing, as if what he'd come for was finished.

"Sam was just catching me up on news from the rez before we both go to work."

"What news?" Cork asked.

"Lots of talk about Big John," Sam said. Cork saw his father give a faint shake of his head, and Sam quickly changed the subject. "I'm headed back to my Quonset hut. Would you like a ride to your paper box?"

"Thanks," Cork said. "Can Jackson come along?"

"Fine by me. You and Jackson go on out. I'll be right with you."

"Come on, boy," Cork said, and Jackson followed eagerly.

He paused on the mud porch. In the kitchen at his back, he heard Sam say, "There's a storm brewing on the rez, Liam. It's not just Big John, but his death is like a lightning rod for a lot of old grievances. When that storm breaks, watch yourself."

Dawn was just a vague promise of azure light along the eastern horizon as Sam drove his truck along the empty streets of Aurora. Cork stared out the window on his side of the cab, wondering about the trouble Sam had said was brewing.

"Does everybody on the rez think my dad should arrest Duncan MacDermid?"

"Seems to be the general sentiment."

"What do you think?"

"Your dad says all he has at the moment is circumstantial evidence. You know what that is, right?"

"Sure."

"He says that circumstantial evidence isn't good enough to convict someone of a crime like a murder, even though anyone who's Ojibwe has seen it happen. But he swears it's not going to happen on his watch. If he's going to arrest Duncan MacDermid or anyone else for murder, he's dead set on getting indisputable proof first." Sam Winter Moon pulled up to the drop box, where two bound stacks of morning newspapers awaited Cork. "He's a man of principle, your father, not an easy thing. So, what are you up to today?"

Cork had no idea. He'd had direction for a while, following crumbs, looking for answers. But there seemed no more trail for him to follow. It left him with an unsettling sense of being without purpose, a feeling he'd never had before. Before, summers had been mostly about doing nothing and enjoying every moment of doing nothing.

"I'll probably just goof around with the guys," he finally said.

"Sounds fun," Sam said.

But it didn't. Not to Cork.

At nine A.M., Liam O'Connor walked into Borealis Outfitters at the end of Oak Street. The building was constructed of white pine logs, and although it had been built five decades earlier, the scent of evergreen still permeated the air. It was filled with racks of outdoor wear, shelves lined with camping gear, and books covering every aspect of roughing it in the great Northwoods. Behind the store were canoes and kayaks and all manner of camping necessities, available for rental by tourists drawn to Aurora because it was the gateway to the vast Quetico-Superior Wilderness, the Boundary Waters.

The two sisters, Sarah Andersen and Kim Krabill, were arguing behind the counter, not an unusual situation in Liam's experience. Both women were smart and strong-willed and seemed to enjoy the little skirmishes that arose in the course of making everyday business decisions.

"Remember what happened last year when we rented canoes to that group?" Sarah said.

The two women looked nothing alike. Sarah was short, brunette, and full of energy, a little powder keg exploding. Kim was tall and blond, and there was a feel about her that made Liam think of how a cattail might bend in the wind but never seemed to break. Their father had owned Borealis Outfitters. They'd been raised in Aurora but had left for college and built lives far away. When their father died, the sisters, both widowed, chose to return to their hometown and take the reins of the business their father had spent his life building. Colleen had told Liam that when they were kids, folks referred to them as the Borealis sisters. When they returned to Aurora, folks slid right back into calling them that again.

Kim, the tall Borealis sister, said, "We should always give folks a second chance."

"They used the canoes like battering rams, for goodness' sake. The bows came back looking like the noses of prizefighters who had no business being in the ring."

"They've all matured a year, and I've spoken to the pastor. He assures me the kids will be more responsible. And, Sarah, they're coming all the way from Omaha. He told me the kids have been looking forward to this trip for a whole year."

"Fine. Let the pastor rent his canoes from Gowdy's."

"Gowdy's canoes are barely floatable."

"Because he rents to kids who use them as battering rams. You were a doctor, Kim, but you can't perform surgery on a canoe that's taking on water in the middle of a Northwoods lake. I've been a businesswoman all my life. Let me handle this business. I'll be diplomatic, I promise."

They both seemed to notice Liam at the same moment and turned to him smiling, as if the spat he'd just witnessed was absolutely nothing. Which, Liam understood, it was.

"Morning, Sheriff," the two sisters said with one voice.

"Morning, ladies. Got a minute?"

"Going to arrest us?" Kim said, sounding as if that might be fun.

"Just a few questions to ask."

"All ears," Sarah said.

"Or mouth, in your case," her sister said.

"About Big John," Liam said, and the two women suddenly became serious.

"We miss him," Kim said. "Miss him terribly."

"Big John was a fine wilderness guide," Liam said.

"The best. Always in demand. We had a waiting list."

"Did he have an outing scheduled sometime around the Fourth?"

"Yes," Sarah said. "A group of businessmen from Chicago. He was supposed to take them out that weekend, but a couple of days before the Fourth he came in and canceled. We gave the job to Ollie Grimson."

"Did he say why he canceled?"

"No, but something was clearly troubling him."

"Did you see him after that?" The sisters shook their heads and Liam said, "Nobody on the rez seems to have seen him either. Any idea where he might have gone?"

The women exchanged a knowing glance and Sarah said, "From the way he looked, all tied up in knots, we figured he was probably heading alone into the Boundary Waters. He always said there was no place so healing to him."

"How would he have gone in?"

"The way most folks on the rez go in," Sarah said. "Up Spider Creek to Moose Lake."

"Spider Creek," Liam said. "A stone's throw from Lightning Strike."

The name brought a dark cloud to the faces of both sisters. Kim said, "We heard that there was something going on between Big John and Mary Margaret MacDermid. We heard that Duncan MacDermid might have had something to do with Big John's death. Is that true?"

"Where'd you hear it?"

"Around," Kim said.

"Don't believe everything you hear."

"It's interesting because MacDermid was in here just after Big John canceled out on those Chicago businessmen."

"What did he want?"

"He was looking for Big John."

"What did you tell him?"

"What we just told you. That we thought he was in the Boundary Waters. Then, just like you, he asked how Big John would've gone in."

"And you told him?"

"No reason not to. Then, anyway." Sarah leaned toward Liam in a manner that felt a little threatening. "Look, Sheriff, we don't believe for an instant that Big John killed himself. Did Duncan MacDermid have something to do with his death?"

Kim stepped close to her sister, and the two women became an imposing wall of outrage.

"In my experience," Liam said, "rumors are like the plague. They spread quickly and they can kill. So I'd ask you both to be careful what you say. But I'll promise you this: As soon as I know anything substantial, I'll let everyone in this county know it, too."

He made a move to leave, but the wall the Borealis sisters had created didn't part immediately. They held their ground for a long moment before finally allowing Liam to pass.

CHAPTER 29

Though it was a normal summer day, nothing felt normal to Cork anymore. He shot hoops for a while with some other boys at the court behind Garfield Elementary, came home for lunch, tossed a ball with Jackson in the backyard, read some more from *War of the Worlds,* delivered newspapers with Jorge, after which they hit Sam's Place for chocolate shakes. These were all things he would have done on any summer day, but that day they felt pointless and empty. Everywhere he went, he carried with him the deep, unshakable sense that there were important questions needing answers, and he was doing nothing about them.

Grandma Dilsey came to dinner that night. Cork could feel the tension around the table. There were so many things he wanted to ask, things he wanted to say, but his mother had instructed him—and Grandma Dilsey—not to talk about Big John or anything that had to do with his father's investigation. So he listened as the women carried on a light conversation about the annual Aurora Blueberry Festival, which was only days away, speculating which of the princesses would be crowned Blueberry Queen, talking about past festivals and past queens.

His father added almost nothing to the conversation, and when supper was over, said he had official business to attend to and left the house.

Cork was on dish duty as punishment for lying, but his mother and Grandma Dilsey cleared the table and stacked the dishes for him. Then Grandma Dilsey made lavender tea, which she claimed helped her to sleep, and sat with her daughter at the kitchen table.

"You know the problem with men?" she said.

Cork could smell the lavender even over the scent of the dish soap that dripped from the plates as he washed them.

"They're like firecrackers," Grandma Dilsey said. "They keep everything inside, then one day they just explode."

"You think Liam's going to explode?"

"I sure get that sense. Don't you?"

"He's always been quiet."

"Quiet, yes. But at dinner this evening, he didn't say three words, Colleen. Did you put the same restrictions on him, no talking about the important things that are happening?"

"I didn't want any arguments this evening. I wanted a normal dinner."

"You think that was normal? The food was good, but the talk was tasteless."

"He wouldn't have said anything important anyway. He's worried that whatever he says will find its way back to the rez."

"Because of me?"

"Well, Mom?"

"If I'm asked to keep something to myself, Colleen, I keep it to myself. If that's not asked of me, I see no reason not to share what I know with my friends and family in Allouette. There's no reason to keep them in the dark about things that affect them directly."

"Like Big John's death?"

"Big John's murder," Grandma Dilsey said. "Do you know

what they're saying on the rez? That Liam sent Sam Winter Moon out asking about Oscar Manydeeds only so that he could muddy the waters, blame an Indian for a crime probably committed by a white man. They're saying that's what white cops have always done."

"Liam has never done that, and you know it."

"What I'm saying, Colleen, is that your husband, the sheriff, needs to be more forthcoming with the things he knows. Otherwise, it just looks like another cover-up."

From the sink, Cork said, "All he has is circumstantial evidence. It's not enough."

"What circumstantial evidence?" Grandma Dilsey said.

"I can't say."

"I'm your grandmother, Corkie."

Cork's mother said, "Wasn't it you who just told me that when you're asked to keep something to yourself you do that? Leave him be, Mom."

Grandma Dilsey said something in her native tongue. To which her daughter replied, "I wasn't blind when I married Liam. I saw beyond his badge and into his heart. It's not made of gold but it's a good heart, Mother."

Grandma Dilsey got up from the table and prepared to head home. She took her cup to the sink and added it to the dishes still waiting to be washed. Then she returned to her daughter at the table and kissed the top of her head. "I'm sorry. I didn't mean to be so hard on Liam. It's just a bad situation on the rez at the moment, and it worries me." A small smile graced her lips, and she put her hand over her daughter's and said quietly, "I never knew anyone, white or Ojibwe, whose heart was made of gold."

Cork watched his grandmother go. She'd always held her back straight and proud, but he saw how she bent now, as if weighted, and he didn't know if it was because of the trouble on the rez or because that trouble was leaking into the O'Connor house, disturbing the peace that had always made it feel so safe.

After Grandma Dilsey had gone, Cork's mother grabbed a fresh towel and began drying the dishes he'd washed.

"Dad said I was supposed to do that."

"I'll take the heat for this one," she said. "Consider it a reprieve."

Cork was scrubbing the pan in which the chicken had baked. "You knew Big John pretty well."

"I grew up with him."

"Everybody says the Boundary Waters was like a second home to him."

"I think he was more at home there than anywhere else. I remember a ceremony Henry Meloux held for him when he was thirteen. He'd run away from the boarding school again, and he vowed he was going to live in the woods and never go back. He and Henry built a canoe together, and together they disappeared into the Boundary Waters. We didn't see them for almost a year. When they finally came out of the woods, Big John looked stronger and happier than any of us could ever remember. But the authorities were still looking for him, so he went back into the woods alone, and we saw him only occasionally over the next few years. He still has that canoe Henry helped him build."

Cork paused in his washing and thought a moment. "His canoe's gone."

"What do you mean?"

"I was at his cabin with Dad after the funeral. Big John's canoe wasn't there."

"Maybe he loaned it to someone on the rez."

"And maybe he didn't," Cork said. "I think it's something Dad should think about."

"Well then, you tell him when he gets home."

"Where'd he go?"

"Ask him that, too. If he wants you to know, he'll tell you."

Cork went back to his washing. That morning, he'd thought he was out of crumbs. But maybe he wasn't.

Duncan MacDermid was already two sheets to the wind. He stood in the doorway of his guest cottage, rocking a little, as if winds were pushing at him from different directions. He had a glass in his hand, and Liam could smell the whiskey.

"What do you want?" MacDermid said.

"I need a couple of questions answered, Duncan."

"Tomorrow. Come back tomorrow."

"What's wrong with right now?"

"Not in the mood."

"I'll be quick, then out of your hair. And you can get right back to your drinking."

MacDermid squinted, trying to focus. "What do you wanna know?"

"How 'bout we sit down? Your deck's a nice spot."

MacDermid frowned, then turned without a word and led the way through the cottage. Liam stepped in, closed the door, and followed.

The deck was softly illuminated, and the lights from Aurora lay like a necklace of multicolored jewels along the black shoreline of Iron Lake. The moon had risen but was still low in the sky, and the stars were diamonds on the black velvet dress of night. Liam thought about Chicago, a city so bright that, as a kid, he never saw stars.

MacDermid sat down heavily in the larger wicker chair, and Liam sat facing him. In the dim light, MacDermid's face was ashen.

"When I asked you about the war, you didn't mention that you'd been assigned to the USS *Indianapolis*," Liam said.

This was clearly not what MacDermid had expected, and he stared at Liam as if trying to see what was in his mind.

"I did a little asking around. It's true, yes? You served on the *Indianapolis*?"

"Lieutenant Duncan MacDermid. Intelligence specialist." He gave a little salute.

"I know the story of the *Indianapolis*. When she went down, nearly a thousand men went into the water. And no one knew you were out there."

"The sharks, they knew. Circled us for days, picking us off one by one."

"I fought in the war, too, Duncan. Airborne. I still have nightmares. I can't even begin to imagine what yours must be like."

MacDermid looked away, across the dark water of the lake. "Don't even try," he said.

"The drink, does that help?"

"I drank before the *Indianapolis* went down. Legacy of my father."

"Was Four Roses his favorite, too?"

"And my grandfather's. Family tradition."

"You know, people in this town think you've got it made. Beautiful estate, lots of money. Hell, you own one of the oldest and biggest mine operations on the Iron Range." He paused and then said, "But you know what I think? I think it's not so easy a life."

MacDermid put his drink down and seemed to be trying to focus.

"I think it's got to be hard being at the top. I think people look at you with all kinds of lofty expectations. I think you must have to work awfully hard to meet those expectations."

"Damn right," MacDermid said.

"And so it must have been a huge blow when Mary Margaret told you about her affair."

MacDermid's face went slack for a moment.

"I know about her and Big John, Duncan. The whole town knows."

MacDermid pressed his lips together in a line as thin as black thread. "That bitch. That slut."

"Did you know about the affair before she told you?"

He picked up his drink again and took a slug. "I knew something was in the wind. She wouldn't let me touch her. I finally dragged it out of her. When I found out it was an Indian, I wanted to puke. Told her I was gonna divorce her, gonna leave her with nothing."

"Why didn't you?"

"Hell, I didn't want everyone knowing my wife was fucking an Indian."

"And then you went looking for Big John."

"Wanted to smash his face in."

"Did you find him?"

MacDermid shook his head. "Must've heard I was looking for him and went into hiding, the coward. Then he goes and hangs himself. Good riddance." MacDermid lifted his glass in a toast.

Liam waited for him to drink again, then said, "Your lighter, the one that Oscar Manydeeds says he found at Lightning Strike, do you have any idea how it might have got there?"

"I hadn't seen it for a while, so maybe someone stole it. I've had things stolen from the house before." He looked darkly at Liam. "As you well know."

"Do you know where Mary Margaret and Big John met to carry out their affair?"

"She told me."

"Can you tell me where you were over the Fourth of July weekend?"

"Hell, that was more than two weeks ago."

"Do you know where you were?"

"Here at the cottage, I'm sure. It's where I spend most of my time these days."

"Can anyone confirm that?"

"Confirm that?" And then it began to dawn on MacDermid, and he looked at Liam as he must have looked at one of those circling sharks in the waters of the Pacific. "Ask my lawyer."

"Nick Skinner?"

"He'll tell you exactly where I was. And you know what, Sheriff? I want you to get the hell off my property. If there's any more talking to be done, you can do it through my lawyer."

By the time Cork went to bed, his father still hadn't returned. Cork read for a while, then heard the rumble of thunder in the distance, announcing the approach of another summer storm. He turned out his light and crawled onto the porch roof and watched as crackling volleys of lightning battered the western sky. He could smell rain on the breeze. His mother had turned in as well, and the light from his parents' bedroom window illuminated a rectangle of porch shingles ten feet from where Cork sat. His mother's shadow cut the light for a moment as she stood at the window, then she drew the curtains and her lamp went out, and Cork knew she'd gone to bed.

Almost immediately his father's cruiser came slowly up the street and pulled into the drive, next to the pickup truck. A minute later, Cork heard the screen door of the mud porch open and slap shut. A few minutes after that, the light in his parents' bedroom came on again, and Cork heard his mother say, "Long day."

His father replied, a grumbling Cork didn't quite catch.

"What did Duncan have to say?" his mother asked.

His father's shadow fell against the curtains and remained there, tall and dark. But again, whatever he said was spoken so low, so quiet that Cork couldn't hear the words, only the tone, which was threatening.

"Did he confront Big John?" Cork's mother said.

The storm was almost upon them. Lightning came with increased frequency and the rumbling of thunder drowned out anything more Cork heard of his parents' conversation. The light went out in the bedroom next to his, and as the first big drops of rain began to fall, Cork returned to his room and to his bed, and finally lost himself in sleep.

CHAPTER 30

When, in the dark of early morning, Liam rose and went to his son's bedroom to make sure Cork didn't oversleep, he was surprised and pleased to see the bed was empty. Downstairs, he found Cork sitting at the kitchen table with Jackson at his feet.

"I see you're all set to go. Big day ahead?" He went to the stove and grabbed the percolator to begin making a pot of coffee.

"Nothing much."

"No pickup baseball game?"

"Maybe."

"The Carruthers had to put their dog down yesterday. Distemper. Your mom's going to make an appointment for Jackson to get a booster shot. Maybe you could give her a hand with that."

"Sure," Cork said in a distracted way. "Dad, I've been thinking. Big John's canoe wasn't at his cabin."

"I know."

"So where is it?"

"I don't know."

"Don't you think we should find out?"

Liam filled the coffeepot and turned from the sink. "We?"

"I mean you."

"Joe and Cy checked at Lightning Strike but didn't find it." He glanced at Cork. "You know Lightning Strike was where Big John and Mary Margaret MacDermid met, right?"

"When they were . . ." His son seemed at a loss for how to say it.

"Having their affair," Liam finished for him. He put the pot on the stove. "She sometimes used her Sunfish sailboat to get there and he used his canoe. Pretty much what we all speculated at my office, thanks to you."

"He used his canoe for lots of other things, too."

"Like going into the Boundary Waters. Which is where he may have been just before he died."

"How do you know?"

Liam put together the coffee in the percolator, then turned on the gas flame. "I'm going to make toast. Want some?"

"Thanks," Cork said.

Liam pulled a loaf of Wonder bread from the bread drawer and dropped a couple of slices into the toaster. "I talked to the Borealis sisters. Big John was scheduled to guide for some businessmen but canceled. The sisters think he might have gone in on his own."

"To heal." When Liam gave him a quizzical look, Cork said, "He used to tell me and Billy that the Boundary Waters was a good place to heal your soul. And he would have used Spider Creek."

Which, Liam knew, was the access Big John used on those occasions when Cork had accompanied him and Billy Downwind into the Boundary Waters. Because the creek was on reservation land, most local Ojibwe used it as their entry point. Spider Creek flowed out of Naabe-Mooz, which in the language of the Ojibwe meant "bull moose." White folks simply called it Moose Lake. It was a large body of water, and at its northernmost point gave access to the rest of the Boundary Waters.

"If he went into the Boundary Waters," Cork continued, "maybe he left his canoe somewhere along Spider Creek. Did Joe and Cy check there?"

"Probably not. But why would he leave it?"

"I don't know. But if he did, that would mean something, wouldn't it?"

"Like what?"

"Something," Cork insisted. "Because he wouldn't just leave it there for no reason."

"I think the most likely scenario is that he loaned his canoe to someone," his father said. The toast popped up. "Want peanut butter?"

"Sure. Can I look for it, Dad?"

"You know where the peanut butter is."

"I mean the canoe."

As he took the jar from the cupboard, Liam thought over his son's request. It was certainly something that would keep him occupied for much of the day, and Liam was a firm believer in not leaving idle hands for the devil to work with. It was also a way for Cork to feel that he was doing something to help, which was important as well.

"Be my guest," he said, and handed Cork a slice of toast and the jar of Skippy peanut butter.

Iron Lake was big, and it took the boys nearly two hours to paddle the O'Connors' canoe to the place where Spider Creek fed in. Along the way, Cork had explained his thinking to Jorge.

Big John had disappeared a few days before he was killed. The Borealis sisters believed he'd gone into the Boundary Waters seeking solitude. If that was true, he probably entered and exited the wilderness via Spider Creek. When Cork and his father found the empty whiskey bottles at Big John's cabin, his canoe wasn't there. So, if he'd gone into the Boundary Waters, as the Borealis sisters believed, and he'd come out, where was his canoe?

Billy was there when they arrived, standing at the water's edge where the stream fed into Iron Lake. He held the bow of the canoe as Cork and Jorge disembarked.

"Did you find out anything?" Cork asked.

"I checked on the rez, like you asked me to," Billy said. "Nobody knows anything about the canoe. So, what's the plan?"

"We know he didn't leave it at Lightning Strike. The deputies already checked. So let's check to see if he left it somewhere along Spider Creek."

"Why would he leave it?" Billy asked.

"I don't have any answers. But maybe if we find the canoe, we'll get some."

The area around the mouth of the creek was marshy, covered with reeds and cattails and dotted with tamaracks. The boys searched both sides of the creek, but to no avail.

"Okay, let's go upstream toward Moose Lake," Cork said.

The creek was not much more than two feet deep and a dozen feet wide. The boys set the canoe in the middle. Cork took the stern, Jorge the bow, and Billy sat in the middle. The current wasn't strong, and they had no difficulty paddling against it.

The Ojibwe called the stream Asabikeshiinh, which meant "spider." It meandered for a couple of miles among bulrushes and cattails and wild rice and tamaracks, a spiderweb of channels that, if you didn't know your way, could take you into dead end after dead end. But as Cork had assured Sam Winter Moon, the boys had all been this way many times. They came at last to the source of Spider Creek, a fast rush of water that poured down a cascade of rocks from Moose Lake. They stepped from their canoe and slid the bow onto dry land, then began to follow the portage that led around the rocks and up to the lake.

The entry to the lake was a small apron of soft earth edged with blackberry bramble. If they'd carried their canoe up, they would have set it on the water there, which was at the end of a long, rocky corridor. A quarter of a mile distant, the corridor opened onto the vast body of Moose Lake. Naabe-Mooz.

"What are you looking for?" Jorge asked.

"I don't know. I thought maybe his canoe would be right here." Cork couldn't hide his disappointment.

"Even if it was, what would that prove?" Billy asked.

"I don't know," Cork said again. "But maybe something. If it had been here."

"What now?" Jorge asked.

"Back to Iron Lake, I guess," Cork said.

"Long way to come for squat," Billy said.

"Did you have something better to do?" Cork didn't try to hide his mood.

They canoed back in a desolate silence, Cork brooding the whole way. What had he expected? Maybe a crumb. What had he found? Nothing.

They were almost to the mouth of Spider Creek when Billy said, "There!"

He was in the bow, and he pointed to his right where a narrow channel cut into tall bulrushes. What Cork saw there would have been invisible to anyone looking for it from the lakeshore. But coming downstream on Spider Creek offered a different perspective. What Billy had seen, what they all saw now, barely visible among the tall reeds, was the curved stern of a birch-bark canoe.

The boys backpaddled, then entered the channel. Almost immediately, their canoe scraped bottom, and they had to disembark carefully and wade through deep mud that sucked at their sneakers. When they reached the canoe, Jorge asked, "Is that his?"

Billy nodded.

The boys stared, and Cork finally said, "What the hell happened to it?"

CHAPTER 31

Ruth Rustad knocked lightly on the frame of Liam's open door. "County attorney wants to see you upstairs, Sheriff."

"Did he say what it's about?"

"Didn't. Sounded unhappy."

"Not unusual. Thanks, Ruth."

Liam went back to the documents he'd been reading, extracts from articles on alcohol absorption when introduced into the human body by various means. The librarian at the Tamarack County Library had been more than generous with her time in locating them.

"He said now, Sheriff."

Liam took his time. When he'd climbed to the second floor of the courthouse, he ran into Nicholas Skinner, who was just about to descend the marble stairway. Skinner's face was the color of an angry sunset sky, and the look in his eyes was like one Liam recalled from the war just before men fixed bayonets.

"You okay, Nick?" Liam asked.

"I just came from our county commissioners' office."

"You don't look happy about that."

Clutched in one of Skinner's hands was a long rolled sheet of heavy paper that Liam figured was an architectural drawing of some kind. More than a year before, Nicholas Skinner and some other investors had bought property on the shoreline of Iron Lake within the town limits. They proposed to build a world-class hotel there, along with an expansion of the town's small marina. His aim, as he'd said in so many of the articles printed about the project, was to increase the allure of the area as a premier tourist destination. At the moment, most accommodations on Iron Lake were cabin resorts or small motel operations. With businesses already closing due to the downturn in the mining economy and new sources of revenue needed in the area, most folks in Tamarack County seemed to welcome the idea. In the local paper, Liam had seen drawings of what the final structure would look like, and he'd been impressed.

"We need a variance for the hotel," Skinner said. "I've been working on it for six months. I thought we were going to get it, but Arne Tikkanen called me this morning. Our county commissioners have decided, quite suddenly, not to grant it."

"Did he tell you why?"

"He didn't need to. I know the reason. Retribution."

"You've lost me."

"All right. What I'm going to tell you doesn't trespass on client privilege, because I'm no longer Duncan MacDermid's personal attorney. I quit last night."

"Why?"

"He called me late, drunk as usual, said you'd been out to question him."

"That's right."

"He said he told you about his wife's affair, her trysts out at Lightning Strike."

"Yes."

"He'd discussed with me divorcing Mary Margaret. I'd advised against it. Divorce would make everything very public. But word seems to have gotten out anyway. Now it's the only thing people around here are talking about. Between that and his drinking, Duncan hasn't been thinking clearly. He said you asked him where he was when John Manydeeds was killed. He said you think it wasn't suicide, and he believes you're looking at him as a suspect."

"He's a person of interest."

"I'm not his lawyer anymore, and like I said, I don't consider what I'm about to tell you covered under client privilege." A look even more inflamed than before came over Skinner's face. "Last night, he ordered me to lie for him."

"How so?"

"He insisted I swear that I was with him during the time you believe Manydeeds was killed."

"We just have a general idea when that would have been. Did MacDermid give you a better idea?"

"Not really. He wanted me to swear we were working together for most of a couple days on a new will, in light of his wife's affair."

"What days?"

"The whole weekend after the Fourth of July."

"And were you, in fact, with him?"

"I was nowhere near him. He's been holed up in that cottage ever since he found out about his wife and Manydeeds. Every time I've called him, to talk sense into him, he's been nothing but belligerent. Honestly, even before he attempted to strong-arm me, I'd had enough of him as a client."

"I'm guessing MacDermid accounted for a significant part of your business," Liam said.

"Once the Four Seasons project is off the ground, if it ever is, that'll more than make up for getting Duncan off my back."

"So, you believe he's behind our county commissioners' decision not to grant you the variance?"

"I know Duncan's handiwork when I see it."

"Thanks for the information, Nick. If I need it, would you be willing to give me a formal statement of everything you've just told me?"

"All you have to do is hand me a pen."

The two men shook hands and Liam continued to the county attorney's office.

"I got a call from Duncan MacDermid this morning," Bud Fassbinder said from behind his desk. He was small and balding, with a pinched face and little black eyes that had always reminded Liam of a ferret. "He told me you've been harassing him."

"Harassing? I simply questioned him," Liam said.

"He said you accused him of some complicity in that Indian's death."

"His name was John Manydeeds."

"Manydeeds killed himself. End of story," Fassbinder said.

"I'm not convinced."

"And why not?"

"Too many inconsistencies."

"Like what?"

"The nature of the man for one thing."

"He was an Indian. What more do you need to know?"

Liam stood up and turned to leave the office.

"Where are you going?"

"To do my job."

"Sit back down."

Liam remained standing.

"Look," Fassbinder said, in a conciliatory tone. "You're not from here."

"What does that have to do with anything?"

"There's always been a certain . . . order . . . to life here."

"And does that order include looking the other way when Indians are killed or when husbands beat their wives?"

"I believe you're wasting your time with this investigation."

"With all due respect, this investigation is my responsibility, not yours."

"There are lines you should not cross."

"And questioning Duncan MacDermid is one of them?"

"There are consequences."

"I'll risk them."

Fassbinder shrugged. "Your funeral."

Liam went back downstairs to the Sheriff's Department, where he found his son sitting with Joe Meese at the deputy's desk. Cork's sneakers were covered in dried mud.

Joe looked up at Liam and gave a slight nod toward Cork. "Wait'll you hear this."

CHAPTER 32

Liam arranged for the use of one of the two launches the Aurora Volunteer Fire Department kept for water rescues. It was late afternoon when he and Deputy Joe Meese boated to the mouth of Spider Creek. They anchored the launch and followed Cork's instructions, wading up the stream to the narrow channel in the bulrushes. They found Big John's canoe lying in the muck among the reeds, exactly as Cork had said.

Both men stood quietly, listening to the song of the red-winged blackbirds flitting among the rushes, then Joe said, "Jesus, what the hell happened here?"

The rear thwart was smashed into pieces, the left gunnel shattered, the whole left side of the stern stoved in. It looked as if an angry giant had slammed a great boulder against the fragile craft.

"Murder," Liam said. "Or the beginning of it."

Joe had brought the department Polaroid, and he snapped photos from every angle. Liam lifted out a Duluth pack, the only item in the canoe, went through the contents, and found more or less what he'd expected, what a man might need for a few days alone in the wilderness. They dusted the canoe for fingerprints, then checked the area for footprints, but the muck had closed over everything, even the evidence of the boys' recent visit. While they did all this, they speculated.

"Someone waited for him at the mouth of the creek," Liam said. "They must have jumped him and tried to hide his canoe here."

"They?" Joe said.

"One man alone couldn't have brought down Big John. I'm thinking the canoe was damaged in the fight."

"When he was hanging from that tree, I didn't see any indication of bruises or anything from a fight."

"I didn't look that hard, Joe. Did you?"

What Liam had seen at Lightning Strike was what his experience had told him he'd see: a man who'd been in the grip of booze before and was in the grip of booze again, a man who couldn't face the harsh reality of what it was to be Indian, a man who had disappointed himself and, in the end, disappointed everyone who'd looked up to him and believed in him.

"We didn't even bother to do an autopsy," Liam said. Thinking, *What kind of cop am I?* "Let's get back to the office, I want to see the photos Cy took at the scene."

"What about the canoe?"

"It's not going anywhere in the shape it's in. We've lifted the fingerprints and we've got the photos and Big John's pack. We'll come back for the canoe later."

At his office, Liam pulled out the file with the photographs Deputy Borkman had shot at Lightning Strike before they cut the body down. He studied them, then handed the Polaroids to Joe. "Nothing. No obvious evidence of a fight, no visible bruising."

"Could have been on his torso," Joe suggested. "Covered by his clothing. Maybe Sigurd Nelson saw something when he prepped the body for burial."

When Liam put that question to the coroner over the phone, Sigurd said, yes, there'd been some bruising on his ribs. "Looked like maybe he stumbled because he was drunk and fell against something hard."

When he set the receiver in the cradle, Liam said, "Bruising on the ribs."

"Consistent with falling into the side of the canoe and crushing it," Joe said.

"Or from someone hitting him good and hard."

"You got anyone in mind?"

"MacDermid for sure. But he had to have help."

"Not if MacDermid drugged him, like we thought."

Liam said, "How would he do that?"

Joe closed his eyes and thought a moment. "He boats to the mouth of Spider Creek and waits there for Manydeeds. Maybe has coffee in a thermos, or cold water, or something as a peace offering, which he's already laced with the sedative."

"Peace offering? You're serious?"

"Or maybe not a peace offering but something he convinces Manydeeds to share while two men who love the same woman hash out what's ahead for them all."

"I can't see MacDermid negotiating on this one."

"For the sake of argument," Joe said.

"All right. For the sake of argument."

"They spend some time together, then Manydeeds begins to feel the effects of the drug, tries to fight what he realizes is coming. They struggle, fall against the canoe, but in the end, the drug knocks out Manydeeds."

Liam nodded and picked up the thread. "MacDermid pulls the broken canoe into the reeds, loads Big John in his boat, heads to Lightning Strike, and makes it look like suicide." He shook his head. "That would require a hell of a lot of planning."

"Yeah," Joe admitted, and it was clear his enthusiasm for the idea was already growing cold. "And he'd have to know more or less when Manydeeds was coming out."

"Or he could simply have parked that big launch of his at the mouth of Spider Creek and waited as long as he needed to." In response to the look of doubt on his deputy's face, Liam said, "According to Nick Skinner, MacDermid asked him to lie about his whereabouts for a couple of days."

"I suppose it's possible. How do we prove any of this?"

Liam stood up from his desk. "We begin by seeing if we can get a warrant to search Glengarrow."

His father wasn't home for dinner. He wasn't home when Cork returned from his weekly Boy Scout meeting at St. Agnes. And he still wasn't home when Cork's eyes drifted shut while he lay on the living room sofa reading about Martians invading Earth. The ring of the telephone in the hallway woke him. His mother answered.

"I was beginning to worry, Liam," she said.

Silence.

"Will he sign it, do you think?" A long pause. Cork rubbed his eyes and sat up. "All right, then," his mother said. "We'll see you when we see you."

When she came into the living room, she saw that Cork was waiting for her to explain.

"Your father. He's putting together a request for a warrant to search Glengarrow. He's hoping to get Judge Jorgenson to sign it."

"Why wouldn't he sign it?"

"It's tricky, Cork." She sat on the sofa next to him. "It's not just about legality. It's also about politics. Duncan MacDermid is a powerful man in Tamarack County."

"Dad says no one is above the law."

"And he's right. But it can be difficult."

"He killed Big John, Mom. He can't get away with that."

"Your father will make sure no one gets away with anything."

Cork wanted to believe her, wanted to believe the things his father had always told him about the law. But bumping up against his father's words were the recent words of Grandma Dilsey: *What I'm concerned about is justice, Liam. That's something I haven't seen much of across my lifetime.*

His father wasn't waiting downstairs when Cork rose to deliver his papers the next morning and headed out with Jackson at his side. As the light in the sky was turning rosy with dawn, he came home to find his father's cruiser parked in the driveway, and his parents sitting at the kitchen table.

"Did the judge sign the warrant?" Cork asked.

His father finished the sip of coffee he'd just taken. Cork saw how tired he looked, drawn and haggard. And old, Cork thought, with a sinking heart.

"He said the evidence wasn't compelling enough. No probable cause," his father replied. "And he said if I ever woke him again in the middle of the night on a wild-goose chase, he'd have my badge."

"He couldn't take your badge away, could he?"

His father offered a weary smile. "No, Son."

"What're you going to do?"

"Get a little sleep, then try to figure another approach."

His mother reached out and put her hand over her husband's. "Things will look better after you've slept."

Liam O'Connor shook his head. "Things will look better when I can cut Duncan MacDermid down to size."

Cork went upstairs and back to bed, as he always did after

his morning route, to try to get another couple of hours of shut-eye, but sleep eluded him. He lay awake, feeling afraid. The world seemed to be changing in front of his eyes, and he couldn't figure out if it was him—that he'd simply been blind before—or if the world was, indeed, shifting, becoming unstable under his feet.

He finally slept, but fitfully, and when he went downstairs for breakfast, he found his grandmother in the kitchen.

"I'm going blueberry picking, Corkie," she told him. "Thought you might want to come along."

His mother was stirring pancake batter, her back to the kitchen table and to Grandma Dilsey. Cork could feel the tension in the air. "Okay if I go, Mom?"

His mother poured the batter onto a griddle and said, "I suppose. But don't spend all day at it. I've made an appointment to get Jackson a distemper booster shot. I'd like you to take him."

Although the day was already hot, the kitchen felt frigid, and when Grandma Dilsey said she needed to use the bathroom and left for a few minutes, Cork asked his mother what was going on.

"I told your grandmother that you'd found Big John's canoe. She wanted to know what your father was going to do about it. When I told her that he was at a bit of a dead end legally, she offered me a few choice words about him. I took issue with her opinions."

"She wants him to arrest Duncan MacDermid, right?"

"In your grandmother's thinking, that would be a good beginning."

"Did you tell her about the warrant Dad tried to get?"

She shook her head. "That's something he wants kept secret for the moment. And I don't want you telling her either. I know exactly what she'll say. That he didn't try hard enough."

"Do you think he did?"

"Don't you go doubting your father. He's doing the best he can. He always has and he always will."

"I know. But couldn't he ask another judge or something?"

"It doesn't work that way, Cork. Give him time. Your dad will come up with something."

She put a stack of pancakes on a plate and set it before him. "Remember, not a word of this to your grandmother."

Later, as he rode with Grandma Dilsey to the rez, Cork stared out the pickup's window, thinking that if the law could be twisted to keep the truth of Big John's death from coming to light and a man like Duncan MacDermid out of jail, what hope was there for the kind of justice his grandmother demanded?

Like lots of folks in Tamarack County, white and Ojibwe, Grandma Dilsey had a secret blueberry patch known only to her and her family. A mile north of Allouette, she turned onto an old logging road that ran east toward a line of low hills known as the Turtlebacks. The woods were pine and spruce and maple, an impressionistic blending of greens, and with the cab windows rolled down, the air that poured in smelled fresh and hopeful to Cork. The forest didn't care about justice. It went about its business in the way it had since the beginning of time. If humans were fickle and not to be trusted, the red burst of wood lilies in a Northwoods meadow could always be counted on to lift your spirits.

Grandma Dilsey parked the truck at the edge of a bog. She grabbed the two metal pails that sat on the seat between her and Cork and got out. In the tall grass that rimmed the bog, she stood waiting for Cork, her face shaded by a broad-brimmed straw hat. When he joined her, she handed him a pail and without a word began circling the reedy marsh. Over the years, Cork had come with her many times in late July in search of the ripe berries. Usually his mother came, too, and it was a multigenerational celebration of a tradition that stretched back even into his grandmother's own childhood. And here again, Cork thought, was a thing that didn't change. Except that this time, his mother hadn't come.

The blueberry bushes grew in a large patch on the far side of the bog. The branches were splashed with berries that looked frosted in the morning sunlight. Wordlessly, Grandma Dilsey began picking, and Cork followed her lead. He had his pail three-quarters full when his grandmother said, "That's enough for now. We need to leave some for the birds and bears."

Grandma Dilsey set the pails in the truck bed and climbed back into the cab. But she didn't start the engine. She sat for a minute, the sunlight warm through the windshield, the rattle of a woodpecker coming from the trees, the fetid smell of the bog adrift in the air.

"Grandma," Cork said.

"Yes?"

"He's doing his best."

Grandma Dilsey took a long time to respond. "It's not your father," she finally said and turned her dark eyes to Cork. "But he's a part of the problem."

Cork gave a nod but not in agreement. It was more because, under her steady gaze, he felt mute and uncomfortable.

"When I was a girl, Corkie, the sheriff or one of his deputies would come to the reservation and take the children away. I remember the day they came for me. I cried but there was nothing my father and mother could do. It was the same for every family. They took me to a boarding school in Wisconsin. It was hard there. The nuns who oversaw us were not kind. I didn't have the courage that Big John had. I never ran away as he did. But I learned something very important. Education is the key to empowerment. That's what I've spent my life trying to do, to educate our children so that they have a sense of what they can do, who they can be."

She put her hands on the steering wheel, old hands, the skin spotted and brittle looking.

"What about my dad?" Cork said.

"In a way, he's what we fight against. On the reservation, we see *zhaagnaashag* bend the laws all the time. We see that enforcement is often arbitrary and unfair. I know your father's heart is in the right place, but in the end, he's still the arm of a system that has oppressed The People for generations."

"He tries," Cork said. "He really tries."

Grandma Dilsey took a deep breath and let it out in a long sigh. "I suppose. So do we all." She turned the key and the old engine coughed to life. "Let's get those berries home."

They returned the way they'd come, and as they passed through Allouette, Grandma Dilsey pulled the pickup to a stop in front of LeDuc's General Store, a small, ramshackle building. On the wooden porch in front of LeDuc's sat a long, low cooler filled, Cork knew, with ice water in which were nestled all kinds of cold drinks.

"How about a grape Nehi?" his grandmother asked. "I'm dying of thirst."

Pulled fresh from the cooler, the bottles were ice cold, and the grape soda as it went down Cork's dry throat tasted like heaven. They stood in the shade under the porch. The town was quiet, the street nearly empty.

"So many gone now," Grandma Dilsey said.

"Some come back," Cork said. "Billy Downwind and his mother."

"Death brought them back. And who knows if they'll stay."

Across the unpaved main street of Allouette, a Chevy pickup sat on blocks, all four wheels removed. Like so many rez vehicles, it was old, rusted, and looked beat to hell. At the moment, Oscar Manydeeds was putting brake pads on the right front wheel, aided by Mickey Broom, the grandnephew of old Broomstraw. Although Billy Downwind's uncle was employed at the tribal-owned lumber mill in the nearby town of Brandywine, he often repaired vehicles on the rez in exchange for whatever was offered—blueberries, maple syrup, deer jerky, a hand-sewn shirt. He caught sight of Cork and Grandma Dilsey and stood. Wiping his greasy hands on a rag, he came toward them across the street. Mickey Broom, who was also called Boom-Boom Broom because of his explosive laugh, followed him.

"*Boozhoo,* Auntie," he said in greeting to Grandma Dilsey.

"*Boozhoo,*" she replied.

Boom-Boom wore a ball cap, which he lifted from his head in deference to Grandma Dilsey, an elder.

Manydeeds eyed Cork and the grape Nehi in his hand, then caught sight of the buckets in the bed of the pickup. "Been blueberry picking," he said. "Nice haul, looks like."

Cork figured he was interested in the location of the blueberry patch but knew he wouldn't ask.

"I'm thinking blueberry cobbler for dessert tonight," Grandma Dilsey said.

"I had your blueberry cobbler at the wake," Manydeeds said. "Best I ever tasted." His tone was friendly, but his eyes, when they settled on Cork, held a threatening look. "When's your father going to arrest the man who murdered my brother?"

"He wants to," Cork said, "but he can't."

At this, Grandma Dilsey said, "What do you mean, Corkie?"

He hadn't meant to say it. It had just come out, a defense of his father, but it was information he knew his father didn't want made public, information he'd promised his mother he would keep to himself.

"Corkie?" his grandmother said, speaking sternly now. "I want to know. We have a right to know these things."

Three faces were turned to him, faces of people who, as Grandma Dilsey asserted, maybe did have a right to know all the facts concerning the death of a man they and their whole community cared about deeply. What was the point of secrecy if it helped to keep the truth in the dark? Was it just another way to twist the law? His mother had asked for his silence, but what was one small broken promise compared to the greater promise of justice for all?

CHAPTER 33

When Cork returned from blueberry picking, his father was gone. Grandma Dilsey brought one of the blueberry buckets into the kitchen and proceeded to explain to her daughter what she now knew about the obstacles to justice erected by those who wielded the power of the law.

Cork's mother eyed him and said, "I thought I asked you to keep that to yourself."

"This isn't his fault," his grandmother said. "I demanded the truth, and Cork's the only one in this house with enough respect and courage to give it to me. And now I'll tell you a truth, Colleen. Unless that man is arrested, there's going to be trouble coming from the rez, trouble like you've never seen before."

"Which is exactly the reason Liam didn't want any of this made public. There's still so much he has to do. At the moment, his hands are tied, legally."

"Legally. Do you know what that word is? An insult to The People. Legally our land was stripped from us. Legally we were marched off to boarding schools. Legally the reservations have been emptied and our people dispersed to the four winds. Where is Liam? I want to say this to his face."

"He's out doing his job."

"Not very well, if you ask me."

"If he does anything in a way that skirts the law, Mom, he risks ruining any case he might be able to construct against Duncan MacDermid. And there goes your hope for justice right out the window. You know Liam. You know he's not going to protect a man just because he's rich or because he's white."

"I'll believe that when I see Duncan MacDermid in handcuffs."

The two women stared at each other, as if there were no words left to say. Or maybe because they both understood the uselessness of words.

Cork had to get out of the house. "Okay if I go over to Jorge's?"

"I told you this morning that I've made an appointment for Jackson's distemper shot. I have work to do, so you'll need to take him."

"And I have to get back to the rez. I've got blueberry cobbler to make." Grandma Dilsey left without a word of goodbye to her daughter.

Cork said, "Come on, Jackson."

He walked to the North Star Veterinary Clinic, on the corner of Oak and Fourth Streets. The practice was owned by Dr. David Svenson, who had a weekly radio show about animal care called *Ask Doctor Dave,* which was how most folks addressed him— Doctor Dave. Inside, the air smelled unpleasantly of medicine and disinfectant. Cork had brought along Jackson's leash and had snapped it onto the dog's collar before entering the clinic. Now he sat in a chair in the waiting area while Jackson sat on his haunches, blinking and unfazed. On the other side of the waiting room sat a woman Cork didn't know with a cat in a cage on the seat next to her. The cat meowed and yowled as if it were in pain. The woman cooed to the cat, "It's all right, Nightingale." And Cork thought it funny that the cat was named for something that could easily be its meal.

A man with a bulldog on a leash came from one of the back rooms, escorted by Sharon Crane, the vet's assistant. She took care of the payment, and when the man left, she said to the woman with the cat, "You're next, Mrs. Bailey." Then to Cork she said, "We're running a little behind. Doctor Dave had an emergency call this morning."

She took Nightingale and Mrs. Bailey to another exam room. When she returned, Cork asked, "What kind of emergency?"

"Distemper in one of the animals at the Wolf Center. Excuse me," she said and went to the reception desk to answer the ringing phone.

In a little while, Doctor Dave came out with Nightingale and Mrs. Bailey. He offered a few more instructions on the cat's care, then turned to Cork.

"Well, hey there, kiddo. Didn't figure to see you with Jackson."

"Mom's got other things to do today."

"I thought teachers did nothing but relax during the summer."

"Not my mom."

"Well, let's have a look at your dog." The veterinarian escorted them to one of the exam rooms and proceeded to check Jackson's coat, teeth, eyes, and ears, all the while carrying on a quiet patter.

"I heard you had an emergency this morning," Cork said.

"Mmm," the vet said, moving his hands in a probing way across Jackson's body. "Got called to the Wolf Center. Had to sedate one of their she-wolves. I suspect she had distemper."

"How do you sedate a wolf, Doctor Dave?"

"Very carefully," the vet said, then gave a laugh. "A couple of options, Cork. Lace some meat with a sedative and wait for it to take effect. Or, in the case today, where we needed to get her down quickly, I shot her with a tranquilizer dart."

"Does she have distemper?"

"It's a tough disease to diagnose. But it's a definite threat to the other wolves. And there's no real cure. To be on the safe side, I advised them to let me put the wolf down and to inoculate the others."

"Did you have to sedate all of them, too?"

The vet nodded and let out a tired sigh. "It's been a busy day."

When Doctor Dave had finished checking Jackson, he said, "He looks fine, but a good thing you brought him in for a booster. He's due for a rabies booster as well, so we'll get that taken care of, too. Tell your mom I'll send her the bill."

Cork left the clinic, happy that his dog was healthy but feeling bad for the wolf that had to be put down. Did she have pups? Did she have a mate? He'd heard wolves mated for life, and if that was true, did a wolf grieve when it lost its mate?

It was well past lunchtime and he could have gone home, but the atmosphere in the O'Connor house wasn't inviting at the moment, so Cork opted for Sam's Place.

He arrived during the lunch rush, and he and Jackson contented themselves sitting in the shade of an aspen on the shore of Iron Lake, waiting for the lines at the two serving windows to thin. Finally, Cork headed up and ordered a Sam's Special from Daisy. He was surprised when Sam Winter Moon himself delivered the big burger and said through the window, "Got a few minutes to talk?"

"Sure."

"I'll meet you at the picnic table. The burger's on me."

They sat in the hot sun while Cork ate his burger and Sam talked to him.

"I heard about what you and Jorge and Billy found on Spider Creek. Good work, by the way. But I also heard nothing's being done about it. I've been trying to reach your dad at the sheriff's office all morning. They keep telling me he's out. Do you have any idea where he's gone?"

Between big bites of his burger, Cork told him he didn't.

"I'm going to tell your father this, and I'll tell you now because you're here. Folks on the rez are pretty upset. Tempers are running high. I think it's best if you and your father and mother stay away for a while."

"You think somebody might do something to us?"

"I'm just saying, and I'll tell your father this when I see him, stay off the rez, at least for now."

"He's your friend. Can't you do something?"

"Indawa Anishinaabe," he said.

I am Anishinaabe. Cork understood. The blood of The People came first.

CHAPTER 34

In the heat of the afternoon, Liam parked his cruiser at Big John's cabin, got out, and walked to the dock on the water where the empty canoe rack stood. He looked across Iron Lake. The far shore was only a thin line of green in the late afternoon light, but he knew exactly where the great estate of Glengarrow lay. He imagined Big John Manydeeds standing alone on this little dock, staring across the water as if staring across a span of universe he could never traverse. He tried to imagine how he might feel if he lost Colleen forever, tried to put himself inside the head of a man who'd lost his heart. And then, as if Big John could hear him, he said, "I'm sorry."

Sorry for the lost love. Sorry for the great divide that separated the worlds on either side of the lake. And maybe sorry most of all for having seen Big John's death from the beginning through a white man's eyes.

He looked for what had brought him there but didn't find it at the dock. He walked back to the cabin, searched the single room but didn't find it there. He went to a small woodshed ten yards into the trees and that's where it lay, a coil of hemp rope.

*   *   *

When he rang the doorbell of the big house at Glengarrow, Mary Margaret answered.

"Is Duncan home?" Liam asked.

"He's at the mine office today," she said. "I don't expect him until dinnertime."

"I'd like your permission, Mary Margaret, to search the boathouse and guest cottage."

"What for?"

"Evidence that your husband killed Big John."

She seemed to wilt before him but he saw no real surprise. "In my darkest moments, I've wondered. I just . . . just didn't want to believe that of him."

"May I search?"

"Yes."

"And will you come with me?"

She drew herself up, as if steeling for an ordeal, and gave him a nod. "But I need to get Carla to watch my mother-in-law. Can you wait a minute?"

She went to the carriage house and returned with Jorge's mother, who said, "Hello, Sheriff."

"Where's Jorge?"

"Delivering his papers with Cork. They're such good friends. Jorge is lucky."

"No luckier than Cork."

"We'll be back soon, Carla," Mary Margaret said and led the way.

They began in the boathouse below the cottage. It was, as Cy Borkman had observed a few days earlier, large enough that a semi could park inside. Almost immediately, Liam found what he was hoping for.

"May I take this?"

Mary Margaret studied the coil of rope in his hand. "Why?"

"Do you know what a boom hitch is?"

She shook her head.

"That's all right. Neither did I until I visited the library this afternoon." He'd brought a small canvas bag with him. He put the rope coil down on a bench top, zipped open the bag, and took out a manila envelope. From the envelope, he drew out a photograph, which he offered to Mary Margaret. "That's a boom hitch."

The photo showed a rope that had been knotted around the branch of a tree. Mary Margaret looked at the photo, then at Liam, clearly at a loss.

"That's an enlargement of a photograph one of my deputies took at Lightning Strike when we first went out there, after my son reported what he and Jorge had found. It's one of the two knots on the rope that was used to hang Big John."

"I'm not sure what you're telling me."

"The knot that was used to secure the rope around Big John's neck was a simple slipknot, one anyone might tie. But that knot, the boom hitch, which was used to secure the rope to the maple limb, is a pretty complicated affair and isn't widely used except by sailors. Mary Margaret, your husband spent five years in the navy and four years at Annapolis before that."

Liam could see that what was clear to him was becoming clear to her as well. He picked up the coil of rope he'd set down on the bench top. "This is marine rope, a special kind. I believe it's going to match the rope that was used to hang Big John. I went to his cabin today, looking for just this kind of rope. All I found was a coil of hemp. See where this marine rope's been cut? I'm hoping that when we get it analyzed, it will match the cut section that was used to hang Big John."

He saw the change come over her, a frightening transformation. A harsh whisper escaped her lips, surprising from so delicate looking a woman. "That son of a bitch. That goddamn son of a bitch."

"I'd like to search the cottage upstairs. Is that all right?"

"Search wherever you need to."

In the cottage, he found another piece of important evidence, a vial of barbiturates.

"They're for Duncan's mother," Mary Margaret explained.

"Why are they here?"

"I don't know. Maybe Duncan uses them to relax."

"Or maybe Duncan used them to drug Big John before he killed him," Liam suggested. "May I take these?"

"Take whatever you want," Mary Margaret said in a voice cold as winter. "And then, for God's sake, take away that man, that monster."

CHAPTER 35

That evening, Grandma Dilsey and Sam Winter Moon showed up at the house on Gooseberry Lane. They came to have a serious talk with Liam about the unrest on the rez.

Cork's mother explained to them that he'd stopped by home shortly before supper and that he believed he'd found enough evidence to obtain a warrant for Duncan MacDermid's arrest for the murder of Big John. He was on his way to see the county attorney.

"What evidence?" Grandma Dilsey asked, looking first to her daughter, then to Cork.

"We don't know," Cork's mother said.

"Did he say when he would be back?" Sam asked.

"Only that he might be late."

"We'll wait," Grandma Dilsey said.

As night overtook Aurora, they sat on the front porch, talking quietly. In the front yard, Cork threw a rubber ball for Jackson until his arm was tired and it was too dark for even Jackson to see the ball in flight. Fireflies had begun to wink on and off. Ten o'clock came and Liam O'Connor still hadn't returned.

Cork sat on the bottom porch step, stroking Jackson, who lay at his feet, and he listened to the others as they talked and speculated.

"Maybe he's already made the arrest," Cork's mother said.

"Would he question Duncan right away?" Grandma Dilsey asked.

"Why not?" Sam said. "I know how eager Liam is to get to the truth."

"If Duncan wasn't drunk, he would have insisted on having an attorney present," Cork's mother said. "That would take a while."

"You could call the Sheriff's Department and ask," Grandma Dilsey suggested.

Cork's mother left the porch for a few minutes, and when she returned, she said, "He's not there. They don't know where he is."

"Has he arrested Duncan MacDermid?" Grandma Dilsey asked.

"No," Cork's mother said. "At least not yet."

They were quiet for a bit, then Sam said, "I knew MacDermid's father. A man as hard as the iron ore that came from his mine."

"I remember the mine strike back in 1916," Grandma Dilsey said. "He brought in armored cars filled with sharpshooters, and the sheriff here then, a man named Wheaton, as I recall, a toady of MacDermid's father, deputized hundreds of men as mine guards. Thugs with badges. Terrible violence from both sides. It was the only time I can remember when people on the reservation were glad MacDermid had a rule against hiring Indians."

"A rule?" Cork said from his place on the steps.

"Nothing official," Grandma Dilsey said. "But everyone knew it. And I suspect he passed that prejudice down to his son. Along with a lot of other unpleasant qualities." She'd been sitting with Cork's mother on the porch swing, but now she stood and said, "I brought blueberry cobbler. I believe I'll have a bite of it. Would anyone like to join me?"

They were in the kitchen, sitting around the table eating

Grandma Dilsey's cobbler, when Sheriff Liam O'Connor walked in the door from the mud porch. He stood just inside the threshold, taking them all in.

"Did you get the arrest warrant?" Cork's mother asked.

Cork's father didn't answer immediately. He seemed to be gathering himself. "I presented our county attorney with everything, and then we went to the judge. He said it wasn't substantial enough to justify an arrest warrant. He said it was all still too circumstantial. He said when it came to a man like Duncan MacDermid, I would need nothing less than an eyewitness or a signed confession. I said, fine. I told him I would bring the man in for questioning and I would get a confession out of him. In no uncertain terms, he said that I was not to harass Duncan MacDermid any further. And then he said, 'Manydeeds was just an Indian. Let it go.'"

Liam O'Connor reached up and unpinned the badge from the blouse of his khaki uniform. He took three long strides across the kitchen linoleum, set the badge on the table, and said, "In Tamarack County, justice is dead."

Cork could hear the low timbre of his parents' voices drifting through his window, and he left his bed. Quietly, he crawled out onto the porch roof and positioned himself near enough to the window of his parents' bedroom that he could hear their words.

"I understand, Liam," his mother was saying. "But this isn't the answer, and you know it."

"I'm tired, Colleen, tired of fighting."

"So, you're just going to give up?"

"Let someone else take the heat."

"And you'll do what? Stand on the sidelines and watch? That's not you, Liam. Come to bed." Cork heard the old bed frame creak. "Lay your head here."

They were quiet for a while, then his mother said, "Now you know what it's like for my people. We've been fighting for justice forever. If we'd given up when it was difficult, we'd be nothing but a memory now."

"There are many of you. I'm one man."

"But a good one, Liam. When I grew up here, the men who wore the badge you wear weren't like you. You make a difference. Get some rest tonight. Things will look better in the morning."

"Nothing will have changed."

"Maybe your outlook. And that's all you need."

The conversation ceased and the chirr of crickets filled the night. Cork returned to his bed and wondered if one night's sleep would be enough for anyone.

He'd just closed his eyes and begun to drift off when the front doorbell rang, followed by a desperate pounding on the door itself. Jackson leaped from where he'd been sprawled across the foot of Cork's bed, bolted into the hallway, and set to barking furiously. Cork followed, entering the upstairs hallway just as his father and mother came from their bedroom, hastily throwing on their robes. He was right behind them as they hurried down the stairs.

"Cork, hold Jackson," his father ordered, switched on the light in the foyer, then the porch light, and opened the door.

Jorge and his mother stood there, supporting Mary Margaret MacDermid, who was between them. The skin around the woman's left eye was a deep purple and the eye itself was almost completely swollen shut. Her lower lip was split, and the dark, clotted blood looked like a leech had attached itself there.

"Good God," Liam O'Connor said. "Come in, come in. What's happened?" He took Jorge's place in supporting Mrs. MacDermid as she walked unsteadily into the living room. He and Jorge's mother eased her down onto the sofa, and Jorge's mother sat next to her and held her hand.

Cork's mother turned on the living room lights and said, "I'll call Doctor Haines."

Cork stood beside Jorge, who looked scared, his face ashen. Like Cork, Jorge was in his pajamas, but he'd managed to put on his Keds.

"Tell me what happened." Liam O'Connor addressed this to Jorge's mother.

"Mr. MacDermid came home late tonight. Somehow he knew that Mary Margaret had let you search the cottage."

"Our county judge, no doubt," Cork's father said.

"He was angry and drinking, and this is what he did to her."

"Is he still at the house?"

Jorge's mother opened her mouth to speak, but no sound came. It was as if instead of speaking, she'd dropped a stone into a deep well, and it felt to Cork like everyone in the room held their breath waiting for the sound of it to hit.

"Yes." It was Mrs. MacDermid who finally spoke. She lifted her battered face to Cork's father and said, "He's still there. He's there and he's dead. I shot the son of a bitch."

PART II

MURDER

CHAPTER 36

July melted into August in heat and humidity that left the North Country on edge. Mary Margaret MacDermid was not charged with murder. Her face and the bruises in other places were proof enough of the brutality of her husband's attack, and the shooting was officially deemed self-defense. That she may have had an additional motive in killing her husband was never brought up, because Liam's suspicions surrounding Duncan MacDermid's part in the death of Big John Manydeeds were never officially made public. But people talked, as people do, especially in small towns, and rumors flew about like harpies.

There was no wake for Duncan MacDermid, just a visitation and a funeral Mass, well attended but tearless. He was buried in the Catholic cemetery, his grave marked with a stone that was ordered by his wife and was undoubtedly much smaller and less elaborate than he might have arranged for himself had he known his fate ahead of time.

Old Mrs. MacDermid died, too, just a week later. Although she'd been in ill health for years, everyone said she'd died of grief. She was laid to rest between her husband and her son.

Billy Downwind and his mother didn't return to California, at least not immediately. Billy told Cork that neither of them was eager to leave the rez again, but what exactly they would do was still up in the air. There were also lingering concerns regarding the truth about Big John's death, which the killing of Duncan Mac-Dermid had done nothing to resolve.

On the second day of August, when Cork was out on his newspaper route with Jackson, the dog tangled with a raccoon and was bitten. As soon as the North Star Veterinary Clinic was open, Cork and his mother took Jackson in.

"Morning, Colleen. Morning, Cork," the veterinarian greeted them in the waiting area, which was otherwise empty. "Sorry to hear about Jackson. Raccoons can be nasty critters."

"We're worried about rabies."

"As well you should be. Follow me and we'll check him out."

As he set about his work, Doctor Dave shook his head and said, "So hard to believe all that business with Duncan MacDermid."

Cork knew this was a subject his mother hated discussing, and she didn't respond.

"We both knew him well growing up, didn't we, Colleen? He wasn't a bad sort when he was a kid."

"He was always a bully."

"I suppose. Although I think that was mostly the influence of his father, who was, if you'll excuse my language, a real bastard. But we were Boy Scouts together, and you got Duncan into the Boundary Waters and away from his old man, he wasn't a bad sort. I remember one time my brother and Duncan and I went skinny-dipping off a point in Moose Lake. Pretty much only us Boy Scouts and the occasional Indian from the rez entered the Boundary Waters through Moose Lake, so we figured we were safe. We were out there having a great time when ten canoes full of Girl Scouts came around that point. Instead of just staying in the water, Duncan climbed bare-assed out of the lake straight up a big face of rock. Got himself great applause from all those Girl Scouts." The vet laughed at the memory. He ruffed Jackson's fur and said, "The bite wound is pretty much superficial. I'll clean it and give you some antibiotic. Just put it in his food. But let me know if it begins looking any worse. No worries about rabies. We gave him a booster just last month. He should be fine." As he saw them out, Doctor Dave said, "And Big John Manydeeds? Liam's closed the book on his death, too?"

Cork's mother said, "Thanks for your help with Jackson."

Cork thought that his father had, indeed, closed the book on the case. He spoke no more about it at home, and neither Cork's mother nor Grandma Dilsey raised the subject.

Then two things happened that changed everything: The Bureau of Criminal Apprehension finally sent the full toxicology report on Big John. And the body of the missing Ojibwe girl was found.

The first Saturday in August, Cork headed out to collect from his customers, those who were home, anyway, and who had both ready cash and the inclination to pay him. Sometimes when he collected, people pulled out wallets and shook their heads and said something like "All I have is a fifty." Cork carried a change bag, but there was never enough in it to cover a fifty. Even if he could see other bills in a wallet, what could he say that wouldn't sound as if he were calling the customer a liar?

He'd had little luck that day when he knocked on a door with a leprous look to it, paint peeling from top to bottom. It was a house on Sycamore Street, with an unkempt yard and a crabapple tree under which fruit, fallen and rotting, attracted a constant buzz of yellow jackets. The customer, Argus Friar, was three months behind on his bill. Cork intended to tell him that there wouldn't be a paper on his porch again until he'd paid what he owed. After Cork had knocked twice, the man opened his door. He wore an undershirt and undershorts, and his hair was all wild wisps of gray, as if the top of his head was smoldering. His angry glare scared out of Cork any determination to demand payment.

"Collecting for the *News-Tribune*, Mr. Friar," Cork said.

"Don't have my wallet, boy. Come back later."

"You haven't paid for three months, sir," Cork ventured.

"I'll pay when I have my wallet."

"I could wait here."

"Later, boy."

"I'll have to . . ." Cork began his threat.

"Have to what?"

Cork summoned all his courage. "Unless you pay me, I'll have to stop delivering your paper."

"Do that and I'll report you," the man threatened.

"And I'll report you," Cork shot back. Though to whom, he couldn't have said. But he was angry, too, and returned the man's glare.

When Cork didn't leave his doorstep, Friar finally said, "What do I owe you?" After Cork told him, he said, "Wait here," and closed the door.

Cork stood on the porch for five minutes, his anger growing as he decided that Argus Friar had stiffed him again. In his head, he was going over the things he would do in response—end the paper delivery, of course, but other possibilities as well, all of them pranks he'd heard about but never tried himself, things involving flaming paper bags full of dog crap or toilet paper wrapped around the crabapple trees or windows on which insults were written in soap.

He was just turning away when the door swung open again and Argus Friar appeared with an old wallet in his hands. He plucked out the bills, handed them over, and demanded his change, which Cork gave him, along with a slip from his receipt book.

The man eyed the receipt, then eyed Cork. "O'Connor? Any relation to our squaw man sheriff?"

It was the first time Cork had ever heard his father referred to in that way, and it was like a rock had been thrown at him.

"He's my father," Cork said, standing as tall as he could.

"Killed MacDermid, you ask me."

Which caught Cork completely by surprise. "What?"

"Hounded the man near to death, is what I heard. That Indian killed hisself a while back? Heard he was screwing MacDermid's wife, and your old man convinced her it wasn't no suicide. Had her believing MacDermid did it. Ask me, she didn't shoot MacDermid cuz he beat her. Men beat their wives all the time and don't get shot for it. Your old man, though, he looks the other way, cuz he's a Indian lover, too. But hell, what can you expect from a squaw man?"

Lava boiled up in Cork, anger so hot he couldn't contain it. "Go to hell, Mr. Friar," he said. "You just go straight to hell." And he turned and stomped across the yard, raising up a flurry of yellow jackets in his wake.

"Yeah and the same to you, you Redskin brat."

After that, there was no more collecting for the newspaper; Cork could barely collect his thoughts. He didn't want to go home and try to explain to his mother in some stammering way why he was so angry. He just walked until his feet, as if with a mind of their own, took him to Glengarrow.

Jorge opened up at his knock and the two boys sat among the monsters in Jorge's bedroom.

"I get it, too," Jorge said. "Beaner. Or Spic."

Cork had heard other boys call Jorge that, though never to his face. "Have you heard me called a Redskin?"

"Oh, yeah. And worse."

"Why didn't you ever tell me?"

"What for?"

"Just to know."

"I thought you knew."

White people and the Ojibwe had been living in the North Country together for so many generations that the intermingling of blood was not uncommon. But Cork knew that, more often than not, people who didn't look Ojibwe didn't broadcast their Native heritage. Indians were dirty, untrustworthy, lazy, drunks. That's what white people thought. A long list of cliché Westerns had drilled into the general public's thinking that Indians were for spur-wearing heroes to kill. Cork realized he wasn't innocent. He'd never made a big point of his own Native heritage. But he'd never heard his mother called a squaw before, or his father a squaw man. He wondered if now, whenever he looked into a neighbor's eyes, he would see some unspoken insult there.

"She's going to sell Glengarrow," Jorge said.

"Mrs. MacDermid? Why?"

"People are saying pretty bad things about her because she was, you know, doing it with Big John. And besides, she told Mom she's always hated it here."

"Funny," Cork said without laughing. "Big John was a good man and Mr. MacDermid was a real bastard. But people thought it was just fine for Mrs. MacDermid to be married to him and get beat up." He stared out the window at the big house, a fortress of gray stone set against the sparkling blue jewel that was Iron Lake. "If she sells, what'll you and your mom do?"

Jorge shook his head. "Maybe she'll marry Nick Skinner."

"That wouldn't be so bad, would it? Especially if he builds that new hotel. You'd be rich."

"I don't want to be rich. I just want Mom to be happy."

"Maybe getting married is the way."

Jorge didn't respond. He took his sketch pad from where it lay in the clutter on his desk and turned to a page on which he'd recently sketched the dark figure they'd seen at Lightning Strike. It was still mostly a thing of shadow but was more detailed than the first drawing he'd done even before they'd found Big John's body. They'd talked about the weirdness of that image coming to him in advance of their gruesome discovery, but it was only one inexplicable thing in the midst of so many.

"Think he's gone for good?" he asked.

"If he was sticking around to make sure we knew the truth, I guess maybe his spirit is finally at peace."

"If it really was his spirit we saw," Jorge said. "Mom told me it was just the clouds and the dark playing tricks. She told me not to let my imagination run away with me. There's one way we might be sure."

"How's that?"

Jorge set his drawing down, went to his closet, grabbed something, and turned back to Cork. What he held was the Ouija board.

"Tonight," he said.

CHAPTER 37

When he got home that afternoon, Cork could tell something was up. He felt it the moment he walked into the house. Grandma Dilsey was there, sitting with his mother in the living room. The curtains were drawn against the August heat and something threatening seemed to be hanging in the air. Jackson rose from where he'd been lying at Grandma Dilsey's feet and trotted to greet Cork, though not eagerly. Cork was afraid someone had died. Turned out he was right.

"How did it go with your collecting?" his mother asked.

He considered telling them about his run-in with the old ogre Argus Friar, but decided against it. How could he explain squaw or squaw man or the anger he still felt? Instead he said, "What's going on?"

"Sit down," his mother said.

He sat on the floor with Jackson, and the dog laid his head on Cork's lap. Cork stroked Jackson's mottled fur, as much to settle his own uneasiness as to caress the dog.

"Do you remember the girl who went missing and her grand-dad came here looking for her?" Grandma Dilsey said.

"Her name was . . ." He thought a moment. "Louise. Louise LaRose."

"She's been found."

"That's good, right?"

"I'm afraid not," Grandma Dilsey said. "She's dead."

Cork absorbed this, a tragic thing, of course, but he didn't know Louise LaRose, and that distanced him from the impact. "How?"

"Drowning, it looks like. You know Sherman Kingfisher and Stoney Bright?"

"Sure. They're both on the tribal council."

"They found her body floating in Naabe-Mooz. They brought her back to Allouette and called Sam Winter Moon. He called your dad."

"Where's Dad now?"

"With the body at Nelson's Funeral Home," Cork's mother said.

"How do they know it's her?"

"They don't, not officially. Your dad thinks she was in the water a long time, three or maybe even four weeks. He's contacted her family down in Leech Lake, and her grandfather is on his way to identify her."

"Naabe-Mooz?" Cork said. "Nobody goes out to Moose Lake unless they're heading into the Boundary Waters. What would she be doing in the Boundary Waters?"

"A good question," Cork's mother said. "And one I'm sure your father will be looking into."

There was a knock at the screen door, and Sam Winter Moon called from the porch, "Can we come in?"

When Sam walked into the living room, Cork was surprised to see Henry Meloux with him, but he could tell that the presence of the Mide didn't surprise Grandma Dilsey or his mother in the least.

"*Boozhoo*, Henry," Cork's grandmother said. "*Migwech.*"

They spoke in their native tongue for a minute, a conversation Cork could understand only bits and pieces of, then Grandma Dilsey rose, as if to leave with the men.

"Where are you going?" he asked.

"To meet Calvin LaRose at Sam's Place and then to the morgue," his grandmother replied. "We don't want the girl's grandfather to be alone in this."

Cork and his mother walked them out to the porch. Cork drew the Mide aside and said, "What's going on, Mr. Meloux? So many bad things all at once."

"And you do not understand the connections," Meloux said.

"Do you?" Cork asked.

Meloux shook his head. "But who sees the spiderweb in the night? So, we wait for the sun."

"Just wait?"

"Just wait. But it is the hardest thing of all."

His mother drifted into the kitchen, and Cork followed her. She seemed lost, in thought, in purpose, and Cork felt unsettled, too. He did his best thinking while he walked, so he told her he was heading back to Jorge's place. She cautioned him to be home in time for supper.

"When will that be?" he asked.

"Whenever your father and your grandma come home," she said vaguely.

As he walked, he tried to put what he knew together in a way that led somewhere, tried to see some pattern woven into all the recent events.

What was a girl on the run doing in the Boundary Waters? How did she even get there? And Moose Lake? The entry through Spider Creek was on rez land, so it wasn't one of the official entry points listed on any of the Forest Service maps. Almost nobody entered the Boundary Waters through Spider Creek and Moose

Lake unless they were part of a Scout troop, who'd sought special permission, or they were Ojibwe. The girl was Ojibwe. So maybe she'd made a connection with someone on the rez.

One thought followed another, and by the time he reached Glengarrow, he'd come to a frightening place in his thinking.

Once again, no one answered his knock at the carriage house. He descended the outside stairway and stood looking at the great stone mansion set on its vast lawn. He'd never been inside, never even wanted to be. It had always seemed like a dark, brooding place.

But now piano music came from the house through an opened window, and Cork heard singing. He recognized Jorge's mother's voice, and he crossed the lawn and stood at the window. It was a large room with vases full of flowers, and in the center stood a big piano, the kind he knew was called a grand. Mrs. MacDermid sat at the keyboard playing a lively tune that sounded Mexican. Jorge's mother stood beside her singing in Spanish, singing her heart out. And there was Jorge with her, also singing, though not so loud or so lovely. It was like one of the gatherings at the O'Connor house when his mother played her concertina, and he and Grandma Dilsey and his father sang the Irish melodies they all knew by heart.

He crept away, not wanting to do anything that might interrupt the happiness of a household in which, for so long, only rage had dwelled. He walked to the boathouse and sat on the dock where the huge motor launch and the smaller Sunfish sailboat were both tied up.

The sun was brutal, and Cork was hot. He kicked off his Keds, pulled off his socks, rolled up his jeans, and dangled his feet in the cool, clear water of Iron Lake. From there he could see the shoreline as it ran past Sam's Place and the rest of Aurora. He could see where Nick Skinner wanted to build his big hotel and enlarge the marina. If it brought more people to town, as everyone hoped,

Aurora would change. But everything changed, even if you didn't want it to.

"Hey!" Jorge called to him and came running. "I saw you out the window. You should have come in." He sat beside Cork on the dock.

"You were all having your own good time."

"Mom wanted to cheer up Mrs. MacDermid."

"She sings nice, your mom. And Mrs. MacDermid's really good on the piano."

"She studied music in college." Jorge had his sneakers and socks off by now and, like Cork, dangled his feet in the water. "She says maybe she'll start teaching piano or something, wherever she ends up. But she's rich enough she wouldn't have to."

Cork let a few moments pass, then gave Jorge the news. "That girl I told you about? The runaway Ojibwe girl?"

"What about her?"

Cork told him everything he knew. When he'd finished, Jorge gave a long, low whistle. "That's really bad." He shook his head. "One more thing in a long line of bad."

"It all feels connected."

Jorge gave him a blank stare.

"I mean," Cork went on, "Big John gets jumped at Spider Creek and hung at Lightning Strike. Mr. MacDermid gets killed before he can get arrested for the murder. And the runaway girl gets drowned at Moose Lake, which is where you end up when you go into the Boundary Waters through Asabikeshiinh. It's a big spiderweb, but the main thread runs up Spider Creek to Moose Lake, don't you see?"

Jorge frowned, then said, "I guess."

"Here's the thing. Almost nobody except someone who's Ojibwe uses Spider Creek to get into the Boundary Waters because if you don't know the right channel to follow, you get lost."

"We go in that way, with the Scouts."

"Yeah, but who else?"

"What are you saying?"

"It had to be someone Ojibwe who took her to Moose Lake."

"Or a Scout."

"Right," Cork said and rolled his eyes. "A Scout."

"Okay, you're saying someone from the reservation took her? So?"

"Sounds like she could have been in that lake nearly a month. Now think about this. Who do we know that was out there around a month ago and was Ojibwe?"

Jorge squinted, but it was not because of the sun. He was thinking hard about Cork's question. Finally, a light came into his eyes and he whispered low, "Big John."

CHAPTER 38

Liam sat in his office with Joe Meese. Both men had been quiet a long time. Then Joe finally said, "Sometimes I wonder why I wanted to be a cop. Bloody car wrecks, people killing themselves, young girls dead in the water and looking like something out of a nightmare."

"I've been doing some thinking, Joe," Liam said.

"Figured. You haven't said a word in fifteen minutes."

"What was she doing out at Moose Lake?"

"Hell if I know," Joe said.

"She was Ojibwe, but not from around here. So how did she know about Moose Lake and how to get there?"

Joe gave a shrug. "Your guess is as good as mine."

"I keep coming back to her and Big John."

It took a moment for Joe to make the connection. "You're thinking Big John took her in?"

"Sigurd Nelson says his best guess is that she'd been in the water three, maybe even four weeks. We're pretty sure that Big John went into the wilderness about that same time."

"Coincidence," Joe said, then caught himself. "Wait. A good

cop never believes in coincidence, right? You're not saying he killed her?"

"Maybe an accident," Liam said. "And maybe he'd have reported it, except that Duncan MacDermid ambushed him on his way out."

"Why didn't he just bring the body back with him?"

"Bodies generally sink in a drowning. Maybe he couldn't locate her body. Or maybe he was afraid to bring her body out."

"Why?"

"An Indian shows up with a dead girl, claims it was an accident. What jury is going to believe him? Certainly not a white jury, at least not around here."

Joe eyed him. "But you're also thinking maybe it wasn't an accident."

"I knew Big John. I respected him. But until I know the truth of what happened to that girl, I have to keep myself open to every possibility." His heart was heavy when he looked at Joe and said, "Don't I?"

That evening for supper Cork's mother made spaghetti. The rich smell of the simmering sauce filled the house for a long time before Grandma Dilsey returned. Cork was setting the dining room table, but he stopped as soon as he saw her face. His mother came from the kitchen and stood wiping her hands on her apron.

"What happened, Mom?" she asked. "Was it her?"

"It was Louise," Grandma Dilsey said. "Calvin LaRose identified her, although it wasn't easy."

Cork stood with the dinner napkins in his hands. "Why not?"

Instead of answering, she said, "I'm going upstairs to lie down for a little while."

"I'll call you when we're ready to eat," Cork's mother said.

Cork watched his grandmother climb the stairs. She moved slowly and for the first time he could remember, looked to him like an old person.

"Finish with the table," his mother said.

His father was a long time in coming. Cork was sitting on the front porch steps when his father's cruiser rolled into the driveway. Liam got out and walked to the porch. The sun had sunk low in the sky and the long, slanting rays were honey-colored. He stood at the bottom of the porch stairs, the low sun at his back, his long shadow encasing his son.

"It was her," Cork said.

"It was her." His father gave a nod.

"Grandma said it wasn't easy to identify her. Why?"

His father sighed heavily, climbed the stairs, and sat beside his son. "A body, when it's been in the water a long time, changes, Cork."

"How?"

"I'd rather not go into it."

"How long was she in the water?"

"Sigurd Nelson thinks maybe as much as four weeks."

"That's about the time Big John would've been out there," Cork said.

His father had been sitting bent with his arms resting across his knees. He sat up now but didn't look surprised. "What made you say that?"

"Henry Meloux said everything's connected, like a spiderweb. I've just been trying to look at the connections."

The screen door opened, and Cork's mother stepped out. "There you are, Liam. Dinner's ready, if you're hungry."

"I could eat," he said without enthusiasm.

"Cork, would you go up and let your grandmother know that dinner's ready?"

Before they stood up, his father looked at Cork and put a finger to his lips.

They didn't talk about the dead girl while they ate. They didn't talk about much of anything. To Cork, it felt as if they were going round and round in pointless circles, not looking at one another. As for him, he barely tasted his food. Finally his mother said, "Why don't we clear the table, Cork."

And that's when Grandma Dilsey began the fireworks.

"You didn't release her body to Calvin LaRose, Liam," she said. "I hope you understand just how hard that was on him."

"My hands were tied. In any case where the cause of death is uncertain, an autopsy is required."

"How long will that take?"

"Sigurd promised to get on it first thing tomorrow morning."

"Her body has already been desecrated enough."

"I want to know the truth of her death, Dilsey. Isn't that what you want, too?"

"You don't believe it was just a terrible accident?"

"What was she doing out there, Dilsey?"

"Why do people usually go into the woods?"

"She was in Moose Lake. I can't imagine that she got there on her own."

Grandma Dilsey absorbed this, then said, "Someone took her in, you're saying? And left her there?"

"I think so, yes."

"Who?"

Cork tried not to react, but his grandmother read him too well. "What is it, Corkie? What do you know?"

"I . . . I don't know anything," he said, but it was a feeble attempt.

"Corkie!" his grandmother said sharply.

"Leave him be, Dilsey."

Grandma Dilsey's hard, dark eyes shot to Cork's father. "You're both in on this. What are you holding back?"

Cork's mother had been standing beside the table with a couple of emptied plates in her hand, ready to head to the kitchen. She put the plates back on the table and sat down.

Cork's father took the napkin from his lap, crumpled it, and set it beside his plate. "All right, Dilsey. Here it is. That girl was in the lake nearly a month. Moose Lake—"

"Naabe-Mooz," Grandma Dilsey said, insisting on the Ojibwe name for the lake.

"Naabe-Mooz," Liam said with a curt nod. "I don't believe she got there on her own. Somebody who knows how to navigate Spider Creek took her there. Unless it's a Scout troop, pretty much the only folks who go up Spider Creek are Ojibwe. And I only know of one Shinnob who might have been in the area at that same time."

Grandma Dilsey sat stone still, never taking her eyes from her son-in-law's face. At last she said, "You think Big John killed her."

"That's not what I'm saying. But I am saying that if he were alive, I would certainly question him."

Grandma Dilsey's voice in reply was as hard and sharp as Cork had ever heard it. "No one from the reservation laid a hand on that girl, especially not Big John. But as soon as this thinking of yours gets around, every white person in this county is going to say, 'Indians killing Indians. What do you expect from savages?'"

"Mom." Cork's mother laid a hand on her wrist.

Grandma Dilsey snatched her arm away. "Am I wrong, Colleen?"

"Some will say that, I'm sure."

"Just listen for a moment, Dilsey. Here's something I haven't told you." His father glanced at Cork, as if hesitant to proceed.

"What, Liam? What haven't you told me?" Grandma Dilsey demanded.

Cork saw his father's face go hard and determined.

"That girl was naked, not a stitch of clothing on her when Sherman Kingfisher and Stoney Bright found her. Although people skinny-dip in the Boundary Waters all the time, it's suspicious. And if the evidence suggests that her death wasn't just an accident, then the question of who took her to Naabe-Mooz is paramount. I'm no believer in coincidence, so the fact that Big John was out there the same time she died is a circumstance that I have to consider. I'm not saying Big John was responsible. I agree that's a hard thing to believe. But it's a thread that has to be followed."

"I can't listen to any more of this," Grandma Dilsey said. "I'm going home." She stood abruptly, threw her napkin on the table, and left the house.

In the silence after the storm, Cork's father looked at his wife and said, "It's not about me being white, Colleen."

"I know."

"And I'm not ready to say anything against Big John. I respected him greatly. But it's something we have to consider."

"It's like I told Dad," Cork said. "It's all part of the same spiderweb."

"You already knew?" Cork's mother said, then cast an accusing look at her husband.

"He followed the same logic I followed, Colleen, and came to the same conclusion I did."

Like Grandma Dilsey, she looked tired of arguing and said, "What about the girl's grandfather, Calvin LaRose? Did he go back to Leech Lake?"

"He's staying with Henry Meloux on Crow Point until I release her body. Henry will do what he can to help the man through this." Cork's father looked down at his plate, where his spaghetti was only half eaten. "I'm not hungry anymore. I'm going back to the office. Things I need to do there."

After he'd gone, Cork's mother said, "Your grandma Dilsey is right. Big John would never have hurt that girl."

"Maybe not Big John," Cork said. "But it sure seems possible that someone from the rez could have, don't you think?"

She didn't respond. She said, "Finish clearing the table, then let's do the dishes."

CHAPTER 39

Near dark, Jorge showed up with his Ouija board. The moment Cork let him in the house, Jorge said, "Man, it feels like death in here."

"A few problems," Cork said. "Let's go outside."

They sat at one end of the porch, facing each other, legs crossed, their knees almost touching. In the soft blue illumination of evening and in the spill of incandescent light through the living room window, Jorge laid the board across their knees and placed the triangular planchette atop it. Before they began, Cork said, "What we talked about today, about Big John and that girl, you've got to keep it to yourself, okay? You can't tell anyone."

"I already told my mom."

"Then ask her not to tell anyone."

"What if she already did?"

"Then tell her not to tell anyone else. It's important."

"Sure," Jorge said.

"Promise."

"I promise, all right?"

They placed their fingertips on the planchette, and Cork said, "If we call him up, I'm going to ask different questions this time."

"Like if he killed the girl?"

"Or if he knows who did. Ready?"

"Ready."

But before they could begin the ritual, Sam Winter Moon pulled his truck to the curb in front of the house. He and Grandma Dilsey got out and strode up the walk.

"Hey, Sam," Cork said. "Hi, Grandma."

"Boys," Grandma Dilsey said in perfunctory voice and led Sam inside. Through the opened window, Cork heard her call out, "Colleen! We have some talking to do!"

He laid the Ouija board aside.

"Sounds serious," Jorge whispered. "What's it about?"

"Big John, I'd guess."

"What about calling up his spirit?"

"That can wait." He put a finger to his lips and whispered, "Just listen."

His mother had joined Grandma Dilsey and Sam, and the conversation had begun quickly and directly.

"I don't know how to keep it from getting out, Dilsey," Sam was saying. "I think it would be best to get word to the rez before anything happens. Maybe we can head off the worst of what might come."

"First it's Oscar Manydeeds. Now it's Big John. White people never blame white people."

"That's not fair, Mom. Liam never accused Oscar of anything. And he hasn't accused Big John either."

"All he has to do is mention their names in conjunction with these deaths and it opens the door to every prejudicial thought abroad in this county."

"All right, Mom, give me another way of seeing these things. Who took that girl to Naabe-Mooz? She didn't get there by herself."

"I don't know. I only know it wasn't Big John or any other Shinnob."

"And does that come from logic or from your heart?"

"Do you think *chimooks* use logic? They convict from their hearts, which in my experience, are more often than not set against anyone who looks Indian."

"Dilsey's not wrong, Colleen," Sam said. "The first thought most white folks in Tamarack County are going to have is that it wasn't one of their own who's to blame. Give them the slightest hint of anything suspicious from one of us, and *boom*, we're guilty. If Liam asks for my help trying to get information from the rez, I'm going to turn him down. Any witch hunt in Indian territory, he'll be going on his own."

"Have you told him that, Sam?"

"I'm going to wait here until he comes home and then I'll tell him."

"That might be a long wait."

"We may not have much," Sam said, "but one thing we Ojibwe have in spades is patience."

"Would you like something while you wait? I made sun tea today. And we have chocolate chip cookies in the jar."

"Both sound good. *Migwech*."

Cork moved away from the window and sat on the porch steps. Jorge joined him, but neither of them spoke.

Cork was thinking that he was just like the *chimooks* Grandma Dilsey railed against. His first thought about the dead girl had been that someone Anishinaabe was responsible. Logic was a part of that, sure, but was something else at work, something dark in him that he didn't want to acknowledge? He was only a quarter Shinnob. Three-quarters of his blood came from European ancestry. Was his thinking swayed by all that whiteness?

"I should be going," Jorge said. "Mom wants me home before it gets too dark."

"I'll go with you," Cork said.

He stepped into the house and told his mother what he was going to do. She said, "Fine, but back by ten. And take Jackson with you. He could use a good walk."

They went slowly through Aurora toward Glengarrow. Lights shone through the windows of the homes they passed, and Cork wondered if all the houses hid worries that no one on the outside knew or cared about.

The moon, nearly full, had risen shortly after sunset, and the boys walked on their own moon-cast shadows with Jackson bounding ahead or lingering behind as his nose and other canine inclinations dictated. By the time they came to the big estate, night clouds had begun to drift in, obliterating for brief periods the bright moon and sections of starlit sky. Shadows thrown down by the clouds crept across the grounds of Glengarrow and climbed the walls of the great house like dark wraiths.

At the wooden steps that led to the apartment above the carriage house, Jorge paused and said, "We could still try."

"Try?" Cork said.

"To call up the spirit of Big John."

Cork was finished with giving himself over to childish games. "Bunk," he said.

"Yeah, bunk," Jorge agreed. "See you tomorrow." He climbed the stairs, opened the screen door, and called out, "Hola, Mama. Esta bién."

But Cork knew that all wasn't well. His head and heart both told him this.

He wandered with Jackson past the big house, where only one light shone, in an upstairs window. Somehow that single light made the place look even emptier. He reached the guest cottage with its boathouse beneath and the dock where he'd sat with Jorge that afternoon and they'd dangled their feet. He stood looking across Iron Lake, which was like a great friend he'd known all his life. Its cool water welcomed him in summer. In winter, he played hockey on its hard, flat face. It could be a mirror and look exactly like the sky above, blue and tranquil. Or it could be a rage of whitecaps and just being near it got his spirit racing. Iron Lake was ever-changing, but at heart it never changed.

Everything else, it seemed, did. And not always slowly. Sometimes it came in an instant, like a lightning strike. Like the death of Big John and everything that had happened since.

The moon slid from behind a cloud and Iron Lake sparkled with a million diamonds. Then Jackson let out a low *woof* and took his pointer stance, his nose toward the big house at Cork's back. Cork felt the hair rise on his neck as Jackson growled low and threatening, and he turned quickly toward whatever it was that was coming.

But there was only the great mansion with its single light, the long empty lawn surrounding it, the carriage house.

"What is it, boy?" Cork whispered.

But he knew what it was. Or who it was. Although he couldn't see a looming figure among the cloud shadows that crept across the grounds, in his heart, he knew. Big John was not yet at rest.

"A little late to be out," Liam said when Cork walked into the kitchen from the mud porch. He was sitting on one side of the kitchen table, Colleen on the other. Cork eyed them both suspiciously and said, "What's going on?"

"A little late to be out, I said." Although Liam had meant it to sound strict, it came out from a place of anger and his son looked stung.

"I stuck around Jorge's place a few minutes longer than I expected, that's all."

"Until I say different, I want you home by dark."

"Why? What's going on?"

"Just do as I ask."

"All right. Where is everybody?"

Colleen said, "Sam took your grandmother back to the rez."

"She's still mad?"

"She just needs some time. She'll cool down."

Cork headed to the refrigerator and pulled out a bottle of milk. "Okay if I have the last piece of cobbler?"

Colleen looked at Liam and raised an eyebrow.

"Go ahead," Liam said. "But take it upstairs. You can eat it in your room."

They were quiet while Cork put the cobbler on a plate and poured his milk.

"Bring those dishes down first thing in the morning," Liam said, again more harshly than he'd intended.

"Yes, sir." Cork practically ran from the kitchen.

When they were alone again, Liam picked up where he'd left off. "I can't just ignore these things, Colleen. They're all part of the investigation. Every move I make, I get accused of being prejudiced."

"That's not what we're saying, Liam. We're just saying you don't understand. How could you? You grew up Irish, white, in a nice, suburban house."

"It wasn't that nice."

"Compared to a shack on the rez, it was a mansion."

"Not everyone on the rez lives in a shack."

"No one on the rez lives in a nice, suburban house."

"That's not my doing."

"Just try for a minute to see things from our perspective. If you hint, even in the least, that one of The People might be responsible for that girl's death, you poison the thinking of so many white people in Tamarack County. And you know this, Liam."

"That girl didn't get to Moose Lake on her own, Colleen. Even Cork could see that. If I have to question someone from the rez, I'll do that. It's my job."

"Are you going to question any white people?"

"If it makes sense."

"Why wouldn't it? Maybe you should ask Father Cam. He uses Spider Creek as an entry point when he goes with Cork's Scout troop."

Liam gave a brief, caustic laugh. "Father Cam? Can you see Father Cam harming anyone?"

"That's my point exactly. He's white, and you can't imagine him doing something so despicable as abandoning that girl out there. But if he were Ojibwe—"

"All right, all right. Let's not keep going over this. It's late. I'm tired. I need to get up early to be there when Sigurd does his autopsy."

Liam pushed his chair from the table and the legs gave a banshee screech as they slid across the flooring. He stood and leveled a cold look at his wife, who had not moved.

"Are you coming?"

"I think I'll lie down on the couch tonight."

"Whatever you need to do."

Liam mounted the stairs as if each one offended him and needed crushing. In the bedroom, he stripped to his shorts, threw on a T-shirt, and headed to the bathroom to brush his teeth. As he passed Cork's room, he glanced in. His son sat with his back against the headboard, hugging his knees. Cork turned his head and looked at his father with eyes full of fear and confusion. What exactly he'd overheard, Liam couldn't say, but he'd certainly heard the volume and the timbre. Liam wanted to step in and offer some reassurance, but there was still an angry fist balled up in his chest, and he simply moved on.

In the bathroom, he splashed cold water on his face and eyed himself in the mirror. Even to himself, he looked like a stranger, a man who could frighten children. He took a few minutes, breathed deeply, and went back to talk to Cork. But the door was closed and there was no light seeping out from underneath. Maybe he was sleeping, maybe not. And maybe it was best, because in truth, Liam had no idea what he might have said, with no comfort to offer. In that moment, he believed he'd never felt so alone.

CHAPTER 40

Like so many rural counties in 1963, Tamarack County had no
medical examiner. Autopsies were typically performed by Sigurd
Nelson, the mortician, who'd been the county coroner for more
than fifteen years. They were rare, but when required, they were
performed in the basement of the Nelson Funeral Home, in a room
typically devoted to embalming. Liam O'Connor was present from
start to finish during the autopsy of the body of Louise LaRose.
The procedure resulted in two major findings: (1) The back of her
skull had been fractured and there'd been massive hemorrhaging
of the brain; and (2) there was lake water in her lungs, which was
the actual cause of death. Liam would have liked to know the blood
alcohol level in the young woman as well, but Sigurd told him
that after so long in the water, that would probably be impossible
to ascertain.

Liam left the mortuary feeling sick to his stomach. He'd seen
death in so many forms, but watching the unnatural procedure
in the unnatural light of that basement room, gazing for so long
upon the horror he would have to release to the young woman's
grandfather later that day, imagining how he would feel if she were

someone he'd watch grow up and had loved, made this one different. Inured as he was to death, this one felt incomprehensively tragic to him.

But one additional notation that Sigurd Nelson had made about the condition of the girl's body filled Liam with an angry determination to get to the bottom of her death.

Before going to the mortuary, he'd left instructions for his deputies to bring in Big John's canoe from Spider Creek, take it to Big John's cabin, and put it back on the canoe rack. He'd given Joe Meese the keys to his pickup truck. When he parked his cruiser in his space at the county courthouse, his pickup truck was there, but the damaged canoe was still in the bed.

In his office, Ruth Rustad explained: "We got a call from Yellow Lake. A robbery at a bar there. Cy and Joe responded. They said they'd take the canoe to the reservation later."

"Tell them not to bother," Liam said. "I'll take it out myself."

When he pulled up to Big John's cabin, he was surprised to see a bicycle that looked exactly like his son's Schwinn leaning against the cabin wall. He got out and checked inside the cabin. The air was cool and there was a dank, unpleasant smell to it, but the room was empty. He stepped out, spotted Cork at the little dock by the canoe rack, and joined him.

"What are you doing out here?" he asked.

"I was headed to Allouette to look for Billy Downwind. Felt kind of wrong just to pass by without, I don't know, paying respects. What are you doing here, Dad?"

"I brought Big John's canoe."

"You don't need it for the investigation?"

"I think we got from it what we need."

"You're done with the investigation?"

"Not yet."

"You did the autopsy on the girl this morning, right?"

"Yes."

"Did you find anything?"

"We did."

"What?"

His son was twelve years old. Liam thought back to when he was that age. He'd come from a family of cops and had been privy to cop talk all his life. He'd heard funny stories and tragic stories and gruesome stories, and he thought that at twelve he'd been given a pretty good idea of how harsh the world could be for some people. He didn't believe his psyche or his young heart had been damaged by this knowledge. He decided to share the truth with Cork.

"Cause of death was drowning. But there was evidence of a blow to the back of her head."

"Somebody killed her," Cork said, as if he'd been certain of it all along.

"That doesn't necessarily follow. She could have fallen, hit her head, tumbled into the lake, and drowned. It's happened before."

"So, you think it was an accident?"

Liam stared across the water. On the far side of the lake, the shoreline of Aurora was just a thin, dark line. "No, I think somebody killed her."

"Why? I mean if it could have been an accident."

Liam turned his eyes on his son, who still had a good twelve inches to grow before he reached his father's height. "This gets grisly."

"I saw Big John's body, remember?"

"And I wish you hadn't."

"But I did. And that was pretty grisly. I can take it."

He could see that Cork's jaw was tight, as if he were biting a strap of leather, preparing for the worst. He hesitated, but he'd already decided his son should hear the truth, all of it.

"One of the things that happens to a body submerged in water for a long time is that the skin becomes soft and can easily peel away. It appeared that something had been tied around the girl's ankles, ropes probably, but as the skin peeled off, the ropes went with it."

"Ropes? What for?"

"I think someone tried to anchor her body underwater so that it wouldn't be discovered."

"Big John?"

"Do you think he was the kind of man who'd do that to a girl?"

"No," Cork said.

"Neither do I."

"Do you still think it's someone from the rez?"

"I think someone from the rez may have guided her in. Were they responsible for her death? I don't know."

"How will you find out?"

"Keep asking questions. After I put Big John's canoe back where it belongs, that's exactly what I intend to do. I'm going to visit your grandmother and a few other people."

"Will they talk to you?"

"Remains to be seen. But I have to try." He put his hand on his son's shoulder. "You okay?"

Cork nodded, then turned his face and gazed across the lake, just as Liam had done earlier. "It feels empty here. Everything feels empty right now."

"It won't always feel this way, I promise." Liam looked down at his son and offered a smile. "How about you give me a hand with that canoe?"

CHAPTER 41

After he'd helped his father at Big John's cabin, Cork biked to the small, BIA-built house in Allouette that was still owned by Billy Downwind's family and where Billy and his mother had been staying since they'd returned to the rez. Billy's mother answered his knock and told him that Billy was with his uncle Oscar in Brandywine, the other settlement on the rez.

Three miles east along a graveled road, Brandywine was a gathering of a few ramshackle homes, mostly BIA built, and like Allouette, with a few old trailers up on blocks. At the heart of Brandywine was the lumber mill, which had been a profitable Ojibwe enterprise for generations. It wasn't large, but the lumber that was milled there was always in great demand because it came from old-growth white pines, a rarity since, by the early part of the twentieth century, most of those great giants had been cut. Cork knew that the Ojibwe logged differently from white companies. They didn't clear-cut but felled selectively and in difficult to reach areas, which made it tough transporting the fallen timbers out of the forest since there were no roads. They'd solved this problem by ignoring machinery and using horses to do the hauling, as loggers had done long before there were trucks in the North Country.

In addition to keeping the machinery of the mill operating smoothly, Oscar Manydeeds was in charge of the horses that did the hauling. The animals were stabled at the edge of a large fenced meadow where they roamed freely when not in harness. Cork spotted Billy Downwind standing at the fence, gazing into the meadow where Oscar Manydeeds was walking a horse while several others idly grazed nearby. The mill wasn't running at the moment, and it was quiet in Brandywine.

"Hey," Billy said when Cork joined him.

"What're you doing?" Cork asked.

"Just watching my uncle. Little Cloud's acting lame. He's trying to figure out why."

Cork watched Manydeeds, who led the horse in a slow circle through the tall timothy and wild oats of the meadow. The horse was big, powerful, but the man beside it was also a powerful giant. The two looked suited to each other. Manydeeds seemed to be speaking quietly to the animal as they walked. It seemed an odd and interesting mix of knowledge, how to heal a horse and how to mend a machine, and it cast Oscar Manydeeds in a different, slightly more favorable light in Cork's thinking.

"Got some news," Cork told Billy. "That girl they found in Moose Lake? My dad thinks she was murdered."

"No way," Billy said. "Who did it?"

"He doesn't know yet. But she didn't get out there by herself. Somebody took her, somebody who knows the way in through Spider Creek."

"That's mostly us," Billy said, meaning all of the rez.

"I know."

Billy looked at him with sudden understanding. "You think one of us killed her?"

"I don't want to think that. But mostly it's Shinnobs who go into the Boundary Waters that way."

"What about your Boy Scout troop? Huh?"

"It wasn't a Boy Scout."

"Okay, who from the rez?" Billy challenged.

"I don't know," Cork said.

"It wasn't one of us."

Manydeeds led the animal toward the stable. Billy headed there to meet him, and Cork wandered along behind. Inside the stable, all the stalls were empty. Manydeeds tethered the horse to a ring bolted into a post. He gave Cork a cold look but said nothing.

"What do you think?" Billy asked.

"He's got a little inflammation in a tendon. Nuthin serious."

"What do you do for that?"

"Make a poultice, wrap it around that lower leg. In the meantime, I'll give him some bute."

"Bute?" Cork said.

"Phenylbutazone. Helps ease the pain. Easy, boy. I'll be right back."

Manydeeds gently stroked the animal's flank, then walked away. He stepped into a room that smelled a little like the vet's clinic in Aurora and was lined with shelves that held jars of medicine, gauze wrappings, rolls of tape, and odd-looking instruments whose purposes Cork couldn't even guess at.

"You won't have to put him down, right?" Billy asked.

Manydeeds gave a short laugh. "Like I said, it's nuthin serious. Little Cloud'll be fine."

Cork said, "Have you ever had to put a horse down?"

"Couple of times, yeah. Hardest thing in the world."

"Did you . . . shoot them?" Cork asked.

"Just put 'em to sleep. Talked to 'em real quiet so they didn't get scared."

He pulled a box from one of the cupboards and plucked out a small packet. He returned to the open area of the stable, grabbed a feed bag from a wall hook, and filled the bag from a sack of oats. Then he tore open the packet and sprinkled the contents into the feed bag. Speaking soothingly, he patted the horse and gently slipped the feed bag over the animal's muzzle. Finally, he led Little Cloud to a stall cushioned with hay.

Then he turned on Cork and said with ice in his voice, "Some reason you're here?"

Billy said, "That girl they found in Naabe-Mooz."

"The one got drowned?"

"Cork thinks one of us killed her."

"Us?"

"Somebody from the rez," Billy said.

"That's not what I said."

"It's what your dad told you."

"Did he tell you who?" Manydeeds said.

"He doesn't know," Cork said. "And he's not saying for sure it was someone from the rez."

Manydeeds turned from the boys and stroked the horse's flank. "Go on, both of you. Work to do here."

Cork offered Billy a ride back to Allouette on his handlebars, but Billy said, "Screw you," shoved his hands deep into his pockets, and began to walk.

Cork walked with him a distance in silence, pushing his Schwinn.

Finally Billy said, "I thought it was over."

"Me, too," Cork said. "The bad just keeps coming."

"It wasn't somebody on the rez. Some *chimook* did it," Billy said. Then he said, "When you know something, you better tell me."

But Cork was afraid he'd already said too much, and he made no promise.

"Come on," Billy said, climbing onto the handlebars of the bike. "Give me a lift home."

CHAPTER 42

After the long, hot bike ride back to Aurora and walking block after block delivering newspapers with Jorge, Cork suggested cooling off in Iron Lake. They often swam off the dock at Glengarrow, but only when Mr. MacDermid wasn't around. He'd made it clear that he wasn't happy with the ruckus they usually created. But Duncan MacDermid was gone now.

Cork kept a swimsuit at Jorge's, and when the boys dove from the dock that afternoon, the water felt like liquid heaven, easing all the sting of the day. They splashed and dove and raced and finally, as the sun hovered above the tops of the buildings in town, lay on the dock staring up at the sun, an unbroken yolk on a blue porcelain plate.

"I don't want to leave," Jorge said. "Ever."

"Maybe you won't have to," Cork said. "Mrs. MacDermid hasn't sold this place yet. Maybe she never will."

"Mom says there are too many bad memories for her here."

"Doesn't mean you have to leave Aurora."

"We have relatives in California. I never met them. Mom says we could start there, and when she finds a job, we could get a place of our own."

"What about Mr. Skinner? You said he might ask her to marry him."

"I don't know."

Cork wasn't sure if that meant Jorge didn't know whether the man would actually propose or if it meant Jorge wasn't sure how he felt about that possibility. It would be a big change in his friend's life. Cork tried to imagine what it would be like if his own father was out of the picture and his mother was considering remarrying. That was too hard and he let it go.

They sat up when they heard a car on the lane to Glengarrow. Nick Skinner parked his red Thunderbird and entered the house.

"He's here all the time now," Jorge said. "Advising Mrs. Mac-Dermid. She told him she wouldn't stand in the way of the hotel he wants to build."

"So, if he marries your mom, you could be rich."

"I don't want to be rich. I like things just the way they are."

"Everything changes," Cork said.

"Come on," Jorge said. "Let's swim some more."

The boys approached Cork as he was walking home late that afternoon. They'd been clustered on the corner of Third and Maple, their skateboards resting on the sidewalk. Older boys, high school. Cork knew them—Rusty Blaine, Buzz Saari, Zack Pelton—guys he didn't much care for. He kept to his side of the street and tried to ignore them.

"Hey, cop kid!" Zack Pelton hollered.

"Squaw kid," one of the other boys yelled. Cork wasn't sure which one. He continued walking.

The boys hopped on their skateboards and cruised down the street to intercept him, blocking his way.

"What do you want?" Cork said.

"Heard about that dead Indian girl," Rusty Blaine said. "What do you know?"

"Nothing," Cork said.

"We heard she was screwing the whole town before somebody killed her."

"You heard wrong."

"So, what's the straight dope?"

"I don't know."

"Your old man's sheriff. If you don't, who does?"

"He doesn't tell me everything."

"How about your Redskin friends?" Buzz Saari said. "Did they do her?"

"Out of my way." Cork tried to push past them, but they shoved him back.

"I heard she was easy," Saari said. "Did you do her?"

Cork squinted at him, his temper rising. "She's dead, for Christ's sake. Leave her be."

"Know what I think, O'Connor? I think the only good Indian is a dead Indian. What do you think?"

Cork swung, his fist connecting with Saari's left ear. The older boy stumbled back, regained his balance, and threw himself at Cork. The two went down together, grappling on the concrete. Saari had Cork by at least twenty pounds, but Cork's fury made up for that advantage. He barely registered the blows Saari delivered as he swung again and again himself. Then he felt big hands pull him up, separating him from Saari. He turned to swing at whoever it was who'd interfered and found himself facing Joe Meese.

"Enough, you two," Meese said.

"He started it," Cork said.

"Like hell," Saari said. "He swung at me, didn't he, guys?"

"I don't care who started it," Meese said. "It's over. Go on. Get out of here."

The other boys mounted their skateboards, but before they headed away, Buzz Saari flipped Cork the bird and said, "Someday, O'Connor."

After they'd cleared off, Joe Meese pulled a clean handkerchief from his pocket and handed it to Cork. "Got a split lip there."

Cork pressed the cloth to his mouth. "Assholes."

"Gonna be a lot of assholes in your life. You can't go around fighting them all. How about a ride home?"

Meese dropped him at the curb in front of the house. Cork held out the bloodied handkerchief.

"Keep it. I got a ton. You okay?"

Cork nodded.

"What was it about?"

"Nothing."

"Big hullabaloo over nothing."

"Thanks for the ride."

Cork moved to get out, but Meese put a hand on his arm. "Things are happening here like I've never seen before. I don't know what's at the bottom of it or why, but I do know that you and your family are at the heart of it. You're kinda like a bull's-eye right now. You be careful."

"I can take care of myself," Cork said.

"I was thinking of your mom and dad, too. Take it easy on them, okay?"

"Sure," Cork said.

Meese looked as if there was more on his mind, more he wanted to say, but he simply released Cork and said, "All right then. Take care of that lip."

Inside the house, Cork could smell meat loaf baking, and the rich aroma made him realize how hungry he was. The table had already been set, but with only two places.

"Wash your hands," his mother called from the kitchen. "Supper's almost ready."

He went upstairs and cleaned himself up. When he came back down, his mother had put a platter of meat loaf, a bowl of mashed potatoes, a boat of gravy, and a bowl of green beans on the table. "Just you and me?" he asked.

"There was a bad accident on Highway One. Your dad will be along later." She'd been dealing with the food, but now she looked at him. "Oh, Cork, what happened to your face?"

"Got into it with a guy. No big deal."

"That lip. It looks like you're chewing on a balloon. Let me get you some ice."

"I'm fine, Mom. Really."

"You can eat?"

"Just try and stop me."

They ate in an uncomfortable silence for a few minutes, then his mother said, "What was it about?"

"Nothing."

"I don't think so. Tell me the truth."

"Some guys were talking trash about the girl who was killed."

"Talking trash how?"

"That she was—" Cork looked away for a moment, trying to formulate the right words.

"Drinking. Whoring. Deserved what she got." His mother's voice was flat and cold.

"Yeah," Cork said. "That kind of thing."

"No woman deserves to be talked about that way, Indian or not. I don't approve of fighting, Cork, but I—" She paused and took a deep, settling breath. "I'm glad you tried to do something."

Cork's lip hurt whenever he put food in his mouth, but he

didn't want his mother to know, so he did his best to eat as if nothing was wrong. Near the end of the meal, he said, "Everything's changing here, Mom. Everything's different. It all feels broken. Here and on the rez."

"I know what you mean. And I don't know how to fix it. Your dad doesn't know either. Nor does your grandmother."

Cork had only one idea about who might. He said, "I know it's kind of late, but would it be okay if we went out to Crow Point?"

After supper, his mother drove the long gravel county road to the double-trunk birch tree that marked the trail through the woods to Crow Point. In the dusk of that evening, they walked the path together. Cork had gone this way many times, and there seemed to him something sacred about the two-mile journey, something that called for quiet contemplation, and he and his mother exchanged not a word as they walked. The evening spoke to them instead. The soft whisper of wind in the pines and poplars. The last song of an oriole and the early cry of a nighthawk. The call and response of the first tree frogs of the night. The low gurgle of water over stones as they crossed the red-tinted flow of Wine Creek. Cork felt a soothing of his soul even before they broke from the trees and stepped out into the meadow on Crow Point.

Meloux's cabin on the far side was backed by a line of birch trees whose leaves had gone dark in the dusk. As Cork and his mother crossed the meadow, Makwa set to barking. Meloux stepped from his cabin with a man at his side. When Cork was near enough, he recognized Calvin LaRose, the dead girl's grandfather.

"*Boozhoo*, Henry. *Boozhoo*, Calvin," Cork's mother greeted the men.

"He told me you'd be coming," LaRose said.

Which, Cork knew, was one of the mysteries about Meloux. He always seemed to know you were coming.

Cork's mother offered Meloux a pouch of tobacco she'd brought from home, and the Mide said, "I have built a fire. Come."

They followed the path that led between two rock outcrops to the fire ring where, not long before, Cork had sat with his father and Sam Winter Moon and Henry Meloux, trying to sort out the truth of Big John's death. A fire already burned inside the ring. More wood had been piled near to feed it. They sat, and from a beaded bag he'd brought, Meloux took a pipe carved from stone. He made an offering of tobacco to the spirits of the four directions, filled the pipe, struck a wooden match, and the pipe was passed. As usual, Cork didn't share in the smoking.

The day was drawing to a close, the sky already shaded in the powdery pastel of evening blue. Makwa lay at Meloux's feet, his huge head cradled on his paws, his eyes holding a sleepy look.

They were silent a long time before Meloux set his warm eyes on Cork and said, "Your heart is troubled."

"Everything feels broken," Cork confessed.

The old man let silence descend for another long while, then said, "Nothing is broken. It is just that we see only in part. We see with a blinded eye."

"Why does everything feel so wrong now, Mishomis?" Cork asked, addressing the Mide as Grandfather, which was how he might address any male elder. "Every time I turn around, I'm afraid something bad is going to happen."

"Fear is not a bad thing in itself, Corcoran O'Connor. It is what we do with our fear that matters. It is like Makwa here."

At the sound of his name, the dog raised his head and gazed up at Meloux, who ran a gentle hand along the dog's back.

"Makwa can bark at a stranger, and that is a good thing, a

warning, what a dog should do. But Makwa can also sink his teeth into a stranger, not a good thing if the stranger means no harm. So, I talk to Makwa when he is barking and together we size up a stranger."

"I should talk to my fear?"

"Why not?" the old man said.

"It's not about Cork's fear," his mother said. "It's about everything that's happening here now, Henry. So much trouble."

"There has always been trouble. It has never broken us."

"Will there be an end?" she asked.

"To this trouble, yes. To all trouble? Only when we have all walked the Path of Souls."

Calvin LaRose had been oddly silent, but now he spoke. "My heart breaks for my granddaughter, that she had to die so young. But the truth is, her life wasn't easy. She suffered. But she ain't suffering no more. And those of us who loved her, we ain't going to have to worry about her no more." He nodded toward Meloux. "Henry here, he's gonna do the burial ceremony for us, and we'll put this trouble behind us. Doesn't mean we'll ever forget Louise. Just . . . well, we can move on."

Cork wondered what Meloux had said to this man. Had they done a sweat together? Had Meloux done a healing ceremony? Because Calvin LaRose seemed to be in a place without fear or anger. At the moment, anyway.

"Your crumbs," Meloux said to Cork. "Where have they led you?"

Cork was surprised that the Mide had not forgotten what he'd said to the boys the night of Big John's wake. He glanced at his mother, then at Calvin LaRose. The place in his thinking where everything had led him wasn't an easy thing to say, because he believed one of The People could have been responsible for the girl's death.

"Like you said, I think I'm still seeing with a blinded eye. I need to sort some things out."

"Find a place where your head and your heart can talk to each other," Meloux advised. "Maybe then you will see clearly."

Cork stared into the fire, absolutely clueless about where that place might be.

CHAPTER 43

Next morning, when Cork and Jackson returned from delivering newspapers, his mother had made coffee and had put out all the ingredients for French toast.

"Hungry?" she asked.

"Is Dad here?"

"Still sleeping. He didn't get home until very late."

"The accident?"

"It was bad. People were killed."

"Do we know them?"

"No."

"What happened?"

"It wasn't entirely clear. They hit a tree, maybe because they swerved to miss a deer."

Cork sat at the table while his mother put the French toast on the griddle. "How does he do it?"

"What?"

"Look at something like that and not get sick."

"He's been looking at things like that for a long time. It was worse in Chicago."

Cork knew part of the reason his father had left his job as a cop in the Windy City was to put the violence of the place behind them. Tamarack County, for all its problems, was a far gentler place to call home. Whenever they returned from a visit with his father's relatives, Cork was glad to be back where the smell in the air was sharp with pine, not the stench of stockyards, where the water was clean, and where you could cross a street without risking life and limb.

They were clearing the kitchen table when a knock came at the back door. Cork's mother opened to Joe Meese, who said, "Morning, folks. Smells wonderful in there."

"We just finished eating," Cork's mother said. "But I could fix you some breakfast, if you'd like, Joe."

"Just coffee would be fine. Is Liam around?"

"Still sleeping."

"You might want to wake him. I've got something he'll want to see." Meese held up a manila envelope.

"What is it?"

"Results of the full toxicology the BCA ran on Big John. They're interesting."

"I'll get him. Cork, pour Joe some coffee."

The deputy took a chair at the table and Cork set a filled mug in front of him. "Were you at the accident scene last night?"

Meese shook his head. "I was following up on a burglary over in Yellow Lake. But I heard it was bad. Two fatalities."

"I don't know if I could do that."

"What?"

"What Dad does. What you do."

"We help people, Cork. That's what we do."

"It gets messy."

"Sometimes. But somebody has to do the job. And I'm here to tell you I'd rather be doing this than standing behind a pharmacy counter all day."

"Have you ever been shot at?"

"Me? No. But your dad, sure. Not here. In Chicago. And the war."

"He never talks about those things with me."

"Probably doesn't want you to worry. I probably shouldn't have said anything."

They heard a murmur of voices and a moment later Cork's mother returned, followed by his father, still in his pajamas. He looked tired, bags under his eyes, his hair mussed.

"What've we got, Joe?" he asked.

Liam sat at the kitchen table with Joe Meese, and Colleen put a mug of coffee in front of him. He pulled the papers from the manila envelope Joe had given him and studied the report. Then he looked at his deputy.

"A barbiturate in his blood, just like we thought."

"But not the one we thought," Joe said. "It's not amobarbital, which is what you found at the MacDermids' guest cottage. The barbiturate in Manydeeds's blood was pentobarbital. It's used mostly for animals, sometimes for sedation or as an analgesic. But most often these days, it's used to euthanize."

"To put them down," Liam said. He drank his coffee and considered. "How would Duncan MacDermid get access to something like that?"

"Probably not that difficult."

"And how would he have given it to Big John?"

"Maybe mixed in with the whiskey."

"Which would mean that Big John and Duncan MacDermid had to have been drinking together?" The sheriff shook his head. "Not sure I can see it."

Cork said, "Could you put a horse down with that drug?"

"Sure," Meese said. He eyed Liam's son carefully. "Why?"

Cork had been standing with his mother, away from the table. Now all faces turned to him.

"It's just that, well, I was out at Brandywine yesterday, looking for Billy Downwind. He was there with his uncle, and his uncle was working with a horse that was kind of lame. We got to talking, and his uncle told me that he put down a horse that way, you know, with a drug."

"Pentobarbital?" Liam asked.

"I don't know."

"Oscar Manydeeds," Meese said with a slow nod. "Not unknown to be a drinking man. Maybe he was drinking with his brother and slipped it in."

"Big John didn't drink anymore," Colleen said.

"All right, then," Liam said. "How would you get alcohol into a man who didn't drink?"

Joe sipped his coffee and offered quietly, as if afraid of interfering in what was occurring between husband and wife, "You could inject him, I suppose."

Liam said, "With a syringe, you mean?"

"Why not?" Joe said. "You knock him out with the pentobarbital, then inject him with enough alcohol to make it look like he was drunk."

"Is that possible?"

"Theoretically," Joe said.

Liam looked to his son, who was still standing with his mother. "When you were at the stables yesterday in Brandywine, did you see any syringes?"

Cork nodded. "Big ones."

"Oh, come on," Colleen said. "You can't be serious, Liam."

"The two men had their differences."

"That doesn't mean Oscar would kill his brother."

"Half brother," Liam said. "And Oscar was awfully eager to put the blame on MacDermid."

"So were you not that long ago," Colleen pointed out.

"It seemed logical then. But maybe things have changed."

"What about the rope you found in his boathouse?"

"The boathouse was unlocked. Anybody could have cut a length from that coil. And he was the one who claimed to have found the lighter at Lightning Strike. Maybe he stole it."

"And maybe Mary Margaret simply dropped it there." She shot out a loud puff of angry air. "You're still looking at everything through a blinded eye, Liam."

"Of course, until I know all the facts. Which is what I'm after. I'm not trying to demonize Oscar Manydeeds. I'm just trying to get to the truth."

"Liam, if you think anyone on the Iron Lake Reservation is going to talk to you about Oscar Manydeeds, you're crazy."

"Then I'll have to figure another way to the truth, won't I?"

They faced off, Liam feeling beat to hell and as tired as sin in his pajamas, his wife standing with her hands on her hips in a posture of pure defiance.

Joe said, "Think I'll head down to the office now. See you there later, Sheriff." He rose and quickly left the house.

Colleen stormed from the kitchen, leaving Liam alone with his son. He realized he'd been sitting with every muscle tensed. Now he relaxed, but his body felt as if he'd just gone a few rounds in a boxing ring.

"Damn," he whispered. Then he looked up at Cork. "I hope you never wear a badge."

CHAPTER 44

Later that morning, after his father had gone to work, Cork's mother said she was leaving to visit Grandma Dilsey, and Cork asked to go along. They were both quiet on the drive. Cork could still sense the heat of a burning anger coming from his mother, and it worried him. The peace in the O'Connor house seemed to be another broken thing.

Although his grandmother welcomed them, Cork could see a pinched look on her face, and there was a sour note in her voice.

"Busybodies," she said, pouring iced sun tea for them both. "Wagging tongues. Mean spirits."

"Who?" Cork said.

"Everyone."

They sat in the bright little living room of his grandmother's small house in Allouette, which was across the street from the community center. She'd told Cork how, when the center had been the schoolhouse, the children had sat with slates and chalk and had learned from her how to read and do sums. She'd taught them the history of the *zhaagnaashag* who had overrun their land and had taught them their own honorable history.

"They babble on about things they know nothing about," Grandma Dilsey complained bitterly.

"Let me guess," Cork's mother said. "Me and Liam." She glanced at her son. "And Cork."

"And me," Grandma Dilsey said. "Because I started it all by marrying an Irishman."

"Dad was respected here."

"Respected but still not one of The People. And now your husband is hunting down Oscar Manydeeds and folks are riled up about that."

"They know?" Cork's mother said.

"Liam was already out here, asking questions. Doesn't help that Oscar's vamoosed."

"He's gone?"

"Nobody's seen him."

"I saw him yesterday," Cork said.

Grandma Dilsey turned a scowling eye on him. "Where?"

"At the stable in Brandywine. He was fixing the leg on one of the horses."

"You told your dad?"

Cork nodded.

"Something you said must've got him dead set against Oscar."

"He simply told the truth, Mom."

"What truth?"

"Big John was sedated before he died. The drug was one that's used to put animals down. Oscar told Cork that he'd put down a horse with a drug. That's all Cork told Liam."

"And your husband leaped to the conclusion that Oscar killed his brother?"

"I know, Mom, I know. But Liam insists that it's a line of inquiry he has to pursue. Oscar and Big John fought. I remember watching those knock-down, drag-outs in front of all of Allouette."

"That was when they were both drinking. Big John put that rancor behind him years ago, along with the alcohol."

"People do fall off the wagon, Mom. And drinking can bring out the worst in them, old grievances that still twist them up."

"You're taking your husband's side," Grandma Dilsey said.

"I'm just trying to make you understand his thinking. I don't agree with it or accept it, but I do understand why he believes he has to ask questions."

Cork had finished his tea. He said, "Okay if I take off? I want to see Billy Downwind."

"Be back in an hour," his mother said. "I'll take you home."

"Let me know if anybody gives you a hard time," his grandmother said. "I'll see to them myself."

August had sweltered and that morning was no different. Cork walked the streets of Allouette under an unrelenting sun, his T-shirt sticking to the sweat on his back. He wished he'd worn a ball cap to shade his face. He was staring down at the dirt of the road, squinting against the glare, when he felt a shove from behind and he stumbled forward. Turning, he saw that he hadn't found Billy Downwind. Billy had found him.

"You son of a bitch!" Billy hollered at him. "You rat fink son of a bitch." And he shoved him again.

"Hey, cut it out," Cork snapped.

"You sicced your dad on my uncle."

"Did not."

"Did too."

Billy set his stance for a fight. "Come on, *chimook*. Let's do this."

"Why'd your uncle run?" Cork said. "If he's not guilty of anything?"

Billy relaxed a little, but his face was still full of fight. "He didn't run."

"Then where is he?"

"I don't know. But he didn't run."

"Look, Billy. Here's the way it stands. Big John was doped before he died, doped with the kind of drug your uncle Oscar uses to put animals down." Cork let that sink in, then added, "Doesn't that make you wonder?"

"No," Billy said. But his face told a different story, and he lowered his fists. "He wouldn't do something like that."

"Maybe not. Probably not. But don't you think it's worth asking him about? Maybe somebody else got into those drugs he uses and maybe he has an idea who."

Billy thought it over and gave a faint nod.

"So, if you know where he is, you could ask him yourself," Cork suggested.

"I don't know where he is. Nobody does."

"Come on," Cork said. "Let's get out of this sun."

They walked to the shore of Iron Lake at the edge of Allouette and sat in the shade of a maple tree near the three docks that folks on the rez used to launch their fishing boats. In season, they netted and spearfished, one of the guaranteed treaty rights that white fishermen hated. The lake held mirror still, perfectly reflecting the blue sky above it. A light breeze came off the water, cooling them as they sat.

"Why would he run?" Cork asked.

"He wouldn't," Billy insisted.

"Then there's another reason he's gone. What would that be?"

Billy stared at the lake, at the blue of the mirrored sky. "He still drinks sometimes."

"Maybe he's just somewhere sleeping it off?"

"Maybe."

"What if . . ." Cork began but stopped.

"What if what?"

"What if someone didn't want him talking to my dad?"

"Who?"

"Good question."

Billy's face tensed as he considered this. "I can't think of anybody on the rez."

"Maybe it's not someone from out here."

"From town?" Billy thought some more, and after a few moments, gave a slow nod. "Uncle Oscar has pissed off lots of white people. He never holds back telling them exactly what he thinks."

Cork picked up a stone at his side and threw it far out into the lake, where it dropped and sent out black ripples. "Maybe why he's gone doesn't have anything to do with Big John. Maybe it's something else. Maybe he just pissed somebody off."

"And what?"

"I don't know. I'm just asking questions here."

"If that's it . . ." Billy looked at Cork. "Geez, it could be anybody, any *chimook*."

Cork sat there wondering how his father or anybody else could ever find the answers to the kinds of questions Big John's death had brought to the rez. He thought about what Henry Meloux had advised, that he needed to find the place where his head and heart could talk to each other. But where was that place?

It was Billy who suggested an answer: "I'm going back to Lightning Strike."

"What for?" Cork said.

"Everything began there, remember? And I felt Big John's spirit there. Maybe . . . I don't know. Maybe I'll feel something again."

"Can I come?"

"Do whatever you want."

"When are you going?"

Billy considered the question. "After dark. After my mom's gone to sleep. Maybe I'll spend the night."

"I'll meet you there."

They separated and Cork headed back to his grandmother's house. His father's cruiser was parked in front. Inside, he found the adults in deep conversation, the air once again thick with tension.

"I'm not trying to accuse anyone here, Dilsey," his father was saying. "I'm just trying to figure out how that drug got into Big John's system. I've been out to Brandywine and checked the medications Oscar keeps for his horses. He's got pentobarbital there. So, at the moment, he appears to be the mostly likely source. And now he's gone. Don't you see how it looks?"

"I don't care how it looks. I know Oscar Manydeeds. He's not a man who'd do that kind of thing to his brother. Or anybody else."

"Then help me prove it."

"How?"

"Help me find him."

"I don't know where he is."

"Ask others out here. Somebody must have seen him. But they're not going to tell me that."

Cork's grandmother sat straight in her chair, as if her spine were made of ironwood. She didn't reply.

"If you believe he didn't do this, help me clear him," Liam O'Connor said.

Grandma Dilsey gave a slow nod. "On one condition."

"Name it."

"I believe in my heart it was no Shinnob who did these things. In your heart, you have to believe that, too."

"I . . ." Cork's father looked from Grandma Dilsey to his wife. "I can't do that. But it's not because I'm a white man."

"It is," Grandma Dilsey said. "And that's the sad truth. But I'll help you anyway, because until you're satisfied, you'll keep asking the wrong questions."

CHAPTER 45

Moments after sunset, Liam pulled into the driveway on Gooseberry Lane and sat a moment in his cruiser. He'd spent the day beating his head against a brick wall, trying to find someone, anyone, who might have an inkling where Oscar Manydeeds had gone. Even Dilsey had come up empty-handed. The man seemed to have vanished completely. Which worried Liam for a number of reasons. He got out and walked slowly to the house, feeling as if he were dragging a heavy ball and chain. In the kitchen, he found Colleen sitting at the table, a notebook in front of her, a pen in her hand.

"What are you doing?"

"Lesson plans," she said. "The start of the school year's not that far away. Thought I'd get a leg up."

He sat at the table with her. "I'm sorry. I can be a stubborn bonehead sometimes."

She laid her pen down. "I knew that when I married you. Any luck finding Oscar?"

He shook his head. "Dropped off the face of the earth."

"You think he's somewhere getting drunk, don't you?"

"It's one of the possibilities."

"Maybe he's somewhere just trying to pull things together. You do that sometimes. For you, it's in a boat, fishing."

"Maybe. But there's another possibility."

"What's that?"

"He may not be responsible for his brother's death, but maybe he knows more about it than he's let on. And maybe whoever is responsible was afraid he might talk."

"You think something's happened to him?"

"I honestly don't know what to think. I'm just posing possibilities."

"You said 'whoever is responsible' for Big John's death. You're sure it wasn't Duncan MacDermid?"

"Since I got the toxicology report this morning, I'm having significant second thoughts."

"Who then?"

"At the moment, no idea." The quiet and emptiness of the house suddenly dawned on him. "Where's our son?"

"He asked to spend the night with his grandmother. Jorge's agreed to deliver papers for him in the morning."

"I don't blame him. I'm kind of hard to be around these days."

"These days?" She leaned to him and kissed his cheek. "Hungry?"

"I haven't eaten since lunch."

"Leftovers okay?"

After dinner, Liam called the Sheriff's Department and checked in with Otto Pendergast, one of the two night-duty officers, who was on dispatch. Pendergast reported that all was quiet in Tamarack County and wished Liam a good night.

"Taking Jackson for a walk," he told Colleen after the call. She was reading in the living room and gave him a distracted wave.

The light of day had faded to a soft blue, and the stars were only just starting to show themselves. The streets of Aurora were mostly empty as folks settled in for the night. Lights shone warm through windows, and Liam thought about these people who'd elected him with the belief that he'd keep the peace in their town, in their county. He wondered if anyone on the Iron Lake Reservation had bothered to cast a ballot, believing that no matter who wore the badge they would still be on their own. He wanted very much to offer them better than they expected, to give them hope for fairness, for justice. In order to do that, he had to do his best to see through different eyes.

He tried once more to put it all together. Somebody who knew how to navigate Spider Creek had led Louise LaRose to Moose Lake, where she'd died. Maybe her death was intentional, maybe not. But they'd tried to keep her body from being discovered. Either way, accidental death or intentional, they'd felt they had to protect themselves. So, who used Spider Creek to enter Moose Lake besides the Ojibwe? The local Boy Scouts sometimes, and on rarer occasions, Girl Scouts. But they always sought permission from the Ojibwe and had to be led by someone who knew their way through the web of marshy waterways. A few white folks probably went in that way without asking permission, because if you knew the way, it was more convenient than a lot of entry points. And if you wanted a big lake pretty much to yourself, free of a lot of other canoe and camping enthusiasts, Naabe-Mooz was a good bet. So, it could have been someone without a drop of Ojibwe blood in them, someone who might not have wanted to be seen with an underage Ojibwe girl in tow. But still someone who knew the way.

As he and Jackson turned to the corner and started back down Gooseberry Lane toward home, he tried to step out of himself and see the situation through different eyes. Okay, he thought, maybe

Dilsey's right and no Shinnob would ever do to that girl what someone had done. Louise LaRose had died at the hands of someone who was white, someone she'd encountered while wandering the streets of Aurora, someone who had a great deal to lose if her death came to light.

And Big John? It wasn't a coincidence that he'd died around the same time as Louise LaRose. Liam had been so focused on nailing Duncan MacDermid for Big John's death that he hadn't really looked at anyone else. But because the toxicology results had shown that the sedative used on Big John wasn't the one Liam had found in MacDermid's cottage, he'd begun to be plagued by doubts about the man's guilt. So, what was the connection between the murder of Big John and the death of Louise LaRose? Did Big John know something about her death and that's what got him killed?

This was as far as his thinking had taken him when he walked up the front porch steps and Colleen met him at the door. Her eyes were full of fear.

"It's Cork," she told him in a strained voice.

"What about him?"

"He's gone."

CHAPTER 46

Grandma Dilsey usually slept like a rock. Whenever she stayed over with Cork's family in Aurora, he could hear her snoring all the way from his own bedroom. It was no different at her little house on the rez. When he heard that rumbling snore, he left the sofa which she'd made up as a bed for him, dressed, and quietly slipped out the front door.

The moon was high, nearing fullness, and the streets of Allouette were empty and bathed in silver. Cork stood in front of the community center, where he'd told Billy to meet him, waiting in the black puddle of his own shadow, which the bright moon cast. The night was warm, the air still, and for reasons Cork couldn't quite name, he felt a deep urgency in his mission that night. From his house in Aurora, he'd brought his pack, which he'd told his mother was full of clothes and things. He wasn't very specific. The pack actually contained a flashlight, a box of kitchen matches, and his official Boy Scout pocketknife. Even though he expected to return to Grandma Dilsey's before daylight, he'd also put in his canteen, his mess kit, a can of Spam, a block of Cracker Barrel cheese, and a packet of saltines. Be prepared, the motto of a Boy Scout.

Billy didn't show. Cork tired of waiting and started for Lightning Strike on his own. It was a three-mile walk, mostly along the lakeshore. Because of the intense moonlight, he had no trouble seeing his way. He crossed Spider Creek, soaking his sneakers, and entered the stand of old white pines that separated Lightning Strike from the lake. When he stepped into the meadow, he stood for a while before the lone maple. His shadow, which no longer puddled under him, pointed like a stubby black finger toward the limb where Big John had hung.

Although Cork had told no one, the fouled flesh of Big John's face sometimes haunted his dreaming. He wondered if Jorge had nightmares, too, but he hadn't asked. He wondered if Jorge's drawing of monsters helped him exorcise the demons that might otherwise haunt him. If so, Cork wished he had some way of getting rid of his own nightmares.

He continued across the meadow to the place where he and Jorge and Billy had built a fire and tried to conjure the spirit of Big John. He spent the next fifteen minutes gathering sticks to build a fire and dried pine needles to kindle the blaze. Then he sat and fed the flames and let the fire grow so that it illuminated an area a good twenty feet in all directions.

He was hungry, always hungry these days. A growing boy, his grandmother said. He took his mess kit and the can of Spam from his pack and fried himself up a few slices of the meat, which he ate with the Cracker Barrel cheese on the saltines he'd brought. It wasn't just a quiet night. It was dead still. There was no cooling breeze whatsoever. Cork sat chewing, studying the ruins of the old logging camp in the moonlight, the sturdy, blackened chimney and the burned remains of the log walls. It could have been just bad luck that had caused the lightning to hit and destroy the camp, but Cork liked much better the idea that there was something powerful and sacred about this place, and that Kitchimanidoo, the Great

Mystery, had caused it to be destroyed. He hadn't heard any stories of anyone being killed in the incident, so it didn't seem to him an act of cruelty. Just a righteous one.

In the bright flow of moonlight, which illuminated even the far side of the clearing, Cork spotted a figure standing beside the tree where Big John had been hung. He couldn't make out details and had no idea who it might be. It wasn't Billy Downwind, that much he could tell. The figure was much larger than Billy, huge in fact, a dark giant. Whoever it was just stood there, motionless, staring hard, and Cork felt a ripple of fear run through him. The figure began to advance slowly across the meadow, its shadow dragging behind like the tail of a panther. A man had been murdered here, Cork well knew, and there'd been no one around to witness it. Where the hell was Billy? Why hadn't he shown? Cork thought about bolting but couldn't bring himself just to turn tail and run. What would he be running from except his own fear? Still, his stomach knotted ever tighter as the figure drew nearer.

A dozen yards away, the figure finally spoke. "Smelled your fire and the food. I'm hungry, if you're willing to share." Two more strides, and Oscar Manydeeds stepped into the light of the flames.

"I didn't run," Manydeeds said. He sat near the fire with Cork and Billy Downwind, who'd arrived a short while after his uncle. "Just needed to come here, get myself straightened out. I used to come all the time, just like you boys." He paused. "Used to come sometimes with John before he went off to war."

They'd shared the Spam and cheese and crackers, and munched on apples now, which Billy Downwind had brought along with peanut butter and jelly sandwiches. He told Cork that his mother had had trouble going to sleep, so he couldn't get away when he'd hoped.

"John used to say this was a place of good spirit." Manydeeds stared beyond the firelight toward the tree where someone had hung his brother. "I believe that, and I don't understand how that spirit could've stood by while John got murdered. Guess that's why I'm here. Trying to figure it out." He glanced at the two boys. "What about you?"

Billy said, "We saw Big John's spirit here. I thought maybe we might be able to talk to him or something. Maybe he'd help us understand."

"Lots of folks seeing his spirit around," Manydeeds said with a nod. He looked at Cork. "What are you doing here?"

"Like you and Billy, just trying to figure things out."

Manydeeds finished his apple and threw the core into the fire. "His spirit's here all right," he said. "He was older'n me, always getting hauled off to boarding school." He glanced at Cork. "Your grandma saved me from that when she started her school here. Convinced everybody, the government and whatnot, that this was better than sending kids off to God knows where. But John, once they got hold of him, they didn't want to let go. He fought 'em. They beat the hell out of him for it, but they never broke him. Then he went into the woods and didn't come out until he was too old for 'em to take back. But the government, they got him another way. Drafted him. When he come back from that war, he come back changed. That's when his drinking started. When I started, too, cuz I wanted to be like him. But the booze brought out the worst in both of us, and with the drinking came the fights and all the bad, hurtful stuff."

Billy said, "You never told me."

"What's to tell? Can't change the past."

"I thought, when nobody could find you . . ."

"What? That I was off drinking somewhere?" He shook his head. "John was always on me to stop. Now that he's gone, I've made his spirit a promise. I'm never touching the hard stuff again. John licked it. So can I." He closed his eyes and breathed deeply. "Feel him? He's here. I know what Henry says about the path to the spirit world, but I think when we go, we always leave something of ourselves behind."

"He didn't kill himself," Billy said.

"I know that. No way he'd kill himself. Was that bastard Mac-Dermid."

"Maybe not," Cork said.

Even in the firelight, a darkness was visible on the face of Oscar Manydeeds. "What are you saying?"

"Somebody drugged him before he died," Cork said. "They used a drug called pentobarbital. Is that the same drug you use to put down horses?"

Manydeeds gave him a hard look. "How do you know this?"

"My dad had Big John's blood tested. Is it the same drug?"

"Yes."

"Could somebody have got into your supplies?"

He thought a moment. "Hell, I got broke into. Maybe three, four weeks back. I guess somebody coulda stole something then."

"Any idea who it might've been?"

"I asked around and nobody knew nuthin. Kids is what I figured, looking for something to get high on. They got no respect these days."

Which was a line Cork seemed to hear a lot from adults, Ojibwe and otherwise, and a little ironic coming from Oscar Manydeeds, whose wildness and disrespect in his adolescence had landed him more than once in juvenile detention.

"Could that be how MacDermid got hold of the drug?" Cork asked.

Before Manydeeds could answer, a sweep of light crossed the dark meadow, and a vehicle pulled to a stop at the end of the old logging road on the far side of the clearing. The headlights died. In the quiet, Cork heard a car door close. A flashlight shot a thin beam toward the ground, and the beam and whoever was behind it came toward the fire. Manydeeds stood, tensed as if preparing to defend himself, or maybe to defend them all. Cork and Billy Downwind stood with him.

"Oscar Manydeeds." The voice from behind the flashlight beam surprised Cork no end. "I've been looking for you."

The beam died and Cork's father stepped into the firelight.

CHAPTER 47

"What do you want?"

Manydeeds's voice was as taut as his body. Liam could see that he was fully prepared to fight.

"To talk," Liam said. "Just to talk."

"About my drugs?"

Liam's eyes settled on his son for a moment, then shifted back to Manydeeds. "The lab test showed pentobarbital in Big John's blood. That's a drug you use sometimes."

"On horses. I'd never use it on my brother."

"I want to believe you, Oscar, I do. But you see how it looks."

"To a white cop, maybe."

Cork said, "Somebody broke into the stables in Brandywine, Dad. They could've stolen the pentobarbital then."

"Is that true, Oscar?"

Manydeeds gave the slightest of nods.

"Why didn't you report the break-in?"

"To you? Would you even give a shit?"

"I'd have investigated."

"And got nuthin. Which is what I got when I asked around. If I couldn't get answers on the rez, you think you could?"

"Why'd you run?"

"Didn't. Didn't even know you were looking for me till your boy told me."

"What are you doing here?"

"You wouldn't understand," Manydeeds said.

"Try me."

"You gonna arrest me, just do it."

Liam stood motionless, his eyes sweeping the three figures facing him in the firelight. It hadn't taken a genius to figure out where Cork had gone when Dilsey called to say he'd vanished. Liam was relieved that he'd read his son correctly. He could have been upset, but Cork had, in fact, helped him locate Manydeeds.

"Can I sit with you?" he said.

Manydeeds didn't give an answer, nor did his face give any clue to his thinking.

"I understand this is a sacred place to the Ojibwe," Liam said. "I want to honor that. But I also have a duty I consider sacred. I'm not here to harass you, Oscar. I'm here in search of answers, and honest to God, I need some help. Someone murdered your brother."

"Hell, yes. That son of a bitch MacDermid."

"I'm thinking it might not have been him."

"Still trying to clear the rich man's name?"

"Here's the situation, Oscar. I figured someone had to drug Big John to set up that phony suicide. One of the reasons I thought it was MacDermid was because we found barbiturates in his cabin. But those barbiturates weren't what the lab test found in your brother's blood."

"He was a rich man. He coulda got pentobarbital any time he wanted."

"Probably. But why use that when it would have been easier for him just to slip Big John something he already had on hand? Look, MacDermid may have been responsible for your brother's death. But what if he wasn't? I want to find out the truth of who killed Big John and bring that person to justice. Isn't that what you want, too?"

For a long time from the far side of the fire, Manydeeds studied Liam. Finally he said, "Sit."

Liam brought out a pouch of tobacco from his shirt pocket and a small pipe carved of cherrywood which had been given to him long ago by Sam Winter Moon. At Sam's suggestion, Liam always kept tobacco and the pipe in his glove box for his trips to the rez. He sprinkled a bit of the tobacco onto the fire as an offering, as he'd seen Henry Meloux do so many times, then filled the pipe. He thrust a stick into the fire and used the flame at the end to light the tobacco. He and Manydeeds smoked together, passing the pipe between them.

After a time of silence, Liam said, "I admired your brother. Big John was a good man, a strong man. What happened to him was the work of a coward."

"What do you know about the man who killed my brother?" Manydeeds asked.

"Not enough, not yet. A couple of things though. It seems to me he must've been waiting for Big John at the take-out point on Spider Creek, where we found your brother's canoe." He glanced at his son and Billy Downwind and corrected himself. "Where Cork and your nephew found the canoe. Whoever it was knew that your brother had gone into Moose Lake and would be coming out that way. Somehow he drugged Big John—I haven't figured that part out yet—then got him here to Lightning Strike. Whoever it was, they planned it carefully. I think they stole the rope from Mac-Dermid's boathouse to implicate him. So maybe it was someone who had something against him as well."

"Half the county," Cork said.

Liam smiled and acknowledged this truth with a nod.

Manydeeds considered this for a while then said, "Maybe it wasn't kids broke into the stables. Maybe somebody had something against my brother. Big John wouldn't go down easy. They'd need something like pentobarbital."

Liam O'Connor said, "How long ago was the break-in?"

"Maybe a month now." Manydeeds scowled as the realization hit him. "Not long before my brother was killed."

"Like I said, MacDermid may have been responsible. He certainly had reason to hate your brother. But I can't help thinking that it might have had something to do with the death of Louise LaRose, the girl from Leech Lake."

Manydeeds thought that over. "I heard somebody bashed her head in, then tried to sink her body."

"Yes."

"They rape her, too?"

"She'd been in the water a long time, so we couldn't tell."

Manydeeds stared into the fire. "Everybody on the rez knows that when my brother went into the Boundary Waters, he always went up Spider Creek to Naabe-Mooz. Who else knew?"

Even though Manydeeds seemed to be asking himself this question, Cork replied, "The Borealis sisters."

"Maybe they told somebody," Manydeeds said.

"I know they told Duncan MacDermid," Liam said.

Billy Downwind, who'd been silent for a long time, said, "Maybe he told somebody."

"Maybe," Liam said. "I'll talk to MacDermid's widow. And I'll talk to the Borealis sisters again. And I'll see if I can't track down where that pentobarbital might have come from. To that end, Oscar, I'd like to ask you to open yourself to the possibility that someone on the rez might know more than they've said. Maybe those kids who broke into the stables, if it was kids. Will you do that?"

"No Shinnob killed my brother."

"But maybe a Shinnob knows something that will lead us to the white man who did," Liam offered.

Manydeeds said nothing in reply, but he finally gave a single nod.

And that's when the wind came out of nowhere, kicking embers up from the flames, embers that spread into the night sky like a thousand fireflies. Liam followed them with his eyes, and what he saw there, he couldn't quite believe.

"Brother," Manydeeds whispered, staring upward in amazement.

CHAPTER 48

"Embers," Liam said. "They were just scattered embers."

His son sat on the kitchen floor, ruffing Jackson's fur while the dog blinked lazily. Dilsey had come that morning, bringing the last of the blueberries that she and Cork had picked together, and she stood at the kitchen counter busily making blueberry muffins. Colleen was slicing tomatoes for the BLT sandwiches that would be lunch.

"I saw his face in the embers," Cork insisted.

"I know what you think you saw," Liam said. "But the mind can play tricks, Son. We often see what we want to see."

"Henry told me to find a place where my head and my heart could talk. Last night at Lightning Strike my head told me my heart was right. Big John's spirit was with us. It was a sign, Dad. We're on the right track."

"I didn't need Big John's spirit to tell me that."

"What are you going to do, Liam?" Colleen asked.

"See if I can track down the source of the pentobarbital in Big John's blood. If it came from that break-in at the stables, we need to find out who was responsible."

"Oscar apparently had no luck with that," Dilsey said. "What are you going to do that he couldn't?"

"Oscar's trying again on the rez. Now that we know what was used to drug Big John, he might get answers he didn't before. And Billy Downwind's going to talk to the kids he knows. I sent Cy Borkman to get a list from Dave Svenson—"

"That's Doctor Dave, right?" Cork asked.

"Yes, Doctor Dave," Liam said. "I sent Cy to get a list of all the people in Tamarack County he can think of whose work requires that they keep pentobarbital on hand. He's out with that list right now, doing interviews. Between us, maybe we can come up with a solid lead."

Dilsey stopped beating the muffin batter and turned a cold eye on him. "Do you still believe someone on the rez is responsible?"

"I can't ignore the possibility." He hesitated, reluctant to say what was on his mind, knowing how Dilsey would react. "Someone familiar with Spider Creek took that girl in."

"There are white people who know the way in. Your priest at St. Agnes, for example. Are you going to question him?"

"Mom," Colleen said.

"No, I'm serious. You think just because he's a priest, he couldn't do horrible things? At the boarding school, we heard the stories of what priests and nuns did to children. He's gone to Moose Lake with Cork's Scout troop, so he knows the way up Spider Creek. And didn't you tell me, Liam, that he knew the girl?"

"I don't want to hear this, Mom."

"No more than I want hear talk of someone on the rez killing Louise LaRose."

Liam said, "She's right, Colleen. If I'm going to be fair, I need to talk to anyone who had contact with Louise. And it's true that Father Cam knows the way up Spider Creek."

"You two," Colleen said fiercely, then swallowed whatever

angry words she was about to say. Instead, she announced, "Lunch is ready. No more talk about killing."

That afternoon Liam stopped by St. Agnes to speak with Father Cam. In the office, Elaine Christiansen, the church secretary, said she hadn't seen him at all that day and didn't know where he was. She suggested his housekeeper might have an idea.

The rectory, a neat, single-story house of red brick, stood next to the church, and when Liam knocked, Nelda Griffin answered the door. The priest's housekeeper was a stern old woman who was clearly surprised to see Liam. He could hear the television blaring in the living room. A soap opera, he guessed from the heavy organ soundtrack. Nelda Griffin didn't appear happy at being pulled away from her program. But Liam couldn't recall ever having seen her look happy.

"I'd like to talk to Father Cam," Liam said.

"Father Ferguson isn't here." She was of the old school, and never referred to him as Father Cam. She thought it was disrespectful.

"Do you know where he is?"

"Canoeing. And working on his Sunday homily. He says the one helps him with the other."

"Canoeing where?"

"Iron Lake, would be my guess. Though he's never told me exactly where."

"When will he be back?"

"Sometimes he stays out all night. I never know. Always takes a bedroll and a knapsack with him."

A large crucifix carved in wood was affixed to the foyer wall, and the tortured figure that hung there seemed to stare at Liam with accusing eyes. Liam turned his face away before he asked the next question. "Father Ferguson, does he drink whiskey, Mrs. Griffin?"

"What kind of question is that?"

"When Father Newton was the priest here, he always said he was proud to drink whiskey from his homeland in the Emerald Isle."

"Father Ferguson's not like Father Newton was. But I never knew a priest didn't enjoy a nip now and then."

"When he drinks, do you know the brand he prefers?"

"What difference does it make?" She looked at him now with a good deal of suspicion.

"In case I wanted to give him a birthday gift, say."

"His birthday's not till October. Ask me then."

"Four Roses?" Liam said.

She finally smiled. "I'm sure he'd prefer whiskey to flowers. Is that all?"

Once again, his father wasn't home for supper. Cork ate with his mother and Grandma Dilsey, then grabbed his receipt book and canvas change bag and left the house to try to collect from the deadbeats on his morning paper route. He'd successfully closed the accounts of two customers and was feeling pretty hopeful when he got to the Crooked Pine. He could tell from the cars in the lot that business was brisk inside. He usually collected in the afternoon, when the bar wasn't so busy. He considered leaving, but he was already there, and he finally decided that he might as well give it a shot. He started around to the back of the building, where he always knocked and waited for Mr. Svenson to open up and give him the usual song and dance about not being able to pay at the moment. "Busy right now, kid. Come back later." Or "I got nothing but fifties and hundreds. Can you make change?"

A woman stumbled out the front door of the bar, caught herself, and stood upright. She wore a black, sequined dress and black high heels. Her hair was blond and hung over her forehead in random strands. An unlit cigarette dangled from her lips, which were so reddened with lipstick that even to Cork she appeared a little clownish. Still, she was a pretty woman, and when she looked at him, he saw that her eyes were a little unfocused.

"Hey," she said in a too friendly way. "Got a match?"

"No, ma'am."

"Not to worry," she said digging into her purse. "Got a lighter here somewhere." She glanced at the receipt book he held in one hand and the canvas change bag he held in the other. "Let me guess. You're collecting the rent on this dump." Then she laughed loud as if she'd made a great joke.

"Collecting for the newspaper," he said.

"Oh, good luck with that, kid. Ben Svenson? I never knew a bigger deadbeat." When she spoke, the cigarette in her lips bounced up and down like a bandleader's baton.

"He hardly ever pays me," Cork said.

"That so?" She seemed to have forgotten about the lighter. She took the unlit cigarette from her mouth and threw it to the ground. "Let's just see about that. Come on, sonny."

She turned and started back into the bar. When she opened the door, the sound of the jukebox and the cacophony of voices spilled out.

"I can't go in there, ma'am," Cork said.

"The hell you can't."

She took him by the arm and pulled him in with her.

Mostly there were men inside. A young barmaid Cork didn't know moved among the tables, delivering drinks. "Fever" was playing on the juke, and as soon as they walked in, the woman began to sing right along with Peggy Lee but in a voice that reminded Cork of how Jackson sounded when he was whining to get outside. He was surprised to see Doctor Dave at the bar. He thought of the Crooked Pine as a place where people came to lose themselves in a liquor haze. Doctor Dave and Ben Svenson were deep in conversation. The woman swept Cork along with her as she strode unsteadily to the bar. Ben Svenson saw her coming and said something to Doctor Dave, who turned on his stool. He didn't seem happy to see the woman, but when he saw Cork, he hauled up a smile.

"Hey, Cork. How's Jackson doing?" he said.

Cork wasn't sure he'd ever been as uncomfortable as he was at that moment. "Just fine, sir. No distemper."

The barkeep spoke around the stub of a foul-smelling cigar smoldering in the corner of his mouth. "Distemper a big problem around here, Dave?"

"I'm still keeping a close eye on things, but I'm sure Cork's dog is safe."

"You're good with dogs, I'll give you that," the woman said and laughed, though it came out like a bark.

"What the hell are you doing in here, kid?" Ben Svenson said.

"He's my guest," the woman said, and put her arm in an uncomfortably familiar way around Cork's shoulders. "And he's here to collect for the newspaper he brings you every day."

"Didn't I just pay you?" the barkeep said.

"That was for April, May, and June. You still owe me for July."

"Damn."

"How much does my brother owe?" Doctor Dave asked.

Adults moved in a different circle from the one Cork occupied, and unless their kids were part of his circle, he didn't pay much attention to their relationships with each other. But he finally put together something that had never occurred to him before, the fact that Doctor Dave Svenson and the grumpy Ben Svenson were brothers.

Cork told him, and the man reached into his back pocket and brought out a wallet. He took out a five-dollar bill and handed it to Cork. "Keep the change."

The woman removed her arm from Cork's shoulders, tried to put her elbow on the counter, but missed and would have fallen to the floor if Doctor Dave hadn't caught her.

"Come on, Moira," the veterinarian said, sounding tired, and maybe even a little disgusted. "It's time we went home."

She pulled from his grasp. "Not yet. Night is young. Right, honey?" She directed this last comment to Cork.

"Go home, Moira," the barkeep said.

"What for?" She looked at Doctor Dave, who, Cork now understood, was her husband. "Just to fall asleep? I came here for some action. So far all I've come up with is a little lamb." She reached out and put her hand against Cork's cheek. Then her eyes moved away, roaming over the men at the tables.

Doctor Dave took her arm once again, but once again she pulled away. "I don't need you or your help." She squared her shoulders and headed for the door.

"Night, Ben," Doctor Dave said and followed his wife outside.

The barkeep took the stub of cigar from his mouth and dropped it in what was left of his brother's drink on the bar. The ember died with a little sizzle. "Drunken cow," he said under his breath. He turned angry eyes on Cork. "What are you waiting for? You got your money, now get out."

"Your receipt," Cork said and tossed the slip onto the bar.

Marriage was a mystery to Cork, one he'd never much considered. He understood that marriage was about love, but love was also about a lot of other things. Marriage was about children, but that seemed to him a consequence, not a reason. Marriage was, he vaguely understood, about sex, legal sex, sex that was okay in the eyes of everybody that mattered, maybe the Church most of all. In the case of his parents, marriage seemed to be about companionship. His mother and father seemed to like spending time with each other. As he walked home in the gathering dark, he thought about Doctor Dave Svenson and his wife, who didn't seem to like each other much at all. He wondered if it had always been that way between them, but decided probably not or why would they have gotten married in the first place?

The evening sky was a satin blue with the first faint stars just beginning to show. As he wandered toward home and neared St. Agnes, Cork saw that his father's police cruiser was parked in the church lot and the light in the priest's office was on. He stopped pondering marriage and thought about what his father had said—that to be fair, he needed to question Father Cam. He didn't know the kinds of questions his father might ask, but he thought Father Cam wouldn't lie. He was a priest. Priests were different from regular people. Although he knew his father wouldn't want him intruding, as if with a will of their own, his feet took him to the door that opened onto the church's administrative and education wing. It was unlocked, and he stepped inside. The hallway was dark, the only light coming from the church office. He moved to it quietly and peeked inside. The room was empty.

The absence of both the priest and his father from the only lighted room gave him an unsettled feeling in the pit of his stomach. He crept down the hallway toward the sanctuary, walking in the dim red light shed by the Exit sign above the sanctuary doorway. He stood near the altar rail, eyeing the great crucifix that dominated the chancel. From the rear of the sanctuary came a low moaning, as if from someone in deep pain. Cork walked slowly down the center aisle, toward the small chapel off the narthex, which was sometimes used for quiet meditation or an intimate ceremony.

As he neared, Cork understood that the moaning was actually a low repetition of words—*Why, God? Why me?*—plaintive in their tone, a kind of chant. A dim, wavering light came through the chapel doorway, and when Cork peered in, he saw that the small room was lit by the flame of a single candle on the tiny altar, before which a figure knelt, hunched so far over that his forehead touched the red-carpeted floor. The figure's feet were clad in boots whose soles were caked with dried mud. The hunched body shook as if in some kind of terrible fit, and Cork stood frozen, torn between fleeing and offering to help.

The figure straightened suddenly and turned on Cork. The face, in dark shadows etched by crude candlelight, was a blackened and twisted mask of horror. Cork found himself staring into the eyes of a madman.

CHAPTER 49

Liam had parked his cruiser in the lot at St. Agnes, entered the building, and walked to the office. He'd seen the light from the street and thought maybe the priest had returned. The office was empty, and the rest of the church was dark. He figured that Father Cam had simply left the light on and gone to the rectory. So Liam had headed across the street and talked with the housekeeper, who insisted the priest still hadn't come back from wherever he'd been.

Liam was already on high alert from all the uncertainty abroad in Tamarack County, and there was something unsettling in the situation. He returned to St. Agnes, walked down the hallway toward the sanctuary, where he heard a painful moaning coming from the back of the church. He moved cautiously in that direction. Then he heard a stifled cry, and as he rushed into the narthex, a body much smaller than his own plowed into him.

"Cork?"

His son looked up, his face awash with relief. Liam looked beyond his son at the grim figure hulking in the candlelight of the little chapel.

"I didn't mean to scare you, Cork," Father Cameron Ferguson said. "You just caught me by surprise."

Liam understood clearly why Cork had fled from the man. The priest's face was smeared with a charcoal coating. His eyes were red from prolonged weeping. His cheeks were streaked as if with scars of white where tears had run. Although his son had probably seen a figure of terror, Liam saw a portrait of deep pain.

"What's happened to you, Cam?" he asked. "Your face?"

"Fasting," the priest said. "Trying to cleanse myself." He spoke in gasps, pulling himself back from his weeping, pulling himself together. "The charcoal . . . Henry Meloux told me about it . . . part of a practice he follows . . . seeking answers through fasting."

"You look pretty scary," Liam said.

The priest ran a hand over his brow and stared at the residue on his fingers. He steadied himself and looked at Cork. "No wonder you ran. What are you doing here?" Then he looked at Liam. "And you?"

"I've been looking for you," Liam said. "A few questions I need to ask. But first, tell me about this cleansing you were seeking. Cleansing for what reason?"

There were chairs in the chapel and the priest said, "Let's sit." When they were all seated, Father Cam said, "You have a great responsibility to the people here, Liam. Does it sometimes feel suffocating?"

"Crushing," Liam said.

The priest nodded as if he understood perfectly. "I have a responsibility to those who come to me for advice and for succor. Sometimes I feel so weighted I can barely breathe. I hurt all the way down to my soul because I don't know how to help."

"Prayer," Cork said. "Isn't that what helps, Father Cam?"

"Sometimes I want to do more, Cork. I need to do more. I think about that girl, the dead girl, Louise. I can't help feeling that I let her down, that there was more I should have done."

"Like what?" Liam asked.

"I should have taken her in. Given her shelter. Helped her find her way. Kept her from . . . from the wolves."

"Cam—"

"And not just her. I see the inequities, the injustice all around me here. And I think, hell, all I do is pray. But there has to be more."

Tears gathered along the lower rims of the priest's eyes, and a wet pearl rolled down through the char of his left cheek. "I'm thinking of leaving, Liam."

"Aurora?"

"The priesthood."

"Cam, that's pretty drastic."

"I went to Henry Meloux a couple of days ago, seeking his advice."

"You went to Mr. Meloux for advice?" Cork said. "But you're the one people come to for that."

"I don't have all the answers, Cork. Sometimes I wonder if I have any."

"Henry suggested the fasting?" Liam said.

Father Cam nodded. "I went to Still Island."

Iron Lake was dotted with small islands. Liam knew the one the priest had just mentioned. He'd heard the Anishinaabe call it Bizaan, which meant "peace" or "stillness." It was said to be a place for contemplation.

"I built myself a fire, took the char, covered my face. For more than a day I fasted and prayed." He shook his head. "Finally, I had to come back. Responsibilities here. But I still have no answers. I keep asking, Why me? What is it you want of me, God? How do I serve you here if my prayers are useless? How do I serve these people who need so much?"

Liam looked at his son and tried to imagine what Cork must

be feeling. When Liam was a kid, he'd believed priests operated on a level elevated above others, called to a higher purpose because of some profound inner strength. He understood the truth of human frailty now, a lesson taught in the war and later in the uniform of a policeman. His son's journey hadn't brought Cork to that place yet. But as the tears streamed down Father Cam's cheeks, Liam suspected that the foundation of so much of his son's understanding was beginning to crumble, and there was nothing a father could do to change that.

"You were in the war, Cam," Liam said. "Me, too. I don't know about you, but somewhere along the way, I lost sight of the why of it, the big picture, I guess you'd say. I did what I did, things that to this day weigh heavily on me, because it was what was expected of me, what I expected of myself. I soldiered on. When I think too much on what I did then, and the darkness comes over me, I comfort myself with something Henry once told me. He said we all stumble in the dark, but that's why the Great Mystery gave us voices, so that we can call out, seeking others in that dark. And we were given hands so that we can reach out to help one another. Alone, the darkness swallows us. But together, we help each other through. So, when things seem bleakest, I tell myself to soldier on. I try to remind myself to call out. I do my best to be ready to offer a hand." He reached out and rested his palm on the man's arm. "You have a strong hand, Cam, and a voice clear in the darkness. No one can tell you what to do, but it would be a loss to this community if you tossed in the towel."

The priest didn't reply.

"Whatever you decide to do," Liam said, "for God's sake wash your face first. Right now, you could scare a goblin."

The priest walked with them back to his office. Before they parted, he said, "Thanks for the hand, Liam. Still a lot of thinking to do."

"Isn't there always?" Liam said. Then, "God be with you, Father."

Outside in the warm night air, Cork said, "You didn't ask him any of the questions I thought you were going to."

Liam paused under the stars. Above him, the pale Milky Way spread across the night sky like a bridal veil. "Do you think I should have?"

"No," Cork said. "He didn't have anything to do with killing Louise LaRose."

"That's what I think, too."

"What now?"

"Now we go home. It's been a long day, Son."

Cork lay in bed that night thinking about what he'd witnessed in the little chapel at St. Agnes. There was so much he was trying to make sense of. The priest who wasn't a killer but had still taken a tumble from the high pedestal Cork had set him on. The Church itself, because if those who were ordained to be the eyes, the hands, the heart of God on earth were only human, what hope was there? And especially his father. Liam O'Connor attended Mass most Sundays when duty didn't call him away, but Cork had never had the sense that he was a true believer. He'd seemed to practice his religion in a dutiful but not particularly devoted fashion, a man going through the motions. The simple, heartfelt benediction he'd offered the suffering priest—"God be with you"—was a ray of light for Cork, illuminating something important, adding another piece to the puzzle of this man who was his father.

CHAPTER 50

The next day was Friday, an evening Liam O'Connor always looked forward to. There was a comforting ritual to Friday nights. Dilsey usually came for supper. After dishes were done, after Cork had returned from whatever outing had called to him late in the day, and after Liam had finally shed his khaki uniform in favor of something more casual, Colleen made popcorn. Then all of the O'Connors settled in to watch their usual Friday night television lineup: *Route 66, The Twilight Zone,* and *The Alfred Hitchcock Hour.* So far north, depending on the weather, the screen could be pretty fuzzy, and Liam had to work constantly at adjusting the rabbit-ears antenna on their Motorola. But that night the images were perfect.

They'd just launched into *The Twilight Zone* when Jackson, who'd settled himself at Cork's feet, lifted his head and let out a low growl. Almost immediately, a hard knocking came at the front door. Liam shot up from the sofa, switched the porch light on, and opened the door.

Oscar Manydeeds stood there, gripping Leroy Kingbird by the arm. Kingbird was a high school kid from the rez who'd given

Liam worries in the past. On the other side of Kingbird stood Billy Downwind. Liam opened the screen door. "What is it, Oscar?"

"Our thief." Manydeeds shoved the kid forward. "Billy tracked him down."

"You broke into the horse barn, Leroy?"

The kid lowered his gaze and said nothing.

"Tell him," Manydeeds said gruffly.

"Yeah, we broke in," the kid said. "Me and Goose."

"Goose?" Liam said.

"Hector St. John," Manydeeds said. "His cousin. Kinda floats between the rez and Duluth these days. He's in Duluth right now."

"You stole things?"

The kid nodded.

"Did you steal drugs?"

"We took stuff we thought could give us a good time."

"You used the drugs yourselves?"

Leroy gave his head a shake. "Goose took the stuff down to Duluth. Said he could sell it there for some good money."

"He took all of it?"

The kid shrugged. "We tried a little. Felt too weird."

Manydeeds put a hand on the kid's shoulder and dug his fingers in deep. "If you're lying—"

"I'm not," the kid said, his face squeezed in pain. "I swear."

"What do you think, Oscar?" Liam said.

"I think he knows what I'll do if I find out he's lying."

"I ain't lying."

"You want me to arrest him, Oscar?"

"Leave him to me."

"What about Hector St. John?"

"I'll take care of him, too."

Liam stood a moment, considering the proposition, then gave a nod. "We done here?"

"For now," Manydeeds said. "Unless you have anything for me?"

"Nothing new," Liam said. "When I do, I'll let you know." Then he turned to Billy. "You tracked him down?"

"Yeah," Billy said.

"How?"

"I knew who to ask."

Liam studied Billy Downwind a long moment, wondering if there was something more that he wasn't saying. Finally he said, "Thank you."

When the porch was cleared, Liam closed the door. He turned, found Cork standing there, and said, "It's always about eliminating possibilities. Come on. The popcorn's getting cold."

"So?" Dilsey said when they returned to the living room.

"Oscar found the kids who stole his pentobarbital. Kids from the rez."

"Who?" When Liam told her, she said, "No fathers, those boys. What will you do with them?"

"That's up to Oscar."

"He has no sons," Dilsey said, and Liam could see that she was turning something over in her head. "Maybe he'll step up to the plate, give those boys some guidance." She worked her tongue at some popcorn stuck in her teeth and added, "I think I'll talk to him about that."

"What about your investigation?" Colleen said. "Does this help?"

Liam settled himself back into his easy chair. "I've got some thinking to do." And he left it at that.

The next morning, after Cork had gone to deliver his papers, Liam sat at the kitchen table with his coffee. He hadn't slept much in the night, arranging and rearranging all the pieces of the puzzle that held the answer to the deaths of Big John and Louise LaRose. There seemed to be so many pieces still missing. He'd been sure that Duncan MacDermid had killed Big John, and he'd been certain why. But the pentobarbital had changed his thinking. He was beginning to believe that Big John had been murdered because he knew who killed the girl. But why the girl had been killed, he had no idea. And no idea either who'd done it.

There was a small knock at the door to the mud porch and Joe Meese poked his head in.

"Saw the light."

"Coffee, Joe?"

"You betcha."

"Help yourself."

Joe pulled a mug from the cupboard, filled it from the pot on the stove, and sat down with Liam at the table. Liam told him about the visit from Oscar Manydeeds the evening before.

"Kids," Joe said, shaking his head. "One of the things a pharmacist always worries about is kids getting their hands on drugs they think'll give them a good high. End up killing them instead. They were lucky, those two boys. Pentobarbital is nothing to mess around with. You talk to Cy yet about that list he got from the vet?"

"Not yet."

"He spent the whole day knocking on doors across Tamarack County." Joe shook his head. "Nada."

"But somebody had pentobarbital, somebody with a reason to want Big John dead."

"Maybe you should talk to Doctor Dave, see if he has any other ideas."

Liam said, "I've got a couple of other interviews I want to do today, folks who might have had contact with the girl. While I'm at it, I'll drop by the vet clinic."

Joe sat, turning his coffee mug idly, round and round on the table, until Liam said, "Something on your mind, Joe? Maybe what brought you here this morning?"

"Okay, you're in charge of this investigation."

"But?"

"We never tried to find the place where the girl was killed."

"And you're thinking there might be evidence there?"

"Yeah. Maybe something that'd tell us who it was. The only thing that makes sense is that whoever killed Manydeeds did it because he saw something he shouldn't have. I think he knew who killed the girl."

"I understand, Joe. I've been thinking the same thing. But have you ever been out to Moose Lake?"

The deputy shook his head.

"Really big body of water. The Ojibwe call it Naabe-Mooz. Means 'bull moose' because it's like an antler, with all kinds of inlets sprouting off the main body. I don't know where we'd even begin to look."

"Where'd they find her?"

"Near the outlet to Spider Creek. But if there's any current in the lake, it would have pushed her body in that direction. And there's no telling when the ropes that held her under slipped off, how far her body might have drifted. We're a small department and we've got other fish to fry."

"I'll go."

Liam turned and found Cork standing in the kitchen threshold. Jackson trotted past him and went to his water bowl in the corner.

"How long have you been there, Son?"

"Long enough to know that somebody should be going out to Moose Lake. I'll go."

"I don't think so."

"Why not? I know the way. I've gone there lots of times with Billy Downwind and Big John and with my Scout troop. And I wouldn't go alone. I'd take Billy and Jorge with me."

"And where would you look?"

"There are lots of places where I've camped. Dad, I want to help."

Joe piped in, "Like I said, Liam, whoever took her in had to have camped somewhere. What could it hurt?"

What could it hurt? As a father, Liam could think of a thousand things that might go wrong. But he looked at his son's earnest face and he understood the impulse, Cork's need to feel as if he was doing something, anything that might be of some use. Hell, he felt the same way. And, now that the thought had come into Cork's head, maybe it would be better to let him go than have him moping around, resentful and fuming because his father had held him back. In truth, Cork was a far more experienced canoeist and camper than Liam, with a bounty of wilderness trips already under his belt. Moose Lake wasn't that far away, and he'd have his two friends, also experienced in the wilderness, with him.

"Two conditions," Liam said. "One, Billy and Jorge have to agree to go with you."

"I know they will."

"And two, your mother has to sign off on this."

"Mom? Why?"

"Because I said so. And because if I let you go without asking her, she'd skin me alive."

Cork gave a reluctant nod.

"Just one day," Liam said. "I'll give you one day out there."

"An overnighter," Cork said. "We'll go out today, stay the night, and be back late tomorrow."

Nothing would come from the expedition, Liam was pretty sure. But so often that summer he'd seen in his son's eyes a look of confusion, of defeat. Now there was fire in them, and Liam didn't want once again to be the one who smothered that hopeful flame.

"It's a deal," he said.

CHAPTER 51

The Crooked Pine opened at eleven A.M. When Ben Svenson turned on the neon Hamm's Beer light in the window and unlocked, Liam and Joe Meese were inside the door even before the man had a chance to take two steps back toward the bar. Svenson turned and blinked at the glare of morning sunlight that burst in along with the two men. "What the—?"

"Morning, Ben," Liam said. "We need to ask you a few questions, if you don't mind."

Svenson opened his arms wide toward the empty bar. "I've got a business to open here, Sheriff."

"Won't take long," Liam said.

Svenson looked unhappy, but then again he usually did.

"I gotta get the register set up. You boys have a seat."

Svenson went behind the bar and Liam and Joe took stools.

Liam said, "The Ojibwe girl who died out at Moose Lake, you knew her, right?"

"Knew her? Wouldn't say that. She hung around for a while till I ran her off. Hitting up customers, trying to cadge drinks, spare change, cigarettes."

"Pretty desperate kid, do you think?"

"Probably. Hell, she was Indian and a runaway."

"Did she look hungry?"

"Looked thin, I guess."

"Did she ever offer you anything in exchange for alcohol or food or maybe spare change?"

"Offer me anything?" Svenson glanced up from the opened register drawer, then mustered a dramatic look of shock. "Like sex?"

"Like sex."

"Sheriff, you got me all wrong if you think I'd do anything like that."

"I wasn't accusing you, Ben. Just asking if she offered."

"No, hell no. No way."

"All right. Any idea if she hit on any customers in that way?"

"I suppose she could have."

"Any of them ever say anything to you?"

"Not that I recall."

"Didn't complain?"

"Well, come to think of it, maybe a few."

"Anyone in particular you remember?"

"That was a while ago now. Couldn't give you a name."

"How long would you say she hung around here before you ran her off?"

"How the hell should I know. A day or two or three, I don't know."

"Got any Four Roses?"

"What?"

"Four Roses. The whiskey Duncan MacDermid used to be so fond of. Him and Big John Manydeeds."

"Sure." He reached to the liquor shelf that ran the length of the wall in back of the bar and pulled down a bottle. "Care for a shot, boys? On the house."

"On duty, Ben. Do you keep much of that in stock?"

"Some. As much as I keep anything, I suppose."

"I'm wondering if I could see the receipts for say the last couple of months of your purchases of Four Roses."

"What the hell for?"

"You told Deputy Meese here that you bought a couple of cases for Duncan MacDermid recently. You told him MacDermid liked to give it out to his mine supervisors."

"Yeah?"

"So, I'm just asking if I could see the receipt for that liquor. I assume someone signed for it. If not MacDermid, then his wife or one of his people at the mine?"

"Hell, you want me to drop everything and go on a scavenger hunt through all my receipts for the last couple of months."

"That's exactly what I want, Ben."

"No way I can do that right now, Sheriff. Like I said, I got a business to run."

Liam looked around the empty bar. "Not much business at the moment. But I'll tell you what. Just hand over all your receipts to Joe here. He'll sit at a table and go through them himself."

"Look, sometimes I'm not as careful as I should be with my record keeping, okay? I don't even know if I've got that receipt. You could go through the whole damn pile, and it could end up just a waste of your time."

"You have the time to waste, don't you, Joe?"

"Nothing on my docket the rest of the morning, Sheriff."

"Hell's bells," Svenson said, but made no move to get the receipts.

"Two more questions for you, Ben, before I leave you and Deputy Meese to sort through those receipts. Here's the first one. Were you a Boy Scout?"

"What?"

"Were you a Boy Scout, here in Aurora?"

"Yeah."

For a man who wasn't doing much behind his bar, Svenson was sweating up a storm.

Liam said, "Here's my second question: How does a man drink a case of Four Roses without leaving any fingerprints on the bottles?"

Doctor David Svenson smiled at Liam as he came up the hallway from one of the examining rooms. An old woman accompanied him. Liam knew her. Astrid Lankinen. She was nearly deaf and had the disposition of a badger. She was a woman with a whole list of complaints, mostly about what people in her neighborhood should not be doing after dark, which she regularly called in to the Sheriff's Department. In her arms, she cradled a cat, gray and with mysterious and unfriendly blue eyes. When they reached the reception area, Doctor Dave said, "Roosevelt should be just fine, Astrid. Sharon will help you with the bill."

The woman buried her old, pinched face in the deep fur of her cat and whispered a couple of endearments, then walked to the front desk without acknowledging Liam at all.

"Any luck with that list I gave your deputy?" the vet asked.

"Nothing so far, Dave."

"He wasn't clear on why he needed it. What's up?"

"There was a break-in at the stables out in Brandywine. Some pentobarbital was stolen. We're just doing some tracking."

"Well, glad I could help."

"Could I ask you a hypothetical question?"

"Sure, why not?"

"What would happen to a man if he were shot with a tranquilizer dart?"

Doctor Dave laughed. "What?"

"Like I said, just a hypothetical question."

"Whoever shot the dart would be in big trouble, I can tell you that."

"But it would be possible, right? And it wouldn't necessarily kill him."

"I suppose so."

"Just one more question, Dave. Were you a Boy Scout?"

CHAPTER 52

When his mother drove to Allouette to fetch Grandma Dilsey so they could pick the last of the season's blueberries, Cork rode along. The whole way, he laid out his case, explaining to her what he wanted to do and why. She told him that she believed it was an exercise in futility and that she wasn't at all on board with him going into the Boundary Waters without an adult along. But Grandma Dilsey, when she heard about it, had a different take.

"Ask me, and I'd say Big John's spirit has been guiding him, Colleen. Who are we to stand in the way of such a big spirit? And what harm can it do?"

His mother argued a bit more but in the end, couldn't stand against both Cork and his grandmother, and she finally gave her permission, but only if, as his father had insisted, Billy Downwind and Jorge went with him.

He spent an hour tracking down Billy, who, it turned out, was helping his uncle put a new oil pump in Oscar Manydeeds's pieced-together pickup.

"*Boozhoo*, Cork," Billy said, His hands were covered in black grease, but he was grinning ear to ear.

Manydeeds lifted his head from the bowels of the truck. His face was streaked with grease in a way that reminded Cork of war paint. "What's up, little sheriff?"

Cork explained what he intended to do, then said, "I need to find out where exactly Mr. Kingfisher and Mr. Bright found the girl's body."

"Just ask 'em," Manydeeds said. Then he seemed to understand Cork's hesitancy. "I'll go with you."

He poured gas from a gallon container over his hands and over Billy's, and the two mechanics used a dirty rag to wipe away a good deal of the caked grease. Manydeeds led the way to an old trailer, which stood on the north edge of the little community. As they approached, a dog hidden in the high grass of the yard leaped to its feet and set up a furious barking. Manydeeds seemed not surprised at all, and simply stood waiting, as if for something he knew would happen.

The door of the trailer opened, and in the entry was Sherman Kingfisher, a broad-chested man with a face that in its color and with its multitude of scars seemed hacked from the trunk of a cedar. He eyed the three arrivals without comment, but to his dog he said, "*Ondaas*, Animikee."

Cork wasn't at all fluent in the language of his ancestors, but he knew that what the man had said was, "Come here, Thunder." And because of the racket the dog had been making, he understood the reason for its name.

Oscar Manydeeds conversed with Kingfisher in Ojibwemowin. Cork understood almost none of it. Finally, Kingfisher leveled a hard look at Cork and said, "She was floatin' not far off Eagle Point. Know where that is?"

Cork said he did.

"Doesn't mean that's where she went into the water. There's current there, flowing out of an underground spring north of the point, so she coulda gone in somewhere up that way, I suppose."

Cork waited to see if Kingfisher had more to say. He didn't. Cork said, *"Migwech. Chi migwech."*

Kingfisher looked at Manydeeds and said, "Joining us for poker tomorrow night?"

"I'll be there," Manydeeds said. "Bringing my lucky rabbit's foot."

Kingfisher finally cracked a smile. "You'll need the whole damn rabbit, the way you play."

Back at the pickup truck, Manydeeds said to his nephew, "Guessing you'd rather go with Cork than muck around here."

"Yeah," Billy said. "Okay?"

"Give you a lift back to town?" Manydeeds asked Cork.

Cork explained that he'd arranged that with his mother.

Manydeeds said to his nephew, "Let your mom know what you're up to."

"Could you do that?" Billy said. "We gotta go right away."

Manydeeds gave a wave of his hand and said, *"Baamaapii,"* which meant "Until later."

Once in Aurora, the boys headed straight to Glengarrow in search of Jorge. No one answered Cork's knock at the door on the second story of the carriage house. He could see Nicholas Skinner's red Thunderbird parked before the big house and thought that maybe Jorge and his mother were inside with Mrs. MacDermid and the lawyer.

Jorge answered the bell and put a finger to his lips. "She's going to sell," he said in a whisper and waved them in.

The adults were in the expansive living room. Nick Skinner sat next to Mrs. MacDermid, hunched forward over a bunch of legal documents that lay on a coffee table made from a great slab of some polished stone. Jorge's mother hovered in the background near a serving table that held a delicate teapot and teacups. She glanced at her son when he appeared with his friends and gave her head a little shake. Jorge stopped where he was, with Cork and Billy at his back.

"And this," Nick Skinner was saying, as he slid a document toward Mrs. MacDermid, "is the agreement that authorizes me to act as your agent in the sale and in the disposition of all holdings here at Glengarrow."

"Where will she go?" Cork whispered into Jorge's ear.

Jorge put a finger to his lips and signaled the two boys to follow him. They returned to the huge entryway, where Cork asked a different question: "Where will you go?"

"She told Mr. Skinner she wanted to sell everything, but that we were to be allowed to live in the carriage house free of charge for as long as we want."

"You can do that?" Cork said.

Jorge shrugged. "I guess. Nick said he would write it into whatever deal he made for the property."

"That's great," Cork said.

"I don't know," Jorge said. "Mom's still out of a job."

"Will she marry Mr. Skinner?"

Instead of answering, Jorge said, "What are you guys doing here?"

Cork explained his plan to find the place on Moose Lake where the girl had been killed.

"It's a big lake," Jorge said.

"We've got an idea where to begin," Billy said. "You in?"

"I have to clear it with my mom. How long you going to be out there?"

"My dad says no more than one night. We'll leave right after we've delivered our papers this afternoon."

"Wait here." Jorge headed back toward the living room. When he returned a few minutes later, his mother was with him and so was Mr. Skinner, carrying a shiny leather briefcase.

"Hey, guys," the lawyer said.

"Is it true, Mr. Skinner?" Cork asked.

"What?"

"Mrs. MacDermid is selling Glengarrow?"

"It's true. In my opinion, it's the best thing she can do. She needs to get away from here and start over." He said it gravely, then he smiled. "So, I understand you guys are planning an overnighter at Moose Lake."

"Yes, sir."

"Lots of lakes in Tamarack County easier to get to. What's so interesting about Moose Lake?"

"Not a lot of people go there, so we pretty much have the place to ourselves." It was lame, Cork knew, but he saw no reason to give away their true purpose to Mr. Skinner. Then he said to Jorge's mother, "Is it okay if Jorge goes with us?"

"Please, Mom," Jorge said.

"It is such a big wilderness," she replied.

"We've been to Moose Lake with our Scout troop lots of times," Cork said. "We won't get lost. And my dad's okay with it."

"Please, Mom," Jorge said again. "It's just one night. Please."

She studied her son a long while, then put her hand to his cheek. "Go. But you be careful."

"I will," Jorge said.

Cork said, "Come on, guys. We've got papers to deliver first."

CHAPTER 53

Liam rang the bell and waited. He could hear music drifting through the screen door, but it seemed a bit distant. He rang again and still got no answer. He left the porch, circled the house, and came to a gate in a privacy fence of cedarwood planks. The music, at the moment Neil Sedaka singing "Breaking Up Is Hard to Do," came from the backyard on the other side of the fence. Most folks in Aurora, if they wanted some privacy, used lilac hedges. But the big house, the privacy fence, the red Cadillac in the driveway made it clear that Doctor Dave had money. His vet practice was pretty lucrative, Liam figured. And maybe he'd made some savvy investments as well.

Liam opened the gate. Moira Svenson reclined in a chaise lounge. Next to her was a little table on which sat a tall glass containing ice, some red concoction, a white straw, and a little blue paper umbrella. A black transistor radio lay next to the glass. Moira wore a yellow polka-dot bikini, just like in the song, and a yellow straw hat with a wide brim that shaded her face. He could tell by the sheen on her skin that she'd oiled herself. Or maybe it was simply a thin layer of sweat. She was leafing idly through a copy of *Life*.

"Moira?" he called, but not too loud, hoping not to startle her.

She turned her head and gazed at him without apparent surprise.

"Liam," she said lazily. "Or is it Sheriff, since you're in uniform?"

"I rang the doorbell. No one answered."

"I heard it. I thought you were the Fuller Brush man. Or one of those dreadful people with some religious tract."

"I wanted to talk to you for a few minutes." He approached her and stood beside the chaise lounge. "I just spoke with Dave. At the clinic."

"Did he smell of dog? He always smells of dog." She gazed up at him, her eyes no longer shaded by the brim of her hat, and she squinted a little, the corners of both eyes showing tiny crow's-feet. "I'd ask you to sit but there's just this." She touched the arm of her chair. Then she patted the green cushion at the edge of her thigh. "You can sit here, if you like."

"Thanks, no. I'll stand." He could smell the coconut scent of whatever she'd used to oil herself. It was not unpleasant at all. The station she was listening to on her transistor radio eased into the soft chords of "Blue Velvet."

Moira shaded her eyes and looked up at the sun. "It's hot out here. Shall we . . . take this inside?"

Without waiting for an answer, she turned off the radio, picked up her drink, and led the way through French doors into the dining room. Compared to the bright sun in the backyard, the house seemed dark and was much cooler.

"Can I get you something to drink?"

"Thanks, no."

"Not even a Coke?"

"I'm fine, Moira. This shouldn't take long."

"Oh?" She put her transistor radio and her drink on the mahogany dining room table, then took off her big hat and shook her hair so that it fell loose over her shoulders. "Liam O'Connor," she said and smiled at him. "That's a fine Irish name. Did you know that my maiden name is O'Malley?"

"I didn't."

"Moira Mary O'Malley. Now there's a name with a lilt to it, don't you think? But what do I do? I marry a Swede. A rather cold race, if you ask me. Compared to us Irish at any rate." When Liam didn't respond, she said, "Svenson. Mrs. David Svenson. Sounds cold. Dead fish cold." She picked up her drink and put her lips around the straw and lifted her eyes to Liam and took a long sip. She lowered her drink, ran her index finger with its polished red nail slowly around the rim of the glass. "I voted for you last November."

"I appreciate your confidence. I need to ask you a question, Moira."

"I'm all ears, Sheriff."

"Was your husband gone the weekend after the Fourth of July?"

She gave a little sniff of disdain. "He took off on his annual fishing expedition with the other two Musketeers."

"Musketeers?'

"That's what they call themselves. Him and his brother and the other one. The Three Musketeers."

"The other one?"

"The lawyer. What's his name?"

"Nick Skinner?"

"That's him. Buddies since they were kids. Musketeers? More like Mouseketeers, if you ask me."

"Do you know where they went?"

"I never pay any attention. All I care about is that for a while I don't have him around here smelling of dog. On the other hand, he usually comes back from his expeditions smelling of fish."

"Did he smell of fish this time?"

"As a matter of fact, no. And he came back early, after only a day or so. I figured the fishing must have been bad this year. I'd planned a big backyard party in his absence, but he made me cancel it."

"Did he seem different to you when he came back?"

"Different?"

"Upset. Nervous. Difficulty sleeping."

"We sleep in different rooms, Sheriff. He has his bedroom and I have mine and I have no idea how he sleeps. Now, may I ask you a question? It's rather personal."

"You can always ask."

She took a step nearer to him and looked seductively into his eyes. "I've heard that policemen use sex as a way to deal with the stress of their job. Is that true?"

"I can't answer for policemen in general."

"I was hoping you wouldn't."

"I take pleasure in my family, Moira. My wife and my son. They provide me all the solace and stress relief I need."

Her face changed. Her whole body for that matter. She stepped back. "Lucky you, Liam." She said this with such sincerity and sadness that he felt moved beyond pity.

"You've been helpful, Moira. Thank you."

As Liam headed to the county courthouse, he thought about Mrs. David Svenson. Moira Mary O'Malley. He wondered if she'd married a different man, would she be a different woman? Was it her marriage that had shaped her into such a needful human being? He thought about Colleen. Sometimes they butted heads, and later would laughingly blame it on the fiery Irish blood that flowed in their veins. But Colleen also had Ojibwe blood in her, and despite all the angry fire she sometimes summoned, she could also be quiet and soothing, able to spread over them both a profound sense of calm and deep contentment. He tried to imagine sleeping in a separate bed, and it left him feeling sad and lonely. And in that moment, he was profoundly grateful for his marriage and all that had come to him because of it.

He'd radioed ahead, and when he arrived at the Sheriff's Department, Deputy Joe Meese was waiting for him.

"Where's Cy?" Liam asked.

"Still up in the county clerk's office, looking for what you wanted."

They stepped into Liam's office, he closed the door, and they sat down.

"What did you find at the Crooked Pine?" Liam asked.

Joe set a slip of paper on the desk. "A receipt for the purchase of two cases of Four Roses from a distributor in Duluth. The purchase was made in person, signed by Ben Svenson himself, and the date matches the general timing of Manydeeds's killing. There was no receipt confirming Svenson's sale of the cases to anyone else."

"What did he have to say about that?"

"Poor record keeping. But get this. I talked to the barmaid, Sylvia Jonsdottir. She told me a different story than her boss about his relationship with Louise LaRose. Apparently, Svenson was much friendlier with her than he let on. And get this. Svenson was gone for three days about the time Manydeeds was killed. He had his backup bartender running things."

Cy Borkman knocked on the door and joined them.

"Did you find anything upstairs?" Liam asked him.

"Just like you thought, Sheriff. That hotel plan Skinner's been pushing? He paid a lot for the land. I mean a lot. But except for the architectural drawings, that's as far as the project's gone."

"And MacDermid's the reason for the holdup?" Liam asked.

"His name's not on any of the documents, but if you ask me, it's sure his handwriting all over every denial for some permit or other by the county."

"Why would MacDermid interfere?"

"Got me," Cy said. "But if I was Nick Skinner, I'd be ready to kill the man."

Liam took a couple of minutes to fill him in on what Joe had discovered at the Crooked Pine, then told them both about his conversation with Doctor Dave's wife. Then he said, "I ran into Skinner just before MacDermid was killed, and he told me he couldn't vouch for MacDermid being at the guest cottage while someone was killing Big John Manydeeds. It seems pretty clear why now. The Three Musketeers were off in the woods, hoping to have a good time with Louise LaRose."

"And something went wrong out there," Joe said.

"And Manydeeds saw it?" Cy said.

"Or saw enough that they thought they had to kill him," Liam said. "I'm not sure why they waited to ambush him on Spider Creek. But it would be easy enough for the three of them to cart his body to Lightning Strike and set up a fake suicide."

"Makes sense," Joe said.

"But a lot of holes in the story that still need filling," Liam said. "I think I should bring in Doctor Dave."

"And question him?" Cy said.

"Or, as we used to say when I was a cop in Chicago, sweat him."

CHAPTER 54

Iron Lake was divided into two halves. From a great height, it would have looked like the impression a man's buttocks might have made if he'd sat in soft mud. In fact, the Ojibwe told the story of the trickster spirit Nanaboozhoo falling from the sky and landing unceremoniously in exactly that position, forming the two, almost equally rounded impressions that had filled with water to form the lake. The northeastern section lay entirely inside the reservation. It took the boys nearly two hours to canoe from Aurora to the mouth of Spider Creek.

They entered the stream and paddled the O'Connors' Old Town canoe through the channels that spiderwebbed the marsh. All around them rose cattails and bulrushes and tamaracks. In the open areas, they passed through duckweed and waterlilies and spatterdock, and startled a couple of herons, who took flight, their long bodies graceful against the blue sky. It was quite late but still hot, and the boys swatted mosquitoes and blackflies and talked little.

The sun had dropped near the horizon and the shadows of the pines were long and broad by the time they finally reached the place where the water of Spider Creek spilled from Moose Lake. It flowed out in a series of small cascades, which required them to leave the stream and portage the canoe a hundred yards up a path to the lake. They shouldered their packs and lifted the canoe over their heads. Cork took the bow end, cradling the gunnels on the palms of his hands. Jorge took the stern. Billy walked ahead carrying the paddles.

The path veered south a bit, away from the rocky cascades, and the ground became mushy from drainage. Near the top of the portage, only a dozen yards from the lake, Billy stopped and bent down to study the path.

"Somebody's been here. Not long ago," he said.

"How do you know?" Jorge asked.

"Footprints." Billy pointed at the soft ground ahead of them. "The prints are still clear and still wet. Not much different from mine, see?"

"Bigger though," Cork said. "Not Boy Scouts. Ojibwe?"

"Hard to tell. We'll probably spot 'em on the lake, then we can see for sure."

They finished the portage and set the canoe in the water of Moose Lake. They were on a narrow, rocky inlet, but a quarter of a mile east, the lake opened up, and the boys could see its broad blue expanse stretching for miles. Billy took the bow, Cork the stern, and Jorge sat in the middle with the packs. Cork shoved them off, and they began down the inlet with green pines walling them in on either side, the sun descending at their backs, and before them Naabe-Mooz, waiting to be explored.

Liam caught Sharon Crane, Doctor Dave's assistant, just as she was leaving the North Star Veterinary Clinic. Her Ford Galaxy was the only car in the lot.

"Doctor Svenson went home a couple of hours ago," she told him. She looked past him toward her Galaxy, and it was clear to Liam that she wanted to be off. Saturday night, and she probably had a big evening planned. "He got a phone call from his brother and left."

"Did he say where he was going?"

"He didn't. He just said to cancel the rest of his appointments."

Liam returned to his cruiser and radioed for Cy Borkman to pick up Ben Svenson at the Crooked Pine and for Joe Meese to locate Nick Skinner and bring him in, too. Then he headed to the house with the cedarwood privacy fence.

Where the inlet opened onto the broad waters of Moose Lake, Billy signaled Cork to pull to shore at a rocky finger of land called Eagle Point. Cork knew it was the first place on the lake where someone might camp, the easiest to reach if you didn't want to go out onto the big water. He'd made camp there a few times with Billy and Big John, though Billy's uncle usually preferred to go much farther onto Naabe-Mooz because the inlet was like a main road, and anyone coming onto or off the lake had to pass there. Big John preferred one of the more isolated spots on almost any of the islands. But the truth was that when they'd camped on the point, they almost never saw anyone. If they did, it was usually someone they knew from the rez, whom Big John would invite to join them.

Billy disembarked first, stepping gingerly from the bow onto a flat, gray slab of stone. He knelt and steadied the canoe as the others got out, and then the boys together slid the tip of the canoe carefully onto the stone to secure it while they explored the point.

From the jumble of rocks along the waterline, Eagle Point rose ten feet above the lake and flattened out in a clear, grassy space approximately ten yards in diameter. It was edged with a cluster of aspen whose white trunks stood as straight as the pickets of a fence. At the center of this small clearing lay a circle ringed with stone and filled with ash and char from past fires. The boys spread out and walked the campsite slowly.

"What exactly are we looking for?" Jorge said.

"Anything out of place," Cork said.

The light was fading, and the boys hunched close to the ground. Jorge found a bottle opener, but it was so rusted that they figured it had been there much longer than a few weeks. Still, Cork put it in his pocket because you never knew. Near the tree line, Billy found brass casings from three spent rifle cartridges. Grass had grown around them and they were filled with dirt. So, like the rusted bottle opener, the boys figured they'd been there a good long while. Still, Cork collected them.

When they were satisfied that there was nothing more that might be useful at Eagle Point, Cork said, "Okay, now to Pine Island. We can camp there."

Jorge looked at the sky. "It'll be close to dark by the time we hit Pine Island. Why don't we make camp here? Get started first thing in the morning."

"Pine Island's only twenty minutes away," Cork said.

"I'm tired," Jorge said. "And I'm hungry."

Billy said, "He's right. We can get an early start tomorrow."

Cork gave in because the truth was that he was tired, too. It had been a long day for them all. And by the time they set up camp and got a fire going to cook some supper, it would be late.

They emptied the canoe of their gear and tipped it on the rocks so that it was secure for the night. They hadn't brought a tent, only a tarp for a lean-to in case of rain. They rolled their sleeping bags out on the grass and gathered wood for the fire. Cork cut shavings while Billy gathered dried pine needles and Jorge began to clear the char and ash from earlier fires, pushing the charcoal pieces toward the stones around the edge of the ring.

"What's this?" he said.

He held up a charred piece of fabric adorned with bright beads, some of which had partially melted.

"That's beadwork," Billy said. "Maybe from a shawl or a purse or a blouse."

Then Billy looked straight at Cork and said, "Louise LaRose?"

Liam could hear the loud music and the raised, angry voices long before he rang the Svensons' front doorbell. The voices stopped, but the music continued to blast. A moment later, the veterinarian appeared behind the screen door. He looked frazzled.

"Evening, Sheriff." He glanced back over his shoulder, then managed to find a polite but tentative smile to put on his face. "Were we being a bit too loud for the neighbors?"

"It's not that, Dave. I'd like to talk to you though."

The veterinarian ran a hand along his jaw and shook his head. "Not a good time, I'm afraid."

"And I'm afraid I'm going to have to insist."

From somewhere deeper in the house, Moira's voice lifted high above the blare of the music. "What'd he do? Rob a bank?"

"Couldn't this wait?" Doctor Dave said.

"No. And we can talk here, but it might be quieter at my office."

"Come on in, Sheriff," Moira called with drunken abandon. "The party's just getting started."

Doctor Dave weighed his choices and finally said, "Your office it is."

CHAPTER 55

"What were they doing in the fire?" Jorge asked.

The boys had raked their fingers through the burned remains in the fire ring and had found another piece of the partially burned, beaded fabric.

"Maybe whoever killed her was trying to get rid of the evidence." Cork had emptied the paper bag in which he'd packed four Snickers bars and now he put the charred pieces of fabric inside. "We'll take them back to my dad. He'll know what to do with them."

They built their fire for the evening, and Cork said, "I brought dehydrated eggs and Spam. And some biscuits. I'll need water for the eggs."

Billy volunteered to get the water and Cork gave him the pot from his Boy Scout mess kit. Because night was almost upon them, he gave his friend a flashlight as well. A dirt path sloped along the tree line from the campsite down to the shore, an easier access to the lake than trying to negotiate the rocks where the boys had landed and stowed their canoe. Billy started down the path, and Cork began taking the food from his pack.

"She was here," Jorge said, in a hushed voice. "This is where it happened."

Cork looked at the darkening campsite and at the great blackening body of the lake. The moon was not yet up, but a dome of moonglow showed where it would soon rise. The evening was still, the woods around them silent, the sense of something tragic palpable in the air.

"Yeah," Cork said, his voice hushed, too. "Think she had any idea what might happen?"

"She wouldn't have come if she did," Jorge said. "She must have trusted whoever she came with."

"Or she was just really desperate." Cork tried to imagine that level of desperation, but it was beyond him. His life had always been safe, always comfortable, always protected.

"Hey, guys!" Billy called from the lake. "Get over here!"

They found him bending far out above the water, the beam of his flashlight prying among the rocks just below the surface.

"What's up?" Cork asked.

"Look." Billy pointed.

Cork watched him sweep the beam of the flashlight across a dark crevice among the rocks beneath the surface of the water half a dozen feet from the shore. "What?" he said. "I don't see anything."

"There!" Billy jabbed the flashlight as if it were a stick he was using to poke into the crevice.

Cork saw it then, a flash of reflected light, a glimpse of gold.

"I can't reach it from here," Billy said.

"Hold the light steady," Jorge said. He kicked off his sneakers, pulled off his socks, rolled up his pant legs, and prepared to step into the lake.

The submerged rocks were sharp and slippery, and Cork cautioned, "Careful."

Jorge stepped gingerly, but even so, his foot turned and he went down with a splash. "Crap!" he yelled and tried to push himself up. Down he went again. This time Cork put out a hand and helped bring him upright.

"Can you reach it?" Billy asked.

Jorge bent slowly, still holding on to Cork's steadying hand, dug between the rocks, and came up with something, which he held under the beam of Billy's flashlight. "A necklace?"

"Kind of big for a necklace," Cork said.

It was a thick gold chain on which hung a gold medallion: an eagle with its wings spread, standing atop a globe, which was superimposed over an anchor.

"Marine Corps," Jorge said. "Eagle, globe, and anchor. My mom has a pin like that. My dad gave it to her."

"What's it doing here?" Billy said.

"Chain's broken," Jorge said. "Must've fallen off somebody."

All three boys exchanged knowing glances. It was Cork who spoke the words. "Her murderer."

Liam let the veterinarian sit alone in his office for half an hour before he and Joe Meese joined him. By then, Doctor Dave was already looking nervous and sweating profusely.

"Pentobarbital," Liam said. "I appreciate the list you gave my deputy of the folks around here who use it."

"No problem," Doctor Dave said.

Liam sat behind his desk with the veterinarian in a chair on the other side. Joe Meese leaned against the closed door behind Doctor Dave. Cy Borkman hadn't yet returned from his assignment to locate Nicholas Skinner.

"But you left one person off that list," Liam said.

"Oh?"

"Probably the one person in Tamarack County who uses it the most."

The vet waited. Liam didn't say anything. Finally the vet said, "Oh, you must mean me."

"You," Liam said.

"Well, of course. I just naturally assumed you understood that."

"If you wanted to put an animal to sleep, but not kill it, how would you do that, Dave?"

"There's a precise formulation, based on the size and weight of the animal."

"How about an animal that weighed, say, two hundred fifty pounds? A strong animal. Would that be a difficult formulation?"

"Not really."

"And what if the animal were dangerous and you couldn't get near it? How would you deliver the drug?"

"I'd probably put it in the animal's food."

"And if you needed to sedate the animal immediately?"

"I'd probably use a dart."

"Are you a pretty good shot?"

"Pretty good."

"Your wife told me you went fishing the weekend after the Fourth of July."

"That's right."

"Where'd you go?"

"Lake Superior. Out of Grand Marais."

"Fishing for salmon?"

"And steelhead. We fish for pretty much anything."

"We? You didn't go alone?"

"My brother and Nick Skinner went with me."

"An annual kind of outing for the three of you, Moira told me. How long do you stay?"

"Five or six days, usually."

"Any luck with the fishing this time around?"

The vet coughed, and the words came out dry and scratchy. "Not this time."

"Moira said you came back early. After only a day or so. The fishing must've been really bad."

"Yes."

"You go far out to catch salmon?"

"Usually."

"What kind of boat did you use?"

"Ben arranged for it. I don't know who supplied it."

"Ben would know though, right?"

The vet tried to answer but the words seemed to catch in his throat.

"Would you like some water, Dave?"

The vet nodded.

"In a minute. Where did you stay in Grand Marais?"

"A cabin somewhere on the shore."

"What cabin?"

"I . . . don't recall exactly."

"Ben made the arrangements?"

The vet nodded.

Liam put his forearms on his desk and leaned toward Doctor Dave. "So, if we followed up on that, we'd be able to find someone in Grand Marais who could verify the cabin and boat rental?"

"You'd . . ." The vet swallowed hard. "You'd have to talk to Ben."

"We'd like to talk to Ben, but he's not around at the moment. Any idea where he might be?"

Doctor Dave's eyes slid away from Liam. The vet stared down at the scarred and wounded top of Liam's desk and shook his head.

"You've known each other a long time, you and Ben and Nick Skinner. Since you were kids, is that right?"

"Yes."

"The Three Musketeers. One for all and all for one. I understand you were Boy Scouts together. Did you ever go with your troop up Spider Creek to Moose Lake?"

The vet coughed and, with the back of his hand, wiped at the sweat dripping from his brow. "That water," he said.

"In a minute. Your brother called you late this afternoon at the clinic."

After a long silence, during which the vet seemed to be waiting for Liam to go on, Doctor Dave swallowed and said, "He wanted some help with something."

Liam continued to wait.

"Some, you know, some . . ." The vet breathed heavily now and couldn't find his next words. His red Ban-Lon sport shirt was soaked through with sweat.

The air was humid, stifling. It would have been dead silent in Liam's small office except for the fast, shallow breathing of the man across the desk from him.

"Do you know how much Big John Manydeeds weighed?" Liam finally asked.

"I . . ." The vet put his fingers to his brow as if he were dizzy and his head needed steadying. "I . . . would guess two hundred and fifty pounds."

"That was before the crows and the maggots got to his body." When Liam spoke next, his voice was gentle, as if coaxing a frightened animal. "Where did you place the dart, Dave?"

The veterinarian swayed a little in his chair, and his blue eyes, when they gazed at Liam, seemed to be swimming.

"The dart, Dave. Where did you shoot Big John Manydeeds with the dart?"

Doctor Dave's face had gone the color of a cauliflower. He struggled to sit up straight, but his body wilted and seemed to melt into his chair. He looked at the sheriff in the way that Liam imagined people in the confessional might look at Father Cam.

Doctor Dave's words, when he finally offered them, were a guttural choking. "In the back," he said. And he began to cry.

CHAPTER 56

The fire lit their faces in shifting yellow hues, and the moon bathed the lake and everything around them in brilliant white. There was a slight breeze, and the boys could hear the gentle susurrus of waves lapping against the rocks on Eagle Point. They'd eaten in a subdued quiet, Cork for his part feeling a little dazed. He understood only too well that they were sitting where Louise LaRose had sat a month before, that the moon he was seeing gave the same light as the moon that had hung above her, perhaps on the night she'd been killed, if she'd been killed at night. Maybe she, too, had heard the soft lulling of the waves. She'd been like him, he thought, and like Jorge, and like Billy, just a kid with her whole life ahead of her. And then that life had ended. Ended brutally. She'd been just a victim before. Now, she was a person, and Cork felt a genuine sorrow, one he wanted to talk about but could not. So, like the other boys, he held to silence.

It was Billy who broke the spell. "Crumbs," he said.

Jorge said, "Huh?"

"Crumbs," Billy said. "It was what Henry Meloux told us. To follow the crumbs. This is where they brought us." He nodded toward Cork's backpack, into which they'd put the burned beaded fabric and the broken gold chain with its Marine insignia medallion. A thoughtful look came over his face. "If it hadn't got so late or if we decided to stay somewhere else tonight or if I didn't take the flashlight with me down to the lake, I wouldn't have seen that gold chain flashing in the water."

Jorge eyed him. "What're you saying?"

"Just that it's kinda strange how things worked out. Like we were supposed to find that stuff."

"My dad would call it due diligence," Cork told him. "We just followed a logical course, and this is where it took us."

"You're dad's a cop, and he's not Shinnob. Me, I'm thinking different," Billy said. "I'm thinking about my uncle. I'm thinking Big John had a hand in this. He wanted us to find that eagle, globe, and anchor. He was no Marine. He wanted us to know it wasn't him who killed her. And he wanted us to find his killer, too." Billy tossed a stick onto the fire. "Maybe now he can finally walk the Path of Souls."

"Not until we know who that gold chain belongs to," Cork said.

"Your dad can figure that out, can't he?" Jorge said.

"Maybe," Cork said. That didn't sound very hopeful, so he said, "Sure."

The flames were diminishing, and Jorge took a long stick from the wood they'd gathered and poked at the fire. As it came back to life, he said, "Who do you think that chain belongs to?"

Billy said, "It's solid gold. No Shinnob would wear something like that."

"Why?" Jorge asked.

"Waste of money," Billy said. "You could probably buy a refrigerator or something with what that chain cost. If I was going to spend a lot of money on something to wear, I'd buy a good pair of cowboy boots."

"Shit kickers?" Jorge said.

"Damn right. Tony Lamas," Billy said. "Girls, they'd go crazy for me."

"They'd have to be looking at your boots, not your face," Jorge said and laughed. "Me, I'd buy a Corvette, just like the one on *Route 66*. Chick magnet."

"You wouldn't be able to drive it till you're sixteen," Cork pointed out.

"Fifteen," Billy said. "But his mom would have to go with him. Some chick magnet." And this time it was Billy laughing.

After a while, Jorge said, "What's California like?"

"Cuz you might move there?" Billy said.

"Maybe."

"Too many people. You'd think nobody would notice you, but they stare. You'd think you wouldn't get lonely, but you do."

"Lots of other Indians from the reservation moved there, didn't they?" Jorge said.

"We never see them. My mom says that's what the government wants. To separate us so we can't be who we are. She doesn't want to go back. Me neither."

"What about your dad?"

Billy shrugged. "It's complicated."

"It sucks," Jorge said.

"It sucks," Cork agreed.

The night seemed suddenly bleaker and more oppressive, and Cork threw more wood onto the fire so that it blazed brightly.

"Scooter Grimes. On Eagle Point. With the lead pipe," Jorge said.

Billy stared at him. "Huh?"

"Like in Clue," Jorge said.

"That's sick," Billy said. Then he seemed to think about it. "But maybe Scooter Grimes. He's creepy and I heard he hates Indians. Won't let 'em pump gas at his station."

"I heard he drinks like a fish. And I heard his wife ran away with some preacher who came through town with a tent revival," Jorge said. "When Scooter tracked her down, he beat her and the preacher both and nearly killed them."

"My dad says that's not true," Cork told him. "And was Scooter a Marine?"

Neither of the other boys could answer that one.

"It was someone who knows how to come up Spider Creek," Cork reminded them. "And who was a Marine. And . . ."

"And what?" Jorge said.

Cork spoke slowly as he put his thoughts together. "Big John must've passed by here on his way into or out of Moose Lake and saw the killer with Louise. Whoever it was, that guy waited for him on Spider Creek, drugged him, took him to Lightning Strike, and strung him up. So, it was either someone strong enough to haul Big John around. Or . . ."

The other two boys waited.

"Or there was more than one," Cork concluded.

"One of them was for sure a Marine," Jorge said.

"And one had some of Uncle Oscar's horse-killing drug," Billy added.

"And they're bastard enough to kill a girl and try to sink her body in the lake," Cork said.

There was a long moment of silence as they all thought this over, then Jorge said, "But who?"

None of them had an answer for that one, and they sat staring into the fire. After a while, they talked about other things and let the fire die down to low flames, then finally rolled out their sleeping bags and lay under the stars.

Cork stared up at the Milky Way, which was half swallowed by the glow of the moon, and he thought about Louise LaRose. Life could be difficult on the rez, he knew, and even harder now that so many Shinnobs had left and gone to cities because the government had promised them jobs and a better life, and families and clans had been torn apart. Which, Grandma Dilsey maintained, was exactly the purpose of the Relocation Act. Alcohol had always been a problem, and it was hard to keep to the old ways. But Big John had broken free of the hold of booze and come back. Maybe Louise would have, too, if she'd lived long enough and if she'd had someone like Henry Meloux to guide her.

Louise was beyond help now. But maybe, Cork thought, just maybe she would have some justice in the end. He and Jorge and Billy had followed crumbs, and they'd found evidence that his father might be able to use. And maybe now Big John could walk the Path of Souls and maybe as he went, he could hold the hand of the spirit of Louise LaRose, and maybe when they reached that place the Anishinaabeg called *Gaagige Minawaanigoziwining,* they could finally be at peace.

Cork closed his eyes and fell asleep, his heart pillowed on that hope.

CHAPTER 57

It had been a terrible thing to carry, Doctor Dave confessed. All that guilt. But it hadn't been his fault, none of it.

"We were supposed to go fishing on Superior, but Ben changed the plan. I didn't know he was bringing the girl along until I got to Spider Creek. I should've backed out then and there. I mean, she was just a kid."

"She went willingly?" Liam asked.

"Yeah. Not bowled over with enthusiasm, but Ben must've made promises. She was pretty quiet. Until he got her drinking."

"Why Moose Lake?"

"Ben wanted to be somewhere we wouldn't be seen with the girl and that wouldn't take us all day to get to. Have you ever been to Moose Lake? Pretty much nobody goes there unless they're Ojibwe."

"Like Big John. What happened, Dave?"

"We got ourselves set up on Eagle Point. That's the first place that's good for camping. Ben brings out the booze right away and pours himself and the girl a drink. And like he was on cue, the Indian comes paddling by and spots us and the girl.

He comes over to the point, climbs up to where we're camping. Ben gives this big hello, all friendly. The Indian just stands there staring at the girl. Then he says something to her in their language. She says something back. He shakes his head and speaks to her a long time, real gentle. But she snaps back at him and waves him off. He looks at us and says he's coming back the next afternoon and we'd better be gone back to Aurora. He makes some noise about talking to the sheriff, contributing to the delinquency of a minor and all that. Then he takes off, paddles out into Moose Lake."

"Did you leave then?"

"I wanted to. I've got a reputation here. Ben said the hell with him. Who listens to Indians anyway?"

"Did Nick Skinner say anything?"

"Not about that. All he could talk about was being pissed off at MacDermid. He'd been trying to get his hotel plan off the ground but MacDermid was putting up roadblocks at every turn."

"Why?"

"Didn't want the hotel to change the face of the town his family built. Something like that. Nick was in deep, pretty much invested everything he had in the project. He started drinking as soon as we made camp. Turned him surly."

"The girl. What happened to her?"

"It was an accident, God's truth. She fell and hit her head."

"How?"

"We'd all been drinking pretty heavily by then. Ben suggested we go skinny-dipping. Nick and I passed, but the girl was fine with that. She and Ben went down to the water, both of them walking pretty unsteady. They stripped, and she tried to go in, but she slipped on the rocks. She went down hard, hit the back of her head. And that was that."

"You mean she was dead?"

"Yes."

"You checked her?"

"I did. I didn't find a pulse."

"How drunk were you?"

The vet shrugged. "Pretty drunk, I guess."

Liam said, "She wasn't dead."

"What?"

"Louise LaRose wasn't dead when you sank her body in the lake."

"No." Doctor Dave shook his violently. "She was dead."

"The autopsy told a different story. There was water in her lungs, Dave. She drowned."

"Oh, God. Oh, Jesus. What did we do?"

"It wasn't an accident. You killed her."

He'd looked ashen before. Now he went perfectly white.

"And you killed Big John because he knew about the Three Musketeers and Louise LaRose."

"I didn't kill him. I just shot the dart. Nick and Ben, they did the rest."

"What about the alcohol in his blood? Did you inject that?"

He shook his head. "I gave them a syringe. They shot him up."

"Why Lightning Strike? Why not just jump him at Moose Lake and sink his body like you did with Louise LaRose?"

"We broke camp at first light in the morning. We knew he was coming back and he'd warned us to be gone. We'd left our vehicles at Lightning Strike. By the time we got back there, Nick was convinced we had to do something about Manydeeds. He knew MacDermid's wife had been meeting the Indian out there, before she called it off."

"And he thought you could make it look like the suicide of a drunk and distraught man?"

He nodded, though he seemed to have barely the strength even for that.

"The rope he used came from Duncan MacDermid's boat-house. Why?"

"That was Nick's idea, too. He figured if there was any question, MacDermid would be the one looking guilty. He was hoping that would happen, in fact. For him, I think it was payback because MacDermid had been doing all he could to keep Nick's precious hotel from being built."

"And the Four Roses?"

"Part of Nick's brilliant plan. MacDermid's favorite. Ben got a couple of bottles from his bar. That's what they used to inject Manydeeds. They left the empties out at Lightning Strike."

"Then your brother bought two more cases in Duluth and emptied those bottles and put them in back of Big John's cabin?"

"Nick's always thought he was smarter than everybody else. He said they'd never look at us."

There was a knock at the door to Liam's office and Cy Borkman stepped in.

"Skinner?" Liam asked.

"Couldn't find him, Sheriff. Looked everywhere. Nobody's seen him."

Liam eyed the veterinarian. "Do you have any idea where he might be?"

Doctor Dave nodded. "That call from my brother this afternoon. He wanted me to go with him and Nick out to Moose Lake."

"Why?"

"Nick thought some kids were heading out there, going to try to locate where the girl died. He wanted to get to Moose Lake ahead of them to make sure there was nothing to find."

"Was there something to find?"

"When the girl went down on those rocks, she grabbed at Ben, got hold of this necklace he wears with a Marine medallion. She pulled it off and it went flying. In all the panic after that, we forgot about it. Nick wanted to look for it or anything else we might have left behind."

"Lock him up, Joe." Liam reached for his phone and called Sam's Place. "Sam," he said when Winter Moon answered. "I need your canoe."

CHAPTER 58

What woke him, Cork couldn't have said. Maybe a noise. Maybe the dream—he'd been having a nightmare about drowning. Maybe just the fact that he had to pee. He opened his eyes and saw that the moon hadn't moved much in the sky, and it still cast long shadows of everything that stood upright in the Northwoods. Tiny flames, like little devil horns, still flickered inside the fire ring. He figured he hadn't been asleep all that long, and he didn't really want to be awake. But there was his bladder, demanding attention.

He sat up slowly, slid from his sleeping bag, and stepped away from the other boys to take care of business. He stood facing the lake, which was just like the sky, a blackness where a million jewels seemed to sparkle and where the moon laid out a path of silver. The wind had died, and everything had grown silent, not even the sound of tree frogs or night birds disturbing the utter stillness.

A hundred yards offshore sat a little island with a few scrub pines, their tips black and ragged against the silver of the lake. As he took care of business, Cork's eyes settled there for a moment. And he saw it. Just a flicker of light among the trees. There for a moment, a sudden flaring in the dark, then it was gone.

He turned back to the nearly dead fire. The other two boys were sound asleep. He could hear Billy snoring softly. He considered waking them but decided against it. He stared intently where he'd seen the little flare of light and decided that it was probably a match that had been struck and that it must belong to whomever had come to the lake before them, to whomever it was that had left the boot print on the short portage up from Spider Creek. Other campers, most likely. But they were so close. Why hadn't he seen them earlier? He wondered if maybe they'd been fishing late into the night on one of the lake's many fingers and had only just made camp. He knew the island and knew it was not a good spot for making camp. Maybe they'd been trying to find their way back to the portage and had got lost and decided to stop for the night before they got lost even further. He tried a couple of other scenarios, but nothing felt quite right. In fact, the whole thing felt off. He decided it had to be checked out. Due diligence.

To reach the island would mean putting the canoe in the water by himself, a difficult maneuver, particularly in the dark. But there was another way, he realized. He could swim there. The lake had been heating all summer long, and Cork didn't balk at all at the idea of entering it in the night. He removed his T-shirt so that he wore only his boxer shorts. He stepped carefully over and among the boulders, making his way down to where they'd secured the canoe. He slid into the water easily, the chill a little startling at first, but he quickly got used to it. Then he began to breaststroke. Around him, the water was liquid silver. As he moved through it, the surface was broken with black ripples. He swam soundlessly, knowing that if he needed to, he could swim this way for miles. He'd grown up swimming in Iron Lake, and earlier that summer, on a dare from Jorge, he'd swum all the way across and back in the course of an afternoon, nearly six miles, while Jorge canoed at his side. The feel of the water was second nature, as if he were part fish.

He neared the island, stopped swimming, and treaded water just off the shore from the spot where he'd seen the tiny flare of light. The island was flat, he recalled, and between the scrub pines the ground was covered with thick brush. But there was a narrow, grassy apron on the near side. Although the area was dark now, under the glare of the moon, he could see a figure standing on that apron of grass. As he watched, a tiny red eye seemed to open in the head of the moonlit figure, and Cork became aware of a faint smell totally out of place in the wilderness: the foul odor of cigar smoke.

He was near enough to shore that his feet could touch, and he stood on the broken rock of the lake bottom, his head and shoulders above water as he tried to make sense of all the elements the moment presented to him. A lot of men smoked cigars, but Cork's thinking settled immediately on one in particular. He was a man who'd used this entrance into the Boundary Waters before, who'd come here as a kid, a Boy Scout. A man Joe Meese had called Devil Dog, which Jorge had told him was a nickname for a Marine. And a man who had always seemed to Cork riddled by a foulness as odious as the smell of his cigars.

Cork knew who'd killed Louise LaRose.

He turned to swim back to Eagle Point but found his way blocked by a canoe. It had come up behind him so silently that he hadn't noticed. The beam of a flashlight shot into Cork's eyes, blinding him.

"Easy there, son. Nothing to worry about." A long pause followed, then the man spoke again. "What say we both head in to shore and talk things over."

Though the light blinded him, Cork knew the voice behind it, and in a way, it didn't surprise him at all.

CHAPTER 59

*T*hank God for the moon, Liam thought.

There were two canoes on Spider Creek. Oscar Manydeeds and Sam Winter Moon led the way in one, Liam and Joe Meese followed in the other. They'd rendezvoused in their trucks at Lightning Strike, launched the canoes, and paddled quickly to the mouth of the stream. Now they stroked in brilliant moonlight, the two Ojibwe in the lead, making their way flawlessly through the web of marshland channels toward Naabe-Mooz. If he'd had wings, Liam would have flown. Although he tried to concentrate on the effort at hand—*stroke, stroke, stroke*—his brain was like an untamed beast.

What could it hurt? he'd asked himself when his son had requested his permission to look for evidence. In all the scenarios that had run quickly through his head, he'd never once considered that the men who'd killed Louise LaRose would end up hunting Cork and his friends. It was supposed to be a harmless outing, something to keep his son busy, to give him a sense of being of some help. *What kind of father am I?* Liam thought. *What kind of lawman? And, oh God, what if . . .* But that was a place he wouldn't let his mind go. Instead, he thought strategy.

The men had camped on Eagle Point. Liam knew the place. A small clearing atop an outcrop where the long inlet that led from the end of the portage opened onto the big lake. If either of the men was watching, both canoes could easily be seen in the brilliant moonlight. But why would they be watching? Who would expect a rescue party in the dead of night? Still, it might be best to pull up short of the point and approach through the trees. Except that they would make noise that way, especially trying to move in the dark. Was there another approach? No, Eagle Point was like a watchtower on the entrance to Naabe-Mooz, and if the men were vigilant, it would be impossible to come at them unseen. If they came swiftly enough, however, even though Skinner or Svenson might spot them, what could those two do except run? And what would be their path of escape? Only to flee into the woods, which were deep and confusing, or take to the lake, and Liam would be waiting there. The real question in all this was would they harm the boys. Or had they already?

On the other hand, maybe Cork and the others had checked Eagle Point, found nothing, and moved on. This was the hope Liam clung to when they reached the place where the water that fed Spider Creek cascaded down from Moose Lake. They shouldered their rifles, lifted the canoes from the stream, and began the short portage up to the lake. The trees broke the moonlight into ragged patches, and they had to make their way carefully. To Liam, it felt as if they were snails.

They set the canoes in the water at the end of the long, rock-lined corridor that led to the body of the lake. Under the moon, the surface was opalescent and dead still. They shoved off, and Liam knew they were only a quarter mile from Eagle Point now. Only a quarter mile from the boys, maybe. A quarter mile from Cork.

They'd gone a little more than halfway when they heard the first of the rifle shots.

*   *   *

Cork waded to shore, the canoe trailing him. He stood with his feet in the water as the canoe glided up beside him. The man who waited for them there, cigar jammed in the corner of his mouth, grabbed the bow of the canoe and steadied it as Nick Skinner disembarked.

"Christ," Svenson said. "We're screwed now."

"Keep your cool, Ben. This is just a slight wrinkle."

"Wrinkle my ass. What do we do with the kid?"

"That depends on the kid." Skinner had turned off the flashlight and he stood facing Cork under the glare of the moon. His face was ghost white, his eyes agleam with moonglow. "What did you do with it, Cork?"

"I don't know what you're talking about."

"We've been watching you since you got here. We know you found the medallion."

"What medallion?"

"Let me explain things, son. What happened out here was an accident."

"You killed her," Cork said.

"No. God's truth, it was an accident. She was drunk. She fell and hit her head."

"And you tied her to a rock and sank her body in the lake."

"It would have been hard to explain things, Cork."

"She was just a kid."

"She hadn't been just a kid for a long time," Skinner said. "When you grow up, things get complicated. When you grow up like she did, things get complicated early. She was already hooked on booze, Cork. That should tell you something."

"She didn't deserve what you did to her."

"You got no idea what we did to her," Svenson said.

Cork thought about her naked body and he did have an idea, but not one he wanted to dwell on.

"When she fell and hit her head, she pulled the medallion off Ben's neck," Skinner said. "We know that you found something in the water. Had to be Ben's medallion. That was it, wasn't it?"

"We didn't find anything," Cork said.

"We don't want to cause you any trouble, Cork. All we want is the medallion." Skinner smiled in a friendly way and held up his hands, showing his empty palms, ghost-white in the moonlight, as if to prove he had nothing to hide.

"Please, Mr. Skinner—"

"Call me Nick." And he smiled a little more broadly.

"We didn't find—"

"Screw this," Svenson said. "Okay, kid, this is what I'll do. I'll go to your camp. I'll round up your two friends. Then I'll start cutting you up, each of you, one by one, until one of you talks or you're all cut into pieces. Then I'll dump those pieces in the middle of the lake. I've learned something from what happened with the girl, and I'll make sure this time nothing comes back up."

"Ben," Skinner said.

"Enough of this shit, Nick. I'm not kidding, boy. I'll slice you good." He reached to his belt and, from a sheath there, drew out a vicious-looking blade that gleamed in the moonlight like a long tongue of silver fire.

Cork took a step back and said desperately, "My dad knows."

"Your dad knows shit," Svenson said.

"What does your dad know?" Skinner said.

"Everything."

Skinner gave a little laugh. "I'll bet he doesn't know about Ben's precious medallion."

He'd spoke derisively and Svenson said, "Hey, I'm proud to be a Marine."

Skinner shook his head. "Once a Marine, always a goddamn Marine." He looked again at Cork, but this time there was no false friendliness in his voice. "One more chance. All I want is the medallion."

The moon, which had been brilliant all night, suddenly blanked out, as if it had moved behind a thick cloud or had slipped behind a mountain. It had been high above the lake at Cork's back. The two men stood facing him but now their attention moved beyond him, and they lifted their eyes, which grew huge. Even in the sudden dark, Cork could see the terror on their faces. He didn't wait to find out what had so frightened them. He turned, dashed into the lake, and dove under the dark water.

Silence. And black. And with each stroke of his arms, a desperate push forward. He'd swum twice the length of the Aurora Municipal Swimming Pool underwater many times, and the press of the lake all around him was nothing he feared. What frightened him, what drove him to go deeper, farther, faster, was the slicing of silver bubbles to his right as bullets penetrated the water. He understood that whoever was shooting at him was anticipating that he would head back in the direction of Eagle Point. Instead, he cut farther to the left, angling toward the corridor that led to Spider Creek.

He swam until his lungs hurt, but when he finally came up for air, he came up quietly, making no splash to give away his position. The moon had returned from where it had hidden itself or had been hidden. The scene before him was once again a milk white island shoreline where the trees and everything else that stood upright cast black shadows. He saw only one figure on the shore and, because of the cigar ember that was like a red eye, knew exactly who it was. But Nick Skinner wasn't with Ben Svenson. Cork tried not to panic. Then he spotted the canoe.

It was far to his right, heading toward Eagle Point. On top of the point where the boys had made camp, he could see flashlight beams. He figured that the sound of the gunfire must have roused Jorge and Billy. He had no idea what kind of madness was in Skinner's mind, but he knew he couldn't let his friends be taken by surprise.

"Jorge! Billy!" he shouted. "Run for it! He's coming!"

Two feet to his right, the smooth surface of the lake was punctured with a tiny splash, followed almost instantly by the report of a rifle shot. Cork dove, swam until his lungs hurt, then came up. Once again, he shouted to his friends to run for it. And once again, when the bullets began to split the water near him, he sought cover deep in the lake.

This time, he did not swim away. The bright moonlight illuminated the water around him all the way to the lake bottom, six feet below. What he saw directly beneath him was a gray cube of stone eighteen inches in width and height, very much like the angular boulders at the base of Eagle Point. But this one was different, because two short lengths of white cord had been bound around it. At the end of each cord was an empty loop. He let himself hang almost weightless as the understanding and impact of what he was looking at dawned on him. He lifted his eyes and stared up at the surface half a dozen feet above him. The moon was an explosion of frost-white in a black velvet sky. Where the water met the air, there seemed a transparent coating, almost like the thinnest sheet of ice. There was no sound except the occasional release of bubbles from between his lips. He had no idea if Nick Skinner had swung his canoe around and would come for him. Or if Svenson would have him in his rifle sight the next time he surfaced. But oddly, it didn't matter. He wasn't even thinking about that. He was thinking about a young girl who'd gone through unimaginable brutality and had been made a prisoner to the lake while she was still alive. He wondered if, with her ankles bound to the boulder's heavy weight, she'd stared up at a full moon like the one above him now and had seen that fragile place where air and water met. He wondered if she'd been afraid, and he hoped not. But he knew absolutely she'd been alone, and maybe that was the worst thing. To die so alone.

His lungs were beginning to burn, and he knew he had to come up for air. At that moment, the silhouette of a canoe passed directly above him and stopped.

Nick Skinner, he thought. And he wondered, *Does he have a gun, too?* He was afraid the man could see him six feet below. He needed air, needed it bad, and he kicked away from the shadow. But the canoe above followed. *He sees me,* Cork thought. He tried to think of an escape plan, but his lungs seemed about to burst, and in another moment, he would have no choice but to surface.

Then a hand dropped into the water and gestured for him to come up.

CHAPTER 60

"Steady, Joe."

Liam sat in the bow of the canoe, as still as he could possibly make himself in that unsteady craft. His Winchester was snugged against his shoulder as he took aim just below the red eye of the cigar end, which was the same place he'd seen the flashes from the muzzle of a rifle. He breathed in. Let the air out slowly. Squeezed the trigger.

Not even in the war had he wanted the killing. But he wanted it now.

The recoil rocked the canoe, and Liam nearly went into the lake. But he saw the red ember fall to the ground and the reports from the island ceased.

In the canoe to his left, Sam Winter Moon dipped his hand into the lake, and when he brought it up, Cork was in his grasp.

"He's okay, Liam," Sam called out. "He's fine."

As soon as he saw his son come out of the water, gasping for air but clearly alive, Liam's whole body went limp and his vision clouded. He'd heard many times that in the moment before dying, a man's life flashed before his eyes. In this moment, it was his son's life that Liam saw. A small red face and wrinkled little body swaddled in a white hospital blanket and nestled against Colleen's breast, and he felt again how deeply he loved them both. A frightened toddler squirming into bed beside him during a thunderstorm, and he remembered the sweet smell of his son's breath against his face as they snuggled. A little boy standing in the firelight, wide-eyed but proud during his naming ceremony, and Liam's own pride at how straight his son stood. A kid with doe-colored hair struggling to hold back tears because his father had spoken to him more harshly than necessary about a lost screwdriver.

"A lost screwdriver," Liam whispered. "Jesus."

And now he was the one struggling to hold back tears. Tears of regret for his pointless anger at a child, tears of gratitude for the blessing that was his son, tears of relief that the ordeal was over and Cork was alive.

"One of those sons of bitches is getting away," Oscar Manydeeds shouted.

"Let him go," Liam said, wiping at his eyes. "He'll have to come back to town eventually. We'll grab him then. Let's make sure the other boys are safe."

The shot had hit its target, Ben Svenson's heart, and the man was truly dead.

They laid his body in the O'Connors' canoe, the one Cork and his friends had taken to the lake, but it would be Cork's father and his deputy who would paddle the body back the next day.

They sat around the fire on Eagle Point, and although they were boys only nearing manhood, Cork felt that he and his friends belonged in the company of men that night.

It had been a long day for them all. When it came time to get some sleep, the sheriff assigned each of his small posse a watch during the night to ensure that Nick Skinner, should he choose to return, wouldn't surprise them.

But Cork couldn't sleep. He lay awake, thinking, still trying to make sense of the world as he saw it now, a place where there was no longer any sure, safe haven. When it was Sam Winter Moon's turn on watch, Cork joined him, and they sat feeding the fire and keeping an eye on the woods and the water. Across Sam's lap lay his hunting rifle, just in case.

"You fought in the war," Cork said.

"Me and lots of other Shinnobs."

"Were you ever scared?"

"All the time. Nothing to be ashamed of."

"I thought I was going to die, Sam. But that didn't scare me so much. What scared me was thinking that Jorge and Billy might be killed."

"You know what that is, Cork? That's brotherhood. It's a precious thing, hard to come by."

"There's something else."

Sam waited with the patience of the Ojibwe while Cork tried to gather his thinking and find the right words.

"I got saved tonight. Nick Skinner and Mr. Svenson, they were about to . . ." He tried to say the words but couldn't quite call them up. "Then the moon disappeared. There weren't any clouds in the sky, but the moon just disappeared. And those men looked up, and it was like they were seeing a monster. That's what gave me a chance to get away."

"What do you think they saw?"

"I think it was Big John. You were out on the lake then. Did you see him?"

"For us, the moon was always there. It lit our way the whole time." Sam let a minute pass. Out on the lake, a loon gave a forlorn and eerie cry. "Crazy as a loon," he said. "That's what white folks would say about Skinner if he told anyone that the spirit of Big John had scared him. If you tell your dad, he'll probably find some rational explanation for whatever blacked out the moon. He's white and Irish on top of that. Stubborn as they come in what he's willing to accept or not. But you, Cork, you're different. You've got Shinnob blood in you. You'll always be a spirit divided, always trying to figure how to put those two worlds together. There's nobody can help you with that one. Not me or your mom or Dilsey."

"Henry Meloux, maybe?"

"Maybe. But knowing Henry, I'm guessing he'll leave it to you to solve that puzzle."

Sam looked away as Liam O'Connor stepped to the fire.

"Time for you to get some shut-eye, Sam."

"Sleep can wait. Sit with us awhile, Liam."

And he did, settling himself so that he was on one side of Cork and Sam on the other. He put a hand lightly on his son's shoulder.

"I wish I could've spared you all this," he said.

But that wasn't something Cork wished. It felt right for him to be there, between these two men. Though one of them was his father, what he felt toward them now was something different, something Sam had called brotherhood. It was a hard place to come to, and he'd left much behind, but there was no going back.

CHAPTER 61

On a Saturday morning three weeks later, Cork O'Connor stood in front of the carriage house at Glengarrow, where a station wagon with a U-Haul trailer attached behind it was parked. Jorge came down the steps from the upstairs apartment, holding a large manila envelope. They walked to the dock beside the boathouse so that Jorge could take one last look at Iron Lake.

Fall was not yet in the air, and the day was warm and exceedingly sunny. Cork had been tapped to be a part of the honor guard for the Boy Scouts of American Voyageurs Area Council later that morning, and he was dressed in his uniform. The two young men sat on the wood planks of the dock, their backs against the upright pilings. The big motor launch and the little Sunfish that had been moored there were gone, sold along with everything else at Glengarrow.

"Four days," Jorge said. "We'll stay tonight in Des Moines, tomorrow in Denver, Monday in Phoenix, and get to California on Tuesday." With his finger, he drew an imaginary line of travel across the weathered boards of the dock. "Wish I had a driver's license. I could help."

"Where will you stay when you get there?"

"Relatives. My mom's cousins. For a little while anyway, till we find a place of our own." Jorge looked across the lake at the distant shore. "Never met them. Hope they're nice."

Cork said, "I'll come and visit sometime, visit you and Billy."

"Right," Jorge said.

"Really, I mean it."

Jorge slapped at a deerfly that had settled on his arm. "Mom got a letter from Nick Skinner. From jail. He said he was sorry for everything."

"Is she going to write back?"

"No. She says she's done with men. From now on, it's all about her and me. Here. This is for you." Jorge handed him the big envelope.

Cork opened it and pulled out several pages torn from a sketch pad. They were all monsters, renderings from Jorge's vivid imagination, except for one they both knew was real.

"I haven't seen him since Moose Lake," Cork said. "Nobody has."

"All he wanted was the truth, I guess."

"He knew the truth. He just wanted everyone else to know it, too." Cork shooed away a deerfly buzzing around his head. "I heard some rich lawyer bought Glengarrow."

Jorge looked back at the grounds of the estate and the mansion. "Ask me, this place is cursed. I don't mind leaving it behind."

Jorge's mother called to him from the carriage house.

"Time to go," he said.

The boys stood and shook hands, and Jorge walked back to the station wagon. He waved once before getting into the passenger side. Then his mother gunned the engine and Cork watched as Jorge rode out of his life.

Billy Downwind was gone, too, back in L.A. with his father and mother. He was no more excited about returning there than Jorge had been about going in the first place. What Cork had told Jorge was true. He fully intended to see his friends again. But intentions could be like cloud animals in the sky, so clear for a while, then shifting, then fading, then gone.

It was Grandma Dilsey who suggested they all visit Crow Point that evening. Cork's father brought tobacco as an offering, and Cork's mother brought two loaves of freshly baked rhubarb bread. They gathered around the fire ring. Henry Meloux's pipe was filled with tobacco and passed. When it came to Cork, he looked to the Mide for permission to join in the smoking. Meloux's dark eyes held on him, expressionless, and Cork figured he would simply be instructed to pass the pipe on. But Meloux's eyes changed, softened, as if they were pellets of iron melting, and he gave a nod. As the light relinquished its hold on the day, Cork, for the first time, joined in smoking from the sacred pipe.

Makwa lay quietly at Meloux's feet. Cork could hear the chirring of crickets from the meadow and the song of tree frogs and the voice of the wind as it spoke in the rustling of the aspen leaves along the shore of Iron Lake. Grandma Dilsey shared a story about Henry Meloux as a young man, one Cork hadn't heard before, and at the end of it, after they'd all finished laughing, Meloux said, "We were young then, Dilsey."

"And had much to learn," Cork's grandmother said.

"We still do." Meloux turned his face to Cork, who'd been silent in the firelight. "It is good when the lessons we learn make us laugh, but it is also good when the lessons make us think. You have much to think about, Corcoran O'Connor."

"I've been thinking about the crumbs. Did you know where they would lead?"

"What I knew is that there is always a way to the truth, but it is not always easy to find. I believed you would find it. But where it would lead you, I did not know."

"Did Big John have a hand in where it led me?"

"What do you think?"

"I guess I think anything is possible."

His father said, "More things in heaven and earth than are dreamed of in our philosophy." He looked at Cork's mother. "Congreve?"

"Shakespeare," she said with a smile.

"Sometimes . . ." Cork said, then paused.

"Yes?" Meloux said.

"Sometimes I wish things would never change."

"That is like trying to stop the dawn," Meloux said. "Better, I think, to open yourself to what each new day offers."

"What if it offers only pain, Henry?" Cork's father said.

"In my experience, pain is never the only offering. What we receive depends on what we open our hearts to."

"We're only human, Henry," Cork's father said.

"Oh, Liam O'Connor, we are so much more than that."

"I haven't seen the spirit of Big John since Moose Lake," Cork said. "Did he finally walk the Path of Souls?"

"I believe his spirit is at rest."

"And the spirit of Louise LaRose?" Cork's mother asked.

"What does your heart tell you?"

"My heart wants peace for her, Henry. But I don't know."

"The spirit of Louise LaRose, of Big John, of you, of me, of every human being comes out of the heart of the Creator. And when our time in this flesh is over, that spirit returns to the place it came from. Our people call that place *Gaagige Minawaanigoziwining*. In your Catholic church, you call it heaven. What does it matter, the name we give it?" His shoulders lifted in a little shrug, as if to confirm that this was of no importance. "Every heart wants to find peace. In the end, that is the place the Creator takes us."

Cork's father shook his head. "Too easy an answer for me, Henry."

"That does not lessen its truth," Meloux replied.

Cork tried to listen to his heart, to understand what it was telling him, but it seemed such a jumble of regret, of hope, of fear, of wants, of uncertainty, that it was just noise to him.

Meloux, as if sensing this, said, "But tonight, around this fire, it is not about trying to understand what awaits us beyond this life. It is about enjoying the gift in this moment together, here under these stars, as the night sings to us. What you are afraid you have lost, Corcoran O'Connor, is not lost at all. The joy of your friendships, of your family, of moments like this when our spirits touch, this will always be with you. When the journey ahead takes you to the darkest of places, the joy in these memories will be a part of the light that helps you see your way through. This I promise."

Even then, Cork thought it was a brave promise. But on that night, in the company of those he loved with all his being, he watched sparks from the fire rising toward the heavens carrying prayers to the Creator, and he chose to believe it.

EPILOGUE

It was a year later, and jack-o-lanterns, black cats, and spiderwebs populated the shop windows of Aurora. Cork O'Connor was nearing his fourteenth birthday. Dark hair had finally begun to appear in those places that he'd always believed would be hallmarks of his manhood. He'd grown four inches and was within spitting distance of standing six feet tall. His mother called him lanky or sometimes rangy. Joe Meese had taken to calling him Bean Pole. With a clear note of pride, his father often said, "Not long and you'll be looking down at your old man."

Across all those months, Jorge had sent him cards from San Diego on which he'd drawn images appropriate for the seasons but with Jorge's bizarre artistic sensibility on display: at Christmas, a grotesquely funny—and irate—elf stomping on toys and declaring "Ain't gonna work on Santa's farm no more!"; an Easter Bunny with a spine and tail like Godzilla carrying a basketful of reptilian eggs; a Fourth of July card dominated by a figure of Uncle Sam that more resembled Nosferatu. In return, Cork had sent him photographs of Aurora and Iron Lake and the Boundary Waters, so that his friend would not forget.

He hadn't heard at all from Billy Downwind, although Oscar Manydeeds occasionally passed along bits of news.

On that day in October when his life would change forever, Cork had already delivered his afternoon routes—he'd been doing them alone since Jorge's departure—and was helping his mother and Grandma Dilsey rake up fallen leaves, which they would burn. They'd just begun when they heard the pop of firecrackers coming from the direction of downtown.

"Leftovers from the Fourth?" Grandma Dilsey said.

The popping continued sporadically for a few minutes, then stopped.

"Must've finally run out of fireworks," Cork's mother said.

Like their neighbors, they'd decorated for Halloween. A skeleton hung from a hook on the porch. In the front windows were pasted the silhouettes of a witch and a black cat surrounded by a flurry of bats. Two carved pumpkins flanked the porch stairs, and a scarecrow stood limp on the lawn, tied with twine to cross poles.

The leaf pile was as high as Cork's knees when a Tamarack County Sheriff's Department cruiser raced down Gooseberry Lane and screeched to a stop at the curb. Joe Meese leaped out.

"Colleen!" he called.

"Hi, Joe," she said brightly, then looked at his face and her tone changed. "What is it?"

"You need to come with me."

"What's happened?" Grandma Dilsey said.

"A robbery," Joe said. "The bank. Liam . . . he's been hurt."

They stared at him, as if the words were a foreign language whose meaning they didn't comprehend.

Cork felt panic grip his chest like the hand of one of Jorge's beasts. "Those weren't firecrackers."

"He's been rushed to the hospital, Colleen. I'm taking you there," Joe said.

"Hurt how?"

The deputy's face showed his reluctance to deliver the truth, but he said, "He took a couple of bullets."

"He's not . . . dead?"

Joe shook his head vigorously. "But badly wounded. We need to go. Now."

"Go on, Colleen," Cork's grandmother said. "You and Cork. I'll call Sam and we'll meet you there."

Cork threw his rake to the ground and followed his mother to the cruiser. The deputy hit his lights and sirens, and the cruiser launched forward, screaming down the normally quiet streets of Aurora.

"What happened, Joe?" Cork's mother asked.

"We got a silent alarm from the bank. I was in the office. Liam and Cy had left for a Code Seven at Johnny's Pinewood Broiler. They were right across the street when a shot was fired inside the bank. Couple of seconds later, three men came running out, wearing Halloween masks, waving guns. They saw Liam and Cy, two uniforms right there across the street, and started shooting. Our guys took cover behind their cruiser, returned fire. The assholes in the masks tried to retreat to the bank, but one of the clerks had locked the door behind them. So they just crouched in the entryway at the top of the steps and kept firing away."

"And Liam was hit?" Cork's mother asked.

"Not then. Astrid Lankinen, you know she's deaf as a post but never wears her hearing aid. She wanders out of the bookstore and into the street, right into the line of fire. Liam left his cover to grab her and haul her to safety, which he did. But that's when he took the rounds."

"Where?"

"In the chest.

"Oh, God."

"He's alive, Colleen. Hold on to that. He's alive."

They parked at the Emergency Room entrance and rushed inside. Cork saw a trail of blood on the white floor tiles. It led through double, swinging doors at the rear of the waiting area. There was already a frantic energy in the Emergency Room, the feel of crisis. A woman and her young daughter sat in chairs against the wall, their eyes gone big and horror-stricken at what they'd witnessed before Cork and the others had arrived.

A nurse blocked their way.

"His family," Joe said.

"You have to wait here, I'm sorry," the nurse said.

"How is he?" Cork's mother asked, her voice oddly controlled.

"I don't know. I know a good team's working on him. Dr. Braddock is there. He's operated on lots of gunshot wounds. Hunting season, you know?"

"But I can't see him?"

"I'm sorry, no."

Cy Borkman came out the doors where the trail of blood led. He looked ashen.

"Cy?" Cork's mother said, studying his face.

"They've taken him into surgery, Colleen. That's all I know."

"You should go to the surgery waiting room," the nurse said. "It will be a while, I'm sure, before we know anything. That's the best place for you in the meantime. Through there," she said, and pointed toward a door.

"Come on, Colleen," Joe said, and gently took her arm.

Throughout the rest of his life, in his worst moments, Cork O'Connor would remember that long wait, recalling disjointed details that, no matter all the years gone by, still had the power to grip his chest so that he could barely breathe. His mother and

Grandma Dilsey were always there in his recollections, and Joe Meese, and Cy Borkman, and Sam Winter Moon.

He would remember Cy telling him that the men who'd robbed the bank had escaped from the prison in Stillwater and had planned to flee to Canada. Troopers from the state Highway Patrol had arrived to assist, and in the continuing exchange of gunfire, one of the robbers had been shot dead. The other two had surrendered.

He would remember his grandmother chanting softly in her native tongue, and although Cork never knew the words she was saying, the sound of them alone provided a measure of comfort.

He would remember the moment, after hours of waiting, that the surgeon came to them, dressed in clean scrubs, and he would remember the gentleness with which the man explained to them all that the bullets had been removed, but that Sheriff Liam O'Connor was in a coma. He couldn't tell them what would happen now, only that more waiting would be required.

Another thing Cork would remember was his anger. At God, at the Creator, at the bank robbers, at deaf old Mrs. Lankinen. And for reasons he couldn't understand, at his father.

In the hours that followed, the new priest at St. Agnes came and sat with the family at Liam O'Connor's bedside. Cork remembered the priest holding his mother's hand as they prayed together. Cork couldn't bring himself to join them, to beg something of a God who, as far as he could tell, offered nothing but pain and hardship in return.

And he would remember forever the final moments as Liam O'Connor slipped away, never having regained consciousness, his wife with her hand gently on his cheek, but her son standing away from that deathbed, unable to accept or understand the sacrifice his father had made, and for too many years after, unable to forgive himself for his own childish anger, his utter confusion, and his soul-shattering desolation.

*   *   *

Liam O'Connor was laid to rest on a cold November morning, when the sky was a mournful gray threatening the first snow of the season. In the days since his father's death, Cork hadn't shed a tear. He felt as if he'd become a thing of iron, a mechanical kid, every move he made stiff and inhuman. His mother, Grandma Dilsey, even Henry Meloux could not reach through that hard armor to his heart.

As the mourners who'd gathered that morning, and there were many, headed back to their vehicles, Cork remained at the grave, staring beyond the coffin into the hole that awaited the empty shell of flesh that had once been his father.

He felt a presence at his back and heard Sam Winter Moon say, "It was a tough road he walked, but he walked it with honor. I'm proud that he called me his friend."

"It was a road that got him killed." Cork didn't like the bitter taste those words left in his mouth, but they spoke an undeniable truth.

"Do you know the Ojibwe word *ogichidaa*?"

"Sure. Warrior."

"That's one interpretation," Sam said. "It also means one who stands between evil and his people. Your father was born *ogichidaa*."

Snow had begun to fall softly, scattered flakes drifting lazily down in the still air. They settled on the polished wood of the coffin and lay there unmelting, little white stars on the dark wood.

"Here's something that you probably can't accept now, but maybe someday." Sam laid a hand gently on Cork's shoulder. "You are your father's son. I believe you were born *ogichidaa*, too."

"I'll never wear a badge."

"Never is a long time."

Cork could hear car doors slamming, engines turning over, the crunch of tires on gravel as one by one the mourners left. But he didn't move. Nor did Sam.

"Years ago your father shared something with me," Sam said. "You were still just a little guy. Your dad wasn't one for dwelling on the past, but we'd been drinking a bit, I admit, and we got to talking about the war and everything that had happened since. You were crawling around the floor at his feet and you grabbed his pant leg and pulled yourself up and stared right into his face. That's when he said it. He said, 'It seems to me more and more, Sam, that we don't choose our lives. Our lives choose us.' Then he picked you up and held you against his heart and he said, 'I'm grateful this life has chosen me.'" Sam took his hand from Cork's shoulder and put it on the coffin, where the white stars settled around it. "Your dad wasn't just honorable. He was also wise. Son, I hope someday you can embrace the life that's chosen you and become the man you were always meant to be."

Sam turned and walked away from the grave, and after a long moment, Cork did, too.